TESTAMENT

BY DAVID GIBBINS

TESTAMENT

DAVID GIBBINS

THOMAS DUNNE BOOKS   ST. MARTIN'S PRESS   NEW YORK

THOMAS DUNNE BOOKS.
An imprint of St. Martin's Press.

TESTAMENT. Copyright © 2017 by David Gibbins. All rights reserved. Printed in the United States of America. For information, address St. Martin's Press, 175 Fifth Avenue, New York, N.Y. 10010.

www.thomasdunnebooks.com
www.stmartins.com

Library of Congress Cataloging-in-Publication Data

Names: Gibbins, David J. L., author.
Title: Testament / David Gibbins.
Description: New York : Thomas Dunne Books, St. Martin's Press, 2017.
Identifiers: LCCN 2016043272 | ISBN 9781250080653 (hardback) |
    ISBN 9781466892569 (e-book)
Subjects: | BISAC: FICTION / Action & Adventure.
Classification: LCC PR6107.I225 T47 2017 | DDC 823/.92—dc23
LC record available at https://lccn.loc.gov/2016043272

Our books may be purchased in bulk for promotional, educational, or business use. Please contact your local bookseller or the Macmillan Corporate and Premium Sales Department at 1-800-221-7945, extension 5442, or by e-mail at MacmillanSpecialMarkets@macmillan.com.

First published in Great Britain by Headline Publishing Group, a Hachette UK company

First U.S. Edition: March 2017

10 9 8 7 6 5 4 3 2 1

Acknowledgments

I'm very grateful to my agent, Luigi Bonomi of LBA; to my editors, Sherise Hobbs at Headline in London and Peter Wolverton at Thomas Dunne Books in New York; to my former editor Martin Fletcher and to Ann Verrinder Gibbins and Jane Selley for their continuing excellent work on my books; to the rest of the teams at Headline and at Thomas Dunne Books, including Beth Eynon, Christina Demosthenous, Emily Gowers, and Emma Stein; to Alison Bonomi and Ajda Vucicevic at LBA; to Nicki Kennedy, Sam Edenborough, Jenny Robson, Simone Smith, and Alice Natali at the Intercontinental Literary Agency; and to my many foreign publishers and translators.

As with my other novels in this series, much of the diving and archaeology that I've written about here is based on my own experiences. My brother Alan has been my companion on many wreck dives in recent years, and his photo of me underwater can be seen in the design cover of this book. Mark Milburn dived with me in Gunwalloe Cove in Cornwall when we discovered the wreck of the *Grip*, and since then we've found much older wrecks in those waters. My excavations at Carthage were carried out under the auspices of the Carthage Museum and were funded by the British Academy, the Cambridge University Faculty of Classics, and Corpus Christi College, Cambridge. I'm very grateful to the staff of the National Archives at Kew and the archivist of the Clan Line for assisting with my research on convoys off West Africa. I owe much to my grandfather, Captain Lawrance Wilfred Gibbins, for having talked to me about his wartime experiences as a Merchant Navy officer. My research on the Abyssinia campaign benefited from assistance I received at the Royal Engineers Library in Chatham, the Cambridge University Library, and the India Office Collections of the British Library, and I'm also grateful to Heidelberg University Library for allowing me to see the original tenth-century manuscript of the *Periplus of Hanno*. Lastly, I owe a special thanks to my daughter for suggesting that we visit Bletchley Park, and for freediving with me off Cornwall just as Rebecca does with Jack in this novel.

AFRICA AND THE MEDITERRANEAN REGION

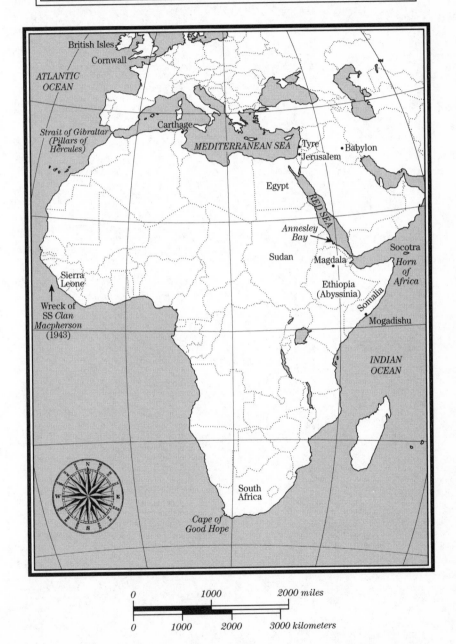

British Isles
Cornwall
ATLANTIC
OCEAN
Carthage
Strait of Gibraltar
(Pillars of
Hercules)
MEDITERRANEAN SEA
Tyre
Jerusalem
Babylon
Egypt
RED SEA
Annesley
Bay
Socotra
Horn
of
Africa
Sudan
Magdala
Sierra
Leone
Ethiopia
(Abyssinia)
Somalia
Wreck of
SS *Clan
Macpherson*
(1943)
Mogadishu
INDIAN
OCEAN
South
Africa
Cape of
Good Hope

0   1000   2000 miles

0   1000   2000   3000 kilometers

Map showing the main places mentioned in the novel, including the Horn of Africa
and the seas beyond the Strait of Gibraltar explored by early Carthaginian navigators.

And the Lord spake unto Moses, saying . . . they shall make an ark of acacia wood: two cubits and a half shall be the length thereof, and a cubit and a half the breadth thereof, and a cubit and a half the height thereof. And thou shalt overlay it with pure gold, within and without shalt thou overlay it, and shalt make upon it a crown of gold round about . . . And thou shalt make staves of acacia wood, and overlay them with gold . . . The staves shall be in the rings of the ark; they shall not be taken from it. And thou shalt put into the ark the testimony which I shall give thee . . .

The Book of Exodus 25:10–16 (King James Bible, Revised Version)

. . . we sailed along with all speed, being stricken by fear. After a journey of four days, we saw the land at night covered with flames. And in the midst there was one lofty fire, greater than the rest, which seemed to touch the stars. By day this was seen to be a very high mountain, called Chariot of the Gods.

Thence, sailing along by the fiery torrents for three days, we came to a bay, called Horn of the South. In the recess of this bay there was an island . . . full of savage men . . . they had hairy bodies, and the interpreters called them Gorillae. When we pursued them we were unable to take any of the men; for they all escaped, climbing the steep places and defending themselves with stones; but we took three of the women . . . we killed them and flayed them, and brought their skins to Carthage.

For we did not voyage further, provisions failing us . . .

The Periplus of Hanno, 6th century BC
(Originally written in Phoenician, translated from
the Greek by Wilfred H. Schoff)

Prologue

Southern Erythraean Sea (present-day Red Sea) during the reign of Nebuchadnezzar of Babylon, 584 BC

The man with the braided beard lurched forward, his hands on his knees, panting hard. Even his breathing seemed cracked, desiccated, like the hard crust of salt on the foreshore around him, as if the skin of the earth were burning and peeling away with his own. The sun had nearly reached its zenith, and it was as hot as the very furnace of Ba'al Hammon in Carthage, at the place of sacrifice where he and his crew had made offerings a lifetime ago at the start of their voyage. For a moment he wondered whether he was back there still, whether the torment of the past weeks had been nothing more than a nightmare inflicted on him by the gods, a punishment for sailing to lands so far beyond the Pillars of Hercules that even the gods themselves held no sway.

He shut his eyes, feeling them smart with the dryness, seeing the white blotches of blindness that had begun to appear over the last few days. He opened them again, blinking hard against the light that reflected off the cracked mosaic of salt around his feet. This was no nightmare, but it was far beyond any reality he had ever experienced before. He turned around, staggering, and shielded his eyes with one hand against the glare, seeing the distant form of his ship where it had heeled over and held fast in the shallows, and in the other direction the hazy forms of his four companions, two of them struggling with their burden as they made their way across the salt flats toward the mountains. The heat shimmer on the flats had made him think of the mirages he had seen as a boy in the desert south of Carthage, and had given him a spark of hope that he might one day make it back there alive. He tried licking his lips, but his tongue was like sandstone. He had to reach the foothills and find water soon, or die.

He staggered forward again, shouldering the sack that contained their meager remaining provisions: a few dried fish, handfuls of wild grain collected during their last foray ashore, some nuts and roots. The other ships of the fleet seemed a distant memory now, ships full of grain and amphorae of olive oil and wine to stock the outposts they had established along the desert shore beyond the Pillars of Hercules, seeking the place the Greeks called Chrysesephon, the Land of Gold. They had found it, a beach where the native traders brought them nuggets of river gold as big as a man's fist, gold they were willing to trade for textiles dyed with the royal purple of Tire. But instead of turning back then, their coffers filled, he had ordered the remaining ships to carry on, past burning mountains crowned with rivers of red, past rivers teeming with fish with teeth like lions', along a desolate sandy shore strewn with the skeletons of whales where the other three ships had all been driven to destruction in a terrible storm, sweeping the men shrieking and yelling into the pounding surf to join the rotting carcasses that lined the shore as far as the eye could see.

His was the only ship to make the southern cape, the very extremity of Africa, a stormy, rocky pinnacle pounded by the surf where they had erected a pillar with a bronze plaque dedicated to Ba'al Hammon before turning northeast and sailing up the far shore. He had wept there, thinking of his brother Himilco. Three years earlier they had stood together at the Pillars of Hercules, drinking wine and eating olives, planning the greatest trading expeditions ever undertaken. Himilco would sail north to the Cassiterides, the Tin Isles, with elephant ivory and textiles and olive oil. If he could find the source of the tin the Greek middlemen brought to Massalia, then they could bypass the overland route through Gaul and ship it directly to the Mediterranean, monopolizing the trade. If himself, Hanno, could sail south and find Chrysesephon, they would be doubly blessed, and great fortune and fame would be theirs.

But then, as they had assembled their ships, from Gades, from Carthage, from their ancestral homeland in far-off Phoenicia, another mission had befallen them. The ships of Tire and Sidon in Phoenicia had brought news of the fall of the kingdom of Judah to the Babylonians, of the destruction of the Temple in Jerusalem by Nebuchadnezzar and the exile of the Jews to Babylon. And one of the ships had brought something else, something that had led him to this place at the edge of existence, an artifact whose form he could just see being carried ahead of him through the haze toward the mountains: the greatest treasure of the people of Judah, the box that contained the holy testament of their God, the golden shrine that they called the Ark of the Covenant.

He swallowed, wincing with the pain in his throat, and glanced back one last time at his ship. She was already settling into the ooze, the painted eyes on either side of her prow staring up at the mountains, her mast raked forward where they had laid it for the final run ashore. She had served them well, her tightly caulked hull waterproof like skin, supple and strong, made from the cedar of Phoenicia that the shipwrights still preferred at Carthage, timber that kept away shipworm and would not rot like the others. No other ship had sailed this far from the Pillars of Hercules, had endured such winds and mighty seas, had kept true to the course when all else seemed against them. He had kissed her prow and wept as he left her, taking a fragment of wood from the hull to place inside the next ship he would construct at Carthage, if Ba'al Hammon willed that he should survive. His last act had been to scratch his name and that of his brother on an amphora sherd and toss it into the sea behind the ship, just as they had done together that day at the Pillars of Hercules, as the sign of their pact.

He hoped that Himilco had been as lucky with his ship, built at Gades by Iberian wrights in the Atlantic fashion, with a flatter bottom so that she could rest upright on the foreshore when the tide was out. He had wondered about the shallow depth of her keel, whether she would hold course with a wind on her beam in the way that his own ship had. When he saw his brother again, when Himilco too had returned from his great voyage, they would use all their newly won experience to design the best ship to withstand the ocean beyond the Pillars of Hercules. Then they would undertake the ultimate voyage they had dreamed of that day together, sailing at the head of a great fleet for the fabled shore they knew lay far across the open ocean to the west.

He remembered the day of their departure from Carthage almost two years before, a morning of shimmering seas when the air was clear of dust from the desert and the sun glinted off the bronze on the temples, the marble blindingly bright. They had rowed their ships slowly through the landlocked harbor, past the crowded vessels of their Phoenician kins-men from Tire and Sidon who had fled the onslaught of the Babylonians. Carthage had suddenly seemed unassailable, the most powerful city in the Mediterranean. They had passed the assembled magistrates and the crowd who were there to cheer them on, showering the deck with flowers and olive boughs for good luck. As the beams were pulled away from the harbor entrance they had heard the first shriek from the great bronze mouth of Ba'al Hammon on the platform above, the first belch of smoke and whiff of roasting flesh. The priests had chosen Hanno's own nephew to propitiate their departure, and he and Himilco had watched from their ships as the infant had been held aloft and then rolled down the maw of the god into the furnace below. The screams came out from the belly as if from a huge trumpet, echoing and rebounding off the harbor walls, and the priests had raised their arms to the mountain of Bou Kornine to the east, a sure sign that the sacrifice had worked. Ba'al Hammon had protected Hanno on his voyage, and he had prayed every day that the eye of the god had been on Himilco too, had kept him safe and well.

He thought again of those ships of Tire and Sidon, and of the cousin from one of the ships who had sought him out one night before the voyage. With him he had brought a robed man who had revealed himself as an Israelite named Ezekiel, a prophet who had fled Jerusalem before the might of Nebuchadnezzar. The king and priests of Jerusalem had entrusted Ezekiel with a sacred treasure, and he and four companions had brought it in the cousin's ship to Carthage. Ezekiel had known of Hanno and his impending voyage, word having spread among the shipmasters of Phoe-nicia, and he had come to him with a proposition. *Forget the riches you might make in trade, in gold and tin and whatever else it is you seek,* he had said. *A far greater reward will be yours if you take on my cargo, if you deliver it to the appointed place.* He had spread out the contents of the sack he had been carrying, gold coins from the kingdom of Lydia, gold chains and bars, gold amulets and scarabs and masks encrusted with dazzling jewels. *All of this now, and twice this amount again when you return.*

He had described the destination, and Hanno had agreed. It was on his course, on the far shore of Africa, not far south of Egypt. Ezekiel had told him what to look out for on the western horizon. He and the priests had chosen the circuitous sea route because the desert to the south of Jerusalem was fraught with danger, the Babylonians having overrun Egypt and the caravan trails infested with brigands. All Hanno had to do was to deliver the cargo to a mountain called the Chariot of Fire, to the followers of Ezekiel who would be waiting there and who would escort him south to another great mountain fastness, an impregnable plateau known only to those who had gone in secret to this place from Judaea to await the arrival of their sacred treasures. There, those who had met them would take the object to a place of concealment and then return with the animal skins that had covered it, giving them to him to take back to Carthage. The skins would be flecked with gold on the inside from the gilding of the object, and would be affirmation to Ezekiel that the deed had been done. Hanno was to set the skins up on poles outside the temple of Ba'al Hammon as if they were trophies from some exotic animals he had taken on the voyage, and then he would receive the remainder of his payment.

And Ezekiel had given Hanno a warning. The hanging animal skin was the Egyptian sign of the *imiut*, a curse-offering from the cult of the black dog Anubis, guardian of the dead. When the Israelites had fled Egypt, they had stolen a portable shrine for their holy objects with a life-sized statue of Anubis on top, protecting the funerary goods that had once been inside. When the Israelite prophet Moses had been instructed by their god to create a receptacle for his commandments, it was this box he had chosen, calling it the Aron Habberit, the Ark of the Covenant. Ezekiel had told Hanno this because he had known of the superstitions of sailors, of those like Hanno who knew many gods. He had said that the power of Anubis was still there, the power of the one who shall not be seen, the one whom the Egyptians always kept shrouded. He had warned that anyone who dared lift the hides and cloths that covered the Ark would be instantly struck dead. Hanno had never once looked underneath, even when they had needed to replace the rotting leopard skins covering it with new hides they found in Africa, flayed from the *gorilla* women his men had hunted on the west coast.

Anubis was not the only god who concerned Hanno. The Israelite god, the one the Phoenicians called the God of the Testament, whose words were said to be in the Ark, was surely as much a cousin of Ba'al Hammon as he and Himilco were cousins of their kinsmen from Phoenicia and Israel itself; with the world's most perilous sea voyage ahead of him, he could not afford to let any god rain down his wrath upon him, Egyptian or Phoenician or Israelite. Like any good Phoenician, he respected the gods of everyone with whom he traded, and always hedged his bets.

He stared ahead, feeling faint. The *gorilla* skins on the Ark might take Ezekiel aback, but by now they would be imprinted with its shape; they would be all the proof that was needed that the Ark had been delivered. He took another heavy step forward, cracking the encrusted shore. There was something more powerful than fear of the gods that had kept him true to his word. Ezekiel's gold had spoken. Hanno was a Phoenician first and foremost, with trade in his blood. Ezekiel's gold and jewels would make him the wealthiest man in Carthage: able to afford the bounty he had promised his sister for giving up her infant for sacrifice, able to dedicate a new temple at the harbor entrance where he would hang the trophies of his voyage, able to make sure his brother Himilco would want for nothing if his own voyage to the Cassiterides had failed to reap a profit. And Ezekiel had also known something else—that the word of a Phoenician was his true word, his covenant, as binding as that between the Israelites and their god. Hanno would do everything in his power to see his cargo delivered, and to banish all thoughts of return until then.

For now, he needed to summon his remaining energy to cross this desolate wasteland, a place where even Ba'al Hammon seemed to have forsaken him. He staggered forward another few steps, his feet crunching through the salt rind, his ankles raw and bloody from pulling them out against the crust. He tried to remember details of their voyage to keep his mind from wandering. He remembered setting up the bronze plaque on the southern cape weeks before. When they had finished, they realized that the native people had emerged from the bush and were watching them, and Hanno had flung himself on the ground as if worshipping the plaque, hoping that the natives would see its sanctity and leave it intact. Their interpreter from the land of the *gorillae* told the people that to damage the plaque would be to bring certain death, just as Ezekiel had told Hanno about the Ark. The people, called Lembana by the interpreter, had seemed suitably awed, and had brought offerings of fresh fruit and meat that Hanno's men had gratefully devoured, caring little that the offerings had been meant to satisfy this unknown new deity rather than their own desperate hunger and thirst.

At the cape his crew had begun to die from a mysterious ailment that had swept through them after they had stopped for water at the mouth of a river a week before. He had taken on two of the native men to bolster the remaining crew, and to help forage ashore. He knew there was every chance that he and his precious cargo might disappear without a trace, and he had decided to leave evidence of their passing. If they succeeded in delivering the Ark, the two Lembana would be released from their bond and told to make their own way back to the cape, taking the memory of what they had seen with them. On the plaque, beneath the message in Phoenician, he had used a chisel to punch in the crude shape of a hieroglyph that Ezekiel had showed him, one that would leave little doubt to any hunting him that they were on the right trail, that he had at least made it that far. To do this had not been to break the pact of secrecy with Ezekiel. The only ones ever likely to follow him would be those sent to recover the Ark, and the hieroglyph was one that only they would understand.

After many weeks of sailing they had veered northeast, around a great promontory that the local fishermen called the Horn, past desolate rocky islands and then northwest through a bay that narrowed to a strait before opening out again. Hanno knew they must have passed into the southern reaches of the Erythraean Sea, with the desert expanses of Arabia on their right and the southern border of Egypt not far ahead. By the time they had reached the beginning of the salt flats, only two of his crew remained alive, barely enough to steer the ship and brail the big square sail. Hanno had pressed on despite their dwindling rations, knowing that if he stopped to forage, he would almost certainly be unable to induce his men to return to the ship, to yet more misery and pain. Every day as they sailed further north he had anxiously observed the sun with his wooden backstaff, waiting for it to reach the highest point in the sky. And then at dawn on this day he had seen it, a ripple of light reflecting off the mountains just as Ezekiel had described it, a burning chariot racing across the western horizon: the Chariot of Fire.

He had steered the ship ashore, and prepared to abandon her. He knew that they had reached a point not far south of the land the Egyptians called Punt, near the entrance to the Erythraean Sea. He had been there years before, on an expedition down the Nile with Himilco to find the finest elephant ivory, and he knew that if they were lucky, he and the two surviving sailors might find a caravan route and strike out across the desert toward North Africa and their homeland. The two sailors and the Lembana had heaved the Ark off the ship, strapping the *gorillae* hides tightly around it and departing ahead of Hanno, who had stayed back to fill the sack with anything they could consume. Parched with thirst, the sailors had underestimated the challenge of crossing the salt rind in the scorching heat. Without the two Lembana, who had shifted the sailors out of the way and taken on the burden themselves, they would have made no more than a few hundred paces, not much farther than Hanno had reached now.

He caught a glimpse of something on the salt flats to the north, and stopped struggling forward, swaying to and fro, staring. It was something glistening, something flashing, a wavering in the haze. For a split second he thought he saw horses, perhaps camels. He closed his eyes, and then looked again, blinking hard. *It was still there.* His heart began to pound even faster than it was already, and he was jarred into action. Riders from the north might bring succor, might bring food and water, might be their salvation. But this was a brutal land, a land where men showed no mercy to interlopers, and more likely they would bring death. He stared back at the mountains, trying to judge the distance. He might be lucky. The riders might still be a long way off, the specter foreshortened by mirage. By marshalling all of his remaining energy he might just make the foothills in time. The others were nearly there already with their burden, barely visible against the mountain backdrop. They could conceal themselves among the ridges and canyons of the foothills, where pursuers would only be able to follow on foot and might quickly give up. Once there, he and his men might find game to hunt, and they would surely find water. They could still make it.

He had sailed farther around Africa from the Pillars of Hercules than any explorer had done before. He had been entrusted with a mission, a cargo to discharge, and as a Phoenician, he could never default on that trust. But he had another covenant, too. It was a covenant with his brother, a pact to return and gaze together once again over the great expanse of the ocean, to tell stories of what they had seen and where they had gone, to exult in their adventures. Himilco, he knew, might reach as far as Ultima Thule, a place where the sky itself was said to be frozen, rippling with blue like the sea ice; in return, he would expect no less of Hanno than the circumnavigation of Africa. They were traders, to be sure, but they were also explorers, driven by the quest to see what lay just beyond the horizon. Hanno would summon up every last drop of energy to push himself forward, to live for the day when he would see his brother again. His was a covenant with survival.

He began to hear a distant beating, like the drums on the walls of Carthage before a sacrifice. He was unsure whether it was coming from the riders or was the sound of the blood pounding in his own ears. Out of the haze from the direction of the riders a camel lurched past, its burden hunched forward, blood pulsing from a gaping wound that had stained his robe a vivid red. Hanno stared at him as he carried on south, watching the spray of salt dust each time the camel's hooves pounded through the crust, then turned again to look at the man's pursuers. One of them, with long dark hair, brandished a whip, and the others had blades that flashed in the sun, their robes billowing behind them like one continuous sheet of white rippling along the seashore. For a moment he was caught between two intersecting worlds: one that would surely see his lifeblood spilled here beside his ship, the other that might offer hope, that might mean a chance of survival.

He dropped his sack and began to run.

Part 1

Part I

1

Marine archaeologist Jack Howard stared down into the abyss, hearing nothing but the hiss of his oxygen rebreather as he floated in the deep ocean swell. Somewhere down there, somewhere in the inky blackness below, lay a prize beyond the dreams of most deep-sea salvors, a king's ransom in gold resting unclaimed in international waters. But at the moment, Jack was far less concerned about the gold than about the diver who had just preceded him. Costas had plummeted in his usual fashion, like a sack of lead, weighed down by the array of tools on his belt. As their rebreathers produced no bubbles, he had disappeared almost without a trace, barely leaving a quiver in the shot line that anchored them to the wreck. After more than twenty years of diving together, Jack had seen his friend disappear down more black holes than he cared to remember, but this time, more than fifty miles from shore in the forbidding waters of the South Atlantic, it had been particularly unnerving. They had the experience to confront virtually anything the oceans had to offer, but Jack knew that what sailors used to call divine providence would always have the final say. Not for the first time over the last few years, he shut his eyes and mouthed the words he always did before a perilous dive into the unknown: *Lucky Jack*.

He opened his eyes and checked the LED display inside his helmet. He remembered the last time he had watched Costas disappear into the abyss, in the Mediterranean five months earlier during their hunt for a pharaoh's lost sarcophagus. Costas had been trapped inside a submersible that had lost its tether and was falling to the ocean floor, and Jack had made a split-second decision to freedive after it, a one-way ticket to oblivion had he failed to reach it in time. Then, there had been no time for reflection, no time for fear. But this time the few minutes he had spent on the surface after watching Costas go had been enough for his heart rate to increase, for his mouth to go dry. His computer had flashed up a yellow warning just as they were about to descend together, too late for him to signal Costas to abort. The diagnostic in his helmet display had shown the reappearance of a glitch in the first-stage rebreather manifold, something that Costas had tried to fix in the support vessel's repair shop before the dive, a fraught few hours during which Jack had been locked in an argument with the captain about the need to keep the shot-line anchor out of the wreckage in order to avoid damaging the sunken hull even before they had begun to explore it.

All he could do now was wait for his computer to complete the diagnostic and hope that it could repair itself. Their communication system was down too, meaning he could no longer talk to Costas, a problem not with their own equipment but with the link to the ship's control room. That and the lack of specialized tools in the repair shop had been just two of the small irritations since they had been winched down by helicopter with their equipment onto *Deep Explorer* the day before.

He rolled sideways, seeing the unfamiliar hull a few meters beyond the shot-line buoy. Instead of *Seaquest*, instead of the support divers from the International Maritime University and the submersible that would normally accompany a dive of this nature, they were operating from a commercial salvage vessel without any of the usual IMU safety backup. They were here because a landmark change in legislation had finally seen British merchant vessel wrecks of the Second World War designated as war graves. They were also here because a researcher for the salvage company had found a secret cargo manifest showing that the ship below them, the SS *Clan Macpherson*, sunk by a U-boat in 1943, had been carrying a consignment of two tons of gold. Without that gold, the salvors would have had no interest in the wreck. With it, they were prepared to destroy the wreck to get at the cargo.

This had been the first case since the legislation had been passed, and Jack had agreed to spearhead the UN monitoring program, knowing that his clout as archaeological director of IMU would ensure that the wreck would be front-page news if things went awry. The salvage company knew that too, and apart from this morning's spat over the anchor chain, relations had been businesslike. They may have thought they were on an easy ride, with two of the world's foremost maritime archaeologists here to verify the wreck and provide guidelines for the salvage, a token requirement that they could make a great show of following while they went ahead and ripped the wreck apart to get at the gold, something the world's press were hardly going to see more than a hundred meters below the sea. Jack was determined to do anything he could to prevent that from happening.

He heard the roar of an outboard engine, and moments later saw a Zodiac swing out from the stern of the vessel with several crew on board and head toward him. He motioned for them to come between him and the ship, a safer option in the mounting swell than being trapped in a narrow space between the two vessels. The crewman at the tiller throttled down and put the engine in neutral as he came alongside. Jack grabbed the rope around the edge of the inflatable and hung on as the project logistics director, a former oil-rig foreman named Macinnes, leaned over. "What's the problem?" he shouted.

Jack was wearing a full-face mask as part of his IMU e-suit, an all-environment drysuit with integrated buoyancy system that Costas had perfected over the years. He was not willing to raise the mask while he was in the water, but he clicked open a one-way valve beside his mouth-piece that would allow him to be heard without letting water in. "Same problem as before with the regulator manifold," he said, bracing himself to stop the swell pulling him under the boat. "My computer's running a diagnostic."

"I thought Kazantzakis had fixed it," Macinnes shouted, staring imperiously at Jack.

"He did the best he could with the available tools."

"Don't blame us. Our remit was to host you, not to provide logistical backup. That's your call."

Jack gritted his teeth, trying to keep his cool. Floating here with a faulty regulator and his friend on the seabed more than a hundred meters below was not the time or place to bicker with these people. He strained his head back upward. "Costas programmed the computer to self-repair if it happened again, so I'm just waiting for it to finish."

The man jerked his head toward the empty ocean beyond the shot-line buoy. "Does he always go off alone like that? Not the best buddy."

Jack ignored the comment. Macinnes and Costas had barely been on speaking terms since they had arrived. Macinnes had made a big show of bowing to Jack's superior archaeological knowledge, but had decided that he knew more about submersibles and remote-operated vehicles than Dr. Costas Kazantzakis, a big mistake. The fact that he had been unable to put down an ROV to do the preliminary recon or to accompany the dive would seem to have proved Costas's case. Jack swung sideways in the swell, holding on with two hands. "What's the story with the comms?"

"It's the *same* story. You brought your own equipment, it didn't match ours. Not our responsibility."

"Is anyone on to it? I can't communicate with Costas."

"It's irrelevant, with the weather getting worse. The forecast has upped from Force 4 to Force 8 in the next few hours. The last thing we need is a botched inspection and a fatality to cloud our press reports. We've come to pick you up."

"Negative. I'm not leaving Costas to do the dive on his own."

"Looks like he was quite happy to leave without you."

Jack tried to restrain his anger. The last thing he needed before a deep dive was aggravation like this. He clicked the valve shut and pushed off from the boat, making a circular motion with his hand and pointing away as he finned back to the shot-line buoy. The crewman at the tiller looked at Macinnes, who raised his hands theatrically and shrugged. He sat back down and the crewman flipped the engine into forward, driving it in a wide arc around Jack and back toward the entry platform at the stern of the ship.

Jack reached the buoy, holding himself against the current, and looked up to see a line of crewmen wearing *Deep Explorer* caps along the foredeck rail. Dealing with these people over the last twenty-four hours had taught him one thing. He had seen more dull eyes and lassitude among this team than he had ever seen on a project before. He was fortunate that IMU had been a purely scientific endeavor from the outset, funded through an endowment from a billionaire software tycoon who also happened to be one of Jack's oldest diving friends. Being here, and witnessing every discussion fall back on the hard floor of profitability, he had seen how the quest for financial gain ultimately drew the fire out of people. What drove Jack on was the urge for adventure and discovery that had pushed humans to explore since earliest prehistory, and a passion for revealing the truth about the past that could make the lowliest potsherd more valuable than any amount of gold that these people might rip out of wrecks like the one below him now.

He glanced up at the railing again, spotting a muscular figure in jeans and a checkered shirt with close-cropped graying hair, leaning on a stick. Anatoly Landor was Jack's oldest dive buddy, the one who had been there beside him when he had taken his first breath from a diving tank in a pool while they had been at boarding school together. At first they had been inseparable, joined by their shared passion for diving, but then they had drifted apart, Jack into archaeology and Landor into treasure hunting. Landor had been an outsider at school, the son of an emigré Russian aristocrat's daughter and a shady British businessman, and that had set the pattern for his future. Early on, before IMU had been founded, he had tried to enlist Jack into his projects, but their differences had been irreconcilable. For the past three years he had been operations director for Deep Explorer Incorporated, the investment consortium that owned the ship. The walking stick was because of a severe bend that had kept him out of the water for almost two years now.

Jack looked at him, remembering the raised arm with an okay signal that would have been there in the past, but knowing that this time there would be nothing. Landor had been a changed man since his accident, still with the upper body strength he had honed at school but with severely weakened legs, and a warning from the doctors that any further exposure to nitrogen buildup in his bloodstream—even a dive to swimming pool depth—would almost certainly result in a spinal bend and permanent paralysis. But it was not so much the physical change that Jack noticed as the hardening of his soul. Landor's knowledge that he would have made this dive himself before his accident only increased the distance between them, fueling a resentment toward Jack that had been bubbling under the surface over the years, and was now plain to see.

His monitor was still only halfway through running the diagnostic, and he looked down into the depths again. The sea here was a strange color, green more than blue, an ominous shade, as if an ugly run-off from the war-torn countries of Africa had spilled out over the continental shelf. It could not have been a greater contrast to the azure waters of Cornwall, off southwest England, where he had been diving only three days before. When the call had come through that *Deep Explorer* had pinpointed the wreck of *Clan Macpherson*, he had just spent an hour in the shallows off the western Lizard peninsula near the IMU campus, excavating a perfectly preserved elephant's tusk that he was convinced was part of a Phoenician cargo. He had been very reluctant to leave the site, and had spent the flight down to Sierra Leone reading *The Periplus of Hanno*, the account of a sixth-century BC Carthaginian explorer who had sailed these very waters off West Africa. It had reminded him of the extent of Phoenician exploration on both sides of the Strait of Gibraltar, stoking his excitement over what he had been excavating and the new story of the earliest explorers that it would allow him to tell.

The Phoenician wreck off Cornwall had been his first big project since returning from Egypt the previous year, and he was gripped by it. But a few hours in Freetown waiting for the helicopter out to *Deep Explorer*, seeing the state of Sierra Leone and its people, had made him realize that his priority for now had to be here. Channeled through the right humanitarian organization, the two tons of gold alleged to be on the wreck below them could make a substantial difference. The wreck was beyond territorial limits, but the IMU lawyers had suggested that a claim of ownership could be made on the grounds that Freetown was the destination of the wartime convoy and there was no documentation to show that the gold was to be transported further. It was a shaky case, but it could buy them time. At the very least, it would garner negative publicity for the salvage company and might deter investors. Nobody would want to be linked to a company that sought personal profit rather than donating a discovery of questionable ownership to one of the poorest and most war-torn countries in the world, a discovery that could provide enough to feed thousands and save countless lives.

He glanced again at his readout. Costas had been gone for ten minutes now, and still there were no comms. It would be at least another five minutes until the diagnostic was complete and he knew whether or not he could follow. He made himself focus on the objective of their dive, running through the details once more. *Clan Macpherson* had been a freighter of 9,940 tons' burden owned by the Clan Line, one of the last of the great East Indies shipping companies. On her final voyage she'd had a crew of 140 men, made up of Indian Lascar ratings, British deck and engineer officers, and Royal Navy gunners to man her defensive armament. Her master, Captain Edward Gough, was a veteran of two previous sinkings, and had been decorated for his courage and seamanship. Her voyage halfway round the world from India to Liverpool was to have been a routine one, plied by thousands of ships during the war. After leaving Calcutta, she had sailed unescorted down the Bay of Bengal and across the Indian Ocean to Durban in South Africa. From there she had joined the first of a succession of convoys that were to take her up the coast of West Africa to Freetown, the staging port for ships heading across the Atlantic to the Americas or north to Gibraltar and home.

The final leg of that route, as part of convoy TS-37 between Takoradi in the Gold Coast and Freetown, should have been uneventful. The weather was fine, clear and overcast, and the 848-mile journey was expected to take five days at the convoy's maximum speed of eight knots. The main focus of the U-boats was in the North Atlantic; it had been more than two years since a TS convoy had been struck. The escort for the nineteen merchantmen when they had left Takoradi on April 26 was little more than a token force—one corvette and three armed trawlers—and there was no air cover. Yet when the first ship was hit, when the first plume of water rose from a torpedo strike, the sight would have been sickeningly familiar to many of the seamen in the convoy. By that stage in the war the Clan Line had lost thirty-two ships—more than half its fleet—and more than 600 men, a rate repeated in the other shipping companies. Many of the seamen in TS-37 would have seen ships sunk in other convoys in the North Atlantic and the Mediterranean, and would have endured the fear of not knowing whether they were to be next.

That first strike by U-515 at 8:55 p.m. on April 30 was followed within five minutes by three others, and then a further three ships were sunk in another devastating five-minute attack in the early hours of the morning. *Clan Macpherson* had been the last to go, straggling behind the convoy, settling down by the head and listing to starboard. Captain Gough survived, but the ship had taken almost her entire complement of engineer officers with her when she finally plummeted to the seabed and came to rest on the edge of the continental shelf more than one hundred meters below Jack now.

Jack ran through a checklist of her cargo: pig iron, groundnuts, linseed, jute, tea. At least there was no record of munitions, other than ammunition for her own guns. Diving into wrecks with unexploded ordnance, their fuses decayed and unstable, was not usually Jack's favorite pastime. But there was no way of knowing for sure. The discovery that she had also secretly been carrying two tons of gold had shown what could be missing from cargo manifests. For a moment, thinking of Costas somewhere below him, risking his life, Jack wished that the researcher in the archives had never found that record, and he felt a flash of anger at the salvage company and its investors. He was damned if he was going to let that gold line anyone's pockets. He would fight tooth and nail to see it go to humanitarian relief, using the considerable weight of IMU's board of directors and their legal team to drag it through the international courts as far as it could go.

And there was another factor that weighed on Jack's mind, the official reason for his inspection. If Landor and the salvage company had imagined that war grave designation was something they could simply brush aside, they would be wrong. It was something else that made Jack want to spin out an ownership dispute as long as possible. New UN legislation currently in its final reading, spearheaded by IMU, would prevent salvors who transgressed from dealing with the financial institutions of signatory nations. To transgress would make them into pirates, only able to sell their finds and launder their money on the black market, making it easier for law enforcement agencies to shut them down. Investors lured into supporting them with promises of sunken treasure would pull out and put their money elsewhere. Jack was here today because this scheme was the best hope of protecting historically important wrecks in international waters. Above all, he would do all he could to protect a war grave from being plundered; persevering with the dive and making a case against *Deep Explorer* was his commitment to the memory of the men who had gone down with this ship on that terrible night in 1943.

He stared into the depths again. He had seen enough wrecked merchantmen from the two world wars to have some idea of what to expect. A ship that was not heavily laden could sink slowly, allowing enough time for its interior compartments to fill with water before it went down; the wreck could be substantially intact, damaged only by the torpedo strike and by the impact with the seabed. A fully laden ship that sank quickly could be another matter entirely, its compartments still filled with air and imploding as the ship sank, leaving jagged masses of metal. *Clan Macpherson* had been carrying more than 8,000 tons of cargo, an enormous dead weight once buoyancy had been lost.

There was one aspect of those sinkings that haunted Jack the most. Men must often have been trapped inside air pockets, alive after the ship had disappeared from the surface. Their deaths would not have been like those portrayed in Hollywood films: a final few moments as the churning waters rose, a gulp of seawater and unconsciousness. Instead they would have been horrific, surrounded by the shrieking and cracking of the hull, the air pockets lasting long enough for the titanic pressures of the ocean to bear down on them, bursting their eardrums and collapsing their sinuses, a final unspeakable agony as the ship plummeted to its grave.

Men who went to sea in ships knew full well the horrors of Davy Jones's Locker. It was what singled them out, what made them tough. Jack came from a long line of such men, sea captains who had defended England's shores at the time of the Spanish Armada, explorers and adventurers who had pushed the boundaries of knowledge during the Age of Exploration, merchants who had built fortunes on the spice trade with the East and the riches of the West. He himself was another, modern kind of explorer, one who had dared to go where his ancestors could scarcely have imagined, who had descended into the world of their nightmares, who had touched the void. His boundary was no longer the distant horizon that had beckoned his forebears, but he knew the same siren call of the unknown as he stared into the depths. He knew their excitement, and he knew their fear.

The LED display on his computer flashed green. The computer had fixed the fault, and the rebreather was good to go. He took a deep breath and steeled himself. It was time to dive.

2

Jack raised his head out of the water one last time and gave a thumbs-down signal for the benefit of the crewmen on *Deep Explorer* who were watching him. The ocean swell was now producing two-meter troughs, and he needed to get below the turbulence. He grasped the shot line beneath the buoy and pulled himself down, feeling the hiss of air into his suit as his automated buoyancy system compensated for the change in pressure, keeping him neutral. Five meters down, he was below the main effect of the swell, but the current was stronger than on the surface, pulling him out almost horizontally from the line. He clicked his buoyancy compensator to manual, pinched his nose through his visor to equalize the pressure, and grasped the line with his other hand, letting it run through his fingers as he slowly dropped spread-eagled into the depths. He had watched Costas do the same, holding on as he plummeted out of sight, and prayed that he had kept hold of the line until reaching the wreck. To let go would mean being swept off site beyond the edge of the continental shelf, and surfacing far from the ship. With no means of communication and the current trending southeast, that could only mean a long, slow ride into the middle of the Atlantic, with little chance of ever being picked up.

Jack was in his element. The tension he had felt on the surface, the slight edge of seasickness in the swell, had disappeared. As he descended further, his intercom began to crackle. "Costas," he said loudly. "Do you read me.

Over." There was still no response. He rolled over, seeing the smudge of
Deep Explorer's hull still visible above him, then turned back to face the
green-blue gloom below. He had reached sixty meters, the safe limit of
compressed-air diving, and was now entering the realm where his life depended on the continuing function of his oxygen rebreather. If the glitch
recurred now, before he reached Costas, his only chance of survival would
be an emergency ascent using the system's bailout regulator, a dangerous
move that would put Costas beyond his help should anything go wrong. If
all went well, the rebreather would allow him an hour at 120 meters, the
maximum depth of the wreck indicated by the sonar. But their expectation
had been for a bottom time shorter than that. All Jack needed to provide
evidence for a war grave designation was to verify the identity of the wreck.

He had kept his helmet headlamps off for the descent, knowing that
the beam from the thousand-lumen bulbs would cut through the gloom
but also reflect off suspended particles in the water, potentially dazzling
him. He wanted to accustom himself to the low light before reaching the
wreck, and then only use the beam for close-up work. He checked his depth
readout again: ninety meters. The gloom was enveloping him, but below
it he began to sense something darker, the mottled shapes of rocky outcrops
on the sea floor. Below him and just off to the right he saw the flashing red
of a strobe. He felt a huge wave of relief course through him. It was a beacon, a waymarker. It showed that Costas had reached the seabed safely.
Then he saw another light, a distant smudge perhaps twenty meters beyond the strobe, along the line of the drop-off where the continental shelf
abruptly ended and the seabed angled into the abyss.

And then he saw the wreck. For a moment it took his breath away. The
vast bulk of the ship loomed below him, its funnel gone and the superstructure a mass of twisted metal but still recognizable as a merchantman
of its era. Beyond it he could see the inky blackness of the water above the
drop-off, and on the other side the level plateau of the continental shelf at
120 meters' depth. The ship had come to rest along the very rim of the shelf,
upright but split in two places where the hull had impacted with ridges on
the sea floor. The strobe light had been placed below the bow; the smudge
of white came from one of the breaks further back in the hull. Jack sank
down toward the strobe, passing the intact four-inch gun still in its mount
on the forecastle, its ammunition box open and ready for use. Seconds later
he came to a halt just above the flashing red beacon, seeing that Costas

had jammed it into a crack in the rock in front of the 200-lb lead weight from *Deep Explorer* that anchored the shot line.

He kept hold of the line and let himself float with the current for a moment, taking stock of his situation. He was 124 meters deep, on the rim of the continental shelf. To his right he could see a jagged seascape of rocks extending east, a plateau that would eventually reach the African coast. To his left was the yawning chasm of the drop-off, no more than twenty meters away. The wreck was blocking the current, a south-trending flow that might exceed four or five knots in the open water beyond the drop-off, too strong to swim against. To stray out there might be to take a roller-coaster ride to oblivion, with the current sweeping down the side of the canyon and taking anyone with it to an abyssal depth before ejecting them far away, beyond the drop-off. He steeled himself, breathing rhythmically, focusing on the task at hand. He was going to have to be careful.

He switched on his headlamps and looked around. The world of gloom and shadows, a place where nothing seemed alive, had suddenly transformed into one of vivid colors and marine growth. It was too deep for most corals, but the rock was covered with living accretion and the water was filled with diaphanous organisms that reflected the light: plankton and diatoms and miniature nudibranchs. He blinked hard, adjusting to the particulate reflection, and then looked up, the two beams of his headlamp converging on the side of the hull above him. The iron was covered with rusticules, extrusions of ferrous material that seemed to drip off the hull like stalactites, with little trails of red streaming from them into the current as if the ship were bleeding. He could now see that the solidity of the wreck as it had first appeared in the gloom was an illusion—that after more than seventy years on the seabed, exposed to a powerful current, the hull plates were thin and friable, not far from crumbling entirely. The force of the current bearing on the hull meant that when the structure gave way, it was likely to be catastrophic, causing large parts to break away and be swept into the abyss. This was not a wreck that Jack would normally wish to penetrate, and the sooner they got out of here the better.

Then he saw the lettering below the port rail some ten meters above him, a few meters back from the gun mounting. It read: *Clan Macpherson*. It was what Jack had wanted to see, the proof that he needed. He checked his readout, making sure that the video camera on the front of his helmet was running. Those letters had probably been the only surviving remnant of her peacetime livery, as if in defiance of the gray uniformity that war had imposed on all ships. The sight of them, nearly clear of corrosion, gave him a strange sense of clairvoyance, allowing him to see for a moment the rusting hulk transformed into the ship as she originally had been. He thought of the men who had crewed her, of those who had gone down with the ship, who were still here now. More than ever he felt that the wreck was a place of sanctity, as deserving of respect as the thousands of other ships that had taken men down with them in the two world wars, whose remains were strewn across the ocean floor.

He angled his head so that his beam panned over the seabed. He could see a thin white line extending from the strobe along the port side of the wreck, the side in the lee of the current facing away from the drop-off. He reached down and gave it a tug. He guessed that it extended to where he had seen the smudge of light partway along the hull, some-where in the green-black haze ahead.

Suddenly his intercom crackled. "Jack, are you there? Over."

Jack felt another rush of relief. "I'm at the bow, over. The manifold glitch recurred and I had to wait on the surface for the computer to fix it. What's the story with the comms?"

"A few moments ago I realized that the problem wasn't with our inter-com but with the diver-to-ship link. I shut that off, and hey presto."

"So *Deep Explorer* can't hear us."

"Just you and me. Like it should be."

"You were on your own. I was worried."

"You won't believe what I've found."

"I saw the ship's name."

"It's incredible," Costas said. "The coordinates in the official report were dead on. Captain Gough fixed the position of the sinking with almost pinpoint accuracy, after having been torpedoed and from an open boat."

"That doesn't surprise me," Jack said. "Back then they were still taught navigation in the same way as Nelson's officers, using dead reckoning with a sextant and chronometer. The best captains had a sixth sense for it, and Gough was obviously one of those. So what have you found? And where the hell are you?"

"Jack, I need you to do something for me. I need you very carefully to look round the starboard side and see how much of the wreck is actually hanging over the edge."

Jack looked to his left beyond the bow over the drop-off, seeing the particulate matter at the furthest extent of his beam rush by at an alarming speed, like a snowstorm caught in a car's headlights. He finned a few strokes past the bow, feeling the edge of the current stream against his body, and peered over. In his experience, most drop-offs were not absolutely sheer, but this one was. The rock at the edge formed a jagged precipice over a darkness as forbidding as he had ever seen. To his right, *Clan Macpherson*'s bow rose high above him, and he could now see the starboard side of the hull hanging over the void. "Just out of curiosity, how stable is the geology?" he asked.

Costas's reply crackled through. "The bedrock's metamorphic, pretty friable. This cliff edge is like a snow cornice on the top of a mountain ridge. Not where I'd choose to park a ship carrying eight thousand tons of cargo."

"You don't want to see what I can see. From here, the hull looks as if it's barely balanced on the edge."

"That's what I thought. But around the other side, where I am, you should be fine penetrating the hull providing you don't disrupt anything. Thankfully our rebreathers don't produce exhaust, so there's no danger of creating air pockets that could crack any weakened structure. It's pretty rusty in here."

"We've seen the ship's name on the bow. That's all we need. We can leave now."

"You'd kill me if I told you what I'd found but didn't give you the chance to see it for yourself. Anyway, I'm in here already. You should be with me."

"I'm trying to see the logic in that."

"It's called the buddy system."

"Right."

"Trust me. Follow the line."

"Roger that." Jack angled his body around, sensing the yawning chasm beneath him as the current took hold of his legs and swung them round until he was parallel with the hull. He knew that he was going to have to fin hard for a few strokes to regain the lip of the precipice, but that once he was in the lee of the wreck again, the water movement would slacken. He finned hard, but nothing happened. In a split second he realized his mistake. In the process of turning, he had allowed the current to take him crucially beyond the protective bulk of the wreck, and he was suddenly being swept along the edge of the drop-off. He felt a lurching sensation, as if he had jumped out of an aircraft, as if the bottom were falling out under him. The current had undulated downward, and he was dropping below the edge as fast as if he were riding a water chute into the void. His computer set off an audible alert and flashed red as it overrode the manual on his buoyancy system and bled air into his suit. The extra lift slowed him down enough for him to right himself and hit the alarm on the side of his helmet, activating a beacon that sent out a continuous sound-wave pulse. He smacked into something, and saw that it was a jagged lava pinnacle protruding from the cliff. He clung on to it, dragging himself up until he was straddling it, perched on an overhang between a mottled wall of rock rising high above and the sheer cliff dropping into the void below.

He looked with horror at his depth gauge: 149 meters. In a matter of seconds he had plummeted twenty-five meters below the level of the wreck. He peered at the rock face above, trying to calm his breathing. There were other protuberances, enough for handholds. It would have been a difficult ascent in the most favorable of conditions, with overhangs that would challenge the best free-climber. Down here, he was impeded by his equipment, by the current bearing down on him like an underwater waterfall, and by his inability to use footholds. He stared at his fins, fought against instinct and pressed the catch at the back of each ankle, causing the fins to draw up and mold around his calves. He would now have no chance against the current if he were swept off, but he knew they would be of little use anyway. At least now he could try to use footholds as if he were properly climbing.

He edged behind the outcrop, feeling the current slacken. There would be pockets of calm close to the cliff, beneath overhangs and inside fissures, and he needed to find those where he could. The air in his suit had caused his arms and chest to balloon out, reducing his maneuverability. He hit the manual override, bleeding off the air until he could move more freely. It was another counterintuitive decision, almost certainly sealing his fate if he were to be swept off, but it was his only chance of making any headway on the climb.

He tapped his intercom. He had heard nothing but crackling since being swept away. "Costas, do you read me. I'm at a hundred and forty-nine meters depth, over the cliff beyond the bow of the wreck, at least fifty meters southwest of my original position. I was swept over by the current and am attempting to climb back. Help would be appreciated. Over."

There was still no response. He guessed that the rock face between them was impeding radio contact, but he knew that the sound waves from his beacon pulsing up the cliff face should be detectable by Costas's homing device. He had to climb now, or give up any hope of survival. He released his hold on the protuberance and grasped another one above him, the jagged edges of the lava biting into the Kevlar of his glove. He pulled himself up, feeling almost impossibly heavy as he swung out against the current, every muscle in his body straining as he reached up with his other hand and found a hold. He kicked his feet back into the rock, finding a ledge and pulling himself onto it. Three meters done, twenty-two to go. He felt his heart pound, his breathing rate increase. He needed to be calm, measured, as he used to be when he had enjoyed rock-climbing, clearing his mind and focusing solely on his objective. He reached up to another handhold, and then another. Slowly, relentlessly, feeling as if he were carrying a sack of lead on his back, he fought his way up against the current, following the line of a fissure that seemed to offer the path of least resistance.

After another five meters he stopped again, his feet and hands wedged into the fissure. He tried another hold, slipped sideways and felt the current swing him around violently, crunching his rebreather backpack against the rock. He stayed still, watching with trepidation as his computer display flickered and wavered, trying not to think of the glitch in his manifold and what might trigger it again. Above him was an overhang he had seen from below but put from his mind, hoping that the fissure would continue through it. Now he saw that the fissure led into a collapsed cavern below the overhang, the remains of a lava tube. He would have to attempt the overhang like a free-climber, using only his hands, dangling over the void. Everything up to now would seem easy by comparison. He would be in the full force of the current again, fighting a downward pressure three or four times greater than anything he had encountered so far.

His arms felt heavy with the strain, and he was breathing hard. He thought of the bailout option, something he had refused to consider until now. He could let go and free fall into the void, no longer fighting the current but hoping that it would undulate back upward and spit him out above the ridge, allowing him to ascend to the surface. But that was hardly a viable plan. Even if he did make the surface, he would probably be miles away, dependent entirely on his beacon for any hope of rescue, being swept relentlessly out into the Atlantic by the heavy seas they knew were on the way. He tensed himself, focusing. He would only let that happen if his body gave way and he could physically hang on no longer. Until then, pressing on and reaching Costas was his only hope.

He pulled himself up, and hit his helmet on something. He shifted to one side, inching further up the fissure, attempting to avoid the unseen obstacle. He hit his head again, this time harder. He swung back, just in time to avoid being smacked in his visor. He stared at what was in front of him, and then felt an overwhelming rush of relief. It was an old-fashioned two-kilogram lead diving weight, suspended from a white nylon line. He looked up, his headlamp beam catching the line where it came down the overhang. He eased his feet out of the fissure, reached down with one hand to click his fins back into position and then grasped the weight with the same hand, letting go of the rock with the other and feeling the current pull him far out over the void. Ahead of him the line stretched taut to a point above the rim where he could just make out a beam of light below the bow of the wreck. He could feel himself being pulled forward, slowly but surely. The current slackened, and he was in the lee of the wreck over the rim of the cliff. He finned along the remaining length of line until he reached Costas, who had belayed it around a rock pinnacle just in front of the bows.

"Look what I caught," Costas said.

Jack looked at the familiar stubbled face behind the visor, hardly believing what had just happened.

"The intercom went down as soon as you went over the drop-off. One of my design team in the engineering lab suggested that beacon with a magnified pulse array. All I had to do was activate my helmet display to locate it, and then go fishing. I think maybe we owe her a beer."

"Roger that. And I'll never make fun of you for fishing again. What other diver would carry a length of line and a lead weight with them?"

Costas patted his tool belt, then coiled the line and stowed it in a pouch. "Always be prepared."

"Thanks, by the way. I didn't think I was going to make it up that overhang."

"The buddy system, remember? Always pays to have a good buddy."

"How much time do we have?"

"How deep did you get?"

"A hundred and forty-nine meters. My readout shows my gas supply's still good for another half-hour bottom time."

"Twenty minutes," Costas said. "We don't want to extend our decompression time. Those bozos on *Deep Explorer* would probably leave without us. Now, where were we? You ready to see something incredible?"

Jack checked his helmet readout and did a quick self-diagnostic. His breathing had returned to normal, and any aches and pains from the climb were eclipsed by the adrenalin. He looked up again at the bow of the wreck, and then along the line Costas had laid into the gloom along the port side. If there was something good to see here, he was damned if he was going to forgo it after what he had just been through.

"How many lives do I have left?" he said.

"That was about your eighth. You've got plenty to go."

"Okay. Show me what you've got."

3

Costas powered ahead beside the sunken hull, the wake of his fins stirring up the silt and monofilaments that were caught in Jack's headlamp beam. To his left the hull loomed high above, blocking off the yawning chasm on the other side. About twenty meters along the line from the bow, Costas veered inside, the yellow of his helmet disappearing from view. He had entered a vertical crack in the hull, some three meters across at the bottom and widening as it went up. Jack turned to follow, spotting Costas's figure where the line led inside, their headlamp beams revealing a jumbled mass of structure and machinery. "Keep hold of the line," Costas said, the intercom crackling. "I tried not to disrupt the sediment when I was in here before, but even so the visibility is poor. Some of the compartments must have imploded during the sinking, and it's a shambles inside."

"I don't see any evidence here of a torpedo strike," Jack said.

"Not here. This is where the hull split when it impacted with the seabed. The cargo holds on either side are filled with iron and manganese ore, thousands of tons of it. There's no way the ship could have survived hitting the sea floor intact carrying that kind of weight. It's amazing that the torpedo didn't do that itself, but these pre-war Clyde-built ships were stronger than the Liberty ships you see splitting in half in the U-boat periscope footage."

"Where did it strike?"

"Toward the stern, just before the number two hold. We're going to get there by swimming beneath the deckhouse superstructure, through what's left of the engine room. Follow me."

Jack checked his computer display. The profile had automatically readjusted to take account of his greater depth and gas consumption during his escapade over the canyon edge, and now gave him only twenty minutes before he needed to start his ascent. The wireless connection meant that the revised data should have streamed into Costas's computer and be showing the same profile on his own helmet readout. "Are you seeing my dive time?" he asked.

"Nineteen minutes," Costas replied. "Once we're finished inside, we can egress from the hole in the hull caused by the torpedo strike. Let's move."

"Roger that." Jack swam cautiously into the wreckage, wincing as he felt his backpack scrape against a girder. A cloud of red from an exploded rusticle filled the water, creating a haze that restricted visibility even further. He lowered the intensity of his beam to reduce the reflection off particles suspended in the water, and looked around him. As often when diving into a wreck his focus became microcosmic, concentrating on the small details, on what he could see clearly only inches from his mask, knowing that the bigger picture might be obscured by the disorder of the structure and poor visibility. He saw a porcelain washbasin free of encrustation, and then a linked belt of fifty-caliber rounds that must have fallen from one of the gun emplacements above. He passed through a collapsed bulkhead into an enclosed space, his beam revealing twisted shapes in the darkness as he swept it around.

"We're skirting the port side of the engine room," Costas said. "Only about ten meters to go now."

Jack pulled himself carefully along the line, keeping clear of Costas's fins. A tapered cylindrical shape appeared below him, its base angled up where the retaining bolts had been wrenched away but with the dial and glass face at the other end still intact. "Did you see that?" he said. "It looks like the engine-room binnacle."

"I checked it out when I was in here before," Costas replied. "It's set at one quarter ahead, twenty revolutions per minute. The officer of the watch must have ordered the ship to slow down immediately after the torpedo strike. It must have been pretty hellish down here, with the explosion having taken place just beyond the next bulkhead."

Jack paused, floating motionless above the binnacle, remembering the report on the sinking. Amazingly, none of the men in the engine room had been killed by the torpedo strike, but four of the officers had gone down with the ship when she had finally sunk. After the strike they had volunteered to stay below to restart the engine, and to close the engine-room bulkheads against further flooding. They would have known that the ship could go quickly once the point of no return had been reached, that the slow wallowing would suddenly escalate into a terrifying maelstrom as the colossal weight of the cargo pulled her down. He closed his eyes for a moment, thinking of those men. This was their tomb, but it was also the place where they had kept the ship alive, where for a fleeting instant Jack could see the gleaming brass and well-oiled machinery instead of the sepulchral gloom and twisted shapes around him.

Costas had disappeared through a gap in the next bulkhead, and as Jack followed, he saw evidence of a different kind of devastation. Instead of damage caused by implosion and by impact with the seabed, he saw the results of a massive explosion—a space some eight meters in diameter where the ship had been disembowelled, eviscerated, leaving only the twisted ends of copper pipes and shattered steel girders jutting out around the edges. To his right he could see through the jagged hole where the hull had been blown open just below the waterline, the plates folded inward like the petals of a flower.

Below him he saw where the line had been tied off to a girder, and ahead he could see Costas straddling something in the wreckage, a long cylindrical shape, his head bent down at the far end. The intercom crackled again. "I just need to finish making this safe," Costas said. "It's what I was doing while you were having your regulator malfunction on the surface."

Jack pulled himself through the bulkhead and swam up behind, staring in disbelief. "My God. You're defusing a torpedo."

"Fuse immunisation, to be technical. And not just any torpedo. This is a *British* torpedo."

"That's impossible. *Clan Macpherson* was a British merchantman, torpedoed by a German U-boat."

"That's the official line. But take a closer look."

Jack inspected the torpedo's propeller and lower body. Costas was right. The torpedo was a British Mark VIII, the standard type launched from British submarines during the Second World War. He stared in astonishment. *How had this gotten here?*

"I know what you're thinking," Costas said. "This must have been the second torpedo of a salvo, penetrating the hole in the hull created by the explosion of the first torpedo but then failing to detonate."

"The odds against that are high, but it's possible," Jack said. "What doesn't seem possible is that a British submarine sank this ship."

"Right now, the origin of this torpedo is academic. We've got a more pressing technical issue."

Jack glanced at his readout. "Twelve minutes bottom time left."

"Okay. I need you to come up on my right side, carefully. We don't want to dislodge this thing."

Jack swam below a fallen girder and slowly finned forward, keeping his breathing shallow in order to maintain precise buoyancy. "Defusing Second World War ordnance is not exactly my speciality. You should know that."

"They didn't teach you this at Cambridge? At MIT, we got the full gamut."

"I was researching for a doctorate in archaeology, remember? You were at MIT on a US Navy secondment to study submersibles technology. There's a small difference."

"You also spent two years before that as a Royal Navy diver and in the Special Boat Service. You'd have thought," Costas continued, wrenching something and grunting, "that some basic ordnance disposal training would have been in order."

"You'll have to take that up with their lordships of the Admiralty. 'By Strength and Guile,' that was our motto. We left the technical stuff to the engineers."

"Well, it's a good thing you've got one here now."

Jack reached a point where his head was nearly level with Costas's chest. The zinc-coated warhead of the torpedo, the forward meter or so, had nearly separated from the main body, presumably as a result of the impact that should have detonated it. The warhead was angled upward, and Costas had wedged himself into a space above it, holding himself against a girder with one hand and trying to force a wrench around the nose cap with the other. Jack tried to edge closer, but was blocked by a mass of wreckage. "What's stopping the torpedo from falling into the hull?"

"That girder below you," Costas said.

"You mean the rusty one that's nearly sheared off at one end?"

"That's the one."

"What do you want me to do?"

"I should be able to make it safe," Costas said, his voice sounding strained as he leaned against the wrench. "Providing the chemicals haven't leaked and the threads aren't too rusted. I just need to be sure of the fuse type. I need you to get down under the rear of the warhead and read out the specs on the base."

Jack looked down, seeing where Costas had meant. He switched his buoyancy to manual and released a few bubbles of air from his compensator, descending half a meter until he was floating just above the rusted girder. He slowly turned his head, barely breathing, until he could read the lettering under the base. "Okay," he said. "There's a red band across the center, which I know means it's filled with explosive. Above the band it says '21-inch Mark VIIIC.' That confirms it's a British torpedo. Below the band, it says 'Explosive weight 805 pounds zero ounces, gross weight 1,894 pounds 9 ounces. Date of filling, February 1943,' two months before the sinking. That at least makes sense."

"The explosive weight means it's a heavy fill, more than three times the TNT fill of a standard warhead," Costas said. "Now I need you to read out the letters immediately above the red line, below the type designation."

"TX 2."

"That's what I'd guessed. It's Torpex, fifty percent more powerful than TNT by mass, using powdered aluminum to make the explosive pulse last longer. These were real killer torpedoes, the most powerful of the war. Whoever ordered this one to be used against *Clan Macpherson* really wanted the ship sunk. Now I know the fuse must be a compensation coil rod contact pistol, Mark 3A. That's all I need."

"You don't actually *have* to defuse it, do you?"

"I'm making it safe so you can see what lies below."

"Where do you mean?"

"Directly below the warhead, in the cargo hold. Take a look."

Jack switched to full beam, and stared down. For a moment all he saw was twisted metal on all sides and a dazzling light in the center, as if he were looking at a reflection of himself in a mirror. He dimmed the light, and gasped with astonishment. The reflection had not been off a mirror but off gold, hundreds of tightly stacked bars on pallets, filling the bottom of the hold. "Well, I'll be damned," he murmured. "So it was true."

"You need to go down and take a closer look."

"I can see enough from here."

"The torpedo blew the tops off the crates and dislodged the bars inside the one directly below us. Trust me, Jack, you need to go down there. You need to see what's inside."

Jack glanced up at Costas, who was still straddling the warhead. "How are you getting on?"

"Almost done. Make sure your video is on. Just watch you don't hit that girder."

Jack carefully backed off, eased his way through a gap beneath the girder and sank slowly toward the gleaming piles of gold. He dropped down until his knees were resting on the bars in the nearest crate, all clearly stamped *SA*, for South Africa. He glanced up, seeing the silhouette of the torpedo some five meters above him, backlit by Costas's beam, then edged over to the next crate. He could see what Costas had meant. The stack of bars had been blown apart, exposing a metal box beneath with its lid also blown off. Something lay inside, nestled in a brown material, some kind of cushioning. Jack dropped head-first as far as he could into the hole, making sure his camera was angled to catch the view. He stared, at first uncomprehending, and then he forced himself to forget the surroundings, to forget the wreck, and just focus on what was in front of his eyes.

It was a thin metal plaque about half a meter square, free of corrosion but not gold, so made of bronze or another copper alloy. It was slightly curved, as if it had once been attached to a column or a post, and had holes in each corner. The metal was beaten, not machine-made, and looked very old, far older than anything else he had seen on the wreck. The most astonishing sight was the four lines of symbols stamped into the metal. For a moment Jack wondered whether he were seeing things, conjuring up phantom images from the shipwreck off Cornwall he had been excavating only a few days before, seeing in a Second World War wreck an artifact that defied all logic or reason.

"I can't believe I'm saying this," he muttered, almost to himself. "But those are early alphabetic symbols, Phoenician letters of the seventh or sixth century BC."

"I thought I recognized them," Costas replied. "I found similar symbols inscribed on a potsherd in the Cornwall wreck on my first day excavating."

Jack reached into the hole, trying to get at the plaque. It was no use; it was a good half a meter too deep. The only way of retrieving it would have been to remove the gold bars, but with less than five minutes left on his readout, there was no time to try. He stared at the plaque, trying to absorb everything he could see. He could just make out a strange symbol at the end of the inscription, a hieroglyph or pictogram, two stick figures with a box-like shape between them. It was something that the Phoenician who composed this had no words for, perhaps. He reached down again, heaving aside one of the bars to make sure his camera got a clear view. As he did so, there was a shrieking and grinding sound from above, and the water seemed to shake. Costas's breathing suddenly became audible through the intercom, and when he spoke, his voice sounded distant, strained. "Jack, we've got a problem."

Jack looked up, and gasped with horror. Instead of lying horizontally above him, the torpedo was now nearly vertical, nose-down. The warhead had closed back down on the main body of the torpedo, giving it the semblance of integrity, but Jack knew that it was attached by only a thin carapace of metal on one side. What was stopping the torpedo from falling further was not obvious, as the girder was nearly broken away. Costas was still straddling it, as if riding it down toward him. For a horrified moment they stared at each other, the warhead only a couple of meters from Jack's head, hanging directly above him.

He cleared his throat. "So that's called making it safe?"

"Jack, you need to get out of there. I can't move, because my extra weight might be what's giving the torpedo its grip on the remains of that girder. I need you to get to my tool belt, take out the length of black nylon line and tie off the torpedo somewhere above me, from the tail assembly."

"Are you telling me that line has at least a two-ton weight rating?"

"One ton. But it might buy us time."

Jack injected a small blast of air into his compensator and rose slowly out of the crate to the level of Costas's belt. His readout began flashing amber, a warning that he had only two minutes of bottom time left. He knew where the line was kept; he opened the pouch and extracted it, then ascended past the girder to the torpedo's tail fin assembly. He looped the rope twice around the cylindrical propeller guard and up over two massive girders above him, then repeated the loop with the remainder of the rope, tying it off at the torpedo. His computer began flashing red. "Done," he said. "If this holds, the torpedo should hang free. But even if it does hold, I can't see it lasting long."

"I'm letting go now. Then we're out of here." Costas let go with one hand, injected air into his compensator, and then released the torpedo completely, floating free above it. There was a sickening screech as the torpedo slipped another half-meter down the rusted girder, pulling the line taut. One of the loops snapped, whipping and coiling in the water. Jack turned away and powered toward the opening in the side of the ship, followed close behind by Costas. As they cleared the hull, there was another ominous creaking sound and a shimmer in the water. Jack watched his warning light revert from red to amber as they ascended the rocky ridge outside to the level of the continental shelf. "At least you managed to defuse it," he said, watching Costas come alongside. "Not much chance of that thing blowing without a fuse, I would have thought. Still, good to be cautious."

Costas cleared his throat. "Well, it didn't go exactly as planned."

"What do you mean?"

"The threads were really rusty. You would have thought they might have coated them with zinc, too. Wartime British expediency, I guess."

"You're saying you didn't defuse it."

"Not exactly."

"Even so, there's not much to worry about, is there? It didn't go off in 1943, so it probably won't go off now. It was a dud."

"Well, when I said not *exactly*, I meant I didn't defuse it, but I did make some progress. I did manage to arm it."

Jack's heart sank. "You *what*?"

"It wasn't a dud. The torpedo mechanic who was meant to arm it didn't screw the fuse in far enough. It was a new type in 1943, and he was probably not that familiar with it. I tried it, just to see, and it went active. Problem was, I couldn't screw it back out again."

"Great," Jack said. "So we've managed to leave eight hundred and five pounds of high explosive hanging by a piece of string from a rotting girder, armed with a live impact fuse."

"We're due for our first ten-minute decompression stop now, at ninety meters. I suggest we get behind this rocky ridge, where we should be protected from the shock wave. Stopping in the middle of the water like we are now is probably not such a great idea."

"Can't be too safe, can we?" Jack muttered, leading them behind the ridge. At that moment there was a huge rending sound, like a deep groaning, and then silence.

"That would be the girder. Next will be the rope. Hold me, Jack."

"Finally lost your nerve?"

"Less chance of one of us being blown through the water. Might be a good idea to activate our ear defenders now."

Jack quickly pressed the sides of his helmet, muffling the sounds from outside, and then clung face-to-face with Costas as low as they could go against the seabed, huddled together behind a rocky pinnacle. A moment later he seemed to be lifted bodily from the seabed, and the water shook violently around them. The sound of a huge detonation followed, a massive muted boom that seemed to course through him. A large fragment of rock tumbled down from the top of the pinnacle and landed beside them, followed by an avalanche of smaller fragments. There was a strange silence for a few moments, followed by an indescribable cacophony, a creaking, screeching and groaning noise as if an orchestra of industrial machinery were tuning up. Then, with a lingering, fading shriek, it was gone, leaving an eerie silence.

"That would be the ship," Jack said quietly after a few moments. "Falling five thousand meters into the abyss."

Costas gazed at him through his visor, wide-eyed. "Whoops."

Jack stared back at him, the water still shimmering between them. "*Whoops*. Is that all you've got to say?"

"So that's what it's like to be underwater when a torpedo goes off," Costas continued, his eyes glazed in wonder. "Cool."

Jack watched his computer readout flicker, and then stabilize. "The explosion doesn't seem to have restarted my manifold glitch, thankfully. Not sure I can say the same about my nerves."

"Did you feel that shock wave?"

"It's a good thing we were behind this ridge, otherwise it would have killed us."

"We'd have been dead anyway," Costas said. "There was enough force in that blast to have ripped our arms and legs off."

"Why does something like this always happen when I dive with you and there are explosives involved?"

"It's called science. What IMU is supposed to be all about," Costas said. "Hypothesis, experiment, observation. Anyway, it solves the problem of who gets the gold, doesn't it? The floor of that canyon is well over a mile down, with who knows how much depth of sediment lying on the bottom. The chances of our *Deep Explorer* friends finding even one of those gold bars again would be pretty close to zero."

"They'll have registered the shock wave on the surface," Jack said. "We'll tell them the wreck contained a consignment of ammunition. There was no record of that, but then there was no record of the gold, either. There were lots of secrets in the Second World War, and this is what happens when you mess with them. I'll radio the Ministry of Defense in London and our UN representative to say that we saw enough to identify the wreck as a war grave, but that they have nothing to worry about, as there's no way the salvage company can now get at her."

"You won't mention the torpedo?"

"That it was British? That's between you and me, for now. There was something strange going on here, something that might have involved the gold and that plaque, and I want to try to get to the bottom of that first."

"We didn't exactly *not* interfere with a war grave, did we?"

"The torpedo should have gone off in 1943. It was going to fall through those rusting girders anyway, and the wreck wasn't going to last long on that ridge. It's all part of the natural process. All we did was help it on its way."

"And nobody's lifted anything from the wreck. Davy Jones's Locker remains sealed."

"Amen to that." Jack looked up, seeing the distant smudge of light from the surface, the shot line bowing above them in the current. His computer flashed green, and he followed Costas up to their next decompression stop, looking down as he ascended and seeing the gloom envelop the seabed. The only evidence of a wreck once having been there was a storm of silt spiraling up from the drop-off, like a huge twister in the sea.

Costas hung on the line, turning to Jack. "What else do we tell our friends on *Deep Explorer*?"

"What else is there to tell? Did you see any gold?"

"Not a glint."

"And your camera malfunctioned."

"Yours too. Faulty IMU equipment. They're used to that."

"Pity about your plan to get the gold to Sierra Leone, though."

"There might still be something good out of this. The guy I went to have lunch with in Freetown while you were sorting out our equipment was an old friend, a former army officer who works for a relief agency. After Rebecca did her stint with UNICEF in Ethiopia last year, I began to think about how I might contribute."

"Taking the cue from your eighteen-year-old daughter? Isn't it supposed to be the other way round?"

"You know Rebecca as well as I do," Jack said. "She's been plowing her own furrow for quite some time now. Anyway, it's about logistics, organization, the kind of thing I can do well, driving a project forward. I even mentioned the combat medic course I had to do in the Royal Navy when I went into the Special Boat Section. A bit rusty now, but I could update."

"You telling me you're going to volunteer for a relief agency?"

"I was just sounding him out. It would only be a couple of weeks a year, between projects."

"Have you spoken to Ephraim about this?" Costas asked. "I have to remind myself that he's not only IMU's main benefactor but also runs one of the largest charitable foundations in the world. After providing IMU with its endowment, he gave away ninety percent of his remaining assets to charity. It's the kind of thing a software tycoon can do and still remain seriously wealthy. When he's not diving with us, he's pretty well full-time with his foundation."

"I talked it through with him when Rebecca first showed an interest. He said the best thing that people like us can do is to provide motivational and leadership skills, to enthuse and inspire. That's something money can't buy."

"Rebecca would be proud of her dad."

"She's too busy even to think about what I'm up to."

"Let's see," Costas said. "Before Ethiopia, she was exploring the hidden libraries of the Mount Athos monasteries in Greece with Katya, after working with her on the ancient petroglyphs site in Kyrgyzstan. How is your old girlfriend, by the way? Ever think of giving her a call?"

"We haven't got external comms down here, remember. Just you and me."

"I don't mean now. I mean topside, with that phone you usually keep in your pocket."

"Katya keeps me in the loop. When Rebecca's with her."

"Huh. Anyway, Rebecca hardly paused for breath after Ethiopia before joining the dig at Temple Mount in Jerusalem, and then flying out to *Seaquest* in the Mediterranean to help Maurice and Aysha sort out the material they'd managed to rescue from the Institute of Archaeology in Alexandria prior to the extremist takeover in Egypt."

"My turn to be proud of her," Jack said. "Maurice is really her honorary uncle, just like you. Egyptology was his life and he was devastated when they had to leave Egypt, really unable to cope. Rebecca being there meant that Aysha could return to London to look after their son. Rebecca was the one who diverted his attention to Carthage, to the old idea he had when he and I were at school together, that it was not the Phoenicians but the Egyptians who had gone west and founded the first colony there. I still don't think he's right, but Rebecca and I encouraged him to check it out on the ground because it gave him a new focus. He's been digging in Tunisia for over a month now, and Aysha's been able to join him again."

"Lanowski's even torn himself away from his computers and gone out there."

"He's been a good friend too. Everyone's rallied round."

"And now Rebecca's been back with Katya in Kyrgyzstan for the final season there."

"She's like I was at her age. Doing as much as she can. It's great drawing off that zest for life, for new experiences."

"Are you going to discuss your plan with her?"

"Once we know we can finance it. Until then, the fewer people who know, the better. But we do often have a bit of time between projects, don't we?"

"Speak for yourself. In the engineering department it's 24/7, three hundred and sixty-five days a year."

"Ephraim thinks you could use a break too."

"I'll think about it. Yeah, I could do that too. You'd need someone to watch your back, for a start. Some of those places are pretty dodgy. But right now, we've got to make sure we're not swept away into the middle of the Atlantic Ocean. Time for the next deco stop."

"Roger that."

Jack made his way hand over hand up the line behind Costas. At thirty meters he looked down one last time, seeing the billowing silt cloud where they had been exploring only a few minutes previously. Costas had been right. That truly was Davy Jones's Locker, a place where nobody living belonged. He looked up, seeing Costas hanging on the line above him, a glint of sunlight reflecting off his helmet, and above that the dark silhouette of *Deep Explorer* rolling and pitching in the swell. He remembered the plaque, and felt a sudden rush of excitement. The wreck might be gone, but their discovery had left indelible questions in his mind. What was a Phoenician antiquity doing concealed in a secret consignment of gold on board a Second World War British cargo ship? What was a British torpedo that could only have been fired from a British submarine doing inside the wreck?

Twenty minutes later, Costas tapped his wrist, and gave a thumbs-up. "Deco's over, Jack. We're clear for the surface. You good to go?"

Jack checked his display. "Good to go." He followed Costas slowly up the line, his body dragged nearly horizontal by the current, feeling the pull of the buoy as it bobbed in the swell. It was going to be a tricky egress into the Zodiac, and there might be an ugly confrontation with Landor and the salvage team over what had happened to the wreck. But he was already racing ahead to the next few days, to what he would do when he got back to IMU headquarters. He prayed that the images from their cameras would be clear enough for analysis. He needed to get the footage to his colleagues Jeremy Haverstock and Maria de Montijo at the Institute of Palaeography in Oxford. He would take them himself, and combine them with a study of Phoenician artifacts in the Ashmolean Museum. And he would go to the National Archives at Kew to dig up anything more he could find out about *Clan Macpherson* and convoy TS-37: any further cargo and crew manifests, secret directives from the Admiralty, German U-boat orders that might have been intercepted and decrypted at Bletchley Park and sent on to the convoy commodore, anything that might help to solve the mystery of the wreck and its cargo.

They reached the chain that held the shot line to the buoy, and then clawed their way up until they broke surface. Jack grasped one of the rope loops around the buoy and glanced up at *Deep Explorer*, seeing the crewmen lining the foredeck looking down on them. He raised his free arm in the okay signal, and saw Costas do the same. The swell was pulling the buoy dangerously close to the hull, and he hoped the captain would have the sense to release his anchor line now that they had surfaced, and to stand off while the Zodiac attempted to pick them up. He glanced toward the stern of the vessel, seeing the Zodiac still raised on its davits. After sensing the detonation, they would have kept the inflatable out of the sea until they knew what was going on. They could hardly have expected them to return from the wreck alive.

Jack tapped his intercom, making sure it was still working. "We're going to have to open up ship-to-diver comms to give them guidance. The ship's going to have to stand off, for a start. The swell's a lot stronger than it was when we went down. Having survived that dive, I don't want us to end up crushed between the Zodiac and the ship's hull."

"Roger that," Costas said. "Anything else before they're able to listen in on us?"

"Here's my plan. Once we're on board, I'm going to radio my friend in Freetown to see if he can get a Lynx helicopter from the British military mission to come out and pick us up pronto. He's ex-army and I'm still a reservist, so he can make it official. British naval officer and American colleague need rescuing from the clutches of pirates, or something like that. Otherwise, with the weather worsening, I can see these guys on *Deep Explorer* refusing to fly us off in their own helicopter, using the weather as an excuse to grill us about what we saw. Landor will think he knows which buttons to press to try to get me talking, but I'm damned if I'm going to give him that chance. He and I are way past swapping dive stories now. And the last thing we want is for them to snatch our cameras and see those images of the gold. There's not much they can do now to recover it, of course, but they could make life very unpleasant for us. We need to get out of here as soon as we can."

"Roger that. Ship comms back on line in two minutes."

Jack twisted around so that he was floating on his back, the spindrift from the waves lashing his visor. By the time they reached Freetown and had stayed a night with the military mission, their nitrogen saturation levels should be safe enough to fly. He would also put in a request for the IMU

Embraer to fly down from England and be waiting for them at Freetown airport.

He felt bone-tired, but exhilarated. He needed to get home, to transport himself back to the darkest days of the sea war in 1943, to a time when the future of the world hung in the balance.

He could hardly wait to see where this mystery would take him.

4

Bletchley Park, England, April 30 1943

A bitter wind swept across the forecourt of the compound, and the woman drew her coat more tightly around her as she hurried toward the checkpoint in front of the entrance. It had only been a twenty-minute walk from the station, but already she was beginning to miss the fug of the train compartment, the familiar smell of stale sweat and wet wool and tobacco, the warmth of the men around her. Most were bomber crew back from weekend passes in London, some still fuddled with hangovers but others pale and wide-eyed and staring through the window into the pre-dawn darkness, knowing what lay in store for them in the skies to the east. At Bletchley they had stayed on board while the train disgorged its other passengers, the silent army she could hear coming up the lane behind her. Many were women, civilians like her or girls of the Women's Royal Naval Service, with a few male army and naval officers among them. As usual she had hurried ahead to avoid lining up in the cold at the checkpoint, and to be the first for a cup of tea at the NAAFI canteen inside.

She reached the barrier and stopped in front of the two military policemen in greatcoats with rifles and fixed bayonets. A corporal came out of the booth, blowing on his hands, and stood before her. "Papers, please."

She knew the drill, and already had her ID, clearance papers and weekend pass in hand. He scrutinized them and then handed them to the officer who had come out of the booth behind him. "Name?" the officer demanded, towering over her.

She drew down her scarf from her chin to show her face, and looked up at him. "Fanny Turley."

"Occupation?"

"Civilian telegraphist clerk, Admiralty."

"What were you doing in London?"

"Staying with my sister in Clapham."

"But your papers give your home address as Shropshire. Why not go there?"

"My sister's husband has just been killed in Burma."

"Did you talk to anyone about your work here?"

"No."

"Did anyone not working here accompany you to Euston station?"

"No."

"What's your division?"

"Hut 9b, Special Operations. Atlantic convoys."

"Supervisor?"

"Commander Bermonsey."

The officer passed back her papers and nodded her through. He had not shown a flicker of recognition, despite the fact that he had spent an evening the week before trying to chat her up in a pub in the nearby village where she was billeted. He was a professional, as they all had to be in this place. The slightest chink in the armor, the slightest lapse in security, could see the whole code-breaking edifice crumble before their eyes.

Even her family had no idea what she was doing. When she had abruptly left her job as a schoolteacher in Shrewsbury to work for the Civil Service in London, they had guessed that it might have had something to do with her aptitude for math, but when they asked her, she had revealed nothing more than her job title and that she worked for the Admiralty. Her sister knew that she was based somewhere an hour or so to the north of London, but that was true for so many girls employed in government departments that had relocated to country houses following the Blitz. Her job title, telegraphist clerk, was a typical Bletchley cover, revealing nothing of her true role. Even within Bletchley there were multiple veils of secrecy, with those in one hut knowing little of what went on in the hut next door. But everyone who worked here knew the official name of the establishment, the

Government Code and Cypher School, and even the military policemen outside who knew nothing of decryption were aware that keeping this place secure was vital to the war effort.

She pushed through the door, grateful for the surge of warmth, went straight over to the canteen, and took one of the mugs of sweet tea that were already being laid out. For a few precious minutes she could ignore the smell of watery cabbage and burned fat that seemed to permeate the place, a residue of lunches past and a foretaste of delights to come. She nestled the mug in her hands for a moment, blowing on the tea, before heading off to the door that led out to the central courtyard and toward the huts, knowing that those coming through the checkpoint behind her would soon be crowding around the canteen.

As she stopped to take a sip, an elegantly dressed young woman came out of the lavatory door beside her, finished applying lipstick, and then snapped shut her handbag, smiling. "Hello, Fan. Good leave?"

"Euston was absolutely packed, even at six A.M.," Fan replied. "There must be quite a lot more new recruits among this lot behind me. I see they've already begun work extending the compound to the north while I've been away. Soon we won't be able to see the old park at all for the Nissen huts."

"There are more Americans here now. Several new ones in your hut."

Fan shrugged and drank some more of her tea. "Can't say I've noticed."

"Come on, Fan. It's an open secret you've got two new American officers. One of them looks quite dishy."

Fan shrugged again, smiling innocently. "I couldn't possibly comment. Top secret, you know."

"You're hopeless. By the way, your Commander Bermonsey knows we're billeted together and has been asking for you. He was here ten minutes ago, chomping at the bit. He wants you to go straight in as soon as you arrive, lickety-split."

"That's why I made sure to take the first train back. He's always like that."

"This time might be special. He was just like my CO gets in Hut 8 after he's been at work through the night, all jittery and nervous. My guess is there's something big on. Just a friendly warning."

"All right. See you this evening in billets."

"With a dishy American in tow, just for me?" She grinned, waved her handbag, and was gone, sauntering out of the door toward the complex of huts adjoining Bletchley House, the stately home that had been the sole building in the park before the war.

Louise Hunter-Jones was from a very different social background to Fan, with a posh Mayfair address, and her frippery could sometimes be trying. But what both girls shared was an aptitude for math, something that had led Louise to Girton College, Cambridge, and Fan on a scholarship to the University of Birmingham, and both had been snapped up by Bletchley when the recruiters had contacted university departments looking for recent graduates with first-class degrees, women as well as men. Louise had gone straight in with the naval code breakers in Hut 8, but then had been transferred to supervise one of the bombes, the inscrutable name given by the Polish intelligence people who had invented them to the electromechanical monsters that churned through the permutations to find the daily settings for the German Enigma machines, clattering and shuddering and reeking of machine oil. It always left her pale and drained at the end of the day. For a while she let it be known that she felt she had drawn the short straw, but then her natural enthusiasm took over and she had made the best of it; the extra effort she took with make-up and clothing was part of that.

Fan, by contrast, had become a statistician, a calculator of probabilities, an adviser to the officer in charge in her hut when they needed to estimate how many of the deciphered U-boat orders they could act on without raising suspicions among the Germans that Enigma had been broken. She did not end each day with her ears ringing and her clothes reeking as Louise did, but dealing with statistics and probabilities took its own toll, the knowledge that what she was doing was not just about saving lives but also making decisions not to, and letting men on the front line in the Battle of the Atlantic sail on into probable destruction and death.

She pushed open the door and started to make her way across the courtyard beside the central pond, the mansion ahead of her and the rows of long wooden huts where most of them worked to the right. Hearing a familiar light step coming quickly up the path behind her, she turned and watched the runner approach. He was wearing only a vest and shorts despite the cold, and his dark hair was matted to his forehead.

"Hello, Alan," she said. He swerved off the path and came to a halt on the grass beside her, his hands on his knees, panting hard. "Good run?"

He looked at his watch. "Better than last time. Set off at midnight."

"At midnight?" she said incredulously. "From where?"

He looked up at her, nonplussed. "London, of course. Whitehall, to be precise. Had a meeting."

"You ran all the way here from *London*? At night? In the blackout?"

"Best time for it. No traffic on the roads. Anyway, it's a full moon." He peered up at the clouds. "Allegedly."

"That's more than fifty miles."

"Early-morning trains are always too crowded these days. Running clears my head."

"You're mad."

He gave her an impish grin. "So they tell me."

"Let me at least get you some tea."

He shook his head, then nodded toward the huts. "Quick shower, then I'm back in there. Work to do."

"Louise thinks there's something on. Bermonsey's been looking for me."

His breathing eased and he straightened up. "You know, it was easier earlier on in the war when it was just code-breaking. Then it was a mathematical problem, an exercise in scholarship. Now it's different."

"I know what you mean," she said. "Now it's real people, real lives."

He stared up at the sky, his hands on his hips, and shut his eyes, the sweat running down his neck in rivulets. Then he looked down and gave her another grin. "See you in the machine."

She watched as he jogged off to the shower block beside the mansion. He had taken to calling their workplace that, the machine, after someone had dubbed him *deus ex machina*, the god from the machine, the device in a storyline that saves the plot. Alan Turing had done that, had done incredible things, had made Bletchley work, but now he was no more than the rest of them, a cog in a machine where genius mattered less than the ability to see human lives as little more than chess pieces, as dispensable elements in the calculus of war.

She turned toward the row of low buildings that formed one edge of the compound. They called them huts, but in reality they were a lot more than that: long, purpose-built structures of interconnected offices and workspaces that could hold a hundred or more workers each, both civilians and service personnel. Hers was officially Hut 9b, but was known informally as the special operations hut. She thought about what Alan had said. More and more, this damp corner of Buckinghamshire seemed to be at the forefront of the war. Sometimes, hunched over the map table, choosing one convoy to save over another, it seemed as if the raging Atlantic were just outside, as if opening the door would reveal the mountainous seas and howling wind, the dark shapes of ships and the throbbing of engines as they battled through the night.

She shivered, and remembered the bomber boys on the train. They were someone else's responsibility, other girls like her and Louise in another secret place, pushing counters across a map, sending some men to near-certain death and giving others a temporary reprieve. She could do nothing to help them. Her boys were the men at sea, the thousands of sailors in merchant ships, British, American, Canadian, Norwegian, Indian and all of the other Allied seafaring nations pitted against the Nazis, plowing their way across the Atlantic and running the gauntlet of the U-boats, living in constant fear of attack. Her twenty minutes in the chill air this morning was nothing compared to the cold felt by those men out there tonight, their ships pitching and rolling as the spray lashed them, trying to maintain station in the darkness. Keeping some of those men alive was what kept her coming back here, day after day, night after night.

She looked up, seeing the milky smudge where the light of the moon was now visible through the morning clouds. The full moon that had guided Alan on his run might be silhouetting those ships in the darkness to the west, making them easier targets for the U-boats. She prayed for cloud over the Atlantic, for rain. She took a deep breath and steeled herself, the adrenalin already coursing through her. She could hear others coming up the path behind her. She pushed open the door and stepped inside.

Fan doffed her coat and warmed her hands at a radiator in the main operations room while she waited for Commander Bermonsey, who was bent over a map table conferring with the two US Navy officers who had so intrigued Louise. They were part of the increased numbers of Americans who had come to Bletchley over the past few months in advance of the planned handover of a large part of the Ultra decryption work to US naval intelligence in Washington. Bermonsey straightened up and saw her, but continued talking to the men. He was awkwardly tall for a submariner, she thought, well over six feet, though with his thick beard and gaunt, handsome features he looked the part. They had been told that before being posted here, he had been the sole survivor among the captains in his flotilla out of Malta, and that his boat had been lost with all hands on its first patrol without him. He had been jittery when he had arrived, pale and haunted, but once he had settled in, he had begun to run the operations room as if he were on the bridge of a ship, something that Fan found she relished; it gave what they were doing the urgency of the life-and-death decisions that she knew he must once have faced at sea.

He strode over to her. "Good. You're here. Follow me."

"Sir."

As a civilian, she was not obliged to show him military deference, but she did so anyway. It helped to keep the nature of their relationship clear, and it was more comfortable for him. She guessed the drill for the morning, because it was the same every morning. First they would go to the main chart table, where the night's decrypts would already have been whittled down to two or at the most three possibilities. There would be an open discussion, and she would provide her analysis. Next, she and Bermonsey would go to the closed operations office at the other end of the hut, where he would make the final decision. At a pre-appointed time, Bermonsey would pick up the phone and call a secret office in the Naval Intelligence Division of the Admiralty's Operational Intelligence Center, where the advice from Bletchley would be recast as the commander-in-chief's orders and sent to the commanding officer, Western Approaches, in Liverpool, or directly to the convoy commodores themselves. Within twenty minutes of Bermonsey picking up the phone, the helmsmen in the ships of the chosen convoy would be changing course. Nobody outside this room would know which other convoys that could have been saved had been sacrificed for the greater good. The steps in the procedure were always the same, like the ritual of a dawn execution, one always with the possibility of a last-minute reprieve.

Fan knew that Bermonsey was in an extraordinary position. As a mere commander, an acting rank at that, he should not have had the authority to issue orders to the highest echelons of the Admiralty. Officially, therefore, his messages to the OIC following these meetings were couched as advice, to be acted on further up the chain if the rear admiral commanding OIC saw fit. Unofficially, his messages were translated into operational orders without exception. Churchill had taken Alan Turing and his team under his wing when he saw that their efforts might be thwarted by those who disliked "boffins," and had issued a personal directive that the outcome of all that effort was not to be hindered by military red tape. Anyone higher up in the Admiralty who kicked up a fuss was removed, instantly. Fan knew that the judgments made in this room were tantamount to orders from the commander-in-chief himself.

She followed Bermonsey to the chart table. She could see that he was on edge, that his hand was shaking slightly as he opened a file. He was probably running on empty again, fueled by tea and cigarettes. Beside him stood Captain Pullen, a retired officer who had done Bermonsey's job during the latter stages of the Great War and had been re-employed to be in charge of the day-to-day running of the hut, but without authority over the Ultra output to the Admiralty. Around the table were a dozen others: girls like Fan, several naval officers, and two of Turing's team who had been shuffled here to make use of them after the main decryption breakthrough, both of them disheveled young men who looked as if they had walked straight out of a Cambridge common room.

The two Americans came and stood in the wings, watching while one of the junior Royal Navy officers arranged some gaming pieces and pencils on the pinned-up chart of the Atlantic in the center of the table. Fan glanced at the shuttered window beside them, seeing that the sun was breaking through. It had been another long, hard winter, the fourth of the war. For the first time she had sensed a cautious optimism while she had been in London over the last few days. The tide had finally turned in the campaign against Rommel in North Africa, and on the Russian front; in Britain, the huge build-up of troops and equipment could only signal imminent invasion plans. And yet for the men actually on the battle lines, that optimism would probably have seemed far-fetched. For those at sea, winter might be over, but the Atlantic was still swept by gales and cold enough to kill a man in minutes. For those men, *her* men, men who so rarely saw the enemy but who lived in his shadow day and night, the war went on, relentless and unchanging, the dark angel of death ever-present just beneath the waves and over the horizon.

Bermonsey glanced at the wall clock, and then at his watch. "Right. 0630 hours. My phone call to the Admiralty is scheduled for 0715. You have fifteen minutes for your assessment. Lieutenant Hardy?"

The naval officer opposite Fan who had laid the counters on the chart sat down and arranged his papers. He was about her age, a recent arrival from the Operational Intelligence Center, one of two officers at the table whose job was to provide a naval briefing to complement her own more mathematical analysis. He had only been here a few weeks, but had already acquired the distinctive flushed, pallid look of long-term Bletchley inmates, a consequence of too little sunlight and too much time in smoky, over-heated rooms. He picked up a ruler and leaned over the table, pointing at the map as he spoke.

"The Ultra intercepts from last night reveal three U-boat patrol lines in the North Atlantic, here, here and here," he said, tapping the map in three places. "To the south, a line the Germans have code-named Amsel, meaning blackbird, comprising eleven U-boats. To the east, off Greenland, Meise, blue tit, thirty boats, covering the northern route. And finally on the western side of the mid-Atlantic air gap, Specht, woodpecker, seven-teen boats, arranged in a line running south of Greenland."

"No wolf packs?" Bermonsey asked.

Hardy shook his head. "No wolf packs. These are not roving attack formations. They are strung-out, static lines, like fishing gillnets."

Bermonsey pursed his lips. "And the convoys?"

Hardy moved the pointer from the pencils indicating the U-boat patrol lines to the backgammon pieces he had arranged across the map. "As of 0500 hours, there were some three hundred and fifty merchant ships in the North Atlantic. Most are within the Western Approaches or off the North American seaboard, well within air cover. The two mid-Atlantic convoys that should concern us most are SC-127 and ONS-5. Patrol line Meise was deployed to catch SC-127, but three days ago the convoy slipped through a gap in the line, completely undetected. SC-127 is by far the biggest prize in the North Atlantic at the moment, an eastward-bound convoy carrying US troops and military supplies for the invasion build-up. But we think it's safe."

"And the other convoy?"

"ONS-5 is westbound, so the ships are mainly in ballast. German naval intelligence knew it was en route, not from decrypting our messages but from long-range Luftwaffe Condor patrols out of Norway that were shad-owing it. Having let SC-127 slip through the net, patrol line Meise was ordered two days ago to reconfigure to catch ONS-5. Yesterday we intercepted a message sent by a U-boat at 1650 hours showing that they had sighted the convoy. We assume that since then the patrol line will have been constricting, tightening the net and making it less likely that this second convoy will slip through. The Germans won't want to make the same mistake twice."

Fan peered at the young officer. Another secret, another fold in the veils that fortified Bletchley, something that even those around this table were forbidden to voice, was that Turing's team had known for some time that their German equivalent, B-Dienst, had broken the British naval cypher used for Allied North Atlantic convoy messages. As a result, not only was Bletchley playing a game of cat-and-mouse with the Enigma decrypts, pushing and prodding to see how much they could get away with, but they were also playing a similar game in the other direction, keeping the compromised British naval cypher open and using it to feed disinformation to the Germans. They had pushed their luck to the point where B-Dienst would be bound to rumble them soon, so a new naval cypher was ready to be activated. But meanwhile the game with B-Dienst went on, seeing how far they could go in acting on their knowledge without exciting the suspicion of their counterparts in German naval intelligence somewhere deep in their own secret operational headquarters outside Berlin.

Bermonsey stood forward, leaning on the table. "What's the strength of the escorts?"

"Mid-ocean escort force group B-7," Hardy replied. "A strong group, British, Canadian, American, some of the best corvette captains we have. They've been buoyed by their success in depth-charging U-boats over the last few months, and frankly, they're spoiling for a big fight. This could be their chance to score a decisive blow, with twelve or more U-boats in that patrol line converging on the convoy and those other patrol lines also within striking range. If the escorts can sink or disable half of those U-boats, then the pendulum really begins to swing in our favor. The Germans simply can't build enough U-boats to make up for losses like that, or replace the experienced crews."

Bermonsey tapped the table with a pencil. "So if we did interfere with ONS-5 and send a warning, we could be preventing a convoy battle that might change the course of the war."

"And even if we did warn them, there's the problem with strung-out patrol lines that they may be too long for a convoy to sail around, and in so doing the convoy might be exposing itself to other U-boats in the area. As you know, it's different with a mobile wolf-pack flotilla or a lone U-boat, where we can attempt to calculate their course from the intercepts and reroute a convoy out of danger's way. If you try that with a patrol line, you're just as likely to reroute the convoy into another submarine further down the line."

Bermonsey nodded. "And as a westbound convoy, with the ships in ballast, ONS-5 is a lower-order priority than an eastbound, laden convoy. As bait for a potentially decisive U-boat battle, the ships in that convoy can therefore be considered expendable."

He paused, looking round for any retort. Fan thought about what he had just said. *A lower-order priority.* She knew the fate merchant seamen most feared, being torpedoed in a heavily laden ship, knowing they could go down in seconds. But they could be just as vulnerable to torpedoing in an unladen ship, when they were less likely to have a guardian angel watching over them. And in the scenario they had just been contemplating, one that would depend on ships being hit in order for the escorts to know where to take action, the merchant seamen would be mere pawns in the battle.

"That's the North Atlantic done, then," Bermonsey said. "It leaves ONS-5 as our one open file, but with the tactical assessment pointing to inaction. Agreed?" There was a general murmur of consent, and he looked at the other seated naval officer. "And now for the South Atlantic." He glanced at the wall clock. "Make it snappy, if you please."

The other man, a lieutenant commander in the Royal Naval Volunteer Reserve who looked as if he might have been an academic in civilian life, pushed up his spectacles and peered at the lower half of the map. "It's more straightforward, thankfully. The other actionable Ultra intercept of the past twenty-four hours concerns *U-515*, which is heading south off the coast of West Africa on a collision course with convoy TS-37, heading north from Takoradi in the Gold Coast to Freetown in Sierra Leone. A couple of ruled lines on compass bearings give the point of contact at about 35 degrees 15 minutes north, 45 degrees 12 minutes east, about fifty miles off the coast of Sierra Leone."

Fan spoke for the first time. "Do we know whether *U-515* has intelligence on TS-37?"

The officer looked up. "It seems so judging by the intercept course, though we don't know how. TS-37 is one of the convoys we've chosen not to contact using the compromised Naval Cypher No. 3, but we suspect the existence of a Nazi spy operation in Durban who may be able to pass on information about convoy departures. Four of the ships in the convoy are carrying large consignments of manganese ore, currently in very short supply for steel and aluminum production and desperately needed to keep production of bomber aircraft up to counter the losses we've been enduring. The current directive from the Ministry of War Transport is that those cargos are to be considered of higher value even than munitions. Manganese is so valuable that you'll see it disguised as pig iron in the cargo manifests of some of those ships in order not to attract the attention of spies whose information might feed back to U-boat headquarters. *Corabella* is carrying eight thousand and sixty tons of manganese ore; *Bandar Shahpour* three thousand tons. *Clan Macpherson* has over eight thousand tons of it, all described as pig iron. In the past, TS convoys have only rarely been hit, with Admiral Dönitz's attention mainly having been in the North Atlantic, but with the U-boat losses there already high this year, and with more effective Allied air and sea cover, he may now look to the South Atlantic for easier pickings. My assessment is that we should do what we can to save this convoy."

"What do we know about *U-515*?" Fan said.

The officer pushed up his glasses again and peered at his notes. "Kapitän-leutnant Werner Henke. An exceptionally capable solo commander who sank nine ships during his first patrol last year. He has already sunk two ships in his present patrol, the British *California Star* off the Azores and the French *Bamako* off northern Senegal. If you were to choose a commander to seek out and hit a convoy on his own, he'd be your man."

"What are our assets in the area?"

"TS-37 has a weak escort, only one corvette and three armed trawlers. That's pretty standard for West Africa convoys at present, with the best ships and captains needed in the North Atlantic. There are two long-range Hudsons of RAF Coastal Command based at Freetown, and the convoy commodore could also call on the US escort carrier USS *Guadalcanal* with its Wildcats and Avengers. But *Guadalcanal* is currently in the mid-Atlantic, too far off to provide any kind of air cover, and barely within range for a reactive strike. By the time the aircraft arrived, the U-boat would be long gone. And none of those aircraft are specialized sub hunters."

Bermonsey glanced at the clock again, and then at Fan. She noticed how pale and tired he looked. "Turley? Your assessment?"

"Sir." Fan took the two convoy files from the officers opposite, one for ONS-5 in the North Atlantic and one for TS-37 off Sierra Leone, and marshalled her thoughts. She opened the files and put the diagrams showing the two convoy orders of sailing in front of her, rows and columns of ships, more than sixty of them in all. That meant perhaps eight thousand crew altogether, many of them with wives and children waking up this morning wondering where they were, with no idea of the machinations being played out that might see them through this day or condemn them to a terrible death. She quickly rehearsed in her mind what she intended to say, and then cleared her throat.

"One possibility is inaction on both convoys," she said. "We know that assault convoys are currently in preparation in the Clyde for imminent seaborne landings in the Mediterranean, at a destination that's still top secret. Any Ultra intercepts related to U-boats potentially targeting those convoys will absolutely have to be acted upon, all of them. Given that, it would be disastrous if by acting on an Ultra intercept now we finally take that one step too far, pushing someone in B-Dienst to realize that we've cracked the Enigma code and to change it just before the assault convoys sail. The destruction of one of those convoys could set back the war incalculably."

One of the two code breakers in the room, an Oxford mathematician named Johnson, pushed his chair back and put his feet up on the table, taking a pipe out of his pocket. "Yes, that's possible, but by deliberately *not* acting you also create a pattern, don't you? If I were a clever analyst in B-Dienst I might notice a welcome but strange increase in the success rate of U-boat contacts with convoys, and I might then be persuaded to look back over the preceding months and begin to suspect that something was not quite right. Do you see what I mean? Inaction means not only do we do nothing to save those convoys, but we might also compromise Ultra completely. *That* might be their key to realizing that we'd broken the code. If I were that analyst, having decided that Enigma had been broken, I might wonder *why* the intercepts were no longer being acted on. I might then begin to suspect that we were protecting our intelligence coup because something big was in the offing, something like a seaborne invasion."

He glanced at the other code breaker, who nodded in agreement, then put his pipe in his mouth, folding his arms and giving Fan a stolid look.

She turned from him and addressed Bermonsey. "I agree. That was going to be my next point. That's why I recommend that we do take action, and redirect TS-37."

She sat back, feeling slightly sick as she always did having chosen one convoy over another, trying not to look at the sailing order for the doomed ONS-5. Bermonsey leaned over and pushed the TS-37 file toward the two code breakers in case either of them wanted to view it. "Does everyone agree? Good." Fan picked up the ONS-5 file, and Bermonsey addressed the table. "Let me tell you where we are today. In March we lost a hundred and twenty merchant ships, for twelve U-boats sunk. In April so far it's been sixty-four ships for fifteen U-boats. Are we turning the tide? The Admiralty thinks so. They think this coming month will be the crunch. But we have to keep our nerve, now more than ever. Any chink in our armor, anything that lets the Germans suspect that we're on to them, and we're *all* sunk. Right, everyone. Back to the next set of decrypts. Johnson, that second file, if you please."

Johnson tapped his pipe on the table, catching everyone's attention. "Come on, Bermonsey. What's it like?"

Bermonsey stared at him. "What do you mean?"

"You're the only one here who's actually done it. Stood behind a periscope. Had a ship in your sights. Given the order. Watched men you've condemned die in the sea."

Bermonsey gave him a cold look. "It's called war. You kill the enemy."

Johnson waved his pipe at the file Fan was holding. "What about when it's not the enemy? What about when a submarine captain has to look through a periscope and murder his own side? How would that feel?"

Bermonsey glared at him. "Keep your mouth shut, Johnson," he snapped. "Now pass me that file."

Johnson leaned sideways, his feet still on the desk, sifted the papers, and picked up the file. "I'm not one of your sailors, Bermonsey. You can't order me around."

There was a sudden tension in the room. Fan saw Bermonsey look at Captain Pullen, who had heard the exchange. "Johnson, a word," Pullen said. Johnson sighed theatrically, tossed the file in front of Fan, pocketed his pipe, swung his legs off the desk, and walked out of the room behind the officer.

They all knew what "a word" meant. Ever since Turing had broken

Enigma, there had been the problem of what to do with his team of code breakers. Some had remained poised for the next decryption, ready in case the Germans altered the machines as they had done with the naval Enigma in early 1942, leaving Bletchley in the dark for almost a year. Others had been reassigned to work on the Colossus computer and Lorenz, the German High Command code. A few of the less socially awkward ones had been flown off to America to teach at the US code-breaker school. Others had been moved to the special operations hut and naval intelligence to help with the cat-and-mouse game they were now playing, using the decrypted intercepts to swing the Battle of the Atlantic in the Allies' favor. Some, like Turing himself, had taken to it well; a few had decided that their talents were being wasted. They were all under pressure and occasionally the pot bubbled over. One thing was for certain: they would not see Johnson in this hut again.

Bermonsey reached over, picked up the file and nodded at Fan. As she followed him to the office at the end of the room, her mind was racing. She thought about what Johnson had just said: *when it's not the enemy.* What could he possibly have meant?

5

Fan followed Commander Bermonsey into the office and closed the door behind them. Through the window she could see others huddled in their coats hurrying up the path toward the mansion and the bombe huts, the result of the second early-morning train having arrived at Bletchley. She shut the blind and turned to the table in the center of the room. She was carrying the file for the mid-Atlantic convoy, ONS-5, and Bermonsey had the one for convoy TS-37 that had been the subject of the altercation with Johnson. She put hers on the table beside his, and opened them both up. Two files: one meant life for the crews, the one that would be left open; the other might mean death. The conference in the operations room had already decided which file would be shut and which left open, but allowing a final reflection in this room as the clock ticked down to the phone call had become part of Bermonsey's routine. He stayed standing, leaning on the table and inspecting the files as he always did, staring at the top pages with the convoy orders of sailing. To Fan it seemed as if he were at sea again, a captain addressing the ships' companies, telling the crews in both convoys that he was not judging their qualities as men but was making a decision based solely on the calculus of war.

She glanced at the clock. Ten minutes to seven. At 7:15 on the dot, Bermonsey would pick up the phone and call the rear admiral commanding the Naval Intelligence Division of the Admiralty's Operational Intelligence

Center in London; minutes later the order would be issued to reroute one of the convoys. What those at sea did not know, could never know, was the existence of Ultra intercepts that were not acted on, the files that were closed in this room and sent to storage stamped *Top Secret*, the result of decisions known only to those in the special operations hut, who were under strict instructions not to put down any of their analysis on paper and were sworn to secrecy for life. Fan had been present when Churchill himself had visited the hut and told them that nothing was more important than securing the Atlantic supply line, that the decisions made here could win or lose the war. Nothing could leak out; nothing could be left to chance.

She watched Bermonsey leaf methodically through the contents of the files—the convoy route plans, the cargo manifests, the secret Admiralty orders to the convoy commodores and escort captains—as if he were registering but not reading them, doing little more than glancing at the headings to make sure that everything was in order. She waited while he stood back, and then she plucked up courage and asked him the question that had been burning in her mind. "What did Johnson mean, sir? Not the enemy?"

He stared at her, and for a moment she thought he would snap at her, too. Then he took out a cigarette, tapped it on the table, lit it and drew in deeply, holding the smoke in and then exhaling upward so that it wreathed the single bare bulb that hung above them. He closed his eyes for a moment, then looked down at her again. "You shouldn't ask questions, Fan, even in this holy of holies. You know that."

"Johnson knew that too, sir. He's wanted out ever since being posted here. He's been badgering Pullen about it for weeks."

"I know. Not calculated to raise my sympathy."

"Sir."

He took another deep drag, and exhaled forcibly. "Even so, I should have thanked him for his opinion. I shouldn't have snapped at him. We owe those men everything."

"They're the genius code breakers, but we girls do this job in operational intelligence at least as well as the men. We're as clever at math as they are, but because academia is a man's world and nobody gave us the professorships and fellowships, we're not used to having elevated opinions of ourselves. It means we're tougher than they are, more used to taking knocks. Put a man like Johnson in this room where the life-and-death decisions are made, and he'd probably go to pieces."

Fan felt her face flush. She had never spoken to him like this before. He gave her a wry smile, took another deep drag and then carefully pressed the half-finished cigarette into the ashtray, putting it out. His look hardened. "You asked a question, and I owe you an answer because of what you're about to be drawn into. What I'm going to tell you now is beyond top secret. I mean, beyond *ultra* top secret."

"Sir."

He glanced at the clock, and then pointed at the mauve-and-red ribbon on the left breast of his uniform jacket. "You know what this is?"

"The Distinguished Service Order."

"I got that after my third patrol out of Malta, in August 1941. We'd shadowed a small Axis convoy out of Benghazi heading north, and we finally got into position in rough seas off eastern Sicily. I put three torpedoes into the largest ship, a converted liner. I knew it was a troopship, but it turned out to be carrying walking wounded back to Italy for convalescence. Two thousand men went into the water, and maybe two hundred were picked up by the escorts."

Fan looked at him. "Walking wounded return to fight another day. You were saving Allied lives."

He pursed his lips, staring at the files on the desk. "War is never black and white, even this one. The virtue of destroying an enemy like Hitler or Mussolini is not in question, but it's what we have to do to get there."

"I can see why Johnson's question hit a raw nerve."

"It wasn't so much that. I was thinking of the decision I'm about to make now."

"My assessment remains the same. We save TS-37."

He reached over and closed both files. "I'm not asking for your opinion any more."

She stared at the closed covers, dumbfounded. "Sir?"

"We're not saving any convoys today."

She felt an icy grip in the pit of her stomach. "I don't understand."

"I'm afraid our convoy conference was something of a sham. I had to make it seem as if it were normal procedure, right down to entering this room with you as usual. We decided to bring you on board some time ago. Do you remember Churchill's visit last month?"

"Of course. You and Captain Pullen were holed up in this room with him for hours. We could smell the cigar smoke for days afterward."

"Pullen is one of very few others at Bletchley who are party to what I'm about to tell you. *Very* few. Do you remember Churchill speaking to you in the hut afterward?"

"I was flattered. He only talked to a few of us, and he chose me."

"It wasn't random. After Pullen and I recommended you, he wanted to check you out himself."

"You *recommended* me? For what?"

He picked up the half-finished cigarette from the ashtray, pinched off the burned end and relit it. He took a deep drag, holding it in for a few moments, then stubbed out the remainder. "One useful aspect of the conference is that it gave you an up-to-the-minute picture of the air and sea assets off West Africa. Well, there's another asset, and it's top secret. One of our own submarines is in position off Sierra Leone."

"In position, sir? Is she a U-boat hunter?"

"She's one of four specialized long-range boats Churchill ordered constructed early last year, soon after the Japanese war began. With the sea war in the Mediterranean swinging firmly in our favor, we took four of the best surviving captains and crews from the Malta and Gibraltar flotillas to man the new submarines. Officially they were men who had stacked up the requisite number of patrols for shore deployment or were being stood down through stress or illness, but in reality they were all reassigned to a top-secret operation. Two months ago we added four American boats to the flotilla, crewed by men with extensive operational experience in the Pacific. It's no coincidence that I'm a submariner too. My assignment to Bletchley late last year was part of this operation. Churchill also vetted me personally."

Fan was struggling to understand. "Why after the Japanese war began? Why is that significant? What have the Japanese got to do with this?"

Bermonsey pulled out another cigarette and tapped it on the table, but left it unlit. He glanced at the door and spoke urgently, his voice lowered. "Four days ago in the Indian Ocean off Mozambique, *U-180* rendezvoused with the Japanese submarine *I-29*. We know about it because a sharp-eyed girl in the bombe cribbing hut spotted an Ultra decrypt about to go on the slush pile with an apparently unintelligible word that she realized was Japanese. The word was Yanagi, meaning Willow. It's the Japanese code name for submarine missions to exchange technology with Nazi Germany."

"I remember another Japanese sub, *I-30*," Fan said. "Last August, wasn't it? Lord Haw Haw in the Nazi radio broadcast made a big splash about the arrival of the submarine at the U-boat base at Lorient, having avoided Allied detection."

Bermonsey nodded. "That was during our dark period, while we were unable to penetrate the new naval Enigma. A really bad time for us; worse for the men at sea. Ever since the Axis Powers' Tripartite Pact in September 1940, Bletchley has been tasked to look out for anything indicating missions like that of *I-30*. We had no way of detecting that one, but since cracking the naval code again early this year, we've been keeping an eagle eye out. The decrypt on the twenty-sixth was the first indication we've had of another exchange, though by then of course it was too late to do anything about it."

"What were they exchanging?"

"In the case of *I-30* last year, it was high-value raw materials and design technology. The Japanese sent mica and shellac, and the blueprints for an aerial torpedo; in return, the Germans sent industrial diamonds, an example of the Würzburg air defense radar, a Zeiss artillery fire director, sonar countermeasure rounds, that kind of thing. Fortunately, most of the return cargo, including the blueprints, were destroyed when the sub struck one of our mines off Singapore. In the case of *U-180* and *I-29*, it's different, even more worrying. After we identified the Ultra decrypt, our intelligence networks have been working overtime to establish what might have been exchanged. It now seems certain that a passenger on board *U-180* was the Indian nationalist leader Subhas Chandra Bose, who has been in Berlin being sweet-talked about how the Nazis would support him should the movement rise against the British in India. His transfer to Japan is a concern, because once there he might be sent to Burma and coerce more Indian Army sepoys to go over to the Japanese and the so-called Indian National Army. But of even greater concern, particularly to Churchill, was what *I-29* was bringing in exchange. Our agents in Penang report that her main cargo was more than two tons of gold."

"Two tons of gold," Fan breathed. "To buy what?"

"That's exactly what worried us. What worried Churchill. We always knew that the German High Command might use the naval Enigma for purposes other than basic U-boat movement orders. Ever since the Japanese entered the war sixteen months ago, we've been keeping an eagle eye out for intercepts that might suggest covert supply arrangements between them and the Germans. The Germans are running out of basic raw materials, especially low-volume, high-grade metals and compounds that might be carried in useful quantities even in a submarine, and the Japanese want materials of their own. With surface shipment being impossible because of our control of the sea lanes, long-range U-boats are the only option. About two months ago, a US naval analyst in Washington linked an Ultra intercept to reports from agents in Tokyo that a special shipment had been requested. The material was radioactive uranium. That's the real reason why those two American officers joined us six weeks ago. They want to be here in case we catch any similar intercepts. The Americans have been involved in a top-secret project to use uranium to make some kind of catastrophic bomb, and the idea that the Germans and the Japanese might be embarked on the same kind of project has put the fear of God into everyone involved."

"Including Churchill," Fan said.

"*Especially* Churchill. When he said the war will be won or lost in the Atlantic, he wasn't just thinking of our merchant ships. He was also thinking of what might break through our defensive screen and reach the U-boat bases at Brest and Lorient. Despite the best efforts of our ships and aircraft, it's still feasible for a U-boat on a long-distance voyage from Japan to reach Nazi-controlled territory undetected, recharging its batteries at night and refuelling from tanker U-boats on the way. The same goes in the other direction."

Fan stared at the files, speaking slowly. "You need me because any operation to take out these U-boats or Japanese subs would be based on Ultra intercepts, and would therefore have to be factored into the calculus that's my speciality. Act on too many intercepts and the Germans will become suspicious. And on the day when one of these special intercepts is acted on, Ultra intelligence related to other U-boat movements would have to be ignored and no convoys saved. Days like today?"

"Correct. We knew you were the right person for the job. Quick assessments will need to be made. You'll continue to do your routine job as part of the operational intelligence team within the hut, the job you have been doing today, but any time one of these special intercepts is detected you will also be wearing this other hat, unknown to most of the others."

"When you said our sub was in position, you meant to intercept *U-515*."

"No. I meant to intercept convoy TS-37."

"To intercept the *convoy*. Now I really don't understand."

"A long-range U-boat is due along that coast in a few days' time. We know this because an Ultra decrypt a week ago showed that a tanker U-boat was heading to a refuelling rendezvous far to the south of the known operational schedules of any other U-boats currently in the Atlantic, including *U-515*. Our sub off Sierra Leone is one of two off the West African coast hoping to intercept the long-range U-boat when further decrypts pinpoint her position. But meanwhile, something else has cropped up. One of the ships in convoy TS-37 is carrying something we do *not* want to fall into enemy hands. Open up the cargo manifest for *Clan Macpherson*."

She shuffled through the papers in the TS-37 file and found it. "Pig iron, hemp, general cargo from India. Pig iron is presumably code for manganese. Ah. It's penciled in at the bottom, to be picked up in Durban. A consignment of gold bullion."

"A very big consignment. We've secretly shipped as much gold as we can from South Africa since the outbreak of war. We need it to build up our reserves, and to fund the resistance in Europe. A consignment of this size would also be enough for the Germans to pay the Japanese for what the Nazi scientists want above all else at the moment: a cargo of uranium ore. The Japanese have opened up a new mine and apparently have a surfeit."

"But how could the gold possibly fall into German hands?"

"Because the German High Command has ordered *U-515* not to sink *Clan Macpherson*, but to capture it. We know that from an Enigma intercept. Despite our best efforts to keep all gold shipments out of South Africa secret, we believe that the Nazi agents in Durban must have caught wind of this one and passed the information up the line. They're the ones we're bluffing by relabeling manganese as pig iron. There is a reason why we haven't shut them down, but that's no concern of ours for now. What we also learned after the ship had sailed is that there are Japanese-trained operatives from the Indian National Army planted among the Lascar ratings in the crew of *Clan Macpherson* who are there to take it over once *U-515* begins attacking the convoy, and who will then cause her to fall behind so the U-boat can come alongside. If the U-boat causes enough destruction in the main body of the convoy, then that's where the escorts will concentrate, leaving stragglers to their fate. We know it's a weak escort, and so do the Germans. We believe that the plan is then for *U-515* to rendezvous with the long-range U-boat at a secret location to transfer the gold aboard. An audacious plan, but ingenious. And we have to do anything we can to stop it. I mean, *anything.*"

Fan suddenly felt sick. "My God. Now I understand what Johnson was saying. Our sub is there to sink one of our own ships. To sink *Clan Macpherson.*"

"That's the real reason I snapped at him. He's one of two cryptographers we brought in on this secret and assigned to spotting the special intercepts. We'd known about the long-distance U-boat program from agents in Japan, but it was Johnson who took that decrypt spotted by the US analyst and put it alongside a number of anomalous movement orders we'd decrypted over the past few months, ones that don't mention a U-boat by name and would normally be put in the slush pile of non-actionable intelligence. The decrypt fingered by the US analyst used a German code word for Japan known to our agents in Tokyo, and by cribbing from that Johnson was able to isolate several dozen previous communications that we realized must have been going to the long-distance U-boats. Bingo, we had the code markers to look out for future messages. It was bloody clever, really. Pity he's turned out to be a loose cannon."

"Alan jokingly calls Bletchley 'the machine,' but he says it's really an analog of the human mind, full of untapped potential but riven by human weaknesses."

"Turing? Well, at least we can rely on him. He's the other cryptographer in on this operation. He can take over Johnson's work as well. He doesn't seem to be affected by stress."

"He runs it off. Hundreds of miles a week. We're all affected by stress, whether we acknowledge it or not." She closed the file. "So what do we do about convoy TS-37?"

Bermonsey tapped the cigarette again. "Officially, you and I came into this office to make the call to order that convoy to be rerouted, and as far as the rest of this hut is concerned, that's what we've done. When they see tomorrow that the convoy has been hit, it won't be the first time that's happened. For every redirected convoy that makes it away in time, there are others that are just too sluggish. And there are U-boat captains who go maverick, changing course without sending signals that we might intercept. In normal circumstances, Werner Henke in *U-515* is just that sort of captain. I know; I was one myself. In this instance, though, with his special assignment, we can be sure that he will stay on course. With the focus in the hut on the big convoy battle that everyone now expects in the North Atlantic, one that we have helped to set up today, the loss of a few ships off Sierra Leone will soon be history, even with their precious manganese ore. That's the brutal truth of it."

She gestured at the phone. "So what do you do now?"

"Anything that comes out of Bletchley on this line is immediately acted upon. Those were the Prime Minister's orders, and this is no exception. The rear admiral commanding the Operational Intelligence Center is another in our group, and as soon as he hears the code word we have agreed for this operation he will act on it, sending the order to our sub. To others at the OIC it will appear to be another Bletchley directive, unusual but in no way betraying what is actually being ordered. By leaving the route of TS-37 unchanged, we can predict that *U-515* on its present course will make contact with the convoy at about 2300 GMT this evening. At that point our submarine will already be shadowing the convoy. Her orders will be to sink *Clan Macpherson* soon after the convoy is hit, to make it seem as if it is another U-boat attack."

"It has to be the ship?"

Bermonsey nodded grimly. "We can't afford to send our sub after the U-boat. That could be a game of cat-and-mouse that we might lose. We've thought of every other possible scenario, and there's just too much that could go wrong. We could order the sub to wait until the U-boat surfaces beside *Clan Macpherson*, the only time it would be exposed and vulnerable, but by attempting to take it out that way, the chances are we'd put a torpedo into *Clan Macpherson* as well. If there were a fight and our sub were forced to the surface, then the whole game would be up, everything we have worked on to try to undermine the gold and uranium trade. The Germans would instantly realize that we'd been on to them, and change Enigma. You know how disastrous that would be. The sub simply cannot allow her presence to be known, either to the escort or to *U-515*. To Henke it must simply appear that another U-boat was in the vicinity, a maverick captain like himself who was keeping radio silence. The convoy commodore and the escorts will know nothing of any of this, and nobody outside our group here or in the OIC will know that my message was an order not for the convoy to be rerouted but for one of our own subs to sink one of our own merchant ships."

"What about our submarine captain? He's going to be ordered to do the unthinkable."

"We vetted those crews for a reason. They know they're a top-secret outfit, under the direct command of Churchill. For them, that will be enough. They're hardened killers. They've all had to do what I've had to do, watched men screaming and burning in the water through the periscope, men you have put there. When you see that, they're no longer the enemy, just men. I know he'll do it because I know I would do it."

He stood up, straightened his uniform and went to the phone. Fan tried to focus, but her mind was in turmoil. The layers of secrecy suddenly seemed like a hall of mirrors, trapping her inside, leaving her uncertain whether she was looking at illusion or reality. In truth, she had little idea what all the others really did here, that silent shivering army who marched in every morning with her from the train, exchanging quick pleasantries over that first welcome mug of tea, then disappearing into huts all over Bletchley with sentries at the doors. For all she knew, her friend Louise could be part of some other top-secret enterprise. She could not even know how far Bermonsey had let her in, whether he had told her the full story. The need to prevent the Germans from getting gold that could pay for uranium was clear enough. But was that really enough justification for sinking a British ship? Was there something else going on, something on that ship other than the gold?

She looked at him standing by the phone, counting down the seconds on his watch. His eyes had hardened again, and she knew that she was not going to get anything more out of him. He had told her what she needed to know to do her job, and that would be it. That was the way Bletchley worked.

One minute to go. She forced herself to think of the Atlantic again, of the ships battling the spray and the swell. It would still be dark, the end of the dog watch. Exhausted men would be falling instantly asleep in their bunks, fully clothed in case they had to spring into lifeboats; bleary-eyed men would be replacing them, clutching cups of cocoa and staring at the dark smudge of the ship in the line ahead, men barely in control of the cold and the fear. Normally it was an image that gave her some comfort, knowing that one file had been kept open, one convoy given a chance. This time it was different. This time, she would be saving nobody.

Bermonsey lifted the phone off the receiver. It was answered instantly. He turned away from her, speaking urgently. "This is Bletchley. Code name Ark. I repeat, *Ark*. Execute."

Part 2

6

The ancient site of Carthage, Tunisia, present day

"Maurice, can you see anything? It's too dangerous. You need to come out now."

Maurice Hiebermeyer watched a clump of mud slowly collapse a few inches from his nose, and listened to the pounding of the blood in his ears. Aysha's voice seemed distant, as if coming from the end of a very long tunnel, and yet she was only a few meters behind him, standing in the excavation trench just above the level of the Bay of Tunis some fifty meters to the east. He had a sudden flashback to his first excavation with Jack, cheek by jowl down a rabbit hole they had widened in a wood near their boarding school in southern England, straining to reach the Roman pottery they had seen at the bottom of the hole and also keep themselves concealed from the teacher who had been sent to find them. A piece of mud slopped over his face, and he snapped back to present reality. It was only the constant scooping of the digger that had kept the water at bay, and with the machine shut down while he investigated the hole, the water was seeping in again, inexorably. He watched it trickle down the mud into the pool that was already lapping the top of his head, and he tasted the sea on his lips. Aysha was right. She was thinking of their two-year-old son Michael as much as him. Being upside-down in a flooding hole beneath several tons of mud did not present ideal conditions for his long-term survival.

"Nothing structural," he shouted back, his voice sounding hollow in the confined space. "But I can see mud from the ancient harbor entrance channel, about a meter below where you're standing. I'm coming out now."

He peered around, confirming that there was nothing more to be seen, no masonry, no artifacts, just the gray-black ooze of the ancient channel below. He could feel his headlamp beginning to work its way off, lubricated by the sheen of mud that covered the strap. He tried everything to keep it on, angling his head forward, butting it against the side of the hole, but to no avail. *"Scheisse,"* he muttered as it dropped into the ooze, shining blindingly back at him. He shut his eyes tight and began to work his way out, crawling backward on his elbows and knees. Over the years he had honed self-extraction to a fine art, displaying an agility that belied his girth. At the last moment he quickly reached back in and grabbed the headlamp, and then he was out on his hands and knees in the glaring sunlight at the bottom of the trench, the bucket of the digger resting in the mud beside him and the anxious faces of the workmen peering down from the top of the trench above.

He struggled to his feet and squinted up, the mud dripping off him. Aysha had evidently satisfied herself that he was all right and had climbed back up to the ledge they had cut in the side of the trench as a platform to oversee the excavation. *"Rien, rien,"* he shouted to the workmen, making a sideways chopping motion with his hand, the third time he had done so since they had begun work just after dawn that morning. Each time the digger had revealed an air space in the side of the trench, a crack or a fissure or a hole, he had gone down to investigate, hoping to find masonry structure that might reveal the shape of the harbor entrance. It was not really what he had come to Carthage hoping to find, but it would be a significant addition to the work Jack had done here years before with a student diving team, recording the foundations of the outer harbor wall that had been inundated by the sea-level rise since antiquity.

The workmen finished their cigarettes, the digger driver got back into his cab, ready to start again, and Hiebermeyer made his way up the ladder to Aysha, who was waiting with a large bottle of water. "Thanks," he said, dumping the water over his head, blinking and spluttering as his face emerged from its mask of mud. Too late he realized that his shorts were flying somewhere below half-mast, and he yanked them up again. They had been a present from Jack years ago at the outset of their careers, a pair of Second World War Afrika Korps shorts Jack had found in a bazaar in

Cairo. The mud would harden in the sun and solidify them, keeping them from falling down again. Nothing would induce him to wear anything else, and Aysha had given up trying long ago.

"I'm off," she said, making as if to embrace him but then looking at the mud and stopping herself. "They're only opening the museum conservation rooms during the mornings this week, and I've got to make the most of it. Call Jack, all right? You may not think that ooze is very exciting, but he'll be very interested if you've hit the harbor entrance channel. It's good for you to touch base with him anyway. Remember, he was the one who set this project up for us."

"He's probably out of touch at the moment. He and Costas are diving off West Africa on a Second World War merchantman, monitoring a salvage company. I'm actually slightly worried about him. The operation's run by Anatoly Landor."

"You mean your old school friend?"

"Hardly a friend. If it hadn't been for Jack's intervention, Landor would have made mincemeat of me. He's held a grudge against Jack ever since I arrived at the school and we started going off excavating together. Normally Rebecca keeps me up to date with what Jack's up to, but she's been a little off the grid herself in Kyrgyzstan."

"I'm sure Jack can look after himself. He's got Costas with him. That always seems to work."

"I just want to find something a bit more exciting for him. He's used to getting calls from me only when it's the big time, right? I don't want to disappoint."

"Nothing from you would ever disappoint Jack. He thinks very highly of you, you know. You may not be a diver, but you're still his oldest friend."

"I feel as if I've got to prove myself all over again since we had to leave Egypt, as if I've got to start from scratch. I hardly know my way around this place."

"Remember what Rebecca told you when she came to us on *Seaquest* six months ago. It was the extremists who forced us out, not anything you did. And remember those of my own family still trapped in Cairo, my brother in the resistance. They're the ones we should be thinking about."

"I know. I only wish I could do something."

"You are. You're doing what you were born to do. Remember what Jack said, too. He said you were a bloody good archaeologist, the best. He

wouldn't have pulled strings to set you up on a site as important as this if
he thought otherwise."

Hiebermeyer gave her a tired smile. "When are we Skyping Michael in
London?"

"Two P.M. My sister will have brought him in from nursery school.
We're doing it from the museum, so you'll have to leave here half an hour
before that at the latest to get there in time. Where's our newly arrived IMU
nanotechnology and computer simulation expert, by the way?"

"Lanowski? At the Roman water cisterns. He's become fascinated by
the water supply system of the ancient city, thinks it hasn't been properly
understood. Typical of Jacob, finding something mathematical to solve. He
really got the fieldwork bug during our final days in Egypt last year, applying his quirky genius to Akhenaten's map of the City of Light. Jack is
going to have a real problem keeping him glued to the screen from now
on. Jacob thinks the established idea that Punic houses relied on rainwater
cisterns and it was the Romans who put in the first aqueduct is wrong,
that the Punic city also had some kind of communal supply. I think he
could be right."

"Did he have guards with him? The cisterns are a bit off the beaten
track."

"Two of them went with him in the van. We've got a bigger police presence here after the bombing in Tunis last night, mainly for the benefit of the
government officials living in the compound, but it increases our security
too. You've still got yours?"

"Waiting in the car. Don't go down any more holes without telling me.
I only came to check up on you because something told me Jacob might
not be here to watch over you. And Maurice, please don't hang your hat
on that thing. Sometimes I really do worry about you. See you later."

He waved, wiped his face on a towel, and put his spectacles on, but left
his hat where it was, hanging from a protuberance in the exposed section
of the trench, while he waited for his head to dry. He watched Aysha walk
off across the overgrown tennis court toward the car waiting at the entrance
to the compound, past the two soldiers with automatic rifles at the checkpoint. For a week prior to opening up this trench, he and Aysha had been
digging only a few hundred meters away at the Tophet, the sanctuary filled
with infant cremation burials where the Carthaginians had practiced child
sacrifice. Many scholars had insisted that the Roman accounts must be

exaggerated, but osteological analysis at the IMU lab had shown beyond doubt that the burials were of healthy infants, not stillbirths and natural infant deaths as had been imagined. The discovery had made him think of their own son, Michael, and how distant they were from a world in which parents would contemplate such an act.

In the lowest layers, dating to the seventh and sixth centuries BC, they had found inscriptions scratched and painted on potsherds giving thanks to the god Ba'al Hammon for accepting the offerings. The inscriptions were similar in date and style to those being found by Jack's team on the Phoenician shipwreck off Cornwall, and had meant that Aysha had been collaborating closely with their colleagues Jeremy Haverstock and Maria de Montijo at the Institute of Palaeography in Oxford to develop a better lexicon for the Punic language at that date. It had been an exciting project for Aysha, and she had been working overtime to finish photographing the inscriptions before they were due to close down the excavation and return to England to be with Michael again at the end of the week.

He wiped his face once more, and watched the guards close the gate behind Aysha's car and resume their patrol of the perimeter. He remembered the mummy excavation in the Fayum oasis in Egypt almost ten years previously where he and Aysha had first met, after she had bombarded him with emails to get on his project. Her trauma at having to leave Egypt six months ago had been even greater than his, with members of her family still trapped there under the extremist regime, some of them joining the guerrilla army to fight back. Egypt was not the only place in the Arab world where archaeology had shut down. Tunisia was heading that way too, with extremist slogans already desecrating ancient sites and museum walls. Gone were the days when archaeologists had come to Carthage in droves under the banner of a UNESCO program that made the site one of the largest and most exciting excavations in the Mediterranean. It was only intensive negotiations by Jack that had made this project possible, under the stipulation from the IMU board of directors that the security arrangements would have to pass their own strict standards. It had helped that much of the suburb of Tunis that covered ancient Carthage was already a high-security military and diplomatic compound, but even so the police presence had been enhanced and extra vetting had been put in place for the local workmen they had employed to clear the spoil and operate the digger at the site.

The sun was burning through the morning haze, and he felt the sweat trickle down his forehead. Soon it would be like a furnace, and the excavation would have to halt until the evening. He picked up his tool belt, a present from Costas before he had flown out. Costas had not been the only one offering to help; everyone had been very kind. He knew they were concerned about his state of mind after having to leave Egypt, but they need not have worried. Carthage had begun to grip him, despite the frustrations. For too long, perhaps, he had been used to the certainties of Egypt, where a tomb was a tomb and a pyramid a pyramid, where so much of the archaeology fell into a predictable framework. Here at Carthage, by comparison, the early history was elusive, disrupted by successive phases of destruction: by the Romans when they leveled the city in 146 BC, by Julius Caesar a hundred years later when he swept away the ruins and rebuilt Carthage as a Roman city, by the Vandals in the early fifth century and the Byzantines a century later, and finally by the Arabs in the seventh century when they built their new capital of Tunis nearby, using the ruins of Carthage as a quarry and never reoccupying it.

At first he had despaired of finding any intact stratigraphy from the earliest Phoenician settlement at Carthage, where he had hoped to discover evidence of Egyptian influence; pottery from that period was more likely to be swept up in destruction debris or used by the Romans as a strengthener in concrete. But then he had begun to see the challenge of it, to see that being an archaeologist at a site like this was as much an act of imagination as of discovery, that his role in being here was to absorb everything he could about the place and then see where his flair for reconstructing the past would take him. After years of rivalry with Jack in which Hiebermeyer's excavations in Egypt had so often produced the bigger artifacts, the show-stoppers and the headline-grabbers, he had begun to think like Jack, to see archaeology in terms of probabilities and hypotheses rather than the certainties that emptying tombs and digging up mummies had brought. And to his even greater disbelief, he had begun to enjoy it. At Carthage, he felt like a novelist trying to tease a story out of the past, using the disparate evidence to create a canvas that could be populated by the people who had made this one of the greatest cities of the ancient world.

It was Jack who had brought Carthage alive for him, standing here on this patch of waste ground beside the tennis court six months ago when they had been negotiating for the excavation permit. Jack had agreed with him that before the founding of the city there may well have been a trade

outpost here, one established by the Canaanite predecessors of the Phoenicians that might have included Mycenaean Greek and Egyptian merchants. That much fitted with what was known about international
maritime trade in the late Bronze Age, at the time of Akhenaten and Tutankhamun, of the Israelite exodus from Egypt. But Jack had steered him
away from any hope of finding Bronze Age remains, and instead toward
the later Punic city and its links with the eastern Mediterranean world, asking him to imagine the site as it had been in the nineteenth century, before
Tunis began to encroach on the ruins, when the clearest evidence of the
ancient city had been the landlocked harbors entered by the channel they
were trying to find now.

Those harbors owed their design to Tire, the mother city of Carthage
in ancient Phoenicia. Another link was child sacrifice, something that associated Carthage with the story of Abraham and Isaac in the Old Testament. Jack believed that sacrifices may have taken place on a ceremonial
platform at the harbor entrance, a place where the terrifying bronze furnace described by the Romans could have been seen from far out at sea,
its belching flames propitiating great voyages of discovery and trade. It
was here, too, that those voyages would surely have been commemorated,
by trophies and inscriptions set up by navigators such as Hanno and
Himilco and others who followed them. An excavation at this spot might
not only reveal the channel itself, literally the portal to those great voyages
of discovery, but also find evidence of rituals that linked the Carthaginians back to the world from which they had come, to the peoples of Phoenicia and the Holy Land who had once been their kin and cousins.

Hiebermeyer picked up another water bottle from the table and took a
deep swig from it. Aysha had been right: he really should call Jack. Having
found the channel, he owed it to him. He stared at the mudbank where
Jack believed the ceremonial platform to have been, and narrowed his eyes.
He would give it another day, just one more. He reached over and took his
battered straw hat from the protuberance in the wall, revealing it to be the
partly exposed tibia of a human skeleton. They had found it on the first day
of the dig, and had decided to leave it *in situ*, to be reburied once the excavation was over. The numerous healed slash wounds on the bones and a
Castilian ring showed the skeleton to be that of a Spanish soldier who had
probably died during a siege of Tunis in the sixteenth century. Hiebermeyer had christened him Miguel, and had taken to brushing the bones

down and watering them every morning to keep them from drying. He had become increasingly concerned about Miguel, about the bleaching of the bones, over the many hours he had spent here alone, sweltering over the trench while Aysha was busy elsewhere and before Lanowski had arrived. He had asked the workmen to build a small awning and to lay on a hose, so that the skeleton could be kept under a constant fine spray, enough also to moisten the sprigs of bougainvillea that he had planted on either side.

He leaned toward the skull, looking around furtively. *"Rien, rien,"* he whispered, wagging his finger, repeating what he had said to the workmen, watching the splayed jaw as if for a response. He sat up, suddenly feeling self-conscious. Perhaps Miguel was not the only one who had become un-hinged. He laughed at the pun, slapping his knee, wishing that Costas had been here. It was good German humor, something that Costas appreciated.

Seeing the digger operator watching him, he quickly got up, straight-ened his hat, and stared into the trench, seeing where the hole had disap-peared under the mud. He made a whirling motion with his hand, still staring. Nothing happened, and he glanced at the digger operator, who was looking at him as if waiting for the next bout of odd behavior. Hiebermeyer repeated the gesture, in some agitation. The operator shrugged, tossed away his cigarette, and the machine roared to life. Hiebermeyer glanced back at Miguel, and then stopped himself. "He's dead," he whispered. *"Miguel is dead."* He was suddenly looking forward to Lanowski returning, to the mathematical digressions, the floppy hair, the lopsided grin. That in itself was serious. He really *did* need someone to talk to.

Twenty minutes later, the excavation of the harbor channel was in full swing again, the backhoe of the digger steadily revealing more gray-black ooze and the workmen clearing the waste ground ahead so that the trench could be extended toward the modern seafront. Hiebermeyer watched the water seep in after each scoop and clumps of desiccated soil fall in from above, coloring the water light brown. Everything here was either extremely wet or extremely dry. The dryness at least was like digging in Egypt. Miguel still had clumps of hair attached to the back of his skull, and mummified skin around his pelvis. Hiebermeyer emptied most of his water bottle on the bones, and then poured the remainder over the back of his own neck.

He looked up just as Lanowski dropped down the side of the cut and strode over, clapping him on the shoulder. "Congratulations, Maurice. I've just seen the gray mud, proving you've found the channel. That about wraps it up here?"

Hiebermeyer gestured at the opposite side of the trench. "I just want to test Jack's hypothesis about the ceremonial platform. If we get nothing today, then I'll assume it was destroyed by the Romans or robbed of its stone after the city was abandoned. It's good to see you back. I was beginning to talk to myself. How were the cisterns?"

Lanowski beamed back at him, nodding. "Good. *Very* good."

Hiebermeyer passed him another water bottle, and then reached into his shorts, remembering the sandwich Aysha had given him that morning. Or was it the morning before? He found it, pulled it out, took off the wrapping and handed half to Lanowski, who took the squashed offering gratefully and wolfed it down. The two had become close friends after Lanowski had revealed his passion for Egyptology the year before, a bond that had been further cemented when he had been instrumental in their escape from the Nile during the extremist takeover.

Hiebermeyer looked approvingly at the other man's gear. Lanowski wore mountain boots, multi-pocketed hiking shorts, and a pair of old army-surplus khaki bags crossed over from each shoulder, like a camel. He had tied his long hair back and was covered from head to foot in dust, a thin film even coating his spectacles. Now he swallowed the last of the sandwich, reached into one of the bags and pulled out a linked belt of a dozen or so 20 mm rounds, the brass ends green with corrosion. "Found these. Pretty cool, eh?"

"*Mein Gott.* You're as bad as Costas."

"As *good* as Costas, you mean. The Roman cisterns were used as tank berms by the British Eighth Army at the end of the North African campaign in 1943, and the collapsed end of one of them contained an ammunition store. It looks as if the berm might have been destroyed by a bomb and then abandoned."

"Leave it for the Tunisian army to deal with," Hiebermeyer said. "I've lost enough people close to me in this place."

Lanowski pushed up his glasses. "Of course. Your grandfather. Insensitive of me. I shouldn't have mentioned it."

Hiebermeyer put a muddy hand on Lanowski's shoulder. "It's part of the archaeology of this place. It can't be ignored." He had another motive for coming here, one that arose from a chapter in his family history more than seventy years ago. His grandfather, a schoolteacher before the war, had been an officer in the German Army engineers under Rommel and had been killed in the final days of the campaign in June 1943, the same month that one of his uncles had gone down with his U-boat in the North Atlantic. His grandfather had no known grave, but Jack had accompanied Maurice during their earlier visit to Carthage to the German memorial and ossuary to the south of Tunis. The juxtaposition of stark gray slabs set against the azure Mediterranean made it difficult to comprehend how somewhere so beautiful could also be a place of war and death that had devastated so many families.

Lanowski bagged the ammunition belt and pointed at the trench. "Got any good stratigraphy yet?"

Hiebermeyer snorted. "Are you kidding? This is Carthage. In Egypt, you can dig through the Ottoman stuff and the Roman stuff to find the real archaeology, everything in nice neat layers. The conquerors there didn't flatten the pyramids and build their own things on top. Here," he said, raising a finger as the analogy came to him, "here, it's as if you're in biology class at school dissecting a frog and some joker of a lab partner has scooped out the entrails and dumped them on the bench for you to sift through, with everything all jumbled up."

"An experience you've had?" Lanowski said.

"That was my introduction to Jack Howard, the day after I arrived at our boarding school. He apologized when he saw that he'd upset me, and said he was only trying it on with the world's most boring biology teacher, not with me. He made it up to me in detention afterward by promising to take me out that weekend to his secret excavation at a nearby Roman site. That nearly got us expelled, but I was hooked."

"Amazing you both made it to Cambridge."

"By then that biology teacher was the headmaster, and he wrote us both shining references. To study archaeology, that is, not biology."

"And now you're both star alumni of the school, highlighted on their website as if you were model pupils."

"That's always the way."

Hiebermeyer heaved himself upward, nearly losing his shorts in the process and quickly grabbing them before they descended to his knees. He pulled them up and tightened his tool belt, checking that everything was there: his trusty trowel, one of the pair that he and Jack had bought with their pocket money at a local hardware shop while they were at school; a geological hammer and a headlamp; various brushes and chisels; and some oddments that Costas had added, items he had found indispensable underwater that he had thought Hiebermeyer might like to have, one of them looking suspiciously like a Costas-designed multi-tool for opening bottles and stirring drinks. He shifted the weight until it was comfortable and then put his hands on his hips, surveying the excavation like a general inspecting a battlefield.

A few moments later, there was a clunking noise from the digger, and the engine revved down. Hiebermeyer and Lanowski hurried to the edge of the trench and peered in. The backhoe had hit something hard, metallic-sounding rather than masonry, not in the trench walls but in the muddy ooze. At that location inside the channel it could not be foundations, but rather something that had fallen or been thrown in, conceivably part of the harbor-front platform that Jack had postulated for the opposite bank. Maurice waved at the digger operator to cut the engine, and felt his excitement rise. *This could be it.*

"My turn," Lanowski said, unslinging the bags over his shoulders. "You promised I'd get the chance when I returned."

"We'll both go."

Lanowski took the lead and Hiebermeyer followed him down the ladder into the trench, past the arm of the backhoe. There was only space for one of them at a time to squeeze between the bucket and the side of the trench, and Lanowski went first, his boots slurping in the ooze that was becoming more liquid as the trench slowly filled up. Whatever it was that had stopped the digger had fallen from the dry soil above, and was covered in clumps of it. Lanowski had made his way in front of the bucket and crouched down out of sight.

"Well?" Hiebermeyer said, forcing his girth through the narrow gap. "Metal or stone?"

Lanowski remained stock still, staring. "You're not going to believe it."

"I'm all ears."

"On the flight here, I boned up on Punic Carthage, and I memorized that famous Roman account of child sacrifice. 'There was in their city a bronze image of Ba'al Hammon, palms up and sloping toward the ground, so that each of the children when placed thereon rolled down and fell into a sort of gaping pit filled with fire.' "

"Diodorus Siculus," Hiebermeyer said, straining forward. "Usually thought of as negative propaganda. Child sacrifice, yes, we know from the osteological analysis that it happened, but a giant bronze furnace shaped like a god?"

"Look what the digger just found."

Lanowski moved as far as he could to one side, heaving his feet out of the ooze that was beginning to grip them like quicksand. Hiebermeyer pulled himself out beyond the bucket and lurched forward, falling on his knees where Lanowski had been standing and splattering them both with mud. He stared at the object in front of him. It was about two meters wide, circular in shape and slightly convex, and clearly made of copper alloy. At first he thought it was a great bronze cauldron, crumpled and misshapen. Then he saw what Lanowski had seen and staggered to his feet.

"*Gott im Himmel,*" he said, astonished. It was not a cauldron but the distorted face of a giant statue, more beast than man, broken off at the upper jaw where a line of jagged teeth, each as big as Hiebermeyer's hand, extended in an arc from the mud. He slid down again, pulling the torch out of his tool belt and shining it inside. "It gets even better," he exclaimed. "It's blackened inside, charred. This was a furnace, no doubt about it."

Lanowski was squatting beside him, staring. "Incredible. So it was true. Fathers like you and me gave up their infant children to be burned alive in this thing."

Hiebermeyer carried on peering inside, flashing the torch beneath the bronze. "There's something else in here. Help me get it out."

Lanowski slumped down in the mud and reached under the bronze teeth beside Hiebermeyer. "The upper part feels dry, desiccated, but where it's become soaked by the water it's almost supple, like leather," he said. "I swear it's hairy."

"It *is* hairy," Hiebermeyer said, poking at it. "It's a dead animal, a skin. It could be very old, if it's been protected beneath the bronze and mummified."

He put his torch between his teeth and they both heaved, pulling the mass out and flopping it on top of the bronze. Large sections of it appeared denuded and leathery, but elsewhere there were patches of dense black hair matted together. Hiebermeyer heaved at a football-sized clump attached to one end and slipped down with it into the mud, staring at one of the most extraordinary things he had ever uncovered in his archaeological career.

He struggled up on his elbows, the clump on his chest, and cleared his throat, seeing that Lanowski was looking in the other direction, still folding down the other sides of the skin. "You said you'd been reading up on Punic Carthage. For Jacob Lanowski, that means reading *everything*. In the original languages. What does your photographic memory have on Pliny and Hanno?" he said.

Lanowski stopped what he had been doing and stared into space. "Well, there are two passages in Pliny's *Historia Naturalis*. The first is the controversial one in which he implies that Hanno sailed from Gibraltar to Arabia, circumnavigating Africa."

"I mean the other one. Book six."

"Ah yes." Lanowski pushed his spectacles up his nose, dropped the hide and slipped back against the side of the trench. "'*Duarumque Gorgadum cutes argumenti et miraculi gratia in Iunonis templo posuit, spectates usque ad Carthaginem captam.*' I think I've got that right. Pliny had clearly read the Greek translation of Hanno's *Periplus*, where the creatures he translates as Gorgons are called *gorillae*. He says that after capturing these *gorillae*, Hanno brought two of the skins back to Carthage, where they were displayed in the temple of Chronos until the Romans captured the city. For Chronos read Ba'al Hammon, the nearest Punic equivalent."

Hiebermeyer heaved the mass on his chest around until it was facing Lanowski. "Well, as our friend Costas would say, get a hold of this."

Lanowski stared, raised his spectacles and squinted, and then gave a high-pitched laugh. "Yep. That would be it. That would be a gorilla. I don't believe it."

Hiebermeyer rolled the head off his chest and quickly extracted himself from the animal's front limbs, which were threatening to wrap themselves around him and push him back into the ooze. Lanowski leaped up and heaved it back, in the process folding over part of the skin so that the interior was exposed. He stopped for a moment, peering, and then turned the rest of the skin over so that the flayed interior was fully revealed, the head lolling backward into the water. "Maurice, check this out."

Hiebermeyer pulled himself forward in the ooze, and stared. In the center of the skin was a rectilinear outline in flecks of gold, with further lines extending out from each corner. He leaned in, peering closely. "Gold leaf or gilding, no doubt about it. I'd say this skin had once been used as a covering for a golden box, a fairly large one, about the size of the Anubis shrine in Tut's tomb. Probably carried outdoors where it was very hot, causing the gold to melt slightly and adhere to the skin. Interesting. Pliny doesn't say anything about *that* in his account."

"Something Hanno brought back from his travels, perhaps?" Lanowski said.

Hiebermeyer felt the ooze creep up above his boots and toward his knees. "Time we got out of here. This is getting a bit too much like maritime archaeology."

"Speaking of which, Aysha called and told me to remind you. Could be time you gave Jack a ring?"

Hiebermeyer wiped the back of his hand across his face, smearing on more mud. "Do you think we've found enough? I don't want to let him down."

"Um, given that we're probably looking at the cover of the next *National Geographic* magazine, not to speak of front-page news around the world, I'd say a big yes. I think Jack would say you've earned your Carthage credentials." Lanowski leaned over, and they shook muddy hands.

"You spotted it for what it was," Hiebermeyer said.

"You stuck with the excavation. It was your perseverance that paid off."

"All right." Hiebermeyer cracked a broad grin, the first for a long time. "We've got to get the digger to raise this whole clump as one mass, and then get it to the conservation lab pronto. Before that, I want to take about a thousand photos."

"Roger that."

"What's that?"

"Oh, just something I've heard Costas say."

Hiebermeyer grunted, heaved himself on to the edge of the bucket, and then sprang up to the top of the trench, grabbing it and pulling himself on to the platform, his shorts miraculously in place. He stomped across to the table, the mud splattering off his boots, and poured a bottle of water over his face. Then he took off his hat and tossed it on to the outstretched tibia, watching it spin as if Miguel were giving it a twirl. He nearly said something, but then stopped himself. It was time to leave Miguel to the past, and to start communicating again properly with the land of the living. He glanced back down at Lanowski and the skin, seeing the strange golden outline. It rang a distant bell, but he could not quite put his finger on it. He would see if it meant anything to Jack.

He picked up his phone, tapping the screen with a muddy finger. Aysha first, and then they would Skype their son Michael. After that, he would call Jack. The adrenalin was coursing through him, the thrill of discovery that had fueled his life since he and Jack had first peered down that rabbit hole, had first reached in and pulled out those ancient sherds. Suddenly he felt on top of the world again.

7

Off the Lizard Peninsula, Cornwall, present day

Jack ducked under the entrance to the tent and sat down on a folding chair, holding the mug of tea that he had just brewed up in the kitchen tent on the far side of the clearing. He took a sip and stared out at the shimmering sea visible through the tent flap, the surf at high tide lapping the foreshore only a stone's throw away. Ahead of him, rising to a grassy knoll above the tents, was the promontory that split the bay into two coves and provided shelter from the prevailing westerlies that could blow to severe gale force even in summer. Today, though, the sea was almost dead calm, as near to flat as he had ever seen it, with only the hint of a swell from the Atlantic pulsing gently against the shoreline. It was Cornwall at its best, the sea warm enough to swim in without a wetsuit and the breeze that ruffled the grass on the edge of the clearing keeping the heat at bay.

He took a deep breath and leaned forward, his elbows on his knees. After their perilous dive on the wreck of *Clan Macpherson* only five days before, he felt as if he had been given a reprieve, and he was still awash with the euphoria that came from survival, still buoyed by residual adrenalin. He knew that the questioning would come soon enough, the quiet discussions with Costas about what had gone wrong and what could have been done better, the occasional sleepless night. But for now he was still riding a wave of excitement over their discovery of the bronze plaque and the mystery it had opened up. The video from their helmet cameras had gone straight to their colleagues at the Institute of Palaeography in Oxford for decipherment of the symbols. Meanwhile Jack had focused on *Clan Macpherson* herself, researching everything he could about the circumstances of her loss and how she might have come to be carrying such an extraordinary artifact.

The IMU campus was only half an hour away, off the Fal estuary on the other side of the peninsula; he had deliberately come across this morning with time to spare before his dive on the Phoenician wreck, his first since returning from West Africa. Apart from a conservator dealing with finds in one of the other tents, the rest of the team were either on the research vessel *Seafire* anchored beside the wreck or underwater working on the excavation. The coastal footpath that passed the camp was quiet, not yet filled with the hikers who thronged it during the summer months, and the beaches were empty. He was itching to get on the wreck, a swim in a pool compared to *Clan Macpherson*, but he had wanted some time to himself in order to run through what he had discovered in the archives over the past few days and to think about what might lie ahead.

He sipped his tea, crossed his legs, and opened the file he had brought with him from the campus that morning. He still could not get the image of *Clan Macpherson* out of his mind. It was not so much their close shave that preoccupied him as the knowledge that something about the sinking, something about the convoy action on that day in 1943, was not quite right. The presence of a British torpedo in the wreck—a torpedo that could only have been fired by a British submarine—was baffling, to say the least. He stared at the two photos clipped to the inside of the file, the upper one showing the ship in her smart peacetime livery on the Mersey, with Liverpool in the background, and the lower one in her drab wartime gray, with guns fore and aft and her lifeboats swung out on their derricks ready for immediate use. He remembered his own first image of the ship, the looming, rusted hull and the twisted metal where the torpedo had exploded, and thought of the last sight of her by the men in the lifeboats, the vessel that had been their home disappearing in a terrifying final plunge that had transformed her into the wreck that he and Costas had seen over a hundred meters deep on the edge of the continental shelf off Africa.

Yesterday he had gone to the National Archives at Kew and had seen the original convoy dossier, including documents that would have passed through the hands of naval intelligence over those fateful days, perhaps even the code breakers at Bletchley Park who evaluated the Ultra decrypts and decided which convoys to reroute on the basis of intercepted German U-boat movement reports. He had been to Bletchley with his daughter Rebecca for a school project a couple of years previously, and remembered sitting behind the desk in Alan Turing's office, looking at the wartime convoy chart on the wall and then out into the main operations room where the deciphered German naval orders were analyzed and passed up the line for possible action. The file he had handled at Kew yesterday had smelled musty, like stale cigarette smoke, and brought home the reality of Bletchley more than seventy years ago in the darkest days of the war: not the sanitized, scrubbed huts of the modern reconstruction but places fugged with smoke and stale sweat, with the wispy rising steam of mugs of tea, where the intelligence work was not just a mathematical puzzle but a deadly calculus of ships and men caught up in the most savage and costly sea war in history.

He sifted through the dossier, scanned copies of the originals. The first part contained the convoy commodore's report, a fold-out *pro forma* with the bare facts of the convoy's progress penned in; clipped to that had been a sheaf of pink and white slips with decrypted radio messages between the Admiralty, the convoy commodore and the Royal Navy escort commander. All of that was standard fare for a convoy file; they showed that the convoy had made a few minor course deviations at the commodore's own discretion, none of them as a result of a rerouting order from the Admiralty. Clearly, if an Ultra intercept at Bletchley had revealed U-boats in the area, the Admiralty's Operational Intelligence Center had decided not to act on it, a decision that would have been based on a risk assessment that such action might reveal to the Germans that Ultra had been broken.

The second group of scans came not from Kew but from the Clan Line archive, a mass of documents that had survived the closure of the shipping company and been preserved as a historical record. The archivist had delved into material yet to be catalogued and had come up trumps, uncovering the report of the master, Captain Gough, after the sinking of *Clan Macpherson*, and an exchange between him and the director of the trade division at the Admiralty.

Jack reread the parts of the master's report that he had highlighted after receiving the documents from the archivist the previous evening. *It is now with very great regret that I report the loss of Chief Engineer Robertson, Second*

Engineer Marshall, Fourth Engineer MacMurtrie and fifth Engineer Cunningham, who went down with their vessel. Gough had described how, after the ship had been torpedoed, three of the deck officers and an apprentice had gone below in an attempt to shore up the breached hold, using sacks of groundnuts from the cargo like sandbags to build up a bulkhead. *No praise is too high for the courageous spirit and dauntless devotion to duty that was shown by my officers, engineers and volunteer crew in their magnificent attempt to save their ship.*

Jack looked up for a moment, squinting against the reflection of the sun on the sea, imagining the grim reality behind Captain Gough's report—soaked and freezing men piling bags as the stricken ship groaned around them, and the engineers living out their worst nightmare, realizing too late that she was going under, desperately scrabbling for air space as the waters rose and the ship buckled and shrieked on its plummet to the abyssal darkness below.

He drained his tea, and then looked at the pages that had kept him awake after first reading them the evening before. Unusually for a merchant captain, Gough had been openly critical of the Admiralty. Jack could picture him as he sat down in Freetown to write his report, after seeing that the survivors from *Clan Macpherson* had been brought safely ashore and then hearing the terrible news that his ship was one of seven from the convoy to have been sunk that night. Even before the attack, there had been concern over the inadequate escort and the absence of air cover. *A very strong feeling exists,* Gough wrote, *that many of these vessels, if not all, have been needlessly sacrificed.* He pointed out that the armed trawlers in the escort could only do eight knots, slower even than the most sluggish of the merchantmen, and that the speed of the convoy was therefore gravely constrained. Jack read Gough's two burning questions, sensing the ire behind the sober phrasing: *whether, knowing there were submarines on the track of this convoy, it was not possible for destroyers to be sent out from Freetown to give the necessary protection;* and *whether the courses which the convoy was instructed to take were, in the circumstances, the right ones.*

Next he turned to the reply from the director of the trade division at the Admiralty. Gough was told that armed trawlers had given good anti-submarine service elsewhere, and that the visibility had been too poor for air cover. *I fully appreciate your distress at the loss of such a fine ship, which I can assure you is shared by all of us at the Admiralty. We are, as you can understand, bound to consider the U-boat war as a whole and view each incident in its right*

perspective. The U-boat threat, for instance, off the West African coast is but a frac-
tion of that in the North Atlantic and we obviously must allocate our limited re-
sources in escort vessels accordingly. Were it possible, there is nothing we would like
better than to give every convoy a really strong escort. And finally: *War invariably*
leads to blows and counter-blows, and it would be illogical not to expect the enemy
occasionally to get in a nasty punch. I can only assure you that we are fully alive to
all the risks that have to be run and are deploying our forces to the best of our ability
to bring about the ultimate defeat of the U-boat.

Jack closed the file, and squinted out to sea again. The response from
the director of the trade division was measured and decent, as compassion-
ate as it could reasonably be. But it was precisely the nature of the response
that had been niggling at him. It seemed odd that at the height of the Battle
of the Atlantic, during those critical weeks in May 1943 when everything
hung in the balance, the Admiralty should have devoted so much care to
the concerns of a single merchant captain from a convoy off Africa, far
from the main focus of attention in the North Atlantic. Jack might have
expected a curt response at best, even a disciplinary one. But instead the
Admiralty had mandated their senior officer responsible for merchant
shipping to give more thought to a response than had apparently been put
into arranging adequate defense for the convoy.

Jack had looked up Captain Gough's war record, and knew he was not
a man to make criticism lightly. He had already been sunk twice, once
when his ship *Clan Ogilvy* was torpedoed in 1941, and then again when the
ship that had rescued the survivors had also been sunk. Gough had been
decorated for his seamanship and courage on both occasions, rallying his
men over many days spent in open boats and on the way rescuing the survivors from two other stricken ships. Most merchant captains, men like
Gough, buckled down and did their job, expecting the navy and the air
force to do their best but accepting that things sometimes went wrong, that
ships and lives would be lost. They were tough men, men who knew well
the fickle whims of war and fate, who asked questions only when they were
truly compelled to do so.

Jack returned to his own part in this story, to a question that Gough
himself could never have imagined possible: how could a British torpedo
that could only have been launched from a British submarine have ended
up inside the hull of *Clan Macpherson*?

He checked his watch, stood, and picked up the VHF radio receiver on the table, tapping the secure IMU channel used on the bridge of *Seafire*. A girl's voice with an accent more American than British crackled in response. "Hello, Dad. Are you ready to come out now? Over."

"Nearly ready. Really looking forward to it. Can you talk?"

"Just stripping off my wetsuit. Give me a moment."

Jack smiled in anticipation. He had not spoken to Rebecca since he and Costas had returned from Africa, and seeing her was another reason why he had been excited about coming out to the site this morning. She had spent the last month working with Jack's colleague Katya at her ancient petroglyphs site in Kyrgyzstan, and had only flown back to England two days before, while Jack had been in Oxford. She had scheduled a week to dive on the wreck before returning to her university summer school in the United States, and Jack was looking forward to spending time with her. He pressed the talk button as he walked out of the tent toward the promontory. "How are you doing? How's the archaeology?"

"I'm studying to be an environmentalist, not an archaeologist, Dad."

Jack scrambled over the old stone wall and onto the rough track that led up to the top of the promontory, enjoying the breeze on his face. "Yes, well, you say that, but archaeology is what you were doing with Katya, archaeology is what you do with Maurice and Aysha, and archaeology is what you've been doing with IMU since you were barely into your teens. It's in your blood. You can't deny it."

"How do you know what I was doing with Katya? She's given up waiting for you to call, by the way. How long ago was it that you two were an item? Anyway, as far as you know, we could have just been having an all-girls party."

"With Katya, beside Lake Issyk-Gul in Kyrgyzstan? I doubt it. More likely learning how to shoot a Kalashnikov."

"I did that last year with her. I didn't tell you. The least accurate rifle I've ever shot. This year it was learning how to hunt with an eagle."

"God help us," Jack said. "You're the daughter of Jack Howard, not Attila the Hun."

"Yeah, well, it's a tough old world out there, got to be prepared."

"Tell me about the wreck."

"It's Phoenician, Dad. You were right, and everyone's sure of it. There are loads of those distinctive Punic amphoras, and other diagnostic stuff. It's what you've dreamed of finding for years. They've left your sector of

the excavation untouched, as you requested, sandbagged over and awaiting your return."

Jack reached the top of the promontory, strode through the thick coarse
grass to the edge of the rocky cliff on the south side, and saw *Seafire* anchored some three hundred meters offshore. "That's fantastic. I've seen the
material in the conservation tent here from the past few days. Pretty early—
late seventh or early sixth century BC. Not a Greek ship carrying Phoenician wares, but an actual Phoenician ship. It's the first one ever found in
these waters, and confirmation that they got to the British Isles at that date."

"Any news on your plaque?"

"I was with Jeremy and Maria all day Tuesday at the Institute of Palaeography in Oxford. They're convinced the symbols are Phoenician too."

"Amazing," she said. "A Phoenician wreck up here and another wreck
off Africa carrying a Phoenician artifact, about equidistant from the Strait
of Gibraltar."

"That's where the Phoenicians went," Jack said. "West from Carthage
through the Strait and out into the Atlantic, searching for tin and gold, exploring, settling. And you know my theory that they went a lot farther
than that, at least circumnavigating the British Isles and reaching the southern tip of Africa, if not circumnavigating that too."

"But you don't know where the plaque came from."

"I'm working on that. All we have to go on at the moment is that *Clan
Macpherson*'s last major port of call was Durban, in South Africa. I think
somehow it got on board there, along with the gold consignment."

"Any progress with the translation?"

"They're working on it, but it's tricky because the imagery isn't that
great. We didn't have much time before the wreck, um, blew up."

"So I heard. And how deep were you? Costas told me about it when he
was here yesterday. How many lives do you guys have?"

"That's what I asked Costas afterward, and he said I still had lots. You
remember *The Lion King*? *Hakuna matata*. It's in the past. I look to the
future."

"You mean to another insanely dangerous dive."

"To a lovely dive with you in less than ten meters' depth on the Phoenician wreck. By the way, have you spoken to Aysha?"

"Just this morning. She left little Michael with her sister in London and
went out to Carthage to join Maurice. She very nearly carried on back to

Egypt, you know. It was Katya who put the kibosh on that during a long satellite call from Kyrgyzstan. She told Aysha that she had a responsibility now as a mother and to Maurice, and that there were plenty of others to carry on the fight against the extremists. It must be hard for Aysha, but Katya knows what she's talking about, with her father having been a warlord and all that.

"As it turns out, Aysha's really got stuck in at Carthage. She says it's just like when they first worked together at the mummy necropolis in the Fayum, when she spotted the Atlantis papyrus. Maurice of course went to Carthage really only to find evidence for an early Egyptian settlement. Poor Uncle Hiemy. He can't get over not being able to work in Egypt anymore. Anyway, what they've actually found is maybe even more interesting. While Maurice has been digging at the harbor entrance, their other dig at the Tophet sanctuary has produced some very old Punic inscriptions, scratched on potsherds. Some of the early alphabetic renderings might help Jeremy with his translation of the plaque."

"Excellent. You can tell Jeremy yourself. He's planning to drive down from Oxford today, to be here by mid-afternoon."

"Huh. First I've heard of it."

"Maybe it's a surprise."

"That is *so* not Jeremy."

"Everything all right between you two?"

"It's kind of hard conducting a relationship when you always seem to be at least three thousand miles apart."

"Tell me about it," Jack said. "Story of my life."

"Katya spoke yesterday to Costas, who spilled the beans about your dive on *Clan Macpherson*. She was worried about you."

"Katya? You must be joking. She's a Kazakh warlord's daughter. Nothing worries her."

"Be serious, Dad. Just text her. Do it now."

"I promise."

"I'll send the Zodiac to pick you up."

"Don't bother. I'll kit up here and swim out myself. I could do with it."

"Okay. I'll be back in the water too. Got to go now. Out."

Jack pocketed the receiver and squinted out to sea, spotting Rebecca leaving the cabin and helping a figure on the aft ladder of *Seafire* coming up from their dive. *Seafire* was much smaller than IMU's two deep-ocean research vessels, *Seaquest* and *Sea Venture*, but had been designed specifically with inshore operations like this in mind, her shallow draft allowing her to anchor comfortably in these depths and her twin Vosper diesels giving her the power of a naval patrol boat should she need to egress quickly in deteriorating weather. *Seafire* was special to Rebecca, as she had been launched just after Rebecca had come back into Jack's life after her mother had died, and she had been allowed to christen her. About a year ago she had quietly taken over a cabin and maintained it as her own, just as Jack did on *Seaquest*, another reason why he took her claim to be an environmentalist rather than an archaeologist with a pinch of salt.

He peered over the cliffs at the shore some ten meters below, seeing the sandy bottom and the dark shadows of rocks that extended underwater from the edge of the promontory. Farther out, more than halfway to *Seafire*, he could just make out the boiler of a steamship that had sunk upright in the cove more than a hundred years before. It was the first wreck he had ever dived on as a boy, and since then he had come here often searching the cove for other wrecks, swimming out over the boiler and sometimes seeing other parts of the hull poking through the sand on either side. The last time he had seen the wreck fully exposed had been the previous summer, snorkeling here with Rebecca, and it had given him renewed hope that the winter storms might one day reveal other treasures in the sands beyond the steamship, a site such as the one they were diving on today.

He shaded his eyes and scanned the coast, spotting familiar landmarks. For miles on either side, the reefs and sands of this shoreline were littered with wrecks, some of ships blown in from the Atlantic, others that had sought shelter along this coast and been caught by a change in the wind. Off this headland alone there were known to be at least a dozen, one of them a fabled treasure galleon yet to be found, others merchantmen and warships armed with cannon that Jack had discovered over the years concreted to reefs and half buried in the sands. But what he had really hoped for, what he had yearned to find since reading of the ancient navigators as a boy, was another kind of treasure, a wreck from the earliest period of Phoenician exploration, when traders from the Mediterranean had first made contact with the prehistoric peoples of the British Isles.

Looking to the west over the bay he could make out St. Michael's Mount, the island where the Phoenicians were thought to have made landfall in the Cassiterides, the Tin Isles, in their quest for the precious ingredient they needed to make bronze. As a boy, Jack had pored over the nautical charts, plotting the likely location of wrecks. He knew that any ancient ship entering Mount's Bay had faced the same risk of being caught by a westerly and wrecked against this shore as the hundreds of later ships known to have come to grief here. He had convinced himself that finding an ancient wreck would simply be a matter of time and perseverance, waiting for that one storm that would shift sand as it had never been shifted before, revealing seabed that might have been buried for centuries. All he had ever hoped for was a few shattered sherds on the shingle and concreted to the seabed, enough to show that the Phoenicians truly had sailed here, and to prove his theory correct.

And then it had happened. Three months ago, after the high seas of winter had abated, he had put on his wetsuit and snorkeled out at this very spot. He had steeled himself for disappointment, seeing that the storms had buried the steamship wreck again up to the boiler. But he had stuck with it, had refused to give up, and had swum out further than he ever had before. He had soon seen encouraging signs. The sand beyond the steamship had given way to shingle, suggesting that the sand that was normally there had been pushed into the cove and piled over the wreck, leaving the seabed further offshore less deeply silted. He swam over a cannon that he had never seen before, concreted to a rocky outcrop. And then he had seen something extraordinary. At first he had thought they were more cannon, dozens of them, but even as he dived down, he knew what he had discovered. They were amphoras, ancient cylindrical jars for wine and olive oil, exactly the type that he and Maurice had seen in the museum at Carthage when they had visited Tunisia earlier that winter. They were at least two and a half thousand years old, from the time before the rise of Rome when Carthage and her traders had vied with the Greeks for domination of the western Mediterranean, when Carthaginian seafarers were pushing the boundaries of maritime knowledge far out into the Atlantic to the north and the south.

For the first time since they had been forced out of Egypt by the extremist takeover the year before, Jack had felt truly elated. He had found far more than just a few potsherds. Many of the amphoras were intact, showing that the wreck had been quickly buried in the sand and protected from the ravages of storm and wind over the centuries. He knew that he had little time to lose if they were not to be buried in meters of sand again, or wrenched from the seabed by storm waters and destroyed. He had immediately put in for an emergency protection order from the government to keep salvors from looting the site, and had secured a license to excavate. Within days an IMU team had arrived, and the shore encampment was established. With the campus only half an hour away, all the artifacts could be taken back immediately for conservation in state-of-the-art facilities.

For Jack it was a dream excavation, as long as the weather held. There were no extremists trying to gun them down, no warlords trying to muscle in on their finds, no treasure hunters pillaging the site at night. At less than ten meters' depth they had little need to worry about decompression sickness. Within two weeks they had stripped away the upper layer of amphoras and revealed gray anaerobic sediment beneath, promising conditions for the preservation of hull remains and other organic artifacts. Suddenly they had found not just amphoras but a site that might be of huge international significance, a wreck to put alongside the best that Jack had ever discovered. For it to be in his own backyard, where he had first learned to dive, made it seem a personal triumph too, as if his career were coming full circle, back to the place where his passion for the past had really first taken hold.

He swept his eyes once more along the coast. So often these waters seemed an impenetrable veil of secrets; one storm might reveal a tantalizing hint of a wreck, and then another conceal it for years. Waymarkers underwater that had seemed so obvious—reefs, cannon, pieces of wreckage—could disappear beneath the sand with the next tide, meaning that exploration constantly had to start over again from scratch. But this time they had a wreck firmly pinned down, one of the best he had ever found, and he was determined to see it through. The weather forecast for the summer ahead was good. He turned to go, running through a mental checklist of the equipment he had brought, suddenly feeling that every moment here was precious. He needed to get in the water.

8

A little over an hour later, Jack walked fully equipped down the beach beside the headland, shading his eyes as he stared out toward *Seafire*. Nestled in the lee of the promontory to his right was the ancient Church of the Mariners, the burial site for many who had washed up on this beach over the centuries: some from wrecks that remained imprinted in local memory, others from ships that had disappeared without a trace. Six months earlier, after returning from Egypt, Jack had stood on the promontory during one of the worst winter storms in recent years, lashed by wind and spray, watching the gigantic swells crash and rumble up the sand and nearly inundate the church. Today, with barely a ripple on the sea, such a scene seemed almost inconceivable; then, it had been impossible to imagine how anyone could have survived being wrecked in this place, with the sea sucking in and out over the jagged rocks and the waves erupting to a height of thirty meters or more against the seaward cliffs, a scene of near-certain death for anyone swept off a ship in such conditions.

He put the image from his mind and concentrated on enjoying the moment. He reached the sea where it gently lapped the shoreline, dipped his mask in the water, and put it on over his hood, running a finger under the edge of the neoprene to make sure the mask was sealed to his face. Unlike his dive on *Clan Macpherson* five days earlier, he was wearing only a wetsuit and conventional scuba gear, all he needed on a warm summer day

off Cornwall with a maximum depth of less than ten meters. It was diving as he had first experienced it as a boy and as he had learned to relish it
again, free from the stress and danger of deep exploration, from the constant nagging fear of nitrogen sickness that was the ticking time bomb
behind so many wreck excavations. Here, with a safe bottom time of more
than two hours, he could excavate almost as if he were on land, and yet
enjoy the physical sensation of being underwater that always seemed to
heighten his awareness and keep the adrenalin coursing through him.

He waded out, pulled on his fins and collapsed into the water, inject-
ing air into his stabilizer jacket and putting his snorkel in his mouth, ready
for the long surface swim out to the wreck. He kicked hard with his fins
to get over a small hump of sand by the shore, and then the bottom gradually dropped away in swimming-pool-like visibility, the sun shimmering
off the ripples in the sand below him. As he swam on, the spurs of rock that
jutted out from the promontory, smoothed and denuded near shore, appeared more overgrown, covered with the more tenacious forms of marine
accretion that were able to withstand the battering of waves and swell.
Several of the larger outcrops had scour pits on the seaward side, and in one
he saw a small crab scurry for cover.

He passed beyond the rocks and floated motionless for a few moments,
the water gently rocking him, letting his breathing and heart rate slow, almost in a state of meditation. Some physiologists argued that humans
were ill-adapted to water, that survival when immersed was a constant and
unnatural struggle; to Jack the reverse was the case, and the fact of being
unable to breathe like a fish seemed secondary to the supreme relaxation
he felt underwater, to a bodily and psychological contentment that he rarely
experienced to the same degree on land.

Five minutes later he stopped, swiveled around, and checked his surface
position, seeing that he had almost reached a midway point in the cove,
equidistant between the seaward end of the promontory with the church
and the tip of the headland to the south. He had seen little except sand since
leaving the rocks, but had begun to swim over patches of shingle where
the winter storms had stripped away the seabed almost to bedrock. He set
off again, and moments later saw the first signs of the steamship wreck
that spanned the entrance to the cove, twisted plates of metal that had been
wrenched from the hull by successive storms. The wreck was only 120
years old, but seeing it still gave Jack a frisson of excitement. For almost

two decades the hull had been completely buried in sand, only the top of the boiler visible, but the winter storms had washed away almost five meters' depth of sand and the wreck was visible in its entirety, sitting on the shingle and bedrock. She was a barometer of seabed exposure elsewhere in the cove, though a fickle one. Three months ago she had been buried when Jack had decided to carry on with his exploration further out to sea, hoping against hope that his dream of finding a much earlier wreck in these waters would finally be realized.

He looked toward *Seafire*, now less than two hundred meters distant, and raised his left arm as a signal, knowing that the dive marshal would have been keeping an eye on his progress since leaving the beach. He remembered the last time he had been in the water approaching a dive boat, five days ago with *Deep Explorer*. Despite all his entreaties, the ship's captain had refused to raise anchor and stand off, and he and Costas had been forced to struggle into the Zodiac in mountainous seas with the ship's hull only meters away. His old friend Landor had watched it all from the railing, seemingly indifferent, but Jack's ire with him once they were aboard had served the useful purpose of allowing him to stonewall any attempt by Landor to wheedle out of them what they had actually seen on *Clan Macpherson*, and within an hour they had been taken off in the Lynx helicopter that had come for them from the British Army base in Freetown.

He tried to put *Deep Explorer* from his mind. He hoped never to see her again, and he did not want brooding about Landor to sully this day. *Seafire* was a reassuring presence, with people on board whose priority was to look after divers, and that was what mattered. He saw the dive marshal watching, and gave him a thumbs-down to show that he was descending. He could have continued swimming on the surface to the excavation site, but he preferred to go down on the steamship wreck and follow the line that had been attached on the seabed from there.

He removed his snorkel, put his regulator in his mouth, and vented air from the inflation tube on his buoyancy compensator, dropping beneath the surface and pinching his nose to clear his ears as he fell to the seabed. Just before reaching it, he injected a blast of air into his BC to regain neutral buoyancy, and for a few moments he hung there, a meter above the sand. Even after thousands of dives he had never lost the thrill he had felt when he first breathed from a tank, and he savored it now, drawing on his regulator and listening to the rush of bubbles from the exhaust. He turned over on his back, took out his regulator and blew rings, watching them expand and explode in a silvery shower against the surface. It felt incredibly good, as it always did.

He turned over and swam toward the steamship wreck, kicking his fins in a languid breaststroke. Within the hull amidships he saw the dark form of the boiler, its top only a few meters below the surface at low tide, as it was now. He turned left toward the stern, marveling at the timbers, which had remained in pristine condition under the sand. At the stern, the screw and rudder pintle were shrouded with old fishing nets and a crab pot from the last time the hull had been exposed, many years before. He rounded it and swam along the ship's port side, on the way spotting the small porbeagle shark that had taken up residence in the shadowy recess of the scour pit, preying on the many fish that had appeared as if from nowhere since the wreck had been exposed. From there it was a short swim to the mass of exposed copper piping beside the boiler that acted as an anchor for the guideline to the ancient wreck.

He followed the line out a short distance, leaving the main bulk of the steamship behind, and then dropped down to a section of deck planking he had not seen before, newly revealed in the last few days. He put one hand palm downward on the wood, feeling how smooth it was. If they could find wood like this on the Phoenician wreck, buried not for a century but for two and a half millennia, they truly would have made a great discovery, one of the outstanding wreck finds ever made in British waters.

He turned back to the guideline and swam further out across the shingle. A giant box jellyfish came by, rhythmically pulsing, making its way with seeming determination to some unknown place. Jack left the line to follow it, swimming beneath its meter-wide body so that he could see the sunlight shine through, marveling at its beauty. Once, seeing a school of these jellyfish over the wreck of a ship-of-the-line further up the coast, a place of terrible loss of life, he had thought that they were like the souls of long-dead mariners, fated forever to remain at sea on an endless voyage.

He watched the jellyfish move on, and returned to the line. He was now in the shadow of *Seafire*, and he saw the dive ladder extended into the water at the stern and the anchor cable beyond that. A diver was ascending the ladder with another in the water behind, evidently a shift returning from the excavation, and a snorkeler was on the surface above him. He rolled over and blew a succession of bubble rings toward her. He could hardly have imagined all those years before that his daughter would one day be freediving in the waters that he had snorkeled in as a boy, but now the slender form in the distinctive blue-and-black wetsuit was almost as familiar to him underwater as Costas. She spiraled down, clearing her ears as she did so, and put a hand on his. She pointed toward the end of the guideline and gave him an okay sign. He did the same in return, and followed her as she swam ahead like a seal, using the fin stroke that he had taught her when they had first swum together in this cove when she was barely into her teens.

As she angled back up toward the surface, Jack saw the ancient wreck spread out before him beyond the staked end of the guideline. There were pottery amphoras in rows on either side, newly revealed as the excavators had dug deeper into the shingle and sand over the past few days. For the first time he sensed the shape of a ship, perhaps eighteen or twenty meters long, six or seven meters in beam. It was incredibly exciting. Everything pointed to this not being the result of a ship capsizing and dumping its contents, but a site that could hold hull timbers as well. If timbers survived in a deeper pocket in the sand, then they must be close to them now, as he could already see outcrops of gray-green bedrock protruding through the shingle.

His mind shifted automatically to the next stage of the project. The discovery of hull timbers would change the tempo completely. Amphoras and small finds could be raised easily enough to *Seafire*, but timbers would require more time to record *in situ*, as well as heavy lifting equipment and onboard fresh-water storage tanks for immediate conservation. *Seafire* was a superb vessel, purpose-built for archaeology, but she was not much bigger than a large dive charter boat, designed for day trips from their Falmouth base and primarily for shallow-water work. *Seaquest* and *Sea Venture* were ocean-going ships, too big to bring this close inshore, and both anyway were committed to projects on the other side of the world, *Sea Venture* to a geological survey in the Hawaiian archipelago and *Seaquest* to deep-water exploration off Sri Lanka. IMU in Falmouth had a barge with lifting equipment that could be towed over the site, but it was an unwieldy vessel, vulnerable to swell and wind.

Always at this place they would be working against the weather, even at the height of summer with the forecast showing calm seas for weeks ahead. At such a shallow depth, so close inshore, a blip in the forecast, a single day of westerlies strong enough to churn up the seabed in the cove, could have a disastrous effect on the excavation, disrupting the datum points and equipment left on site and sweeping away any artifacts left exposed. Shallow-water excavation had many benefits, but it came with increased risk of exposure to the elements, precisely the factors that had caused so many shallow wrecks in the first place and dispersed wreck material that had not become quickly buried in protective sediment.

Jack finned slowly over the edge of the site. Two of the four stone anchors they had discovered were still there, crude triangular slabs of igneous rock weighing an estimated quarter of a ton each, with holes in one corner for the rope and in the other two for double-ended sharpened stakes to hold the anchor to the seabed. The IMU geologists had taken a thin section and sourced the rock to the volcanic Lipari Islands to the north of Sicily, a region under Punic control where the Carthaginians were known to have quarried stone for their anchors. Seeing one of these anchors poking through the shingle on that first dive three months ago had been a huge excitement for Jack; they were a shape unchanged since the Bronze Age, and put the wreck well back in the first millenium BC, before Admiralty-style wooden anchors with lead stocks came into common use.

They had found one of those too, a lead bar a meter and a half long with a rectangular hole for the anchor shank in the center, the wood having perished long ago. That had tightened the date, and stoked Jack's excitement even further. The earliest lead-stocked anchors from datable wrecks in the Mediterranean were from the first part of the sixth century BC, at the time when the western Phoenicians, the people the Romans called Punic, were the dominant power in the Mediterranean. Any Phoenician captain worth his salt would have wanted the latest anchor technology, and the presence of both types in the wreck suggested a date very soon after their inception.

For Jack this opened up an extraordinary historical possibility, a porthole into one of the most famous episodes in maritime exploration. The sixth century BC was the most likely date for the voyages of the Carthaginians Hanno and Himilco. That was the reason why he had been reading the surviving account of Hanno's voyage down the west coast of Africa during his flight to Freetown the previous week. Himilco's voyage was known only through a brief reference by the Roman historian Pliny more than five centuries later, but the possibility that he had gone north and reached the Cassiterides, the fabled Tin Isles, had tantalized historians ever since. Jack had hardly dared think that this might be a wreck from Himil-co's expedition, and he would let the archaeology speak for itself. Hanno and Himilco were explorers, to be sure, but they were also driven by the Phoenician passion for trade, and the discovery of a wreck filled with the kind of goods that the British in Cornwall might have traded for their tin made the possibility too compelling to put aside.

He saw the lead anchor stock now, cushioned between sandbags on the seabed, and sank down to look at the symbols cast on one side. They were a Phoenician letter B, an early type with an angular form, and a small bu-cranium, a shape like bull's horns. Jack was certain that they were apotro-paic, to ward off misfortune, a common function of symbols on later Greek and Roman anchors, in this case the B perhaps referring to the Phoeni-cian god Ba'al Hammon and the bucranium to the sacred bull's-horn shape seen in the mountain peak to the east of Carthage. If so, they had failed in their purpose, but seeing them did made Jack ponder the nature of the wrecking.

The anchors they had found were in the bow, facing the shore. He knew this because the other end of the wreck contained pottery and small finds, indicating the crew's living area, a stern deckhouse where they would have cooked and taken shelter. The absence of anchors in the stern suggested that those must have been lost in an attempt to hold the ship against a westerly wind, the most likely cause of the wrecking. Unlike the steamship, therefore, which had been blown into the cove sideways and sunk beam-on, the Phoenician ship had gone down facing the shore. Jack had stood on the headland trying to put himself in the mind of the captain, imagining the sea as he had seen it during that winter storm. Laying out the anchors astern, knowing they would drag, might not have been an act of desperation but that of a skilled navigator, one who had sounded the seabed and knew there was no hope of holding in the sand but that he might at least prevent the ship from going in beam-on, allowing her the small chance of being thrown intact onto the beach.

What the captain could not have known about was what Jack saw dur-ing the storm, the sucking undertow down the beach that followed each huge wave as it crashed in, momentarily exposing the seabed at low tide almost as far out as the wreck site. In such extreme conditions, with the anchors still holding her bow-on to the shore, the ship might actually have been grounded rather than sunk, driven hard into the seabed while the next towering wave built up behind her. In that instant, with shore only a stone's throw away, the captain must have known that they were doomed, that there would be no time to hack away the anchor ropes and hope for the best. The next wave would have inundated the ship, smashing away the mast and rigging and breaking the bodies of any men still aboard even before they were thrown on to the rocks.

It would have been a terrifying end, following hours of fear clinging to the ship as it was driven ashore, lashed by spray and lurching sickeningly in the swell as the anchors dragged remorselessly. But like those who had gone down in *Clan Macpherson* off West Africa, like so many who were buried along the clifftops and sand dunes of this coast, the Phoenicians were men of the sea who would have known the fate that might lie in store for them, that no manner of apotropaic sign or pleading to the gods was going to help them when the storm waters were raging and all hope was lost.

Rebecca dropped down again, pointing at the stern part of the wreck and swimming on her back toward it, looking at Jack. He gave an okay signal, and watched as she turned over and followed another huge jellyfish that had appeared overhead. He looked at where she had pointed, and felt a surge of anticipation. The project supervisor had seen his frustration the week before at having to leave his corner of the excavation incomplete when he had been called to *Deep Explorer*, and had left it sandbagged over for his return. He restrained himself from swimming straight for it, and continued to float slowly over the site, taking in everything that had been exposed while he had been away.

Instead of being covered with a latticework of grid squares, the only fixed structures on the site were twenty red-topped metal stakes that acted as datum points for the sonic high-accuracy ranging and positioning system they used to map the wreck. The system had been refined by Jacob Lanowski, IMU's resident computer genius, and meant that with a click of a sonic gun an excavator could record the exact position of any new find. The data went straight into the master plan, and combined with photo-grammetry and sonar mapping meant that a detailed 3D rendition of the site with up-to-date finds was available for anyone who could log on to the project website. Above all, it meant that the huge amount of time that used to be spent measuring and recording finds by hand was no longer required, a factor of supreme importance at a site exposed to vagaries of the weather where rapid excavation was of the essence.

Jack swam over the main area of the cargo hold, looking at the amphoras that had yet to be raised. The main type was for olive oil, a speciality product of the eastern coast of Tunisia to the south of Carthage; the few fish sauce and wine amphoras were probably for use by the crew. A number of the amphoras had been bound up by the excavators in protective wrap to cover inscriptions that had been found painted on the shoulders or bodies in pitch, most of them describing the contents or marking amphoras for export. One of the tents in the shore encampment was filled with buckets where broken sherds with inscriptions had been put to soak in fresh water prior to being taken to the conservation lab at IMU.

He saw the area of the excavation where Costas had been working the week previously, the lead weight with his name tag and a sand-filled gin bottle still there where he had staked out his territory. On the phone yesterday Jack had reminded him of his comment during their dive on *Clan Macpherson* about finding a sherd from the Cornwall wreck that might have had an unusual inscription, and Costas had promised to go fishing in the finds buckets in the conservation tent when he arrived this afternoon so that they could have a closer look.

Jack flashed through the other finds they had made, preparing himself for anything he might discover. One of the most amazing artifacts had been a small, thick-walled jar with a deep blue residue that the lab had quickly identified as dye from the murex shell, the famous "royal purple" from Tire that was a closely guarded Phoenician secret. It was a hint of the dyed textiles that the ship might also have been carrying, and a reminder of the close ties that the western Phoenicians retained with their Semitic homeland, with the peoples of the coast of ancient Canaan that extended from modern Syria and Lebanon to Israel. They had also found three distinctive Massaliot amphoras, made by the Greek settlers of modern Marseilles and containing high-grade wine, as well as a batch of beautiful black-glazed drinking cups from Corinth, showing that the Phoenicians were not above diversifying their cargos with goods acquired from their trade rivals.

As if that were not enough, beneath the amphoras they had found piles of crushed galena, the lead sulphide used in the cupellation process to extract tin from ore, a material that would have been of huge value to the ancient miners of Cornwall. And to cap it all, a copper box in the stern contained two bronze steelyards and multiple sets of balance-pan weights, bronze with lead cores, as well as some of the earliest coins ever made, stamped lumps of electrum from the kingdom of Lydia in Asia Minor from about 590 BC. To Jack, all of this indicated a merchant captain not only well stocked and prepared for every type of transaction, a Phoenician through and through, but also one who was speculative, plumbing new markets before the demand for certain products had become established, something that had made him think again of Himilco and Hanno and the very dawn of Phoenician contact with the late Bronze Age peoples of Britain.

He reached his own area of the excavation, about five meters along the port side from the stern of the ship, at a place from which all the amphoras had been removed. He released a small amount of air from his BC to make himself negatively buoyant, and carefully lifted away three small sandbags from where he had left them, covered with silt during the past days. To his right was one of the water dredges that served as their main excavation tool, powered by a pump on *Seafire*; the water was pumped down a hose into one end of a solid plastic tube two meters long that floated just above the seabed, creating a vacuum that sucked water and sediment in at that end and spewed it out at the other, beyond the edge of the excavation. He pulled it over, careful to keep the exhaust end pointing out of the site, and brought the nozzle close to the area of shingle that had been covered by the sandbags, wrapping his right arm around it and getting ready to waft with his left hand. He looked up, knowing that Rebecca would have been watching him, and made a whirling motion with his left hand. She made an okay signal, swam to the surface and signaled the boat. Seconds later, the dredge erupted into life, lurching and bucking until he got it under control. He glanced back, seeing the blur in the water at the exhaust end, and then turned back. It was as if he had never left, as if the past week and the dive on *Clan Macpherson* were a dream, part euphoric and part nightmare, something he had parceled in his mind along with all the other dives he and Costas had done over the years where they had pushed the envelope as far as it would go.

Seconds later he had exposed what he had started to uncover last time, tapering expanses of polished white, his excitement mounting as first one, then the other was revealed. They were the ends of huge elephant tusks, lying flat and extending under the sediment. They were an extraordinary find, unquestionably the premium trade item of this cargo. But what was more incredible was their origin, revealed in the analysis of a sample Jack had taken the week before. Many archaeologists had assumed that the elephant ivory traded by the western Phoenicians came from their outposts on the Atlantic shore of Africa, acquired from native middlemen from sources far inland south of the Sahara. But the analysis had pointed to an East African origin, to modern-day Somalia or Ethiopia, the place known as Punt, where the ancient Egyptians had obtained their ivory. And there was something else, something Jack had wondered whether he had really seen on that last dive, but here it was again, as clear as could be. Both of the tusks had been inscribed with the alphabetic symbols for the letter H, twice over. Ancient Phoenician merchants were assiduous markers of their own trade goods, so there was nothing exceptional in that. It was the letters themselves that made Jack's mind race. HH: Hanno and Himilco. *Could it be?*

The tusks were one of the most sensational finds of the excavation, left *in situ* until his return and now ready for recovery and conservation. It was extraordinary for Jack to see them again, but what really set his pulse racing now was to imagine what might lie beneath. Elephant ivory, especially the prized East African variety, would have been enormously valuable, and would have been packed in dunnage in the safest place on the floor of the cargo hold, below the amphoras and immediately above the ship's timbers. The tusks were resting on a gray-black layer, revealed now across the entire space beneath them as he wafted the sediment away. The color indicated anoxic conditions, suggesting that this layer had survived undisturbed below the cargo. If timbers existed on the site, this layer might be the first place to find them.

He wafted again, and the water turned black, staining his fingers. That was an excellent sign, evidence of metal oxidization, exactly what he would expect from decayed iron nails and rivets. He wafted once more, waiting for the dredge to clear the water, and then he saw it. About fifteen centimeters below the tusk was the surface of a wooden strake, with another beside it, running precisely where they should be, parallel to the likely location of the keel. Another waft revealed a frame. Peering closely at the side of the first strake, he saw a stamped letter A, the crossbar sloped in early Phoenician style, clearly a shipwright's mark. He put his palm on the wood, just as he had done half an hour earlier at the steamship wreck, feeling the same surge of excitement, the thrill of watching the sea give up her secrets. He could suddenly see the ship in his mind's eye, wide-bellied, sturdy, with close-set frames, her shaped timbers carpentered together with pegged mortice-and-tenon joints, so well preserved that he could imagine her released from the sands and surging forward, square sail billowing and helmsman at the steering oar, a brilliant image of human endeavor from the time when Carthage and her mariners ruled the waves.

He pushed back, easing the dredge out of the excavation, and looked up. Rebecca was there again, pointing excitedly into the hole, giving him the okay sign. He did the same, gave a thumbs-up to indicate that he was about to surface, and then made a whirling motion at the dredge again. She acknowledged his signal and rose to the surface, and seconds later the dredge stopped sucking. He had finished where he had left off a week before, done what he had needed to do; now it was the job of the excavation team to take up where he had left off. Jeremy and Costas would be at the camp by now, and he needed to be ready for what Jeremy had to say about the plaque from *Clan Macpherson*.

He tied off the dredge, rose above the seabed and then looked up, seeing Rebecca spread-eagled on the surface above him, silhouetted by the sun, wreathed by bubbles from his exhaust. He felt a supreme sense of contentment. This had been one of the best dives of his life.

9

Two hours later, Jack sat outside the beach café finishing his Cornish pasty and tea, feeding the last morsels to the black-and-white collie from the local farm who had been his companion on many visits to the cove over the years. He got up, waved at the farmer's wife who ran the café, and gave the dog a final stroke, then strode across the lane to the dunes and along the track toward the church behind the headland. Just before the graveyard he veered right into the grassy compound behind the old dry-stone wall that served as the shore headquarters for the IMU project, protected from the prevailing westerlies by the steep rise of the promontory. Rebecca was at the entrance talking to several hikers on the coastal path who had stopped to look at the information board they had set up in the lane about the Phoenician wreck. He smiled at the walkers and nodded at her, knowing that she would join him as soon as she could.

He waved at the group of local divers who had parked their van in the lane and were beginning to kit up for their dive. They were friends he had known for years, stalwarts of his team, and had been responsible for many exciting wreck discoveries. Over lunch he had talked with them about the logistical challenge of raising timbers from the wreck, and together with the project supervisor they had sketched out a plan that would see the hull exposed and all the timbers raised and safely back in the IMU conservation facility within two weeks. He glanced up at the sky, feeling the

early-afternoon breeze on his face and seeing the clouds beginning to
accumulate. Everything depended on the weather; for that they were as
much in the lap of the gods as the ancient mariners had been. But he had
the best possible people on the job, and he knew he could rely on them to
make the right decisions and take the project forward, whatever the forces
of nature chose to throw at them.

He ducked under the flap of the operations tent and put his notebook
on the trestle table in the center. A tall, tousle-haired young man with
glasses was arranging his papers and laptop at the other end of the table,
having brought them in from his car a few moments before. Jack smiled at
him and shook hands. "I saw you arriving from the café, but thought you'd
probably want to go and say hello to Rebecca first."

He looked slightly flustered, and pushed his glasses up his nose.
"Haven't really had the chance yet. I wanted to get everything ready here
first."

"Are we going to see you in the water this time?"

"That's the plan. What's the temperature like?"

"Warm. Barely need a wetsuit."

"That's Jack Howard for 'cold.' You're as bad as your daughter. She barely
feels anything. I think I made a mistake in having Costas teach me to dive
in the Red Sea. It's completely spoiled me."

Jack grinned at him. Jeremy Haverstock had become an integral part
of the IMU team since he had first arrived from Stanford as a Rhodes
Scholar almost eight years before, to work with Maria at the Institute of
Palaeography in Oxford. Since then he had completed his doctorate, published the first volumes of material from their two greatest manuscript
discoveries—the secret medieval library in Hereford Cathedral and the lost
library of the Emperor Claudius in the Villa of the Papyri at Herculaneum—
and had recently become assistant director of the Institute. He had also
become interestingly close to Rebecca, something that had slowly devel-
oped as Rebecca had grown into a woman and that Jack pretended to watch
with bemused indifference.

The flap opened and Rebecca came in, finishing off an apple. She tossed
the core into a bin and wiped her mouth. "Is Costas here yet?"

"Half an hour away," Jack said. "He called to say he was caught in
traffic."

"Hello, by the way," she said to Jeremy. "Nice of you to call."

Jeremy coughed, glancing at Jack. "Surprise. Sorry. Been really busy with this translation."

"Right. I only hope it's good. We'll talk later." She turned to Jack. "We really need Costas here to find that inscribed sherd. There are more than two hundred buckets next door containing amphora sherds with painted inscriptions on them, and the conservation people have their hands full now with everything else that's coming up."

"He says he can find it straight away."

"Costas is pretty important, isn't he? He always seems to have the key to unlock things, even if he doesn't realize it himself."

"I've been coming to that conclusion myself."

"I hadn't realized it was Costas who actually discovered the plaque on *Clan Macpherson* last week. I'd say he counts as a fully fledged archaeologist by now."

"Not sure if he'd be pleased to hear you say that. The tough-guy engineer, you know. The Greek immigrant brought up on the mean streets of New York. The practical man who leaves the ideas stuff to wishy-washy people like us."

"I think he'd be pleased, even though he might not show it," Rebecca said. "Anyway, getting a PhD from MIT does *actually* involve a few ideas. In fact he's probably the smartest of all of us. And as for the tough-guy stuff, take it from me, he's a softy underneath. It's a toss-up whether Uncle Costas or Uncle Hiemy will be reduced to tears the quickest when small children are around."

"Speaking of Uncle Hiemy, how's he getting on?"

"I spoke to Aysha in Carthage again over lunch. She's been pressing Maurice to call you. He's found something interesting in the harbor excavation, but he's decided not to disturb you until you're settled back here following the *Deep Explorer* trip. She says it's going to need your full attention."

"I can't wait," Jack said. "Maurice only ever calls me when it's good."

"Leave it for him to get in touch with you. Remember, this is his comeback after Egypt, and he should be allowed to drive things at his own speed. When he's ready, he'll do it."

"You're probably right. You've spent more time with him recently than I have, so you know his state of mind."

"They've been excavating at Carthage for almost a month now. It took a long time to pull him out of his frustration and shock after they had to leave Egypt last year. Everything that's happened since then with the extremists makes it even less likely that he'll ever be able to return."

"Do you think he's going to find evidence of Egyptians at Carthage?" Jeremy said, looking up from his laptop. "It was the Phoenicians who founded it, early ninth century BC, wasn't it?"

"That's what the Roman historians tell us, and the archaeology so far doesn't contradict it," said Jack. "If there was some kind of earlier Egyptian presence, it's more likely to have been merchants or trade representatives in an outpost run by the Canaanites, proto-Phoenicians. They seem to have been the ones in charge of maritime trade in the late Bronze Age, just as their descendants were at the time of our wreck here. If Maurice does find Egyptian artifacts, it doesn't necessarily signify an Egyptian settlement."

"Aysha says that he's like you: when he has a gut feeling, he won't be happy until he's dug a hole right down to bedrock," Rebecca said.

"I remember it well from when we were at boarding school together, sneaking out at weekends to dig up part of the local Roman villa. We shouldn't have done it, but we did record everything meticulously and eventually published it. Watching out for the landowner while Maurice's rear end was sticking out of a hole in the ground is one of my abiding memories of those days. I called him the human mole."

"He surely couldn't have found anything Egyptian there," Jeremy said.

"Oh yes, he did. It turned out that the villa had been built in the second century for a retired centurion who was a follower of the cult of Isis, a favorite among Roman soldiers. I can still remember the look of indescribable joy on his face when he emerged from his hole clutching a little faience statue of Anubis. That was how he caught the Egyptian bug. That summer he absconded using some money an aunt in Germany had left him and was next heard of in the Valley of the Kings, having been taken on by an American director who had never come across an eighteen-year-old with such an encyclopedic knowledge of ancient Egypt. In fact, he was sixteen, not eighteen, and getting him home nearly caused an international incident. But after that, he never looked back."

"The question with his idea about Egyptians at Carthage is whether it's gut instinct or wishful thinking," Jeremy said. "For a man designed to be down a hole, imagining you might have to spend the rest of your career studying artifacts in museums would be pretty devastating. I can see why he might want to find Egyptians everywhere he digs."

"At least he's got Jacob with him," Rebecca said.

Jeremy peered at her. "Lanowski? You must be kidding. I thought he was at some big nanotechnology conference in California. Giving the keynote lecture, about pressure-resistant polymers used in diving suits or something. He and Costas were burning the midnight oil over it a few weeks ago."

"He canceled that as soon as Aysha invited him out," Rebecca said. "I think she thought he'd be good for Maurice. Ever since Maurice learned about Jacob's passion for Egyptology, the two of them have got on like a house on fire. And they're both recent fathers, so they can share the trials and tribulations of having small children."

"Nothing like the trials of having an older child," Jack said.

Rebecca narrowed her eyes at him, and he turned to Jeremy. "Speaking of the plaque, what have you got?"

Rebecca coughed, and put up a hand. "Before that, there's something I want to show you. Something from *my* part of the excavation that came up yesterday. I've been saving it to tell you in person, Dad."

Jack smiled at her. For a moment he saw her mother Elizabeth sitting in front of him, the dark eyes and hair, the olive skin of her Neapolitan background, taking him back to the time when he had last seen Elizabeth almost eight years earlier, at the ancient site of Herculaneum shortly before her murder by the Mafia. But he also saw in Rebecca's eyes a steely determination that he knew was Howard through and through, a resolve to see things to the end whatever the odds, to follow a trail she was set on as far as she could, to never give up. He leaned forward, picked up a pencil, and tapped it on the table, nodding at her. "Okay. What have *you* got?"

She went to a rack behind her and carefully lifted a large finds tray with a cloth cover from one shelf, putting it on the table in front of her chair. "Those elephant tusks you found were cool, Dad, *really* cool. Congratulations, by the way. So I just thought you might be interested in what I found. I took this out of the fresh-water tank in the conservation tent just to show you, but it'll be back in there pronto when we're done."

She lifted the cloth and picked up a bubble-wrapped object about half a meter long. Jack could see the end of a tusk poking out of one end. Her sector of the excavation was on the opposite side of the ship's hold to his own, and this showed that there was even more ivory than he had imagined stowed beneath the amphoras, an incredibly valuable cargo. She unwrapped it, leaned over, and handed it to him, a long, straight tusk with a twist in it. "The tusk must have been broken during the wrecking," she said. "The lower part's still *in situ*. Altogether it's more than two meters long, more than your height. And there's another one on the site next to where I found this."

Jack stared in astonishment. It was not quite what he had imagined. "Well I'll be damned," he exclaimed. "That's not elephant ivory. It's narwhal."

"I sent pictures to the marine biology department at IMU, and they confirmed it. And they said that another broken fragment I found next to it was walrus."

"Narwhal and walrus," Jeremy said. "Not exactly African creatures, are they?"

"There's something else." She took back the tusk, carefully replaced it on the tray, and handed Jack a smaller bubble-wrapped package. "Open it."

Jack did so, and gasped. Inside was a lump of translucent honey-colored material the size of his fist. He lifted it to the light, seeing the bodies of insects trapped within. "Amber," he said, turning it slowly. "That's one of the largest pieces I've ever seen. Amazing."

"It's from the Baltic, probably the eastern shore. There are other pieces, probably originally a basketful, and I sent a sample to the lab for analysis. There's a lot of excitement over the potential of those mosquitoes for DNA analysis, especially if they contain the blood of extinct megafauna. But what was most fascinating to me was what these finds, narwhal and walrus and amber, might say about the voyage of our ship."

"They could have been high-value trade goods, acquired by the Phoenician merchant in Cornwall and destined for the Mediterranean," Jeremy said.

Jack's mind was racing. "Undoubtedly there would have been a market for this kind of exotica in the Mediterranean, and it's possible that these were trophies to take back to Carthage, proof that they had reached further north than anyone from the Mediterranean had ever gone before. But there may be another explanation. Think of the rest of the cargo; there's nothing of British origin. We're looking at a cargo ready to trade with the tin merchants, not the result of that trade. If she'd been outward-bound after trading then I might not even have spotted the wreck at all, as most of the goods we've found would have been traded and the only visible cargo might have been lumps of tin ore, real treasure to the Phoenicians but barely recognizable on the seabed."

"These finds show that she hadn't arrived here direct from the Mediterranean," Rebecca said.

Jack weighed up the amber in his hand, staring at it. "I think this shows that the ship had sailed first to the Baltic and then somewhere far to the north, where they obtained the narwhal and walrus ivory. I think it shows that she circumnavigated the British Isles before putting into Mount's Bay and coming to grief on her way to the tin traders. This ship was wrecked as she was heading *into* Mount's Bay, to the shore marts where the British miners would have brought their tin ore, not as she was sailing away."

"The ship not just of a merchant, but of an explorer," Rebecca suggested.

"Yet with trade never far from his mind," Jack added. "If I were a good Phoenician, still with my Mediterranean goods on board and looking for tin, I'd see the amber and tusks I was offered by sea peoples in the north as potential items for barter as well. Down here among the Britons of Cornwall, these goods from forbidding lands hundreds of miles away might have been as exotic as they were to people in the Mediterranean, and as desirable."

"You always tell me that history is driven by powerful individuals, Dad, that prehistorians dealing with large expanses of time often lose sight of the effect that charismatic and motivated individuals can have on technological innovation, on colonization, on exploration. When I saw this ivory and thought about the fantastic voyage they must have undertaken, I thought immediately of Himilco and Hanno."

Jack handed back the amber, and watched as she carefully wrapped it and then submerged the package in the tray with the ivory, replacing it on the rack. She sat down again and turned to Jeremy. "You've been quiet. What do you think?"

Jeremy spun his laptop round so the other two could see it. "I can only add my assessment of the literary evidence. You'll recognize this page from *Codex Palatinus Graecus* 386 in Heidelberg University Library. It's the oldest extant text of Hanno's *Periplus*, bound together with the *Periplus Maris Erythraei*, the Roman merchant's guide to the Red Sea and Indian Ocean of the first century AD. Some Byzantine monk in the tenth century AD decided to make a compendium of all ancient voyages of exploration that he'd come across, copying the bits that interested him from original manuscripts that are now lost. Hanno's *Periplus* is usually dated to the sixth or fifth century BC, and in my estimation is within the earlier part of that range, the first half of the sixth century BC. It was originally written in Punic Phoenician, but the Heidelberg version is a Greek translation. Hanno's voyage, and that of his brother Himilco to the north, is mentioned by Pliny in his *Natural History* of the first century AD and by several later authors, confirming that the *Periplus* was not just made up by a medieval monk. It purports to be a first-hand account of Hanno's voyage down the west coast of Africa, but ends abruptly when he turns back before reaching the Cape."

"It's as if an editor has slashed a red line across a text without actually considering the flow of the narrative," Jack said. "It doesn't ring true."

"Maybe there was a complete account, but it never made it into the official version," Rebecca said.

"What do you mean?" Jeremy asked.

"Trade secrets. If you've found something good and want to put people off discovering it themselves, you write an account that does just that."

"Pliny mentions that Hanno made it round to Arabia," Jack said. "He's a pretty reliable source, and may himself have seen that fuller account."

"And Himilco?" Rebecca asked.

"Much less clear," Jeremy said. "The first mention of him is by Pliny, who says that when Hanno went around Africa, Himilco was dispatched north to explore the outer coasts of Europe. A number of historians have speculated that they were brothers. He crops up again in Avienus, a Roman author of the fourth century AD, who mentions him as having made a voyage to the Oestrumnides, the Western Isles, his term for a land known to the early Greek and Phoenician explorers as the Cassiterides, the Tin Isles. The voyage was fraught with dangers, full of sea monsters and fog. Avienus has us believe that his source is a lost account by Himilco himself, something also implied by Pliny. But there's no indication of tablets with that account having been set up in Carthage as well, odd because circumnavigating the British Isles would have been just as noteworthy an achievement as Hanno's."

"Maybe the trade secret was too valuable for any of the voyage to be made widely known, with British tin being in such high demand," Rebecca suggested.

"Or maybe Himilco never lived to trumpet his success," Jack said. "A sparse account, maybe only half believed, may have come down through others in his fleet who did survive, assuming that his was not the only vessel to set out. But without the great man to sell his story, without the Columbus or the Cabot or the Vasco da Gama, even the most compelling claims of exploration could fall flat."

"So it could be that Himilco perished in a shipwreck," Rebecca said, eyeing Jack. "A shipwreck off Cornwall."

"The thought has crossed my mind."

A familiar voice shouted greetings to the divers outside, and a few moments later Costas appeared at the tent flap, clutching a huge sandwich and wearing a battered straw sombrero, his signature Hawaiian shirt, and baggy technicolor shorts. He waved, took an enormous bite of the sandwich, and made his way round the table. He had the rolling gait that Jack had seen among his cousins on the Greek island where he had been born, bred into them over the generations from working on small boats as fishermen and sponge divers. He pulled up a plastic chair between Jeremy and Rebecca and sat down. He looked particularly grizzled today, Jack thought, with at least a week's worth of stubble, but he had the contented look he always had after a few uninterrupted days in the engineering lab at IMU. He took another bite and inspected the oily stains on his forearms. "Sorry," he said between mouthfuls. "Changed into my beach gear, but forgot to wash."

"Nice sandwich," Rebecca said. "New York deli in Cornwall. Always good to sample the local cuisine."

"She always does them for me at the café," he said, swallowing. "I call ahead the day before, she gets the stuff in. I spear her fresh fish from the steamship wreck as payment. It works."

"Better watch out for the shark," Jack said.

"He doesn't like flatfish, I do. I leave him the rest. It's called working with nature."

"That something you learned on the mean streets of the Bronx?" Jeremy said.

Costas took another bite. "Spearfishing with my uncles as a boy when we went back home to Greece on vacation."

"When you weren't sipping gin and tonic by the pool on the deck of your father's two-hundred-foot yacht?"

"That was a different kind of learning. Learning how to enjoy myself. Speaking of which, barbecue on the beach tonight?"

"Depends how we get on here," Jack said. "Might have to head off this afternoon."

Costas grunted, pushed the final part of the sandwich into his mouth and wiped his hands on his shorts, staring at Jeremy's laptop showing the transcript of Hanno's *Periplus*. He read it while he finished munching, and nearly choked. He stared again, swallowing hard. "Check this out," he said, and read out a passage.

" 'In this gulf was an island, resembling the first, with a lagoon, within which was another island, full of savages. Most of them were women with hairy bodies, whom our interpreters called "gorillas." Although we chased them, we could not catch any males; they all escaped, being good climbers who defended themselves with stones. However, we caught three women, who refused to follow those who carried them off, biting and clawing them. So we killed and flayed them and brought their skins back to Carthage. For we did not sail any further, because our provisions were running short.' "

He looked up, his expression deadpan. "Hairy women who bit and scratched? How long had these guys been at sea? They must have been desperate."

"That was probably in the region of Senegal, so maybe several months after leaving the Strait of Gibraltar, longer if they'd stopped to trade and establish outposts as the text implies," Jack said. "This is the *Periplus* of Hanno the Carthaginian, sailing down the west coast of Africa."

"Gorillas? Really?"

"That's the actual word, in Greek," Jeremy said. "In fact it's one of the reasons for believing in the authenticity of this document. What we have here is a Greek translation of the original Phoenician inscription set up in Carthage by Hanno after his return, in the early sixth century BC. The Greek historian Herodotus in the fifth century BC knew of Hanno's *Periplus*, as he describes a method of bartering along the West African coast that closely mimics an earlier passage in the *Periplus* and for which he could have had no other source, as there had been no further exploration along that coast after Hanno. Perhaps a Greek traveler who had been in Carthage made a copy and showed him. The word 'gorilla' would have been otherwise unknown to the Greeks and must have been copied from the original Punic inscription. It's a rendering of the Kikongo word *ngo diida*, meaning a powerful animal that beats itself violently, so Hanno must have got the word from the Africans he met."

"Not so nice of him to kill and flay them," Rebecca said.

"It's fascinating, because it's actually the first recorded instance we have of a natural history specimen being brought back from a voyage of discovery," Jack said. "Men like Joseph Banks on HMS *Endeavor* and Charles Darwin on the *Beagle* would have approved. Pliny tells us that the gorilla hides were still on display in Carthage when the Romans sacked the city in 146 BC."

Costas dug a can of Coke out of his shorts pocket and popped it noisily, taking a deep drink. "Okay, the gorilla story may be real, but I don't believe that final sentence, about turning back."

"We were just talking about that," Jeremy said. "It doesn't fit the narrative."

"I don't know about that," Costas said. "But when I was in the US Navy we deployed along that coast, and I do know about wind and currents. The Phoenicians were supposed to be great navigators, right? Trying to battle back against the Canary current and the prevailing northwesterlies would have made no sense at all. Hanno would have carried on, rounded the Cape and gone up the east coast of Africa."

"That's what Pliny said he did, reaching the coast of Arabia," Rebecca said.

"Speaking of circumnavigating Africa, take a look at this." Costas typed something into the laptop, and swung it round so Jack could see. "Our favorite salvage ship *Deep Explorer* has left her position off Sierra Leone, and is now heading past the Cape of Good Hope. Lanowski forwarded this image."

"Lanowski? From Carthage?"

"He's a one-man mobile command and control center. Never goes anywhere without his Landsat link."

"Anything more?"

"About an hour ago she turned north-northeast, making fifteen knots at twenty-five degrees, and she's maintained that course some thirty nautical miles off the coast."

"That means she's heading to the northern Indian Ocean."

"The Horn of Africa. Any idea why? That's a pretty hot place, and I don't just mean temperature. Pirates and Iranian missiles. Not sure I'd want to be there now."

"I had a few moments alone in the chart room on *Deep Explorer* just before our dive," Jack said. "I didn't think much of it at the time, as all eyes were on *Clan Macpherson* and we assumed *Deep Explorer* would be there for weeks attempting a salvage operation. But judging by the charts that were lying around, that figures as their next destination."

"Another Second World War wreck? That seems to be their speciality."

"They've got an excellent researcher in London, Collingwood, the guy who put them on to *Clan Macpherson*. He was at the same college as me at Cambridge, doing a doctorate on Allied convoy operations in the war. He always struck me as a little weak and naïve and he never managed to secure an academic post, so he makes his money where he can. In fact I met him at the National Archives yesterday, when we were ordering the same box of declassified Admiralty files, and we had a guarded conversation in the café afterward. I was certain he was there yesterday as a result of the *Clan Macpherson* project going bust following our dive. I invited him to contribute any additional documentary evidence he had for my report to the government on the wreck, and then I plugged him with some innocent-seeming questions. It turned out that he'd just returned from the Deutsches U-Boot archive that morning, and he was quite excited about some kind of all-expenses-paid holiday to the Indian Ocean in a few days' time. Seeing this Landsat image, I wouldn't be surprised if that meant a trip out to *Deep Explorer*. I got the impression that he'd been mandated to find evidence of *any* lost cargo of value, especially U-boats."

"They're going to be desperate after the failure to recoup from *Clan Macpherson*," Costas said. "A ship like *Deep Explorer* costs thousands to operate per day, and there are going to be some pretty noisy investors out there. He's probably going to be looking for anything marketable, not just gold."

"Landor's always operated on a knife edge," Jack said. "But if he's heading up to the Horn of Africa, he might just have got himself in too deep this time."

"Landor?" Rebecca said. "You mean the guy you and Maurice were at school with? I thought he was in prison somewhere in South America."

"I didn't have a chance to tell you about it before we were called out,"

Jack replied. "He's operations director for Deep Explorer Inc., his latest in-carnation. He keeps bouncing back."

"No wonder you had to grit your teeth to go out there and do that dive. He had a bend, didn't he?"

"A bad one, in his spine," Jack said. "It was on a First World War wreck off Scotland two years ago, hunting for a consignment of silver bars. He pushed the envelope too far, dropped too deep and took a gamble with his air."

"Sounds familiar," Rebecca said wryly.

"The hyperbaric specialist who dealt with him told me about it. He had the choice either of running out of air underwater and dying, or of surfac-ing too quickly, knowing he was going to take a hit. He was diving alone from a Zodiac without a support vessel, and by the time the boat driver got him to the recompression chamber at Oban, the damage was done. He can't even do a ten-minute dive to ten meters without risking a fatal hit, and hasn't dived since."

"If his passion for diving was anything like yours, I can imagine what that might do to him."

"It's hardened him, made him bitter. I don't recognize him any more." Jack paused, thinking for a moment. "He and I were inseparable for about a year, both obsessed with diving. I did my first ever open-water dives with him, and I can still remember the excitement. But then Maurice arrived at the school and I found someone I could share my archaeology interests with too, and Landor and I drifted apart. He was charismatic but rebel-lious, always with a dark edge, self-destructive. He dropped out of school and drifted off to Africa, worked for an aid agency at first but then as some kind of mercenary, and then he got into treasure hunting. For a long time I felt bad about him, guilty that I'd let him down by turning away from him at school.

"He came to see me once when I was a student and I agreed to dive with him again, on a galleon he'd found off Colombia. Then the Gulf War intervened and I was called up from the naval reserve, and the next I knew he was languishing in a prison in Bogotá. But he's always been good at pull-ing in credulous investors. He's made fortunes, lost them, made them and lost them again. I'm godfather to his son, who lived with his mother after Landor left her; father and son have never spoken since. I kept my distance from him on *Deep Explorer*, but what I saw I didn't like. Maybe agreeing to go out on *Deep Explorer* was part of my old guilt trip with him, and he knew it. But once I was out there, seeing him standing at the ship's rail doing nothing while Costas and I battled to get into the Zodiac, I realized I didn't owe him anything."

"Did the researcher give you any more hints about what they might be after?" Costas said.

Jack took a deep breath, and shook his head. "Very secretive. But if we're right and they are heading toward the Somali coast, we could do a bit of ferreting about and work out if there were any Allied vessels or U-boats in the vicinity with valuable cargos. And I might just have a word with a friend from navy days who's currently commanding officer of Combined Task Force 150, the anti-piracy flotilla operating out of Bahrain. I can at least warn him about Landor and what might be going on."

"I've got some spare time after diving while I wait for deliveries to the engineering lab," Costas said. "I can do a search online."

"Meanwhile, keep Lanowski on to it. I'd like to be updated on *Deep Explorer*'s progress. Get him to stream it through to my account as well."

"He could probably hack into the CIA and order in a drone strike if you like."

"Don't tempt me," Jack said. "So where are we, Jeremy?"

Jeremy picked up an A4-sized envelope and looked at him. "I think it's time to tell you about the bronze plaque from *Clan Macpherson*."

Costas finished his Coke, exhaling noisily and crushing the can under his foot. "And you haven't seen my sherd with its inscription yet. I found the bucket before coming in here, and the conservator will bring it in as soon as I call her."

Jack leaned forward, tense with anticipation. "All right. Show us what you've got. The plaque first."

Jeremy slid the envelope toward him. "That contains a sharpened still from your helmet video inside *Clan Macpherson*, along with my translation. Remember what we were saying about Hanno the Carthaginian, whether or not he circumnavigated Africa? Prepare to be amazed."

10

Jack stared in astonishment at the photograph that Jeremy had put in front of him, showing the bronze plaque from *Clan Macpherson* in the upper part and Jeremy's translation below. "Are you certain about this?" he asked, rereading the text, hardly daring to believe what was before his eyes.

"Absolutely," Jeremy replied. "It's the early Punic alphabet, pretty well identical to Phoenician from the Levant, the text reading from right to left. You can see the early form of the Punic letter A, toppled over on one side. There's no chance of this being some kind of forgery, because there are distinctive features of the letters *bet, tet,* and *mem*, the equivalent of the Greek *beta, theta,* and *mu*, that are only found elsewhere on the potsherd inscriptions from our Phoenician wreck, and we know from the Lydian coins and the datable Greek painted pottery in the cargo that our wreck sherds date to the early sixth century BC. We've run a thorough paleographic comparison between the early alphabetic letters on the plaque and those on the wreck inscriptions, and have concluded beyond doubt that they are contemporaneous. Both the plaque and the wreck date to the most likely time period of Hanno and Himilco's voyages, about the 590s or 580s BC."

Jack slowly read out Jeremy's translation: " 'Hanno the Carthaginian affixed this at the southernmost point of the Libyan regions beyond the Pillars of Hercules, having commanded fifty ships and now only having one, before setting off up the far shore with his cargo to the appointed place at the mountain called the Chariot of Fire. To Ba'al Hammon he dedicates this plaque.'"

Jeremy leaned over and pointed at the photo. "And then there's that symbol crudely stamped at the end, looking like an Egyptian hieroglyph of two stick-figure men carrying a box on poles between them. It's a pictogram, certainly. I haven't yet asked Maurice if he's seen one like it in Egypt, but will do so now that his excavation at Carthage is coming to a close and he'll have more time to check for comparisons."

"That's exactly what I found on my potsherd," Costas said. "I think Jenny from the conservation tent has just left it outside." He got up, hurried out of the tent and came back moments later carrying a bucket full of water. He reached in and pulled out an amphora sherd, carefully patting it on his shirt and placing it on the table between them. "You can see that the letters are scratched, not painted, so that's one difference from the other amphora inscriptions. But if you look carefully, you can just make out that pictogram among the scratchings. You see?"

Jeremy pushed up his glasses, leaned forward and peered at it. He looked up, staring into the middle distance, and then looked down again. "My God," he said quietly.

"Let's deal with the plaque first," Jack said, still focused on the photograph. "Have you got the text of the *Periplus of Hanno* to hand?"

Jeremy cleared his throat, still gazing at the sherd. "Yes, of course." He turned to his laptop, tapped the screen and swiveled it toward Jack. "The Heidelberg manuscript."

"It mentions a mountain called Chariot of the Gods, toward the end."

Jeremy nodded. "Here it is: 'And we sailed along with all speed, being stricken by fear. After a journey of four days, we saw the land at night covered with flames. And in the midst there was one lofty fire, greater than the rest, which seemed to touch the stars. By day this was seen to be a very high mountain, called Chariot of the Gods.'"

Jack looked at him. "Could Chariot of the Gods and Chariot of Fire be the same thing?"

"I'm certain of it. Remember, the Heidelberg text is a copy made more than fifteen hundred years after the event of a Greek translation that may itself have been copied from earlier translations, each time offering the possibility of mistakes and corruption. 'Chariot of the Lord' or 'Chariot of God' is most familiar as the translation from Hebrew into Greek of the conveyance in which the Israelite God appears in the Old Testament Book of Ezekiel. It's possible that the monks in the scriptorium, steeped in the Bible, would have seen the Greek word for 'chariot' and inserted the familiar biblical phrase, restricting reference to fire to the other fiery images in that passage. But with the evidence of the plaque, in Phoenician and dating to the time of Hanno, we can be certain that the original phrase was the one that I translate as 'Chariot of Fire.'"

"There is a geographical problem, though," Jack said, thinking hard. "In the Heidelberg text, the chariot appears on the *west* coast of Africa, just before the land of the gorillas. The image of rivers of fire is usually equated with an active volcano that Hanno must have seen in the region of modern Senegal. And yet the text in the plaque indicates that it was set up hundreds of miles to the south, at the Cape of Good Hope, and that the chariot lay ahead of them, somewhere up the *east* coast of Africa."

"That's why the plaque is a game-changer," Jeremy said, talking intently. "It suggests that the fiery passage in the Heidelberg text is a conflation, combining the Senegal volcano with something awesome to come, something that Hanno chose not to present accurately when he returned to Carthage and composed his *Periplus*."

Jack nodded slowly. "And yet something he could use to embellish his description of the volcanic region, making it seem even more terrifying, even more as if anyone traveling there would be transgressing in the realm of the gods."

"Exactly." Jeremy turned to Rebecca. "Earlier you mentioned the idea of trade secrets, of the explorers extolling their achievements but being careful not to give away too much, to make sure they were not providing a route map for their rivals. Well, here I think we have evidence that the Heidelberg *Periplus* is a truncated version of the truth, one that Hanno himself connived in, making a decision not to tell the full story when he came to present it to the world on his return to Carthage."

"How then do you account for Pliny's assertion that he *did* reach Arabia?" Rebecca said.

Jeremy shrugged. "Perhaps several of his sailors survive with him, and they can't keep their mouths shut. Perhaps Hanno himself lives to old age, when he no longer has anything to lose, and it becomes important for him to tell the truth of his achievement, to keep the names of Hanno and

Himilco high in the annals of exploration. The tablets of the *Periplus* remain unaltered, sacrosanct in the temple of Ba'al Hammon, but rumor spreads, soon becoming a fixed truth among Carthaginian mariners, men who would have revered the memory of Hanno, just as later ones did Vasco da Gama or Captain Cook. When the Romans sack Carthage, the story is still there, surviving with enough authority for Pliny to present it as fact in his *Natural History*."

Costas put up his hand. "But I see another problem. There's nothing volcanic up the east coast of Africa that would fit the description."

Rebecca shook her head. "You don't have to look for volcanoes. When I was in Ethiopia two years ago with my school group working for the aid agency, we used to get up at dawn to see the first light of the sun on the mountain ridges of the plateau. During the dry season, when the wind whips up the dust, it creates a dramatic light effect, a kind of ripple on the western horizon as the sun lights up the mountaintops. The ripple can be seen most clearly at a certain place where there's a line of ridges angled northwest, so the sun progressively lights up the ridge from south to north over a span of several seconds. On a clear day, where you can see the distant mountains over the plain from the sea, I guess to an ancient sailor that might look like a chariot racing across the sky—a Chariot of Fire."

Jack stared at her. "Can you pinpoint the place?"

"Absolutely. It covers the ancient mountaintop plateau of Magdala, where the Ethiopian King Theodore had his last stand against the British when they invaded Abyssinia in 1868 to rescue those European hostages. You should know about that, Dad."

"I certainly do. Our ancestor the Royal Engineers colonel inherited a box with some material relating to the campaign from a fellow officer in India. My father only told me about it just before he died, in a long list of other family documents he hadn't had time to catalog. Apparently there's a handwritten diary and some kind of fabric, a piece of tapestry or something brought back from the campaign. The archive's been in disarray over the last few years, with the new building at the campus under construction, but maybe now's the time for me to delve into it. My father always told me they weren't just fighting a war, but were on the trail of biblical antiquities."

"Another thing puzzles me, though," Rebecca said. "I get why Hanno might have abbreviated his story when he got back to Carthage. He was probably under strict orders from the magistrates or whoever to keep quiet about his circumnavigation. Who knows what gold and other riches might lie in East Africa. But why then should he give the game away in a plaque he erects at the Cape, saying exactly where he's going?"

"He would have been in a different mindset then," Costas said. "That plaque reads almost like a last journal entry—'We were fifty ships, now we're one.' I went round the Cape several times when I was in the navy, and I can tell you that the proposition in a simple square-rigged sailing ship would be little short of terrifying. He didn't know whether he'd make it back. Revealing trade secrets was the last thing on his mind. At the Cape, faced with the fearful prospect ahead, all that mattered was to leave something that showed his achievement, and perhaps a waymarker for those who might have followed to find out what had happened to him."

"What happened to his cargo, you mean," Jack said. " 'The appointed place' shows that whoever had entrusted him with this cargo had a fixed destination in mind, the mountain called the Chariot of Fire."

"If that was in Ethiopia, it wasn't entirely off the ancient map, was it?" Rebecca said. "The Egyptians knew of the Land of Punt to the south, and explorers seeking ivory and precious metals must have known about the rich wildlife and the gold to be found in the Ethiopian highlands. Perhaps someone had a treasure they wanted spirited away, to some hiding place at the edge of the known world but not beyond the bounds of recovery."

"And important enough to send it on a voyage all the way around the continent of Africa to get there," Costas said.

Jack gazed at the pictogram of the two men with the box. An idea was forming in his mind, something almost too incredible to contemplate. "The early sixth century was a very unsettled time in the Middle East, in the Holy Land," he said. "Nebuchadnezzar of Babylon had conquered the old Phoenician lands of Canaan, and Carthage had become the new capital of the Phoenician world. It's exactly the time you would expect navigators like Hanno and Himilco to be sent on great voyages of exploration to the west, to assert Carthaginian dominance over a new world where they would not have to contend with the ancient powers of the Middle East, a region as intractable then as it is now."

"And Nebuchadnezzar did something else, didn't he, Dad?" Rebecca said quietly, eyeing him. "Remember, I worked at Temple Mount in Jerusalem last year, and we were digging through those layers. He destroyed the Temple, and forced the Jews into exile. Something went missing, didn't it? A great treasure, the greatest, most sacred treasure of the Jews. So here's what I'm thinking. With the Phoenicians fleeing their homeland for Carthage, who better for their kin in Judah to entrust their treasure to than the greatest navigators of the world, men like Hanno, who might take it safely away from the cauldron of the Middle East and on an extraordinary voyage to that appointed place, somewhere for it to remain concealed until the time was right for its recovery."

Jack stared at the pictogram, his mind racing, and Jeremy looked at him. "I think we need to examine Costas's sherd now."

Costas leaned forward eagerly. "Can you read it?"

Jeremy picked it up and angled it into the light. "The inscription has been scratched into the outside of the sherd, hastily but decisively," he said. "There's no doubt the language is Phoenician, of the same time period as the painted sherds from the wreck and the plaque. It has the same toppled letter A, among other similarities."

"Another reference to the contents of the amphoras, like the painted inscriptions?" Costas suggested.

Jeremy shook his head emphatically. "The markings on those amphoras had been put on where they were filled or at the wharfside. As a result, where we've got broken sherds with those markings, from amphoras that shattered during the wrecking, they're like a jigsaw puzzle, with each sherd only containing part of an inscription. Your sherd is completely different, unique on the wreck so far. It's a complete inscription, squeezed into the available space, scratched on a sherd that was already broken. It was made by someone who had picked up a broken sherd and used whatever he had to hand, a ring or a knife perhaps."

Jack took the sherd from Jeremy, inspecting it. "The odd amphora might shatter in the normal course of a voyage, creating a mess that might be swept into the scuppers. But I don't think that accounts for this sherd. On a voyage such as this one, with the cargo needing to be stowed as well as possible to avoid breakage, with everything needing to be battened down and shipshape, any breakages would have been cleared overboard. And with the presentation of the cargo being of prime importance for trade, the last thing they would want would be to invite merchants on board to see stinking, messy scuppers. So my money is on this sherd being from an amphora that shattered in the final lead-up to the wrecking."

"That's consistent with the poor quality of the incisions," Jeremy replied, taking the sherd back and pointing at it. "They look as if they were scratched by someone being thrown violently about, who maybe knew they weren't going to make it."

"A message in a bottle," Rebecca said.

Jeremy nodded. "That fits with what the inscription actually says."

Jack leaned forward. "Go on."

Jeremy placed the sherd in the center of the table, pointing as he spoke. "It contains ten words, in four lines. The first word is 'Chimilkat,' evidently the name of the writer. The second word means 'made this,' like the Latin *fecit*. So that first line reads 'Chimilkat wrote this.' "

Jack stared, stunned. "You sure of that name?"

"You can read it for yourself."

"Chimilkat is the Phoenician name that the Greeks rendered as Himilco."

"Correct."

Costas looked at them. "Himilco the Navigator?"

Jeremy pointed at the sherd again. "The second line also contains two words. The first means 'go round,' but in a specific nautical sense, 'circumnavigate.' The second is the Phoenician spelling of the word we know from Greek as Cassiterides, the British Isles. So that line means 'circumnavigated the Cassiterides.' "

" 'Himilco, who wrote this, circumnavigated the British Isles,' " Costas said.

"That's amazing enough," Jeremy said. "But the third line says something truly astonishing. The same word for 'circumnavigate' appears, though with a suffix indicating a future sense, something that will happen. There are two other words you might recognize from the plaque, the word for Africa and, amazingly, the word for Chariot of Fire, the mountain. Then there's a name, barely visible, and another word."

Jack picked up the sherd and angled it again for a better view. "My God," he said quietly. "It's Hanno."

"And the last word in the line signifies their relationship. They're brothers."

Costas translated again. " 'Himilco, who wrote this, circumnavigated the British Isles. Hanno, his brother, has gone to circumnavigate Africa, to the Chariot of Fire.' "

"And now to the pictogram at the end, and the two words below," Jeremy said. "The pictogram is clear enough, but it must have been incised in his final moments. One slash becomes a gouge that trails off to the bottom of the sherd, as if it were done at the moment the ship struck."

"It's very moving," Rebecca said. "Two brothers, half a world apart, sending the same message to the world, both under duress. Hanno punches that pictogram into a bronze plaque at the Cape of Good Hope, as if to make absolutely sure that any who might follow him would know his purpose. He may not have been facing the same immediate terror as Himilco, but he must have wondered whether he would survive. For Himilco that pictogram is the last thing he'll ever inscribe, and he knows it. Leaving that message for posterity is the uppermost thing in his mind. Whatever it represents, it must have been something incredibly important. And he's thinking of his brother in his final moments."

Jeremy nodded and leaned forward intently, staring at Jack. "And now the final two words. Prepare yourself for one of the most extraordinary revelations of your archaeological career."

11

Jack felt his pulse quicken as he peered at the ancient potsherd, watching Jeremy trace the faint remains of the inscription with his finger. He cleared his throat and looked up at Jack, his face flushed with excitement. "The two words below the pictogram are 'Aron Habberit,' the same in Phoenician as in Hebrew."

"Aron Habberit," Jack repeated, his voice taut with excitement. "The Ark of the Covenant, the Ark of the Testimony. Well I'll be damned. That makes absolute sense of the pictogram."

Costas leaned back, closed his eyes and began to recite. "'And Bezalel made the ark of acacia wood; two cubits and a half was the length of it, and a cubit and a half the breadth of it, and a cubit and a half the height of it: and he overlaid it with pure gold within and without, and made a crown of gold to it round about. And he cast for it four rings of gold, in the four feet thereof; even two rings on the one side of it, and two rings on the other side of it. And he made staves of acacia wood, and overlaid them with gold. And he put the staves into the rings on the sides of the ark, to bear the ark.'"

"The Old Testament Book of Exodus, chapter 37, verses 1 to 5," Jeremy said. "Well remembered."

"The benefits of a strict Greek Orthodox upbringing," Costas said. "The only things that really interested me were the stories of treasure, and

I memorized them. I'd wanted to find the Ark of the Covenant way before I first met Jack. This is incredibly exciting."

Jeremy tapped on his laptop, opening a black-and-white photo and swiveling it round so that they could all see. "Recognize that?"

"The treasury in the tomb of Tutankhamun, as it looked just after Howard Carter stepped inside in 1923," Rebecca said. "That's the so-called Anubis shrine, made of gilded acacia wood, the wood that the Israelites called *shittim*, with carrying poles almost three meters long. The shrine is corniced, decorated on the sides like a palace facade covered with hieroglyphic text, and on top there's that frightening live-sized statue of Anubis, canine god of the dead and guardian of the burial chamber and the pharaoh's canopic equipment. That's what was found inside the shrine: sacred materials and equipment used in the mummification process. It was really a kind of portable treasury."

"You *really* know your Egyptology," Jeremy said.

"I've spent a lot of time with Maurice and Aysha. Being with Maurice is like living inside a virtual museum of ancient Egypt."

Jeremy cleared his throat. "I've put this image up because the Anubis shrine is the closest we have archaeologically to the description of the Ark of the Covenant. There are a lot of obvious similarities, including the box-like shape, the gilded wooden construction and the carrying poles. They're of very similar date as well, if we follow Maurice in believing that the Pharaoh of the Book of Exodus is Akhenaten, the likely father of Tutankhamun."

Costas looked at him quizzically. "So what you're suggesting is that when the Israelites came to think of a sacred box for the tablet of the Commandments, they had an obvious model in the type of shrine they would have seen being carried around in processions in Egypt."

"Precisely," Jeremy said. "Many of the Israelites of the Exodus had probably been in Egypt for generations, and as slaves, their own material culture would have been very sparse. Even though they may have despised Egyptian religion and the pharaohs, when it came to conceiving of a receptacle, their imaginations would have been fueled by the treasures they had seen around them in Egypt."

"There's another factor, something that Maurice always talks about," Rebecca added. "Look at how we use the words. When we call a box a shrine, we give it extra stature, extra strength, the power to protect what's inside. In the case of the Anubis shrine, it was the sacred canopic equipment; in the case of the Ark, it was the two stone plaques inscribed with the Ten Commandments. The Egyptians were past masters at invoking everything they could to protect their sacred objects. Anubis was the black dog of everyone's nightmares. In that photo you can still see the shroud that was found covering the dog's body, probably one of several that would have covered the head as well. People knew what lay beneath, they feared it, but they were probably told that to remove the shroud would be to bring down the wrath of the god upon them. The figures on top of the Ark in the biblical account, the so-called cherubim, probably a pair of winged lion-bodied creatures like the sphinx, had much the same function, and the Ark was also meant to be covered with shrouds or skins in a way that sounds very similar."

"The Book of Numbers, chapter 4," Costas said. "The Ark was to be covered with skins and a blue cloth, and to touch it was to die."

"Rebecca's right," Jack said. "Maurice and I often argue about the extent of Egyptian influence in the ancient Mediterranean, but in this case I agree with him. At the time when Egypt had its greatest involvement in ancient Mediterranean trade, during the New Kingdom in the late second millenium BC, the time of the Exodus, we should expect to see Egyptian artifacts being copied by other peoples. And remember how close Phoenicia was to Judah, geographically as well as culturally. The Phoenician god Ba'al Hammon had similarities with the early Judaean God, and we know that the concept of one overarching deity may be closely associated with the cult of the sun god Aten under Akhenaten. Even the western Phoenicians would have felt this influence. Hanno and Himilco would have been closely connected with the Phoenician homeland, and as we've seen from our wreck find of elephant ivory, they may even have traveled up the Nile themselves in search of trade goods. To me it's no surprise that when they come to inscribe a pictogram of the Ark, it looks very like an Egyptian hieroglyph, partly because the Ark itself is an Egyptian form."

Jeremy swiveled the computer back and tapped the keyboard. "There were two additional points of comparison that struck me when I was looking at the Egyptian material. The first was the association with mountains. We know that Moses was given the Commandments on a mountain, and we're told that the hiding place of the Ark was to be in a mountaintop cave. Well, Anubis was also known as the mountain god, Tepy-dju-ef, 'he who is upon his mountain.' The second point concerns the animal skins. I remembered Pliny's reference to the gorilla skins brought back by Hanno being hung up for display on his return to Carthage. Looking through the other artifacts found in Tut's treasury, I saw those two strange gilded sculptures of decapitated animal skins hanging from poles, part of the *imuit* fetish. That too was associated with the cult of Anubis."

"Are you suggesting a connection between Tut's tomb and the gorilla skins?" Costas asked incredulously.

"It's as Jack was saying, tendrils of influence that spread out from Egypt by way of the Near East, through Canaan and Judah, through the Phoenicians. The *imuit* fetish may have lost most of its meaning outside Egypt, but the imagery and symbolism could have remained, even a lingering memory of its power, a hint of the fear that Anubis instilled. And there may have been a more practical meaning. Perhaps Hanno had been instructed to set up the skins as a secret message that he had carried out his task, a message to the priests and prophets of Judah who may have retained a memory of Egyptian cult practices from the time of the Exodus."

"Gorilla skins might not have been quite what they had in mind," Costas said.

"It probably didn't matter, so long as they could see them and know they'd been used as a covering for the Ark."

"And the connection with Ethiopia, with the mountain called the Chariot of Fire?" Costas asked.

"I heard about the Ark when I was in Ethiopia, from the village elders in the mountains," Rebecca said. "And the Lemba people of South Africa, the Mwenye, claimed that they had the Ark and carried it deep into the mountains, hiding it in a cave. The Lemba called it *ngoma lungundu,* 'the voice of God.'"

"It sounds as if you were doing a bit more than relief work on your trip," Costas said.

"Yep. I'm an archaeologist's daughter."

"I remember that story," Jeremy said. "I went to a seminar in Oxford on the analysis of Lemba Y chromosomes that appeared to reveal a haplogroup similarity among samples from one clan with those of Semitic peoples of the Levant. There was a lot of talk of the lost tribes of Israel, and some pretty wild speculation. It could never have occurred to me at the time, of course, but Semitic DNA could mean Phoenician, not Jewish."

"Maybe Hanno's crew at the Cape made friends with the local women," Costas said. "Might have made a nice change from gorillas. Probably easier to catch."

"If our bronze plaque was set up in the Lemba homeland at the Cape, isn't it most likely that they would have safeguarded it?" Rebecca said. "They might have seen Hanno setting it up and making offerings to Ba'al Hammon, something he might have done extravagantly to try to keep the locals from tampering with it."

"And then they remove it and hide it away when they see it being threatened," Costas said. "That could have happened two thousand years later, when the next navigators from the Mediterranean arrived at the Cape."

"You mean Bartolomeu Dias in 1488," Rebecca said.

"And then someone gets hold of it during the Second World War and conceals it among a consignment of gold on a British merchant ship in 1943," Costas said.

"Who do we know who was snooping around looking for Jewish antiquities at that time?" Jack said, eyeing Costas.

Costas gave him a grim look. "I can think of one unsavory outfit we've come across before."

Jack stared at the photograph on the screen, his mind still on the ancient past. "We shouldn't discount a direct connection between Judah and Ethiopia as well," he said. "Remember, the early Christian kingdom of Axum was founded in the region of Ethiopia, maybe with an earlier Jewish presence. Perhaps some Jews fled south following the conquest of Jerusalem by Nebuchadnezzar, seeking the Promised Land. It might have been too dangerous for them to take the Ark and the other sacred objects from the Temple, with the risk of being apprehended by the Babylonians as they went south through Egypt, or of being waylaid in the lawless desert to the south. Perhaps they were a small number of the hardiest people, tasked with finding a secure place to hide the treasures. And once they had done so, it's possible that some of them returned and made arrangements for the transport of the Ark by sea, all the way round Africa. What fuels all this speculation is that phrase 'the appointed place' in the plaque inscription. It seems clear that the Chariot of Fire was an actual place, and that there might have been a reception party awaiting Hanno."

"So how do you fit the Lemba people into this scenario?" Rebecca asked.

"Only with more speculation," Jack replied. "But if Hanno arrived at the Cape with his fleet depleted to only one ship, then he may have had a problem with disease as well as with shipwreck. The *Periplus* shows that they were making forays inland on the way down the west coast of Africa, and every time they did that, they would have been exposed to potentially fatal new diseases against which they would have had little resistance. You only have to look at the miserable time with disease on board the ships of the early European explorers to imagine the scenario. If Hanno encounters people at the Cape who are tough, friendly, and persuaded that the Phoenicians are some kind of messengers from the gods, then he might have recruited some of them to join him for the final part of the voyage. He would have needed strong men to carry the Ark from the shore into the mountains, for a start. And then once their job was done, they may have left Hanno and his surviving crew to carry on overland to Carthage, and made their own way back south to their homeland."

"Taking with them the story of having transported the Ark to a cave in the mountains," Rebecca said.

"And also taking with them some of the Jewish customs that researchers have identified among their beliefs," Jeremy said. "Perhaps the Jewish refugees who formed the reception at the Chariot of Fire tried to convert them, to keep them in awe of the sacred nature of their mission and to impress on them the need for secrecy."

Costas leaned forward. "All of this is consistent with the idea of the Ark being in a church in Ethiopia, isn't it? Search online and that seems to be one of the most common conjectures. Maybe its hiding place in the mountains was revealed at some point in recent history and it was secretly taken there by those who had been entrusted with its safety."

"It's exactly the kind of thing that King Theodore of Abyssinia might have done, the one who took on the British in 1868," Jack said. "Maybe knowledge of the original mountaintop location of the Ark had somehow percolated out, and reached the ears of some of the adventurers in the British expedition against him. There were men like Stanley there, later of Livingstone fame. Maybe there was more to that expedition than meets the eye."

"You might have the key to that in those nineteenth-century documents you have," Rebecca said.

Jack stared at her, his mind racing. "That's one direction I want to go in. The other is to find out what the hell was happening in 1943. There's a crucial backstory to all this in what happened to *Clan Macpherson*, and I still need to get to the bottom of that." He sat upright, checking his watch. "That's fantastic work, Jeremy. And to Costas, for finding the sherd. Absolutely incredible."

"Okay," Costas said, standing up. "If we're done here, it's time to dive."

Jeremy gave Jack a hesitant look. "Jack, can I borrow your drysuit? We're about the same height."

Jack shook his head. "Sorry, I only brought my wetsuit. You're going to have to brave the icy North Atlantic."

"Some of us don't even need a wetsuit," Rebecca said, giving Jeremy a challenging look. "Maybe you should go back to hot cocoa and a hot-water bottle at the Institute."

"No way," Jeremy said. "I want to see those carpenter's marks on the timbers. I want to see every last inscription this site produces."

"Well then," Costas said, gesturing at the tent flap. "Are we good to go?"

"Good to go," Rebecca replied firmly, watching Jeremy close his computer and stash his papers in his briefcase. "You still want us back here at four P.M., Dad?"

Jack nodded. "Before then, I've got some phone calls to make. When I was at Kew I met up with an Imperial War Museum friend who is an expert on the intelligence files. She says there's someone still alive from Bletchley Park in 1943 who *might* be able to shed light on what was going on with our convoy. It's probably a long shot, but worth a try. If I can set up a visit, I'd like all of us to go. It sounds as if she's quite a character."

"I've got to stay here, Dad. I'm taking over from the site director next week while he's away."

"It'll have to be Costas and Jeremy, then. Apparently she's quite fond of men."

They all got up and went toward the tent entrance. Costas hesitated, and then turned back, pointing at the sherd. "Rebecca was right, Jack. It was a message in a bottle. That guy Himilco must have known that no-body in his lifetime would ever find that sherd, so he was looking to the future, to some distant time when others might pick up the trail. He was leaving it for us. For *you*."

Jack was alone again, as he had been that morning after arriving at the site. He picked up the two objects, the photograph of the plaque and the inscribed potsherd. They were fragmentary messages from the past, made at the furthest extremities of the known world over two and a half thousand years ago. He thought of Hanno and Himilco: the one standing at the Cape as the waves lashed and the wind howled, and yet somehow surviving his voyage; the other pulling off an equal feat of navigation but falling foul of the weather just as landfall must have seemed certain. They were two men determined to bask in the glory of their achievements, undoubtedly, but whose main audience was perhaps each other, driving the one to survive his ordeal against the odds in the hope of meeting his brother again, and the other to devote his final moments to scratching a message that could only have been intended for people in the far-distant future—people who might tell the world what he too had done and erect a monument on the harbor front at Carthage, where he would expect there to be one honoring his brother as well, the two men equal in stature and achievement, forever celebrated side by side.

Jack held up the potsherd, imagining Himilco in those final moments. History from the age of sailing was full of dread images of mariners being driven inshore with full knowledge of what was likely to happen but refusing to believe it until the very end. He remembered the image of the ship he had conjured up when he had discovered those timbers on the wreck site. Somewhere over the promontory in front of him, in a raging sea with death all but inevitable, a man had scratched those words, words important enough to be his final message, to his brother, to the world, words that revealed an extraordinary secret that Hanno too had felt compelled to record for posterity on his own inscription set up at the very extremity of Africa more than seven thousand miles away.

Jack put down the photograph and the potsherd and pulled out his phone. Secrets were meant to be forever, but the passage of time so often weakened that resolve; it was the human propensity to break the pact, to leave something for the future, that had been the lynchpin of so many of his quests, and this one now needed a veil to be lifted, a veil that had concealed one of the most secretive enterprises in history. He remembered what Costas had said: *one unsavory outfit we've come across before.* It was not just the extraordinary enterprise of Allied intelligence and counter-intelligence that he needed to break into, but the operations of a Nazi organization, one that had recruited archaeologists, fantasists, and the most diehard fanatics into its fold, an organization that would have been farcical had its purpose not been to help justify and instigate the worst crime against humanity ever committed.

He took a deep breath, tapped a saved number, and listened while it rang. A woman with an accent straight out of the 1940s answered, and he spoke. "Hello, Miss Hunter-Jones. My name is Dr. Jack Howard, and I'm calling from the International Maritime University. I believe that our mutual friend Dr. Gordon from the Imperial War Museum may have contacted you and explained that I'm researching a merchant ship lost off West Africa during the war. I've listened to the recording you did for him about Bletchley Park for the museum project last month, and I was fascinated. To help me with my research, I'm very much hoping that you may be willing to talk about some aspects of your work at Bletchley during the early part of 1943. We have an archaeological mystery to solve, and I'm hoping you can be part of it."

Part 3

Part 3

12

Off Madagascar, East Africa, present day

The man ducked against the downdraft of the rotor as he made his way from the helipad to the main deck of the ship, clutching his briefcase against his chest and holding his glasses on with his other hand. A crewman who had been waiting guided him past the ROV derrick and salvage machinery on the aft deck, steering him clear of the port railing where spray from the bow wave lashed the deck as the ship plowed through increasingly heavy seas. They clattered up the metal stairs and along the gangway toward the bridge, where the crewman opened the door and waved him inside. He dropped his suitcase, took off his glasses, and wiped them on his shirt, almost losing his balance as the ship pitched forward and another huge wave broke over the bow. A man wearing a baseball cap with the company logo and the four gold bands of a captain on his shoulder boards came over from the binnacle to greet him. "Dr. Collingwood. Welcome to *Deep Explorer*. Mr. Landor is waiting for you in the chart room. This way, please."

Collingwood picked up his briefcase and followed him toward the door at the back of the bridge, staggering as the ship lurched forward again. The captain opened the door and ushered him inside, closing it behind them. The noise of the spray against the bridge windscreen was blocked off, but they could feel the ship shuddering and groaning beneath their feet as it powered forward. Collingwood steadied himself and looked around.

As well as the captain, there were two other men present: Landor, whom he knew from their meetings in London before the *Clan Macpherson* project, and another he did not recognize, a wiry younger man chewing gum who looked Somali, dressed in a tracksuit and cradling an assault rifle. Collingwood stared at the gun, discomfited, and then back at Landor, who got up from his chair and limped over to shake hands. "Dr. Collingwood. The captain you already know, and this is the boss. He's our contact in northern Somalia, where he runs a fishing trawler. Don't worry about the Kalashnikov. It's the tool of the trade in these parts, wouldn't you say, Boss?"

The Boss spat his gum into a bin, then took out a handful of green leaves from his pocket and stuffed them into one cheek. "Whatever you say, man."

Landor turned back to Collingwood. "Drink?"

Collingwood lurched sideways again. "I think I'll pass."

"Straight to business, then. As soon as you called us three days ago with the heads-up on the U-boat, I took a gamble and set us on this course. You'd better be right."

Collingwood sat down heavily on a chair beside the chart table in the center of the room, bringing his briefcase up and opening it. "I've never had a lead as exciting as this one in all my years researching."

Landor sat down again opposite him and leaned forward, eyeing him intently. "I need everything you've got, and I mean *everything*. We're only forty-eight hours from Somali territorial waters and we need to be ready to strike fast and get out of there as soon as we can. This time we're not waiting for some joke UN inspection like we did with *Clan Macpherson*."

"Is that where your friend comes in?" Collingwood gestured at the Somali. "Keeping away unwanted attention?"

"You call him the Boss."

"That's right." The man spat a jet of green juice into the bin. "You call me the Boss, I call you English. The only names we need."

Collingwood looked at him uncertainly, and back at Landor. "Right. The Boss. I've got it." He clutched his briefcase to stop it sliding down the table, and then delved inside it, passing over a sheaf of papers and a file. "That contains copies of all the original source material I unearthed from the Deutsches U-Boot archive, and my summary and assessment. There's nothing more."

Landor arranged the material into a neat pile in front of him, and then put his hands on it. "Okay. I want a quick briefing. First, the U-boat."

The ship lurched again, and Collingwood swallowed hard, gripping the table. "*U-409*. She was a top-secret Type XB cargo boat designed to be used in the trade in raw materials and gold between the Nazis and Imperial Japan, laid down in November 1942 and first deployed four months later. She carried out two successful runs right under the noses of the British and Americans, despite the fact that at least one operative at the German B-Dienst intelligence facility believed that the Allies had broken Enigma and were on to the secret trade. Luckily the operative wasn't believed, otherwise the Battle of the Atlantic might have gone catastrophically wrong for the Allies in the middle of 1943. Not only that, but with Enigma being shut down, some of the secret U-boats that were intercepted and destroyed by the Allies on the basis of Ultra intelligence might have got through with cargos that could have changed the course of the war."

"You mean the cargos you told me about on the phone. You're certain of that?"

"We already knew that the U-boats on this mission were used to transport uranium ore to Japan. None of it, thankfully, was ever put to any use, other than one consignment captured by the Americans that probably went to the Manhattan Project, the A-bomb program. But the risk was always there, the terrifying possibility of the Germans or the Japanese developing a nuclear weapon. And the risk with material that remains unrecovered is still there today, only the enemy is different and the value much higher, now that we know how uranium can be used to make dirty bombs as well. A consignment of uranium worth two tons of gold back then would be worth ten times that now, and a number of potential customers have those kind of resources."

"That's my business, not yours," Landor said testily. "Otherwise I wouldn't be here, about to risk my ship in a potential war zone. Just tell me about this U-boat."

"According to my informant, the last time anyone heard of *U-409*, right at the end of the war, she was heading toward the Horn of Africa off Somalia with as much gold as she could carry, as well as a secret cargo, very possibly uranium ore. Judging by the consignment captured by the Americans, it would have been unrefined, and sealed inside lead cubes to minimize radiation. There was no record of her sinking. She vanished without trace."

"And you're certain about the secret U-boat pen on the island?"

"It was built just before the war under instructions from the Ahnenerbe, Himmler's so-called Department of Cultural Heritage. That in itself was odd. I can only assume that the Ahnenerbe were intending to store artifacts in it from their crazed expeditions around the world to find lost treasures, a kind of halfway house before working out a way to get them to Germany. Perhaps the captain of *U-409* had been involved in transport for the Ahnenerbe at some earlier point in the war and knew its location, and then remembered it as an ideal place to stash his loot—better than surrendering to the Allies or carrying on to Japan, with the Nazi war over. I feel certain that's where he went."

"Your source?"

"As I told you on the phone. A verbal testimony from a former SS Ahnenerbe man who gave himself up after the war and spilled the beans to an American interrogator, in return for an assurance that he would not be executed for other crimes. Unfortunately for him, the assurance he was given could only be empty, as he had gone on to work for the SS Einsatzgruppen liquidating Jews in Ukraine; but fortunately for us, his death meant that the story stopped there until I uncovered it. Any account mentioning the uranium transport was considered so secret that no written record was ever made of it. I know about it only from speaking to a former US naval intelligence interrogator who died a decade ago. I kept the story to myself, and was only able to link it to *U-409* after my visit to the Deutsches U-Boot archive last week."

Landor held up the file. "Once again, you can assure me that nobody else knows about this?"

The ship lurched, and Collingwood gripped the table again, looking pale. He shook his head. "Listen, I'm not doing too well here. Maybe I will have that drink. Water."

Landor opened a drawer behind him, put the file inside and locked it, then turned back to Collingwood, relaxing in his chair and smiling pleasantly. "Water won't help. What you need is to get off this ship."

"Jack Howard sends his greetings, by the way. Said you were old friends."

Landor's demeanor suddenly changed. "Jack Howard? How? You've been talking to him?"

"I met him at the National Archives yesterday."

Landor glared at him. "What do you mean, you *met* him?"

"Quite by chance. I'm always meeting people there. He and I had ordered the same box of convoy files to look at, and had to work out between us who was going to see them first. He was looking at a file on *Clan Macpherson*."

"What the hell for?" Landor exclaimed. "*Clan Macpherson* is a done deal. He and his sidekick Kazantzakis saw to that by doing whatever it was they did to sabotage the wreck during their dive. I never bought the story they spun about unstable munition cooking off. It's too much of a coincidence that the wreck should blow up and slide into the abyss just after they happen to be there. I should never have agreed to that inspection. Howard has let me down once too often, and now he owes me big time."

"I don't know anything about that," Collingwood said. "But remember, Jack's an archaeologist and historian, not a treasure hunter. If he was trying to get to the bottom of something in the archives, it's not because he's after gold."

"I know full well what Howard is. He's someone who has cost me far too much. Not recovering any gold from *Clan Macpherson* has put the whole Deep Explorer operation in jeopardy. We're out here now on a wing and a prayer because of him."

"All he was doing was tying up loose ends. He's going to have to make a report to the British government and the new UN committee regarding the identification of the wreck as a war grave. That's what he and Kazantzakis were out there with you to ascertain, and he'll finish the job properly. In fact, he asked me to come on board, to contribute anything I'd found on the convoy attack to help flesh out the report. We were graduate students together at Cambridge, and he knows the quality of my work. I agreed to go down to the IMU campus to collaborate with one of their researchers."

"You agreed *what*?"

Collingwood looked nonplussed. "I thought it would look good. To have my name on the report would make it look as if we'd had a productive collaboration, as if Deep Explorer had done everything it could to facilitate IMU. It would give you a clean bill of health and make it less likely that you'd be interfered with next time."

"I don't need a clean bill of health. Not at the risk of Howard having insider knowledge of where I might be going next. I know exactly what he's doing. He's playing you." Landor slammed one hand on the table, staring angrily at the chart, and then got up and limped over to Collingwood, glaring at him. "Did you tell him *anything* about our new operation? That you were coming out to visit us?"

Collingwood looked uncertain, and shook his head. "I don't think so."

"You don't think so. What does that mean?"

"He didn't ask."

"He wouldn't, would he? Did you tell him you'd just been to the U-boat archive?"

Collingwood brightened. "That's when he asked me to contribute to the report. We were both lamenting the fact that the National Archives contain little on the U-boats, and he asked me whether I'd been to the Deutsches archive. I told him I was there several months ago to research *U-515* and the West Africa convoy, in the lead-up to *Deep Explorer* finding *Clan Macpherson*."

"And did you also tell him that you were there again a few days ago, *after* he and Kazantzakis had done their dive?"

Collingwood looked nonplussed again. "Why not? I'd just flown in from Dusseldorf that morning, gone straight from Heathrow to Kew. Jack saw my Deutsches Archiv pass and said he was wondering whether to visit himself. I gave him the contact details of the guy there who looked after me. They're incredibly helpful, and I knew they'd be flattered to hear from Jack Howard."

Landor raised his arms in the air in vexation, and then let them fall. "So. Jack now knows that I sent you to the U-boat archive *after* we knew that *Clan Macpherson* was a write-off. That'd be just enough for him to wonder where we were going next, to keep an eye on us via Landsat. He has an American who does that for him, the geek with long hair who looks such an idiot in those IMU films. So by now Jack will know we've come up this coast, and he'll be putting two and two together. He'll have guessed that you found something new as a result of your visit to the U-boat archive that has led us here."

The captain turned to him. "We've probably got nothing to worry about. We're in international waters, and there's nothing he can do to us with the resources he has to hand. The nearest IMU vessel, *Seaquest*, is at least four days away in the Palk Strait off Sri Lanka. And even if Howard has friends in Somalia, I don't think that should concern us. The few patrol boats that comprise the Somali navy hardly ever leave port and they don't seem to have the guts to confront anyone. And with things heating up with Iran, the anti-piracy Combined Task Force 150 is going to be looking elsewhere. We should have a free hand."

Collingwood looked at Landor. "All I've done is what you wanted. I've found you a prize far more valuable than *Clan Macpherson*. You'll be able to recoup your losses easily and sail out of here rich men."

Landor stared at him coldly. "You're right. You've told me everything I need to know." He turned to the captain. "Dr. Collingwood has a flight to catch. Can you slow the ship for a helo launch?"

The captain nodded and went through to the bridge. Landor looked at the Boss, jerking his head toward the door, and the two men followed the captain, shutting the door behind them. After a few moments, Landor opened the door again and gestured for Collingwood to follow. "All right. The helo's revved up, ready to fly you off. Our pirate friend is going with you because he needs to get back to his village and get ready for the next phase of our operation."

"He's a *pirate*. You didn't tell me that."

"The Kalashnikov is as good as a skull and crossbones. But we're paying him more than he'd ever get from kidnapping and ransoming any of us. Just don't provoke him."

Collingwood shut his briefcase, then hesitated. "About my payment. Fifty percent on contract, fifty on coming up with the goods. That was our agreement. I think this counts as the goods."

Landor paused for a moment, and then took Collingwood by the shoulder, steering him out onto the bridge. "I'm going to do one better than that. I'm going to cut you in on a percentage of the gold, ten percent, the same proportion as the captain and the operations director, Macinnes. Does that seem fair? It'll make you a millionaire. Our banker will be in touch once you're back in England. Have a good flight."

Twenty minutes later, Collingwood sat beside the Boss in the rear passenger seat of the Lynx as it clattered away at low level from *Deep Explorer*, the downdraft from the rotor kicking up spray from the sea. The helicopter gained altitude, tilted forward and roared off, soon leaving the ship far

behind. There had not been enough intercom helmets, so the two passengers were just wearing ear defenders. As Collingwood looked out, clutching his briefcase, he saw that they were still heading east, into the Indian
Ocean. He turned to the Boss, tapping on his ear defender. The Boss raised
it, and Collingwood shouted into his ear, "We're going in the wrong
direction. The African coast is west, and we're going east."

The Boss, who had been listening to music, rocking with the beat, took
out his earbud headphones. "Eh?" he said. "No, this is the right direction."
He pointed down to the waves. "Very dangerous, English. Very dangerous."

Collingwood lifted his defenders, struggling to hear against the roar
of the rotor. "What do you mean?"

"Very dangerous, lots of sharks. No fishermen come out here, no navy,
no Americans, no Obama, no English, no nobody."

"I get it," Collingwood shouted. "A very dangerous place. So a good
time for the pilot to turn around."

"Hey, English." The Boss prodded him with the muzzle of his Kalashnikov. "You know how to swim?"

"Not very well, actually. Time I learned."

"Yes, English, you learn. You learn now." The Boss reached over,
unclipped Collingwood's harness and prodded him hard. "Now get up."

Collingwood looked at him in alarm. "What do you mean? What are
you doing?"

The Boss curled his finger round the trigger and aimed at Collingwood's chest. "I mean, *get up.*"

Collingwood did as he was told, dropping his briefcase and grasping
for handholds as he swayed in the confined space. His briefcase slid toward
the door and he lunged for it, nearly following it out. He turned back to
the Boss, enraged. "What did you do that for? That had everything in it,
all of my notes, now lost in the sea."

"Yes, the sea," the Boss said, spitting a jet of green at him and wagging
a finger. "Very dangerous. Too many sharks."

Collingwood banged hard on the glass partition between the passenger compartment and the cockpit, but the pilot remained unperturbed,
staring forward. He turned back to the Boss, holding on to the rail above
the door, the downdraft ruffling his clothes. "Okay, let's end this game.
We've come far enough."

"Yes, English. Far enough." The pirate raised the rifle and fired a single round into Collingwood's chest, the blood spraying out behind and whipping away in the wind. Collingwood seemed frozen in shock, unable to breathe, and then his legs collapsed and he fell away, tumbling round and round into darkness.

13

Herefordshire, England

J ack followed Costas and Jeremy toward the main entrance of the nursing home, a red-brick Georgian mansion set in beautiful grounds in the
rolling Herefordshire countryside, the Malvern Hills visible on the skyline
to the east. It had taken them a full two hours to drive here from the Institute of Palaeography in Oxford, but it had been a chance to go over the
Periplus of Hanno again and to scrutinize Jeremy's translation of the golden
plaque from the wreck. Jack's excitement had been mounting during the
drive, knowing that they were now on the trail of a story more remarkable
than he could ever have imagined when he and Costas had glimpsed those
symbols underwater less than a week before. The new evidence they had
discovered for the voyages of Hanno and Himilco would rewrite the history of early exploration, and he could hardly hope for more. And yet they
now knew from the pictogram and the two words beneath it that an even
more extraordinary story lay behind those voyages, one that opened up the
possibility of discovering what had really happened to one of the greatest
lost treasures of antiquity.

For Jack, the biggest mystery now lay not in the ancient past, but in the
darkest days of the Second World War. He had crossed his fingers as they
had turned into the lane, hoping against hope that what they heard here
today would provide the key to unlocking that mystery, an explanation for
what he and Costas had found on the wreck of the *Clan Macpherson* and its

link with the voyage of a Phoenician mariner and his astonishing cargo more than two and a half thousand years ago. He took a deep breath, remembering his phone conversation with the woman they were about to meet, and stepped through the entrance.

The receptionist took their names and pointed up the grand staircase to the first landing. "She's expecting you. She's been looking you up on the internet. You should expect a grilling from her. Jenny will take you up."

They followed the nurse up the stairs and along the first-floor corridor, past doors on either side surrounded by food trolleys and medical gurneys. "Lunchtime," the girl explained. "Louise has already had hers. She's quite excited by this. Her family come over a lot, children and grandchildren and great-grandchildren, but when you get to her age, there aren't many old friends left."

"How is she?" Jack asked. "I mean, her health?"

"Up and down. She's in her wheelchair today, with an IV. It's important not to tire her. But her mind's sharp as a tack. And you should be prepared," she said, her voice dropping to a whisper. "She *really* likes men."

She led them through the open door of what had once been a grand bedroom, its wide windows looking out toward the Malverns. On one side was a bed, on the other a desk with a computer; the space in between was crammed with bookcases covered with artifacts and framed photographs. An old woman sat in a wheelchair looking out of the window, wearing a gaily colored skirt and a Norwegian sweater, an IV drip extending into her left wrist. The nurse stood aside and gestured toward the three men. "Louise, your guests are here. I'll pop back in five minutes to see that everything's all right."

She left, and Louise turned. She had silver hair done in a 1940s fashion, and was still a beauty. She pressed a button on her armrest and the wheelchair advanced to the low coffee table in the center of the room. "You know, I'm nearly a hundred," she said, flashing a smile. "All my old friends from boarding school have gone, and there can't be that many left from my time at Cambridge either. There are still a few of us from the war, of course, old crocks like me by now. And yet sometimes," she said, eyeing the three men, "I don't feel a day over twenty-three."

She spoke with the crisp accent of her era and background. Jack smiled, holding out his hand. "I'm very pleased to meet you. I'm Jack Howard, and this is Dr. Costas Kazantzakis and Dr. Jeremy Haverstock, both Americans. They're colleagues of mine."

"Ah, Americans," she said, shaking their hands in turn. "We had Americans at Bletchley, you know. They were *so* much more civilized than our chaps, at least to begin with, less desperate to get under our skirts. Not that I minded that, but so many of our chaps had been in the war before being assigned to Bletchley and were haunted by it, still expecting to be knocked off any minute. Those first Americans had a bit more time for romance. Are any of you gentlemen married?"

She looked inquiringly at Costas, who coughed. "Um, not yet, ma'am."

"I'm Louise, not ma'am. And why not? You'd be a good catch for the right sort. I've looked you all up on the IMU website, you know. Some girl out there's bound to go for that Hawaiian look. It happened for the German chap, despite his shorts, with his delightful Egyptian wife, and even for the one who looks as if he's out of *Star Trek* . . . what's his name?"

"That would be Lanowski, Dr. Jacob Lanowski," Costas said.

"I think he's lovely. Well?"

Costas looked rueful. "Never seems to last beyond the beach. Where I have my holidays, that is. Romance and the engineering lab don't mix too well, I find. Too much grease and oil."

"Never stopped me at Bletchley. I was covered in it from operating the wretched bombe. You should try harder."

Costas coughed again, glancing at Jack. "Yes, ma'am. I mean Louise."

"And you, young man?" She turned to Jeremy.

"Not yet either," he said. "Well, I've got a girlfriend. Actually, it's Jack's daughter Rebecca. We might be engaged."

"Engaged," Jack exclaimed. "First I've heard of it."

Costas turned to him. *"Might be* engaged?"

Jeremy pushed up his glasses, looking uncomfortable. "Well, it's a little tricky. It's kind of hard pinning her down."

"That's because nobody pins my daughter down," Jack said. "She's a Howard."

"Nobody pins you down either, it seems," said Louise, looking at Jack. "I've read two of your books on your underwater adventures. They're over there, on the table. Costas is in them a lot, and so is Jeremy, and Maurice and Aysha and that lovely *Star Trek* man. But in one book there are quite a few pictures with one woman, and in the other book another woman. One looks central Asian, the other Spanish. Katya and Maria."

Jack scratched his chin. "That's a bit tricky to explain, too."

"No, it's not. You're dithering. You need to make your mind up. A girl likes to be chosen."

Jack nodded. "Yes, she does. Damn right."

"Okay." Her eyes twinkled with amusement, and she gestured at the three chairs that had been placed on the other side of the table. "Now that we've got that sorted out, let's get down to business. How can I help you?"

Twenty minutes later, Jack sat back, having told Louise about their dive off Sierra Leone. On the coffee table were two large photographs of the wreck, one showing the ship's name painted below the bow, the other the gaping hole caused by the torpedo explosion. He had not yet shown her the intact British torpedo that had been resting inside the hull, or the gold. He was still feeling for what she might know, and did not want to press her too far.

She had been mesmerized by the images. "Fascinating. You know, I'm glad my friend Fan won't be seeing these. She felt personally responsible for the men lost in that convoy."

Jack looked up from the pictures. This was what he had wanted to hear. "Was she also at Bletchley?"

"We called it the special operations hut. Commander Ian Bermonsey."

"You worked together?" Jack said cautiously.

Louise shook her head. "Not exactly. We were in digs together, though. Fan always thought I did something frightfully mysterious, but really all I did was what I told her, supervising the Wrens operating one of the bombes. It was stinking, dirty, noisy work. Computers then were not like they are now. Not the obvious thing for a cosseted girl like me, but we all got on with what we were told to do. There was a war on."

"So Fan was more the mathematician of the two of you?"

"Not at all. We both had first-class degrees. To some extent it was luck of the draw where they put you in Bletchley. They wanted clever people everywhere, even oiling the bombe. But Fan was exceptional, a really clever statistician. And she'd had an actual job before the war, teaching math at a school. I'd gone back into London society after Cambridge and was in danger of becoming a flibbertigibbet. Really, Bletchley was the best thing that could have happened to me. You could say I drew the short straw getting the bombe, but mucking in with the Wrens was probably just what I needed."

"Do you remember the thirtieth of April 1943, when *Clan Macpherson* went down?"

"I remember it well. It was cold, unseasonably so. Summer wasn't yet in sight. Fan came back to our digs that evening terribly upset about something, but of course she couldn't talk about it. I knew that her hut was where the decrypts were put into action, as it were, sent down the line to the Admiralty. Maybe they'd tried but failed to reroute a convoy. There were two battles that night, I remember, one in the mid-Atlantic and one off West Africa. Later I saw on her bedside table that she'd copied down the names of the ships lost in that West African convoy, and had underlined *Clan Macpherson*. I'd never seen Fan cry before. It was odd. She was usually so tough. I suppose we all have a breaking point. It never happened again."

Jeremy opened the tablet computer he had brought in with him. "Have you got wireless in this place?"

"Wouldn't have allowed them to move me here if they hadn't."

"Okay. I've got the stats here for the two convoys that night. ONS-5, the mid-Atlantic one, Liverpool to Halifax, forty-two ships and sixteen escorts, with a total of forty-three U-boats in two patrol lines arraigned against them. The ensuing week-long battle saw thirteen merchant ships sunk against seven U-boats destroyed and six damaged. The African convoy was TS-37, Takoradi to Sierra Leone, a fairly short hop on the West African route from Cape Town to the UK. Seven merchant ships sunk by *U-515,* one of the biggest tallies of the war for a solo U-boat attack. No U-boat losses."

Jack thought for a moment. "The evening of the thirtieth of April, when Fan came back distressed, was before these losses had actually been incurred. Maybe she was upset because she knew a decision had been made *not* to act on the Ultra decrypts that day. I can see why that decision might have been made for ONS-5. The S designation means that it was a slow convoy, and altering course would have been a long-winded business. Even if Bletchley did have decrypts showing the position of U-boats, with over forty boats out there they might have been redirecting the convoy straight into another line of U-boats."

"Think about the overall context, too," Jeremy said. "The escort corvettes by that point had become very proficient at killing U-boats. Dönitz's fleet was already losing more boats than could be replaced. As the Bletchley intelligence people might have anticipated, the ONS-5 battle was hard-fought, with bad losses, but turned out to be one of the decisive battles of the war."

"You're saying they *wanted* that battle to happen," Costas interjected. "That the merchant ship losses in ONS-5 were a price worth paying to bring the navy and the U-boats together. If she knew about that, no wonder the girl was upset."

"It's harder to explain a decision not to save the other convoy, the one with *Clan Macpherson*, TS-37," Jack said. "A single U-boat, a distant route off the main battle area that had rarely been hit. Given that, you might have thought it was safe enough for a decrypt to be acted upon without exciting German suspicion."

"Maybe they didn't have an Ultra signal showing the position of *U-515* clearly enough," Jeremy said. "Maybe her captain was on silent patrol, lurking. Sometimes U-boat captains did that when they didn't want to be reined in by Dönitz. I've been reading a lot about it over the past few days."

Jack pursed his lips. "I'd agree with you, except that the girl appears to have been specifically upset about that West African convoy and *Clan Macpherson*, suggesting that they *could* have rerouted that convoy too."

While they were talking, Louise had been struggling to reach a framed group photo on her windowsill. Jeremy quickly got up to help her, placing it on the table so they could all see. "There," she said. "That's the only picture I've got from Bletchley. Actually, it's not *at* Bletchley, as hardly any photos were taken there, but it shows a group of Bletchley cryptographers just after the war back at Cambridge, members of a chess club. Those were some of our chaps."

"Seems a fairly unlikely-looking bunch for a girl like you," Jeremy said, pushing up his glasses and sweeping back his hair. "I mean, romantically speaking."

Costas peered at the picture and then inspected him. "You should talk. The only thing missing is a bow tie. Otherwise you'd fit in perfectly."

"You'd be surprised," Louise said, pointing at the photo. "That one there could really do the business, once you showed him the ropes. He became my husband."

"Ah," Jeremy said.

"You never took his name?" Jack asked.

"Too independent for that. Also, my postwar job. You couldn't show you were married for risk of being compromised. I can't really talk about it."

"Understood. We don't want you to say more than you're comfortable with."

"Jeremy's right, though," she went on. "Before the Americans arrived, it was a question of going with what you'd got. The cryptographers could be pretty awkward, but then the alternative was those poor men in uniform who'd been wounded or traumatized, burned-out submariners, that kind of thing. Bermonsey had been one of those."

"Did you know him personally?" Jack asked.

"I invited him for a drink in the pub near our billets soon after he arrived, in early autumn of '42, I think. I'd known his sister before the war in London, and she asked me to look out for him. He was very nervy, wouldn't talk much. By that stage we'd been at war for three years, and there were a lot of men like that. It sounds harsh, but that's why the arrival of the Americans was such a breath of fresh air for us girls."

"Did Fan ever talk about him?"

"He had the hots for her, you know. Never did anything about it at Bletchley, far too professional, but I could tell. Of course, they got married after the war."

"Ah," Jack said. "Did you keep up contact?"

"I was a witness at their wedding," she replied. "It was at Southampton registry office the day before they were due to sail, in late 1947. He'd resigned from the navy and they were going to start a new life in Canada. Happened quite a lot with people from Bletchley. Not the marriage, I mean, but getting away. We were all supposed to walk off that last day when Bletchley shut down, to go back to our civilian lives and never talk about it. Oddly, it wasn't such a problem for the cryptographers like my own future husband, as to them Bletchley was like a kind of special extended research fellowship, and afterward they returned to their universities and carried on doing much the same kind of thing. For the rest of us it was different. It would

have been nice for me to tell my children growing up that I'd done something for the war effort."

"They must know by now," Costas said.

She nodded. "I told them when the whole Alan Turing story became
public. But other than the fact that I worked on the bombe, I haven't
revealed any details. We were sworn to secrecy."

"Where did Fan and Bermonsey go?" Jack asked.

"To British Columbia. I went to visit her there about twenty years ago,
after Ian had died. They'd both been schoolteachers. We had a lovely week
together, went whale-watching. I hadn't realized then that she'd been ill,
too. She died soon after I returned."

"Sorry to hear it," Costas said.

Jack leaned forward. "Did she ever talk to you about the work that she
and Ian did at Bletchley? It might help with the *Clan Macpherson* mystery."

She gave him a sudden steely look. "As I said, we were sworn to secrecy."

"Of course."

She paused, staring at the photos on the table for a moment, her hands
shaking slightly. "But the answer is yes. I didn't tell you about it when we
spoke on the phone, as I wanted to size you up in person. But this is the
reason why I wanted you to come here." She looked at Costas. "There's a
little key in a matchbox in the top drawer of that desk beside you. Find it
and use it to open the lower drawer."

Costas did as he was told, taking the key and pulling the drawer open,
revealing a few neatly stacked notebooks and a small pile of envelopes.

"I don't keep many papers, as you can see," Louise said. "A legacy from
Bletchley days. But there's a brown envelope with my name and address
and a Canadian stamp on it. Fan sent it to me just after I returned from
my visit to her."

"Got it," Costas said. "Do you want me to open it?"

"Pass it over to me, please."

She took the envelope and pulled out a three-page typescript letter. She
paused, and eyed Jack. "What do you know about the Ahnenerbe?"

"Himmler's Department of Cultural Heritage, based at Wewelsburg
Castle in Bavaria. We've bumped into them a few times—their legacy, I
mean. They were on the hunt for a couple of artifacts that interested us."

"The menorah," Costas said.

"Sacred golden candelabra of the Jews," Jeremy added, looking at

Louise. "Stolen by the Romans when they looted the Temple in Jerusalem, and then vanished."

"I know what the menorah is," she said. "Anyway, everyone knows it was stolen from its secret hiding place in Constantinople by Harald Hardrada of Norway. He had it with him when he failed to conquer England in 1066, then took it across the Atlantic to the Viking colonies of Vinland and down to the Yucatán in Mexico, where he had a show-down with the Maya. What happened to it then is anyone's guess. Probably melted down by the Maya and became part of the gold stolen by the Spanish five hundred years later, then lost in one of those shipwrecks off the Spanish Main." She gave Jack a mischievous look. "Am I right, Dr. Howard?"

Jack pointed at one of his books on the table. "I'll even sign it for you if you like."

Costas smiled. "It's a great story. One of my favorites. And I can vouch for it, as I was there, trapped inside an iceberg looking for a Viking long-ship."

"I'll have your signature too, then."

Jack smiled, and then looked serious again. "Why do you mention the Ahnenerbe?"

Louise coughed, suddenly looking frail, and reached back toward the table behind her. Jack saw the small water bottle and got up to pass it to her, unscrewing the top first. She took a sip and then put it in the cup-holder on the arm of her wheelchair, her hand shaking badly. "You know," she said, "we'll never have the full story of what really went on at Bletchley. As more of us go, the secrets will die with us. But when Fan wrote that letter, she had decided to tell me everything she knew about that particular op-eration. She's left the trail open for someone to follow. Perhaps for *you* to follow."

"Will you read it to us?"

"One of you read it. My eyesight's not so good any more. Fan always typed her letters, so it's clear enough." She handed the letter to Costas, who was nearest to her, and turned back to Jack, her eyes suddenly gleaming. "You asked about the Ahnenerbe. Prepare to be amazed."

14

My dear Louise,

We had such a lovely time last week, didn't we? We always talked of traveling together after the war, and finally we've done it. So sad that Ian wasn't here to enjoy it with us, but then we always did want a "girls only" outing and it did mean we could talk a bit more about Bletchley. With Ian that would have been impossible, because he was haunted by the war, especially during his final illness. He had nightmares where he saw the men from one of the ships his submarine had sunk in the Mediterranean swimming toward him desperately, and he was unable to rescue them.

I know it was frustrating for you, but you were lucky to be just working on the bombe (if that's *really* all you were doing . . .). At least you didn't have to deal as directly as I did in human lives. After being posted to the special operations hut, I had a hand in how the U-boat decrypts were used. Sometimes they saved lives, and sometimes we chose not to act on them if we thought the Germans might become suspicious. I'm able to tell you this because I know you must have guessed it already. You must have seen how upset I was on occasion. I felt that those men in the merchant ships were my responsibility, and I still think about them every day, about those I couldn't save and the grief of all of those children growing up without having known their fathers, living out their lives forever under that shadow.

I will, though, never reveal to anyone how we reached those decisions. You and I were both sworn to secrecy, and keeping that bond has become part of who we are. Somehow it has helped me to live with it, feeling that what we did at Bletchley, the *way* we did it, could still save lives in a future war. But after you left last week, I thought about it and have decided to tell you about one operation that no longer has any bearing on national security. It was an operation within an operation, one of those folds of secrecy at Bletchley, and you'll understand that I still can't reveal anything about the bigger picture.

The operation was called Ark. That was the code name used for it by B-Dienst. Their naval intelligence division was involved in all German seaborne operations, and this was one of them, albeit a highly unusual one. When the word first appeared in the Ultra decrypts at Bletchley it was thought to be a code name for a new U-boat patrol line, a wolf pack. The patrol lines surrounding convoy OMS-5 in late April 1943, for example, were named after birds: Meise, blue tit, and Specht, woodpecker. But then an army intelligence officer attached to Hut 8 recognized it from one of the Colossus decrypts of German High Command communications from Berlin, and sourced it to the Ahnenerbe. The SS at Wewelsburg Castle had their own signals section, whose communications were channeled through the High Command, and with Colossus having cracked the Lorenz cipher, we were able to decrypt them. The Ark communications were specifically sourced to a Nazi agent established in Durban in South Africa before the war. They concerned an Ahnenerbe operation to smuggle something back to Germany on an Allied merchant ship. The first of these communications was deciphered toward the end of March 1943.

As you will know, many of the Ahnenerbe expeditions were

attempts to find evidence for an Aryan precursor civilization, to substantiate the Nazi fantasy of an Aryan master race. Even within the Ahnenerbe there were many who knew this was absurd, but who could see it as a useful cover for the more plausible business of searching for Jewish treasures from antiquity lost or concealed around the world. Prime among their interests was the Ark of the Covenant. To find that, to bring it back to Germany and display it in Berlin, would have been the ultimate symbol of dominance over the Jews. That was what most worried our intelligence people about the Ahnenerbe, and it went to the very top. Churchill had little interest in fantasies of an Aryan master race, but he was deeply concerned about anti-Semitism, about the way Hitler and his cronies used it to stir up and strengthen Nazi belief. Once when he visited us he said that the discovery and parading in Berlin of a single artifact from the Temple in Jerusalem would be the equivalent of losing two or three army divisions to the Nazis, such would be its effect on German military morale. The horrible consequences of Nazi anti-Semitism were also becoming known. By 1943 we were aware of the mass murder of Jews by the SS Einsatzgruppen in the east, and reports of death camps in Poland were beginning to gain credibility.

By then the Americans were of course major players in the war; the American Jewish lobby had been a powerful factor in pushing Roosevelt to commit against Hitler in the way he did. Few people realize how much Churchill worked his will on those people during his early visits to America, and how grateful he was to them. For us in Allied intelligence to have failed to prevent an artifact central to Jewish identity from reaching Nazi Germany would have been a terrible blow. Hitler would have presented it as a huge triumph, just like the Roman emperor parading the spoils of the Temple through Rome after the sack of Jerusalem. He would have used it to try to humiliate and degrade the Jewish people. Imagine the scene: goose-stepping SS officers carrying the Ark past the Reichstag just like the legionaries shown with the menorah at the Arch of Titus in Rome, and the Ark then being defaced or destroyed. It would have been ghastly. Churchill by this stage in the war had taken many decisions for the greater good that required our men knowingly or unwittingly to sacrifice their lives, and Operation Ark would be one of those.

Whether or not the Ark had truly been found by Ahnenerbe agents we may never know. But the intelligence was good enough to put our intelligence people in South Africa on it. Nazi agents were often clumsy and obvious, and we'd rumbled the Durban operatives before the war even began. Our people determined that something had been secreted on board the British merchant ship *Clan Macpherson* during her port stay at Durban in mid-April 1943. After she sailed, only two days before her sinking, one of the Nazi agents was snatched and interrogated. He revealed that the plan had been an elaborate set-up involving another Nazi cell in Bombay, one that we had not previously rumbled. A month earlier, *Clan Macpherson* had stopped there and picked up a new draft of Lascar seamen, among whom were six former Indian Army sepoys who had gone over to the Japanese in Burma to join the Indian National Army against the British.

We now know that the Nazis, with Japanese assistance, recruited a number of these Indian nationalists for nefarious purposes; this was one of the few plans that came close to fruition. The six men were experienced soldiers trained in unarmed combat who were meant to kill the ship's gunners, arm themselves, and take over the bridge. This was to happen at the coordinates we had learned from the Enigma decrypt mentioning Ark, when the ship was part of convoy TS-37 halfway between Takoradi and Sierra Leone. The usurpers were to slow the ship to cause her to straggle behind the convoy, and to signal engine trouble to the escorts. That would allow *U-515* to distinguish her from the other ships when it attacked the convoy. The captain of *U-515* was ordered to hit as many ships as possible, so that the escorts were entirely focused on the threat amidst the main body of the convoy and on picking up survivors. The U-boat was then to slip back, rendezvous with *Clan Macpherson* and take off her precious cargo and the six men. After standing off, she would torpedo the ship and machine-gun any of the crew who happened still to be alive in the water. She was then to rendezvous in the mid-Atlantic with a supply boat,

U-409, that was to take the cargo directly to the U-boat base at Lorient on the French coast, at which point the precious cargo would be flown on to Berlin.

Ian was able to tell me all this because Churchill had personally selected him to be part of a directive within Bletchley whose remit encompassed the Ark operation. Enigma intelligence, as you know well, was Ultra, for ultra top-secret; this organization was one stage of secrecy above that, and never had a name. The only others in on the operation at Bletchley were Captain Pullen, who you will remember, Alan Turing and another cryptographer, and me. I was recruited by Ian just before TS-37 was hit, so I was with him when he put through the call that sealed *Clan Macpherson*'s fate, though not as the Nazis had envisaged it. Unknown to me, Churchill had vetted me already when he spoke to me during one of his covert visits to Bletchley a month or so earlier.

I mentioned that there was a bigger picture, the wider remit for our group that Ian and I agreed never to speak about; the operation against the Ahnenerbe was, if you like, a fold within that picture, though closely intertwined with it. All I can say is that because of that wider remit, we already had in place a line of specialized hunter-killer submarines off the west coast of Africa, one of them off Sierra Leone. By the time we knew of the Ark plan from the interrogation of the Nazi agent in Durban, it was too late to warn *Clan Macpherson*; without knowing the names of the six men, it would have been impossible for the captain to take effective action, and worse still, it might have alerted B-Dienst that we were on to them and had possibly broken Enigma.

Churchill himself made the final decision. Our submarine would shadow the convoy, wait until it saw a ship straggling, and then torpedo it. With *U-515* meanwhile embarking on its attack on the main body of the convoy to the north, nobody would be any the wiser. History would record *Clan Macpherson* as just another one of *U-515*'s victims on that terrible night. Whatever the treasure was, whether or not it was the Ark, would be lost forever, and another small victory would have been scored against the Nazis, unknown to history and cloaked under a veil of secrecy that would see almost all of those in the know taking the story with them to the grave.

And that's what happened. *Clan Macpherson* went down at about 0540 on May 1. The takeover by the six men was put down to a mutiny by disaffected Lascars influenced by the Indian nationalist movement, at a time when Lascars on other British merchant ships were refusing to serve in the North Atlantic. Even so, the survivors were met by naval intelligence officers who had been flown out to Freetown to swear them to secrecy for reasons of national security, on the grounds that knowledge of a mutiny would be utilized for propaganda by the Nazis and might result in even more widespread disaffection among the Lascars, a potential disaster at that critical point in the Battle of the Atlantic. The captian of *Clan Macpherson*, who survived the sinking, agreed to go along with it, and to write critically to the trade division at the Admiralty about the weakness of the convoy escort in order to deflect any wayward attention from the circumstances of *Clan Macpherson*'s sinking, the reason why she might have fallen back behind the convoy.

Months later, Ian told me what the captain of *Clan Macpherson* had reported about the fate of the mutineers, an account that was never written down and never made it into the official documentation. The first torpedo from our sub blew a hole in the side of the ship but failed to sink her. A second torpedo had been fired, but lodged in the hull without detonating. Our sub could not linger after that to launch any more torpedoes for fear that it would be seen and recognized for what it was, a British sub and not German. Meanwhile, most of the crew had got off in the boats, leaving the six mutineers on board. The captain and his officers conferred and determined to get back on the ship, ostensibly to try to save her but in fact to attempt to finish the job and scuttle her, knowing that the mutineers' success would otherwise become known and be a propaganda coup for the enemy. Four of the engineer officers volunteered to return and pull the stopcocks. In the event, they and the mutineers went down with the ship. Whether the engineers saw the unexploded torpedo and realized it was British, we shall never know. But those merchant seamen finished our job for us, sinking their own ship.

When you saw me upset that evening of April 30, Louise, it was not just because I knew that *Clan Macpherson* was doomed. It was also because this operation had sealed the fate of those other ships in the convoy that were torpedoed by *U-515*. That morning, Ian had orchestrated the usual conference to decide which of the previous night's Enigma decrypts to act upon—which convoys we could try to save and how much we could "push the envelope," as they would say nowadays, without arousing German suspicions that we had broken Enigma. We made the decision not to intervene with ONS-5 but to reroute TS-37. What I didn't know until Ian took me into his office for the telephone call to the Admiralty was that it was all a charade. What he was involved in, what I then became part of for the remainder of the war, was so secret that not even the other people in that very top-secret hut could be allowed in on it. They would see the next day that TS-37 had been hit but would just think it was bad luck; not all convoy rerouting worked. But what we did that day, what we chose not to do, cost hundreds of lives, and that still keeps me awake at night.

The losses in ONS-5 were one thing; I can live with that. We probably could not have intervened successfully with that convoy anyway, and the ensuing battle proved to be pivotal for the Atlantic war. But TS-37 was a different matter. We knew the likely interception point with *U-515*, and we could have saved those ships. I can name them all from memory: *Corabella, Bandar Shahpour, Kota Tjandi, Nagina, City of Singapore, Mokambo,* and of course *Clan Macpherson*. You can go to the Merchant Navy Memorial beside the Tower of London and see the names of the men, including the four engineers. I just hope that whatever treasure it was that went down with *Clan Macpherson* was worth their lives to keep it from the Nazis.

There you have it. Maybe there will be a trail still to follow. Perhaps divers will one day find the wreck of *Clan Macpherson*. It's astonishing what's being discovered nowadays in the ocean depths, though the images sometimes give me nightmares. Seeing those tombs in the sea brings it all back, what we were really doing at Bletchley. We may have done our bit to win the war, but it wasn't all about those euphoric moments you see in the films. And poor Alan. I can still picture him running at night on the road to our digs outside Bletchley, passing us with a grin. I can still see him there, if I shut my eyes.

With love from

Fan

15

Louise took the letter back from Costas, and then showed them a hand-written note from the same envelope. "Fan included this as well. It's personal. It's where she tells me she only has a short time to live." She tucked the note and the letter back inside the envelope, and then turned to Jack, eyeing him keenly. "Well? Was she right? Is there a trail to follow?"

Jack leaned forward on his elbows, his mind racing. "It's an incredible story. What I can do now is show you three more photos from the wreck of *Clan Macpherson*. I was holding back on these until we knew where we were going with this." He picked up the folder from the table, took out another A4-sized print and handed it to her. It showed a mass of twisted metal covered with rusticules and marine accretion, and in the center a long cylindrical object nestled in the wreckage. It was the extraordinary view that had confronted Jack when he had followed Costas into the sunken hull off Sierra Leone a week earlier.

"It's a torpedo," Louise said, her hand shaking slightly. "I can see the propeller."

"Unexploded, inside the hull," Jack said. "Now take a look at the markings."

"I can see numbers and words, in English. It's a *British* torpedo."

"A Mark VIIIC, to be precise," Costas said. "A submarine rather than an aerial torpedo, much bigger. We'd already concluded that the sub that fired this must have launched a pair of torpedoes almost simultaneously, and that this one entered the breach in the hold created by the explosion of the first. We were baffled at how a U-boat could have got hold of British torpedoes. Fan's letter solves *that* mystery for us."

"And the second photo?"

Jack pulled it out, and paused. "The next two are a bit blurred. By the time I got to this part of the wreck we had only minutes left in the hull. We had something of a close shave."

She gestured at his books on the table. "So what's new?"

"All I needed to do was to unscrew the torpedo fuse," Costas said. "Then everything would have been fine."

"No it would not," Jack said firmly. "Rebecca would not have had a father. Your beach friends would have missed their volleyball partner." He turned to Louise. "The warhead had nearly come off the torpedo when it drove into the hull, which is how you can see those markings on the base. In the process of fiddling with the fuse, my dive buddy here caused the torpedo to dislodge, fall through the wreckage and come to rest with the warhead facing downward, held in place by a few tendrils of rust. One accidental brush, one waft with a fin, and boom."

"I thought you two always worked as a team?" she said, her eyes glinting with amusement.

Costas nodded enthusiastically. "I go ahead where there are explosives to defuse, and Jack goes ahead where there's archaeology to be found. That's teamwork for you."

Jack gave him a wry look. "In this case, teamwork got us out just in time and behind a ridge of rock before the torpedo broke free and detonated, causing the entire wreck to slip down the drop-off into the abyss."

She pointed at the first picture. "So this is all gone?"

"Well, it's still there, in a manner of speaking," Costas replied. "Only it's more than a mile deep, strewn down the slope of the massive canyon that lay next to the wreck."

Jack passed her the second photo. "And that includes what you can see here."

She stared at the image from Jack's helmet camera, her hands shaking. "Crikey," she said quietly. "So they really *were* on board. Gold bars."

"That's the reason we were diving on the wreck in the first place, as I explained to you on the phone. A researcher for the salvage company we were monitoring had got hold of a bill of lading, evidently made by an over-scrupulous clerk in Durban, who must have filed it away before the security people supervising the lading could see and destroy it. It showed that *Clan Macpherson* was in Durban to pick up a consignment of South African gold."

"There are a lot of bars there."

"About five hundred million pounds in today's money."

"Crikey. The salvage company can't have been too pleased about your little escapade, then."

"Not too pleased, though we told them nothing about seeing the gold. Apart from a select few at IMU and those of us here in this room now, nobody else has seen that photo or knows what we found. As far as the salvage company is concerned, we drew a blank and the explosion was just an unhappy accident with unstable Second World War ordnance. Being a treasure salvor is generally like that, one disappointment after another."

Louise's eyes glinted. "You can rely on me. I'm a Bletchley girl. I'm pretty good at keeping secrets."

Jack looked at her intently. "I'm thinking of those Nazi agents in Durban that Fan mentioned. In a major port like Durban, their day-to-day work would presumably have been spying on ships' movements and cargo lading. The arrival of such a large consignment of gold from the mines would have been difficult for the authorities to conceal."

"What are you suggesting?" Jeremy said.

"I'm suggesting that there might be more to this than meets the eye. More than Fan was able to tell in her letter. Bletchley was all about folds of secrecy, right? Every time something is revealed about the workings of that place, it seems to point to another operation. Open the wrapping and you reveal another layer."

Costas eyed him. "You mean the story of *Clan Macpherson* is not just about the Ahnenerbe and ancient antiquities. Ask me, and we're talking about a heist. A Nazi gold heist."

"A heist, yes, but one that fits into the wider picture, the operation that Fan and Bermonsey had sworn never to reveal. An operation that would have been a far greater concern to Churchill than lost Jewish antiquities. The reason why I think there was a British submarine on station off Sierra Leone in the first place."

"Go on," Costas said.

"You mean the Yanagi program," Louise said quietly.

Jack turned to her. "You know about it?"

"I was the one who spotted the decrypt," she said.

"I'm astonished. I shouldn't be, of course, knowing what went on at Bletchley. But you were adamant that you'd only worked on the bombe."

"In the bombe hut. Once the thing was up and running, clanging and belching away, there could be hours when there was very little to do, and eventually someone in Hut 8 decided that the more mathematical of us in the bombe rooms should be put to use cribbing, trying to find patterns in the code that might fit with words we knew should be there. I spotted the Japanese word *yanagi* on one of the decrypts, and passed it on. My father was a British trade attaché in Japan while I was growing up, so I know some Japanese. I knew this was the word for willow, though I had no idea until after the war that Yanagi was the code name for the Japanese exchange program with Nazi Germany."

"Did Fan know about your role in this?"

"I never told her. I was sworn to absolute secrecy. There was a fear that the Soviets had got hold of Japanese encryption machines in Manchuria, and after the war, anything to do with Japanese code breaking was a closed shop. I was still in the game then, you know."

"I didn't know. I thought it ended with Bletchley."

"For Fan, yes. For me, not quite."

"The Yanagi program," Costas said. "What kind of stuff was exchanged?"

Jeremy tapped on his computer and scanned the page. "From Germany, mainly technology: weapons and blueprints, optical glass, radar equipment, jet engines and so on. An exchange of scientists and engineers. Oh, and some Indian nationalist leader, traveling from Berlin to Tokyo. From the Japanese, mainly raw materials: rubber, tungsten, tin, zinc, quinine, opium, coffee. Oh, and here we go. Transferred from a Japanese submarine to a U-boat on the twenty-sixth of April 1943. That's only four days before *Clan Macpherson* was sunk. Two tons of gold."

"Holy cow," Costas said. "Where?"

"Off Mozambique. Transferred from Japanese *I-29* to German *U-180,* and destined for the U-boat base at Lorient on the western French coast and then Germany."

Jack sat forward, speaking slowly. "Two tons of gold. And we believe there were also two tons of gold on *Clan Macpherson*. Look at the dates. *U-180* would have passed the Cape of Good Hope and been up the west coast of Africa exactly in time to rendezvous with *U-515* after she'd hit the convoy."

"What are you suggesting?" Costas said.

"Got it," Jeremy interjected, staring at the screen. "*U-180* was a Type 9D1 transport U-boat. That means she was a cargo carrier. *U-515* may have been the boat tasked to take the gold off *Clan Macpherson*, but she was an attack sub, not a cargo carrier, and it would have made sense for her to transfer the gold as soon as possible to a specialized U-boat in the vicinity designed to take that kind of load."

Jack nodded. "And at that point, all going well, *U-180* parts company with *U-515* and makes her way undetected to Lorient, with a whopping four tons of gold on board. Two tons come from Japan, and the other two tons could be considered Japanese booty, the heist having been carried out on *Clan Macpherson* by Japanese-trained agents."

"Hold it there," Jeremy said, swiping the mousepad and staring intently at the screen. "I think I might just have seen the bigger picture. The one that Fan couldn't reveal to us."

"Go on," Jack said.

Jeremy cleared his throat. "I mentioned that most of the German export seemed to be manufactured products, high technology. Well, it wasn't always that way round. When the long-range cargo submarine *U-234* put out for Japan in December 1944, she was indeed carrying examples of the latest military technology, including a crated Me 262 jet fighter. But she was also carrying twelve hundred pounds of uranium oxide."

"Good God," Jack said, sitting back. *Of course.* "That explains all the secrecy at Bletchley. That's what the gold was for."

"Uranium for what purpose?" Jeremy said.

Jack pursed his lips. "In April 1943, the Manhattan Project was still a good way from coming to fruition, and there would have been a lot of concern about the possibility of similar research being carried out by physicists in Germany and Japan. By then Germany was beginning to receive the full brunt of the RAF and USAAF bomber offensive. The Americans in the Pacific had not yet taken islands close enough to put Japan within easy range of the US bombers then available. Japan would have been a safer bet for research and development, and the Germans may even have entered into some kind of scientific collaboration. They may never have been close to developing a fusion bomb, but uranium oxide could have been used to make a radiological weapon, a dirty bomb. If a few of those had been shipped back to Europe and put on top of V-2 rockets, Hitler could have devastated the population of London. That terrible possibility would really have stoked the fire under Churchill."

"And it explains why a line of Allied submarines were lying in wait off the coast of West Africa," Costas said. "They were hoping to catch those Japanese and German cargo subs."

Jack turned to Louise. "Some of those American officers you had your eye on at Bletchley might actually have been there to keep close to the action on this too. Roosevelt would have been as horrified by the possibility as Churchill."

"Fascinating," she murmured. "We didn't even know about the Manhattan Project, of course, though I do remember overhearing some of our Cambridge chaps in the pub talking about physicist friends who had disappeared off to America. It was only after Hiroshima and Nagasaki that we realized the reason."

Jeremy turned to Jack. "Back to *Clan Macpherson*. So what we're talking about here is a really audacious heist. The Nazis loved Hollywood gangster movies, didn't they? A high-seas robbery worthy of Al Capone. Japanese-trained agents take over the ship, transfer the gold to the U-boat, and ship it to Germany in payment for vital raw materials, maybe for a consignment of uranium."

Jack nodded. "And meanwhile British submarines, alerted to Yanagi by encoded Enigma decrypts, were strung out along the coast of Africa waiting to pounce on long-distance U-boats heading to or from Japan."

"So the sub that hit *Clan Macpherson* was diverted from that task, but actually by sinking the gold it was all part of the same game."

"The diversion ostensibly being because of the Ahnenerbe treasure on the ship, but actually to sink the gold as well," Jack said. "Quite astonishing. If we're right about this, then Fan really was only pulling away one veil on a much bigger story."

Louise picked up the third photo from the wreck of *Clan Macpherson* that Jack had taken out to show her. "Goodness me. Is that it? Nestled in among the gold bars?"

She placed the photo on the table, and Jack leaned forward. "It's an incredible find. Jeremy is certain that the lettering is Phoenician, and relates to the voyage of the Carthaginian explorer Hanno around Africa in the early sixth century BC. We think the Phoenicians set up markers to record their voyages at various waypoints, just as the Portuguese did two millennia later. It's not exactly a planting of the flag, but it shows those who might follow, colonists or traders, that they were on the right track. A big excitement from Jeremy's reading of the text is that it shows Hanno about to head north again, suggesting that this was set up at the Cape of Good Hope. The surviving medieval rendition of Hanno's *Periplus* stops somewhere on the west coast not far south of Senegal, and this is the first evidence that he went further and probably circumnavigated Africa, as many like me have suspected."

"Assuming that the plaque is authentic," Louise said.

Jeremy turned the laptop around and showed her his rendition of what could be seen of the text. "We went through that yesterday. I'm certain that these letters could not have been forged or duplicated. They're identical in style to letters we've been finding on amphoras from a Phoenician wreck off Cornwall. I did a reverse analysis, taking letters from the wreck inscriptions and re-creating the text on the plaque. It's virtually identical."

She clapped her hands. "So you used the Cornwall text as a crib. Just as we used to do at Bletchley."

"My doctoral supervisor, Jack's friend Dr. Maria de Montijo, made me learn all of the Bletchley code-breaking material when I arrived in Oxford to study ancient paleography. She said it would train my mind and would be bound to come in useful one day."

"So how does this relate to the Ark of the Covenant?"

Jeremy increased the magnification and pointed. "Take a look at that symbol at the end. It's not Phoenician but a hieroglyph, and indeed is probably Egyptian in derivation. To be more exact, it's a pictogram."

She stared at the little image of the two men carrying the box, and then sat up, smiling broadly. "Well, that really *is* satisfying. Everything *does* interconnect."

"Say again?" Jeremy said.

"Well, I've seen that image before."

Jack stared at her. "You've seen that pictogram before?"

"Not the original myself, but someone else's drawing of it."

"Go on."

The nurse came in, and checked Louise's IV. "Ten minutes, no more," she said. "Your physio is coming at two."

Louise waved her arm irritably. "No time for that. What's the point, at my age? It's keeping my mind active that matters, and I haven't had this much mental exercise in ages."

"We're almost done," Jack said. "It's been a marvelous visit."

"Well, I'm not done," Louise said. "Fan had her say in her letter, and now it's my turn."

The nurse turned to Jack, mouthing the words to him. He nodded, and she left. He turned back to Louise. "Do go on."

"When I dug up Fan's letter after you called, I thought about what she said at the end. About following the trail. I can't exactly go traipsing about like Indiana Jones, but I can do a bit of research of my own." She pointed to the desktop computer on the other side of the room. "You see, I've up-graded since the bombe. My grandchildren asked me how on earth we managed without the internet. Well, at Bletchley we wouldn't have trusted it an inch. It's a seedbed of misinformation and disinformation. The stuff we fed the Germans and the way we did it makes today's hackers look like amateurs. But mum's the word about that."

They watched as she wheeled herself to the keyboard and began typing. A few seconds later, a scanned document appeared on the screen. "Fortunately, what I wanted was available as an original document online. This is part of the Nuremberg Trials records. I wanted to check out Fan's story, to see if I could take it further."

"You didn't trust Fan's account?" Jeremy said.

"I trust her implicitly. But what anyone says is only as good as their sources. You're a paleographer, aren't you? Well, you deal with it too, all those scribal errors, deliberate changes and additions that are then copied down the line and become received wisdom, just as you get everywhere on the internet. Always go back to the original sources. Always verify, always double-check. The cardinal rules of intelligence gathering."

"Indeed," Jeremy said.

"This is the final part of the interrogation report of May 17 1947 on one Ernst Schnafel, a former Obersturmbannführer in the SS. That's not the army SS—the Waffen-SS—but the ones who ran the concentration camps and the Einsatzgruppen murder squads on the Eastern Front. A nasty piece of goods from a nasty bunch. Before that he had worked for the Ahnenerbe as a kind of bully boy who accompanied the archaeologists on their expeditions and roughed up any natives who stood in their way. I know about this because Ian Bermonsey had been at Nuremberg as part of the naval interrogation team shortly before he resigned and went to Canada with Fan. He spoke about it when we met up in Southampton for their marriage, and mentioned this unsavory character and his Ahnenerbe connection. Ian was something of an amateur archaeologist, having read classics at university before joining the navy in the early thirties.

"The transcript shows that Schnafel did indeed briefly mention his time in the Ahnenerbe, specifically an expedition involving agents in South Africa. At that point he became agitated because the chief interrogator showed no signs of accepting this information as a bargaining chip, and he clammed up. Apparently he'd already been interrogated by an American officer at the time of his capture in 1945, but I couldn't find a record of that anywhere. After the end of the interrogation at Nuremberg he was left with Bermonsey for half an hour to clarify some details about Kriegsmarine movements at the end of the war in the Baltic, where he had been captured. That night Schnafel found a way of killing himself in his cell. A pity, really. I mean a pity that he cheated the hangman, but also that he didn't say more."

"Is that how Fan knew about the code word Ark?"

"Ian must have got that out of him in that last half hour, after the official stenographer had left. Having mentioned agents in South Africa, that was clearly what he was about to reveal to the chief interrogator when he became agitated."

"Nothing more?"

"Not from Schnafel. But then I had a brainwave. I remembered hearing about someone who'd worked at Wewelsburg Castle, Himmler's headquarters for the Ahnenerbe. Not one of the SS, but a civilian girl who'd been a typist. Almost all of what she typed up was deliberately destroyed by the SS as the Allies closed in on the castle, but she told what she remembered to the intelligence officer of the US unit that finally took Wewelsburg in April 1945. None of it was of tactical value, and most of it was accounts of Ahnenerbe expeditions that the interrogator found too far-fetched to believe, real Indiana Jones stuff. So the officer didn't do a transcript of the interview and only made a brief report. It was one of my friends in the old West German intelligence service who came across it when she was remitted to archive the surviving Wewelsburg material on the Ahnenerbe, and I told her what I knew of Bermonsey's interrogation of Schnafel."

"You had friends in West German intelligence?" Jeremy said.

"I told you that my work didn't end with Bletchley. It was another war, another veil of secrecy. It helped that I'd studied Russian at university alongside math." Her monitor began flashing red and emitting a low alarm. "Oh blast," she said irritably. "This thing's telling me I need some meds. I do apologize."

The nurse entered the room, walked over, checked Louise's pulse and eyes, and hooked another tube into the IV on her wrist, taping it back up. Then she turned to Jack. "It's time to go. She needs a rest."

"Not likely," Louise said. "I haven't had this much fun since Bletchley. Anyway, I'm not *she*, I'm Louise."

"Yes, Louise. My apologies. Five minutes then, no more."

Jack nodded at the nurse, and she left. He leaned forward. "So where did you see that pictograph?"

"During her interrogation at Wewelsburg, the girl jotted down several images, and that symbol was one of them. She said that in late 1942, just after she arrived at Wewelsburg, she was assigned as typist to a Dr. Pieter Ritter, an archaeologist working for the Ahnenerbe. I looked him up. He seems to have been one of the more sane ones of the group, a genuine scholar, and also seems to have paid the price for it, probably for speaking out against some of the nonsense, as he disappeared in early 1944 and was never seen again. Anyway, all the US interrogator noted down was that Ritter had been in charge of a program called Ark, and that it concerned the Nazi hunt for the lost Ark of the Covenant."

"Anything else?" Jack said.

"The girl was well educated, a student of history at Heidelberg University before the war, so what she remembered can be taken seriously. She told the interrogator that the Ark had been in Ethiopia. No great surprise there, as the present-day Ethiopians believe it is hidden away in a church at Axum, as doubtless you know. But she also said that it had been discovered in the mid-nineteenth century by King Theodore of Abyssinia, in a cave in his mountain fastness at Magdala. She said there were those among the British expedition against Theodore in 1868 who knew the whereabouts of the Ark and were intent on discovering it themselves. One of them was the journalist Henry Stanley."

Jack stared at her. "But that expedition was to rescue British hostages."

"All I know is what the American interrogator decided to write down, what he found plausible, before closing the file. The war was still on, and his job as his battalion's intelligence officer was to collect any tactical information about German positions and movements ahead, not what he would understandably have viewed as fairy-tale Ahnenerbe nonsense."

"So we don't know whether they went there and hunted for it," Costas said.

Jack took a deep breath. "What we have to go on is that plaque. The Ahnenerbe archaeologists scoured southern Africa for artifacts in the years before the war. Some South Africans of Boer origin were not exactly sympathetic to the British, and there were many poor local people who might have been persuaded to part with artifacts that no longer had cultural meaning for them. Let's imagine that the plaque falls into the hands of the Ahnenerbe that way, perhaps aided by a thug like Schnafel. The war has started, and the problem is how to get it undetected back to Germany. The opportunity finally presents itself with the shipment of that gold consignment in 1943, and the plan to get it onto a U-boat. The Ahnenerbe archaeologists might have been able to make some headway with translating the Phoenician, and they may well have recognized the pictogram for what it was. Before that, aided by information we haven't yet got, something perhaps from Stanley, they may have gone into Abyssinia while it was under the control of their Italian allies, and made it up to Magdala. What happened then is anyone's guess."

The nurse returned and stood with her arms resolutely folded. Jack gathered the photos and stood up, Costas and Jeremy doing the same. "Thank you so much, Louise. Whatever happens next, you've played a very big part in this story."

"Game on?" she said, pointing at the books. "You see, I really *have* read them. How do my grandchildren put it? I can talk the talk."

Jack smiled broadly. "You can talk the talk. And yes, game on."

"Do you have to go yet? You haven't even had any tea. Let me get you some."

Jack saw the yearning in her face, the frustration. "We'll keep you in the loop. I'll email you with any updates."

She reached down into the bag hanging on the side of her wheelchair and held up a phone. "Texting is better. You can send pictures, too. And video clips."

"It's a promise. And then we'll come and see you again when it's all over."

"I *so* wish I were coming with you."

Jack leaned down and kissed her on both cheeks, and she smiled up at him. "Now I *like* that." Costas did the same, and then Jeremy. "My lucky day," she said. "You know, I don't think I've been kissed by as many men on one day since the war. That reminds me. There was a chap I used to meet behind the bombe hut—*not* my future husband, I fear. One day I wore lipstick and he forgot to clean it off. There was hell to pay from his commanding officer. Compromising hut security cavorting with a girl from another hut, or some such nonsense. Never did see him again, but there were plenty of others in the queue. Cheerio!"

Ten minutes later, Jack accelerated down the narrow paved lane that led from the house toward the main road, over cattle grids and through fields dotted with sheep and cows. "I've got my work cut out now," he said. "Do you remember me discussing with Rebecca the 1868 Abyssinia material in the Howard archive? It contains a manuscript by a Captain Edward Wood, a fellow officer of my Royal Engineers ancestor, but there's also some correspondence from Henry Stanley the explorer, among others. I glanced at it for the first time properly before we left Cornwall yesterday and it looks like fascinating stuff. I really want to get my teeth into it this evening and reconstruct the full story, to move from 1943 to 1868, to immerse myself in it. I'm quite excited by that, as I love those time shifts where there's an unexpected thread running between them, but most importantly I think there's a good chance of finding material in there that will help us make major headway with our quest."

"What you're saying is you've got that feeling," Costas said.

"I've got that feeling."

"That's good enough for me."

"You'll be busy too," Jack said.

"Not much call for submersibles engineers up in the mountains of Ethiopia, if that's where you're thinking of going."

"I meant while I'm in the library, you're going to be in charge of the Phoenician wreck," Jack said.

"What do you mean, in charge?"

"I mean in charge. Archaeologist."

"You must be joking. I can barely spell the word."

"Maybe, but after all these years you can talk the talk, just as Louise said. Anyway, Jeremy will help."

"Me?" Jeremy said, looking up from his tablet. "Bit nippy in the sea off England, I find. If you want any help in the Indian Ocean, though, I might be persuaded."

"I need you on site in case any more inscriptions come up. And in case Costas needs help spelling that word."

Jeremy's phone vibrated. "Will Rebecca be there? Anyway, I thought she was taking over the site."

"You should know. It seems you're engaged. Anyway, I'm going to need Rebecca's help with the Abyssinia material. Maybe that's her calling you now."

"Nope. Text from Maurice," Jeremy said, munching an apple and trying to read the screen as the vehicle bounced over a cattle grid. "Seems a bit miffed that you're not answering your phone. That's all."

Jack glanced at his phone. There were no new texts or phone messages, just missed calls. His pulse quickened. That meant Maurice would only speak to him personally, and that usually meant something big. He remembered Rebecca saying that he was saving up something he had found at Carthage. He pulled the vehicle up on the grass verge before reaching the main road and quickly returned the call. A familiar voice answered, cursed in German as the phone seemed to go flying and then issued instructions loudly in French, the sound of a muezzin's call to prayer competing with the roar of machinery in the background. Jack clicked on the speaker phone. "Maurice, is that you? Costas and Jeremy are here too. Tell us what you've got."

Part 4

16

Captain Edward Gillespie Wood of the Madras Sappers and Miners stood with his telescope on a ledge behind the battlefield, staring at the wide saddle that separated his position from the great granite plateau of Magdala less than half a mile to the west. It was an extraordinary sight, at the end of an extraordinary expedition. For more than two months since leaving their forward supply base at Senafe, he and his sappers had reconnoitered ahead of the main force, surveying, taking photographs, and tracing the road that had been hacked out of the rock for the animals to get through. On the way they had encountered almost every physical obstacle known to man: scorching salt pans on the coast, nearly impenetrable juniper forests in the foothills, terrifying ravines and defiles beset by rock falls, and almost impassable scree slopes, an obstacle course that only seemed to get worse as they ascended ever higher to the upland plateau of Magdala, a dead end that had made it nearly impregnable as a fortress.

Day by day the army behind them had progressed, inch by relentless inch, the ridges getting higher and the canyons deeper until finally, three hundred miles from the sea, they had reached the mountainous spur he was standing on now. He raised his telescope, training it on the entrance to the fortress. The crenellated mud–brick battlements seemed almost inconsequential set against the grandeur of the place, with sheer cliffs and vertiginous scree slopes dropping thousands of feet on all sides of the plateau except for the saddle in front of him. He had only ever seen anything like it at the ancient fortress of Masala in the Holy Land, another place where the besieging army of a mighty empire had forced an enemy into a desperate last stand, one from which escape was beyond all possibility.

He looked down to where he could see the entrenched troops on the edge of the saddle, his engineer's eye taking in all of the details. They were the vanguard of a force of nearly twelve thousand; among them were hundreds of mules from India and Egypt, dozens of camels from Arabia, still snorting and stamping from the noise of the battle, fifteen elephants, and the Armstrong guns that were shortly to be used to attempt a breach in the walls of the fortress. All of that had come grunting and bellowing and sweating from the sea, through sweltering days and freezing nights, through mountain passes that rose ever more precipitously until at the end there was only a narrow fissure above, barely wide enough to squeeze the elephants through. Even after they had reached the tablelands the rigors had not let up, as frequently they had been obliged to descend thousands of feet between the plateaus only to ascend again, pushing men and animals to the limits of physical endurance. And always there had been the nightmare of supply; they had found some grass and barley and meat and wood on the way, but not nearly sufficient, meaning that a continuous mule train of provisions was snaking behind them over the hundreds of arduous miles to and from the coast, making that same soul-destroying journey over and over again.

The smell of the battlefield was beginning to permeate the air unpleasantly; the sulfurous reek of gunpowder had been replaced by a sickly-sweet odor that he knew would only grow stronger. It always astonished him how quickly bodies left on a battlefield began to decay. Already the vultures had begun to pick away at the corpses; another day in this heat and the stench would be intolerable. It had only been a few hours since General Napier's disciplined infantry with their Snider–Enfields had lined up against the Abyssinians, pitting the latest breech-loading rifles capable of ten rounds per minute against shields and spears. It had all been over in a matter of minutes, leaving more than seven hundred of the enemy dead and many more wounded, the remainder having been driven back into the fortress at the point of the bayonet. With King Theodore's force now so depleted, it had become feasible to think of an artillery barrage and a frontal assault using infantry, a tactic straight from medieval warfare that Wood had never imagined he would see being acted out for real in a place so far removed from civilization as this.

The young sapper who had been struggling up the slope with the camera apparatus finally reached the ledge and dropped his burden, panting hard and sweating profusely. His skin was darkened by the sun and by the dust that seemed to penetrate every pore, finding its way into every conceivable part of the body, within and without. Wood offered him his water bottle, and the sapper took it gratefully, drinking deeply and then passing it back. "Excellent work, Jones," Wood said. "Now let's get the thing set up while the light's still good."

"It's too bloody hot, sir," Jones said, sinking back against a rock. "And I can hardly breathe."

"It's the altitude. We're over ten thousand feet up. There's about a quarter less oxygen in the air here than there is at sea level."

Jones gestured at the plateau ahead. "Down in the camp they say he's got gold up there, tons of it—mad old King Theodore."

"We're here to rescue missionaries, Jones, not to loot gold."

"Speak for yourself, sir, if you don't mind me saying. I'm not leaving this godforsaken place without something for my troubles. Anyway, I didn't join up to rescue missionaries, or anyone else."

"Why *did* you join up, Jones?"

"Well, sir, I joined the sappers to learn stuff." He gestured at the camera. "To learn photography, sir."

"Precisely. And now it's time you put your learning to good use and set that thing up. I believe that in short order we'll be called out for the final assault, and I want to get some pictures before that."

"Sir." Jones struggled to his feet and began breaking down the crate with the camera and extending the tripod.

Wood took up his telescope again, scrutinizing the plateau, and then lowered it and gazed at the battlefield. He thought about what Jones had said. They might just as well have been here to loot gold, given the absurdity of the real reason. The hostages had been taken by the Ethiopian king because his request to Queen Victoria for arms to defend his borders had gone unanswered: arms from the queen who had personally sent him a revolver as a present and had led him naïvely to believe that the weapons needed for his army would follow.

There was no doubt that Theodore was a sadistic monster, given to acts of bestial cruelty. A week before, Wood and his sappers had come across several of the king's native hostages, including the son and daughter of a local chieftain who had wavered in their loyalty and had their hands and feet chopped off and hung around their necks. They had been a pitiful sight, dumped provocatively in front of the British column, and Wood had shot them both out of mercy. Yet part of him felt slightly sorry for Theodore, perched up there in his eyrie with no chance of escape, with no hope of an honorable exit now, and with the scribbling newspaper journalists ensuring that his ignominy would soon be the talk of the world. They were here to save missionaries, unquestionably a humanitarian cause, even a noble one, yet they were really here to slap an ally on the wrist for flying too close to the sun, for being too cocky and for expecting Her Britannic Majesty to answer his call. Wood peered at the battlefield, seeing the dark haze that he knew was millions of flies beginning to swarm over the corpses. It was a slap on the wrist that had already cost over a thousand Abyssinian lives all told, with many more doubtless to join them rotting in the sun before this affair was over.

A small, dapper figure, not in uniform but wearing a pith helmet and a Colt revolver on his belt, came and stood beside Wood, notebook in hand, surveying the battlefield. "That's quite a sight," he said, his accent a curious mixture of Welsh and American. "I haven't seen anything like that since the Battle of Shiloh in '62, during the Civil War."

"Well, Mr. Stanley, you should be able to add your own memories of the sensations of war to your description, and make a fine account for the newspapers."

Wood remembered other battles he himself had seen, ten years ago in India during the Mutiny. The sickly-sweet smell had brought back images of horror, of women and children butchered, of fighting without mercy, of mutineers hanged and blown from the guns. He remembered not just the carnage of war but how shockingly quickly the veneer of civilization had fallen away: how the women who had come out from England, the memsahibs, those who had tried to create a fantasy of Wimbledon or Kew in the sweltering cantonments, had become hardly recognizable as human beings, tattered, begrimed, emaciated, their countenances lost in the settled vacancy of insanity. He remembered how the stench of the unwashed mingled with that of the corpses, the flies swarming around the living and the dead alike, a pestilence from Beelzebub himself.

No matter what the cause, no matter what the trigger that drove men to war, the outcome was always the same. Ten years ago, it had been a terrifying breakdown in order that had swept across a continent, seemingly unassailable, merciless; here it was the ludicrous business of a few missionaries taken hostage, and the delusions of a pitiful king. But looking at the battlefield now, Wood saw little that was different from the scenes of ten years ago: the same hideous wounds, the same rage and anguish, the same smell of fear and adrenalin, the same baying for blood long after the reason for war had been forgotten in the exhaustion and the scrabble for survival.

Another man joined them from the slope, an officer Wood recognized from General Napier's staff but did not know personally; a soldier labored up behind him carrying a large sketchpad, a folding chair and a satchel. "Baigrie, Bombay Staff Corps," the officer said, proffering his hand. "I've seen you and your men often enough ahead of us, but I don't think we've met. Wood, isn't it?"

They shook hands, and Wood gestured at the soldier's load. "I've seen you at your watercolors before. I understand that the *Illustrated London News* has taken them, and I offer my congratulations. It seems that you and I and Mr. Stanley are all of a mind being on this ledge and recording our impressions of this place, though my photographs are of a more prosaic nature, I fear, as part of an archive for the School of Military Engineering."

"Have you tried developing pictures out here?"

"Tried, but failed. A damned nuisance really. One of them was a picture I took two months ago at Annesley Bay before the main force had disembarked, while my company was employed building landing stages across those infernal salt flats. Right out at the edge while sinking a beam we discovered the frame and planks of a wreck, a very old one I believe, with a painted eye on the bow and alphabetic symbols incised into the timbers that I think were Phoenician. Some of the timbers had already been pulled up and reused by my sappers in the revetments, and what was left will, I fear, by now also have been destroyed, for the same purpose."

"You have an interest in antiquities?"

"I traveled on leave to Jerusalem and widely in Palestine last year."

"Then you'll know what they're saying about this place." Baigrie nodded his head toward the fortress. "About the treasury of King Theodore."

Jones had been listening intently. "Here you go, sir. I told you. Gold."

"Sapper Jones here has a particular interest in filling his pockets with loot," Wood said.

"As do two thousand other British and Indian troops encamped below. After what they've been through, they feel they deserve a bonus."

"Too right, sir," Jones said. "A bonus. For all my efforts."

"You'll get nothing if you don't set that camera up before sundown."

"Sir."

Baigrie watched as his batman opened out the tripod canvas chair and the satchel, laying out his brushes and paints. "What they're saying," he continued, "is that his treasures include ancient antiquities of the Israelites, brought here by the lost tribes of the Exodus as they fled the Babylonians after the sack of Jerusalem."

"Soldiers' rumors, no doubt," Wood said.

"Napier had a local chieftain in his camp last night, one of those who have been helpful to us. He had a priest with him who said there's a tapestry in the church at Magdala depicting a procession coming ashore carrying the Ark of the Covenant. He claims that the tapestry is exceedingly old, older even than the ancient Christian kingdom of Axum."

"We don't want some old bit of cloth," Jones grumbled. "We want gold."

"I think we'll all get our share," Baigrie said. "Napier has told everyone to pool what they find, and then he's going to hold a drumhead auction. The proceeds will be spread about the entire expedition according to rank."

"There are said to be ancient manuscripts in the church too," Wood said. "I just hope someone sensible gets in there first and keeps them from being destroyed."

"Not that I'll see any of it," Jones said ruefully. "Not much call for a photographer in the first wave of the attack. Those are the lucky ones who'll get their hands on the best of it. And I can tell you, not all of what they find is going to some drumhead auction, orders or no orders."

Baigrie took out a pipe and tobacco; he packed it and lit it while contemplating the grim scene below. "You know, after the Mutiny, I thought I'd never see anything like this again. Indeed, I rather hoped I would not."

"Where were you?" Wood asked.

"Central India Field Force, under Sir Hugh Rose."

"Sagar Field Division, under Whitlock. I know what you mean."

"I had a close friend in the Light Dragoons. We shared a tent on campaign. I was going to resign with him after the war and join him on his father's sheep station in New Zealand to start a new life. In the event I never did; I stayed on in the Staff Corps. But I'd had enough of war."

Stanley looked up from his notes. "Truth be told," he said, "I never was much one for war either. I left Wales to find a new life in America, but by unfortunate timing I became settled in New Orleans just in time for our great national conflagration. I believe I have the unique distinction of having served in the Confederate Army, where I had my baptism of fire at Shiloh; in the Union Army, after being having been captured and turned; and then in the Union Navy, from which I am sorry to say I jumped ship. Indeed, I garnered no military glory whatsoever from any of those unhappy adventures. It was journalism that saved me, and then I found I had a taste for exploration."

"I rather wanted to be an explorer too, and one thing this expedition has done is to give me a renewed taste for it," Wood said. "During my next furlough I'm determined to go north into Afghanistan to follow the River Oxus to Lake Aral. I want to see if there are any traces left of Alexander the Great's expedition."

Baigrie pointed the stem of his pipe at Jones. "And what about you?"

"Me, sir? Sapper Jones might become Corporal Jones, and Corporal Jones might become Sergeant Jones. That is, if the loot in that fortress doesn't make me King Jones."

They all smiled, and Wood glanced up at the sky. "Look, the sun has that brown halo around it again, the corona."

"Down in camp, they say it's an omen of blood," Jones said. "They say that King Theodore sees it too, and knows it signals his end."

"It's an atmospheric phenomenon, a result of the rising dust. The next time we have one of those terrific thunderstorms, it will go."

"Or the next time *we* create a thunderstorm, you mean, tomorrow when we take that place."

One of the local girls they used as messengers came running up the slope from the headquarters encampment and handed Wood a slip of paper. He read it, looked up and paused for a moment, then scribbled his name in

acknowledgment and gave it back to her. He watched her run off, mesmerized as always by the long, effortless stride and the ability of the girls to
run fast even at these altitudes without losing breath.

"Anything interesting?" Stanley asked.

"That was from Napier," Wood replied. "Apparently there are no other
engineer officers available to effect the breach. They don't expect the Armstrong guns to punch their way through, and want a charge to be taken
up. It looks like my lucky day. One photograph, and then I should report
to headquarters."

"Good luck to you," Baigrie said. "Not worth coming all the way up
here just to get killed."

"Hear, hear," Stanley said. "And bring me back a good story."

Wood put his head under the black cloth that Jones had set up, adjusted
the camera, and composed the scene. Shorn of sky and people the image
looked bleak, elemental, with hardly any vegetation or other evidence of life.
On the sides of the ravines rose high sandstone cliffs, scarped and water-
worn, so different from the mountains on the frontier of India that he was
used to; here, the weathering gave a certain sinuous beauty to the landscape,
almost a voluptuousness, but it was fragile and ephemeral, the slopes
and pathways liable to be swept away at any time by the torrential rains
that beset this place. This was what he had wanted to photograph, not
Magdala itself. He slotted in the holder containing the plate, removed the
lens cover for three seconds, then replaced it and got out from under the
hood, nodding at Jones to begin breaking the camera down.

He stared out at the encampment and the battlefield again, thinking of
what lay ahead. From the outset this had been an engineers' war, a war of
logistics and transport, of construction and mapping and reconnaissance,
as arduous as any they had ever experienced. They had built piers, roads
and railways, and condensers by the sea for fresh water; they had triangu-
lated, measured and photographed, had blown rock and spanned rivers and
ravines. For the first time he had felt as if he had used everything he had
been taught as a young officer, almost as if this campaign had been designed to parade the engineer's skills. But what he had been asked to do
now would be different, something that no amount of training could prepare him for. It was about inching forward, about finding his way up a re-
doubt under fire, about setting and blowing charges, with the bayonet and
the revolver taking the place of the pick and the shovel.

He pulled out his own revolver from its holster, checking the cylinder, pleased that he had replaced the old cap-and-ball Adams that had served him through the Mutiny with a new cartridge version, harder-hitting and far faster to reload. One thing they had learned from the Mutiny was that men crazed by fanaticism were very hard to put down, would pick themselves up and keep coming. And the Abyssinians had more to them than that, an obstinate, suicidal courage that they had shown in the battle that morning, a courage that had kept them charging again and again against a murderous fire until hardly any were left standing.

Holstering the revolver, he knelt down and helped Jones pack up the camera, then put a hand on his shoulder. "Oh, and Jones."

"Sir?"

"It looks as if you might get first pick at the loot after all. I'm going to need someone to help me carry up the charges, and then to cover me while I lay them. When was the last time you fixed a bayonet?"

17

Captain Wood shifted slightly to the right, wedging his body against the boulder at the edge of the precipice to stop himself from slipping any further down. He rested his revolver on a rock and pulled out his pocket watch, checking it and quickly resuming his position. It was a quarter to four in the afternoon; the main wave of the assault was due to begin at four. Before then the storming party was meant to have breached the thick timber doors and stone archway of the Koket-Bir, the entrance to the fortress, using the powder kegs that should have been brought up to him by now.

Already he and Jones had endured the initial British cannonade, a pulverizing salvo from the Armstrong guns and the eight-inch mortars on the saddle and the mountain guns and naval rocket battery on the ridge behind, the rounds bursting against the parapet and steep ground in front of them, showering him with rock fragments and leaving his ears ringing. Being put in charge of the reconnaissance party at the outset of the campaign had meant a pleasant alternative to the toil of joining the main expedition through the mountains, but in the past hour or so it seemed as if he and Jones were having their comeuppance, finding themselves at the sharp end of the assault against an extraordinary natural fortress and a deranged king who by now had no hope left and was bent only on his own destruction.

The wind wafted over the ridge from the precipice below, bringing with it a sickening stench of decay. Wood leaned over and glanced down the vertiginous slope, seeing the sprawled cascade of bodies at the base of the ravine, hundreds of them, all without hands or feet. The day before, Theodore in a rage had ordered all of his Abyssinian captives to be mutilated and thrown over the cliff from the plateau. Several of the corpses had already bloated in the heat and split open, the source of the terrible smell. He pulled out his pocket telescope and peered at a ledge about a hundred yards ahead, above a sheer drop at least three times that. Among the twisted, swollen limbs he had seen movement, someone still alive. He thought of taking Jones's rifle and finishing the poor devil off, as he had done the two pitiful wretches on the road a week earlier, but to do so would risk revealing their position to Theodore's few remaining marksmen on the ramparts above. The time for mercy was now over, to victim and perpetrator alike. All he wanted now was to see this day over and the enemy destroyed.

"What are we doing here, sir?" Jones said, ducking as a bullet whizzed by. "I mean, why are we trying to take this place?"

"For God's sake, man, this is hardly the time," Wood exclaimed, peering over the boulder and spotting the man with the musket on the parapet. Here, give me your rifle."

Jones passed it over and lay back against the rock, looking up at the sky. "I mean, old Theodore released the European hostages yesterday. That's what we came here for, isn't it? And it looks as if the Abyssinian hostages are all done for . . . or rather it smells that way. It positively reeks. If you ask me, sir, it's time to pack our bags and go home."

"That's a change of tune. Yesterday it was all talk of loot."

"That was before they started shooting at me."

A musket ball ricocheted off a boulder beside them, and Jones ducked down, his hands covering his helmet. Wood opened the breech cover of the rifle, checked there was a round in the chamber and snapped it shut again, then slowly brought the muzzle to the side of the boulder until it was facing the parapet. With the bayonet fixed it was going to be difficult to shoot accurately, but the parapet was near enough to give it a try. He pulled back the hammer, curled his finger round the trigger and waited, knowing that the marksman had an old muzzle loader that took him at least a minute to reload. On cue a few seconds later the man reappeared, poking his barrel above the parapet. Wood aimed quickly and fired, the kick of the rifle pushing him down the slope. He saw the man lurch forward, blood spilling from his chest, and then hang head-down over the parapet with his arms dangling, his musket clattering to the rocks below and discharging. The smoke from the rifle wafted back over Wood, pleasantly sulfurous after the ghastly odor from below. He pulled himself up and handed it back to Jones. "That's your job from now on. You're supposed to be here to provide covering fire."

"Sir." Jones fumbled with the cartridge box on his belt, and Wood turned around on his back, staring down the slope at the troops marshaling for the assault. The expedition had an overwhelming force of arms, but even so they had been lucky. The battle on the saddle the day before had swept away the finest of Theodore's warriors, and most of his artillery had been abandoned on the retreat up the slope. Had he chosen not to meet the British in open battle but instead to occupy and fortify one of the rocky ridges further back along the escarpment, he could have poured down a murderous fire and inflicted many more casualties.

The Abyssinians had shown extraordinary bravery, but Theodore was no tactician. The fortress looming above Wood now should have been impregnable, but the Abyssinian defense had been fatally weakened by the loss of most of Theodore's muskets and rifles on the saddle below. He had never faced a European army in battle before, and he had expended too much in pomp and show, all that was usually needed to subdue his recalcitrant chieftains. Somewhere up there was his greatest folly of all, a mortar of monstrous dimensions named Sevastopol, dragged all the way up here from the plains to the north. Even if his gunners could manhandle the half-ton ball into the muzzle, the quantity of powder needed to propel it any meaningful distance would blow the gun to smithereens. It was the farcical side of his madness, though at the moment any thought of that was subsumed by the murderous cruelty revealed by the horror spread across the ravine below.

Wood watched as the regiment chosen for the assault, the 33rd Foot, formed up below, seven hundred men in ten companies, with those on the flanks in skirmishing order, all with bayonets fixed, wearing the khaki uniforms and white pith helmets that had been an innovation on this campaign, far preferable to the old red battle order. Ahead of them he saw the storming party making their way up the slope, some thirty men of the 33rd alongside turbaned Indians of his own regiment, the Madras Sappers and Miners. A few minutes later, the officer of engineers accompanying the party scrambled up to his position, panting and dripping with sweat.

"Le Mesurier, Bombay Sappers," he said breathlessly. "I've got bad news, I'm afraid. The girl carrying the message to bring up the powder kegs and scaling ladders was shot down by one of Theodore's muskets. We're simply not going to have them in time for the assault."

"For God's sake." Wood snorted in anger, but then remembered the girl he had watched yesterday bringing the message from General Napier; he hoped she was not the one who had been hit.

Another officer joined them, a subaltern of the 33rd, and Wood could see the rest of the storming party spread out among the rocks just below them, awaiting orders. He turned to the two officers and pointed up at the parapet. "Do you see beyond where that body's hanging, about ten yards to the right? A tall man might stand on that outcrop of bedrock below the wall and pull himself up, or push a small man above him. There's a rather nasty-looking thorn and stake hedge on top of the wall, but I think it could be done. If we're not going to be able to blow our way through the gate, then this might be our only way up."

The infantry officer followed his gaze, and nodded. "I think I've got just the men for the job." He turned and whistled. "Private Bergin and Drummer Magner. Up here, at the double."

Two soldiers detached themselves from behind the rocks and scrambled up the slope, falling back against the boulder beside Wood with their rifles at the ready. One man was very tall, the other very short. The tall man crinkled up his nose. "That's a God-almighty stench, sir, if you don't mind me mentioning it," he said in a rich Irish brogue.

"That it is," the other man said, his accent equally thick, his free hand over his nose. "Positively disgusting, it is."

"Well the sooner you get on with the job I've got for you, the quicker you'll get away from it," the officer said. "You see that low point in the parapet ahead? We're going to storm it. You, Bergin, are going to stand on the rock, and you, Magner, are going to stand on his shoulders. How sharp are your bayonets?"

"Razor-sharp, sir. We ground them yesterday evening."

"Good. Because you're going to need them to cut through that hedge on the top. Understood? There'll be a medal in this for you if we get through."

Both men looked distinctly unenthusiastic. "Sir."

The officer spoke quickly to a sergeant who had come up behind him. The sergeant saluted and slid back down the slope, and the remainder of the party began moving up from their positions. The officer turned back to Wood. "Half of my men and all of the sappers are going to the gateway as originally planned, to try to find a way around it. From here it looks as if it's been blocked from behind by a mass of boulders, so your gunpowder might not have done much good anyway. The rest of my party is forming up here. I'm assuming that you and your sapper will be joining us?"

"Wouldn't miss it for the world," Jones muttered, tightening the bayonet over the lug on his barrel. "Just what I signed up for."

"Good. I don't see any more of the enemy actually on the parapet. They may have fallen back to the second wall, the one that leads into the fortress. If we keep our wits about us and abstain from unnecessary fire, we might achieve an element of surprise. Agreed?"

Wood and Le Mesurier nodded. Wood checked the chambers in his revolver and got up on his haunches. "I'm the senior officer here, so leading this assault should be my job." The infantry officer nodded, raised his arm, and held it ready to signal his men to advance, his own revolver at the ready. Wood knelt up, peered round the boulder and put a hand on Jones's shoulder. "Right, Jones. You're with me. Let's move."

Ten minutes later Wood emerged scratched and grazed from the thorn thicket on top of the parapet. Bergin and Magner had hacked their way through easily enough, but there had been no time for finesse and there were many vicious thorns still to negotiate. He dropped down on the other side, taking cover next to the two Irishmen, and waited while Jones came up cursing and grunting behind. Ahead of them lay about seventy yards of dead ground between the two walls, much of it variegated and rocky like the slope below, but more level. The inner wall itself had clearly been built for show rather than defense; Theodore could hardly have expected any attacker to get this far. Wood scanned the ground, revolver at the ready, looking for the few final Abyssinian defenders they assumed must be here. The imminent fall of the fortress now seemed certain, but they had all seen the suicidal bravery of the Abyssinians on the battlefield the day before, and they were taking no chances.

The officer of the 33rd slid down beside Wood, one side of his face scratched and bloody. At that moment there was the whoosh of an incoming shell and a deafening detonation some twenty yards to the right. Three Abyssinians who had been concealed there were flung into the air like rag dolls, their limbs and heads flying away and hunks of flesh splattering all around. The officer turned to the man who had followed him through the hedge. "Get the colors up now," he yelled. "On the parapet!"

He turned to Wood. "I'm not supposed to do this until we've taken the fortress, but it might stop our own side from shooting at us."

The soldier did as instructed, raising a pole he had been carrying and unfurling the colors of the 33rd, a Cross of St. George with a wreath in the middle and a Union Jack in the corner. They waited for a few tense minutes, but no further shell came. All eyes were on the patch of ground where the shell had burst, near the path from the outer to the inner gateway. Suddenly an Abyssinian got up, yelling and ululating, sword in hand, and then another; both were instantly shot down.

The officer turned to Wood. "Right. An old-fashioned bayonet charge should finish the job." He drew his sword and bellowed at his men. A pistol cracked from somewhere ahead, and he stumbled back, the bullet grazing his forehead.

The dozen men of the 33rd who had made it over the wall got up and charged forward, yelling and swearing, Wood following close behind. Two more Abyssinians appeared brandishing their weapons, one of them firing a flintlock pistol that sent a ball whizzing past Wood's ear. The Abyssinian stumbled backward and fell, and Wood heard a string of Irish profanities as Bergin lunged at the writhing body with his bayonet. Another soldier barreled into the second Abyssinian, dropping his rifle and clutching the man's head by the ears, smashing it again and again into a rock, bellowing himself hoarse. Wood could see that the Abyssinians had been well dressed, chieftains rather than foot soldiers, Theodore's last loyal guard. The rest of the army seemed to have melted away.

The soldier who had smashed the man's head was ripping the gold brocade from his robe; others were picking over the bodies ahead, several holding up shields and daggers as trophies. Looking back down to the outer entranceway, Wood could see that a route had been found around the boulders and the first of the main force were already through, their bayonets glinting. It could only be a matter of moments now before all resistance ended and Magdala fell.

He reached the path that led toward the inner gate, seeing that there was no door in this one to bar their way; through the passageway he could make out the thatched roofs of the houses on the plateau beyond. He and Jones advanced inside, hardly expecting further resistance now but still being cautious. Suddenly a man appeared in front of them, standing up from a cleft in the rock, a pistol held muzzle-down by his side. Wood aimed his revolver at the man's chest, but he had recognized his face and did not fire. The golden mantle, the braided hair, the wispy beard, and the white robe were all familiar from the illustrations that had garnished newspapers the world over for months now; only the eyes were different, not wide open in some caricature of madness but somehow anchorless, the eyes of a man who no longer knew the measure of himself, who had lost all grip on reality.

King Theodore looked at Wood, the pistol still by his side, and spoke in English. "Your queen has destroyed me. But you will not have our greatest treasure. It is no longer here, and will never be yours." Then he raised the pistol, put it in his mouth, and fired. A large chunk of skull and brains exploded from the back of his head and he collapsed on the ground.

Wood remained transfixed for a moment, watching the blood rapidly puddle around Theodore's head, then reached down and picked up the pistol, the smoke still curling up from the muzzle. It was highly ornate, with etching on the lock plate and silver inlay in the grip, and had the king's name on the escutcheon plate. He realized that it was one of the pair that Queen Victoria had sent to Theodore as a present, and that he had just witnessed the grotesque irony of the king using it on himself in the last desperate act of war against his erstwhile benefactor. He dropped the pistol beside the corpse, suddenly repelled. Someone else would claim it, for certain, but for now there were more pressing treasures to safeguard.

The officer of the 33rd came up beside him, his head swathed in a bandage. He stared at the corpse and then turned to the soldier who had hurried up behind him. "Get our Abyssinian. Tell him to call out that Theodore is dead. That should put an end to it."

Moments later the chieftain's son who had come along for this purpose with the storming party raised his voice and shouted, a high-pitched, penetrating sound that reverberated off the walls, repeating the same mantra again and again. Wood advanced past the corpse into the fortress, coming out among a cluster of thatched huts. In front of him was the gaping maw of Sevastopol, the huge mortar that Theodore had dragged up here at immeasurable cost in lives and energy and yet never fired, mute testament to the futility of the enterprise. To his left a group of emaciated Abyssinians stood with spears and shields on the ground in front of them; others were coming forward from the huts, dropping weapons and putting their hands in the air. Wood gestured to Jones, who advanced with his rifle raised and directed the men toward the others with his bayonet.

The rest of the storming party came streaming through the entranceway, the sergeant ordering several of them to take over from Jones in guarding the prisoners. The standard-bearer appeared with the colors he had brought from the parapet and now proceeded to mount them on the highest point he could reach above the gateway, making sure they would be clearly visible to the main force below. Seeing the red, white, and blue fluttering in the breeze, Wood knew that this really was it, that the game had been up the moment Theodore had put the pistol into his mouth.

He quickly took stock. There were wounded soldiers among the 33rd and the sappers, men such as the officer who had been grazed by the pistol ball, but, incredibly, they appeared to have forced one of the most formidable natural fortresses ever known without suffering a single fatality. That at least was something to be thankful for. Officially, the orders to the sappers on taking Magdala were to destroy the guns, mine the gates, and burn everything that was flammable: the huts, the palaces, the storerooms, only the church to be spared. But Wood was here as a reconnaissance officer, not in charge of a sapper company, and for a few crucial minutes before the main force arrived he might be able to limit the desecration that he knew was about to happen.

He turned to the officer of the 33rd, who had come up beside him. "For the time being I'm the senior officer present, so I'm taking charge. I want you immediately to post a guard around the church to prevent looting."

The officer nodded. "Understood. But it won't work."

"I'm obliged to try."

The officer told his sergeant to take a section of eight men across the plateau to the thatched building with the cross on top visible on the far side. They left on the double, Wood and Jones following some twenty meters behind. Wood's heart sank when he saw what transpired once they reached the church; the officer had been right, of course. The soldiers immediately stacked their arms and went inside, ignoring the remonstrations of the sergeant, who was the only one to remain at the entrance. Jones passed his rifle to Wood, ran ahead and went inside as well. Already other soldiers were spreading out over the plateau with firebrands, lighting one thatched roof after another, the flames flickering and crackling and leaping out with the wind, igniting the adjacent buildings. Wood could see that there was no way the church could escape that holocaust either, regardless of General Napier's orders, and that attempting to save it was going to be a lost cause. All he could do now was join the melee and try to rescue what he could.

He reached the entrance, holstered his revolver and leaned Jones's rifle against the others. Three soldiers came out carrying great handfuls of objects in gold and silver and brass: crosses and chalices, shields and crowns, vestments covered in filigree and gold. A boy stood at the entrance, weeping, seemingly not caring as the soldiers jostled him in their eagerness to get out with their booty. Wood ducked inside and immediately smelled smoke. Above him part of the thatch was already ablaze, spreading as he watched it. Some soldier had clearly been overzealous with his firebrand. He seized a handful of rolled manuscripts, passing them to another man, who rushed with them to the entrance, and then turned around looking for more. The smoke was billowing, catching in the back of his throat. One of the roof timbers crashed down on the altar, crushing a metal chest and spreading the fire to the rushes on the floor. He realized that Jones was nowhere to be seen, and then he saw that the soldiers were coming up with their booty from a hole in the ground, evidently some kind of crypt. He crouched down over it, and shouted, "Everyone out. The church is burning. Everyone out now!"

Two soldiers came struggling up the rock-cut stairs, attempting to carry a large painted triptych between them but dropping it. Another timber came down from the ceiling, bringing with it the ornate bronze cross that had stood on the roof. One of the soldiers lunged for it, but immediately sprang back, clutching his burned hand, and staggered away to the entrance, helped by the other man. Jones appeared behind them, carrying scrolls that spilled from him as he struggled up the stairs. One of the scrolls was larger than the rest, and Wood grabbed it, pulling Jones up with his other hand and pushing him toward the entrance just as another beam came crashing down.

They stumbled out into the open air, coughing, Wood still clutching the scroll and Jones a handful of others, all that he had managed to rescue. Wood picked up Jones's rifle, the last remaining one outside the church, and pulled him farther away, well beyond the flames that were now licking off the roof. They came to a halt under a stunted acacia tree some twenty yards farther on, and both went down on their knees, coughing and catching their breath. Wood peered at the other man. "I never thought I'd say this, Jones, but I had expected you to go for the treasure, and instead you would appear to have done a selfless service for mankind."

Jones dropped his armful of scrolls on the ground and began counting them. "It's not quite what it seems, sir, but thanks all the same. Yesterday evening at headquarters, when our role in the storming party became known, the archaeologist, Mr. Holmes, the one who often comes and talks to you, took me into his confidence and asked whether I would rescue scrolls for him, knowing that we would be among the first to come up here. He would have asked you, but he thought you might be constrained, sir. He promised to pay me straight up, no questions asked, five shillings per scroll, no need to put them in the kitty for the drumhead auction. Twenty scrolls here, that's five pounds, sir, not bad for a hard day's work, wouldn't you say? He wants them for the British Museum."

Wood coughed, and shook his head. "Well I'm glad there's something in it for you. It's still a good deed you've done. God know how many of them have been lost in that conflagration."

Jones gathered up his load again and stood up. "I've got to be going now. Two fellows from the 33rd are ahead of me, taking the other scrolls I managed to get out before you arrived. I've promised them both a cut of the proceeds. None of the soldiers think the old parchment and vellum is of any value, so nobody should bother them as they go down. But I need to be there to give Mr. Holmes's name should they be in any way harassed."

"And then you need to retrieve the camera. I want to take some pictures of the entranceway and the revetments. It's too late for much of value to be photographed inside the citadel, with everything going up in smoke, but we'll do what we can."

"Sir. I'll be at the bottom of the slope in an hour. Thank you, sir. I'll send the money home to my poor mother in Bristol. She'll be ever so grateful, she will."

"Right, Jones. I'll look forward to the postcard. And mother or no mother, you'll have to take your rifle, otherwise you really will be in trouble."

Jones looked at the rifle, then at the scrolls. He sighed, dropped the bundle of parchment, slung the rifle over his shoulder and laboriously gathered the scrolls up again, dropping one and nearly losing the rest as he stooped to retrieve it. Then he seemed to remember something. He stopped and turned. "Sir."

"What is it?"

"That one you've got. The big one."

Wood looked at the scroll he had picked up. "I don't think you've got space for it."

"Perhaps, sir, if you could, you might show it to Mr. Holmes? He might pay more for it, see, being bigger."

"Don't push your luck, Jones. Remember, what you're doing here is actually contravening General Napier's orders. If anyone finds out, that drumhead auction will also be a drumhead court martial for one Sapper Jones, never to be Corporal Jones or Sergeant Jones, and certainly not King Jones. Now get on with it."

"Sir. Thank you, sir. Bottom of the slope, one hour."

Wood watched him hurry off down the path beside other soldiers struggling with their own loot, then looked at the scroll he had kept. He could immediately see that it was not in fact a scroll but some form of tapestry. He undid the leather cord and rolled it out, holding it up under the shade of the tree so that he could see the design more clearly. It was obviously very old, the colors faded, and was an impressive antiquity, showing a scene that was perhaps biblical: two men carrying a shrouded box between them the size of a seaman's chest, another behind who looked patriarchal, with a braided black beard, and then behind him a cluster of horsemen, one with a lasso or whip and long hair.

He looked up, seeing that the boy who had been at the entrance to the church was watching him, standing by the tree. Perhaps he was the son of the priest, someone who might know the significance of this scene. Perhaps, indeed, this might be one for Holmes, for the British Museum. Holmes had become something of a friend on the occasions over the last weeks when Wood had been able to come down from the forward party and spend time with the headquarters staff of the expedition. It was he who had inspired Wood to think of planning his own archaeological expedition into Central Asia, something that he now had firmly in mind for his next furlough, an expedition for once without the dismal context of war and death and destruction, but purely for knowledge and gratification and discovery.

He turned from the boy and began to roll up the tapestry. As he did so, he saw the diminutive figure of Stanley coming up the path toward him, his pith helmet askew, clutching his notebook and pencil. "Mr. Stanley," he said. "We meet again. You have seen the body of Theodore? He took his own life. I saw it myself."

Stanley was covered in dust and looked shaken, pale. "There is nothing redeeming in what has happened here. Nothing redeeming at all."

Wood thought for a moment, and gestured at Stanley's notebook. "It will make a good story. Your readers will lap it up. That's all."

The acrid smell of burning thatch was beginning to disguise the reek of squalor and death that had pervaded this place. Soon, once the regiments of the expedition had returned to their stations in India, the proceeds of all that loot would be squandered in the way of soldiers, in the brothels and taverns of Mhow and Nowshera and Peshawar, drained away as if it had never existed. Well before then, a few hours from now, the smoldering remains of Magdala would be quenched by the torrential rains of the late afternoon, and the place would appear cleansed, the memory of this day swept down the eroded channels of the hillsides, flushed down the ravines to the sea.

Wood took out his handkerchief and rolled the tapestry inside, careful not to get any of it dirty. Looking down, he saw that his tunic was splattered with blood, and realized that it must have been Theodore's. He squinted up at the sun, seeing the curious brown corona still there, ominous and looming, and remembered what Theodore had said about his greatest treasure, wondering what he had meant. He tucked the tapestry under his arm; at least he had managed to save something. He took one last look at the burning church, seeing the black smoke twisting and writhing up toward the corona, then nodded at Stanley and turned to go.

18

Magdala, central Ethiopia (formerly Abyssinia), present day

A little over twenty-four hours after leaving Louise in the nursing home, Jack stood on the plateau of Magdala in the central Ethiopian highlands, the site of King Theodore's last stand against the British in 1868. Earlier in the afternoon he had scoured the saddle in front of the plateau for evidence of the battle, finding three corroded Snider–Enfield cartridges where the British line had stood their ground; further up the slope he had discovered the broken tip of a bayonet where the Abyssinians had been forced back by the British charge.

It was a beautiful summer day, the plateau and the ravines green with the vegetation that had not yet sprouted in the month of the 1868 siege, making it difficult to marry what he had seen with the bleak landscape in the photographs taken by the Royal Engineers just before the assault. But what had brought home the reality of the siege for him was the seven-ton bronze monster in front of him now, the mortar that Theodore had dubbed Sevastopol after the Crimean War battle of the previous decade. It had never been fired, and had remained on the plateau ever since, half buried and nearly forgotten. It was a reminder that Theodore, too, had engaged in a Herculean undertaking to get here, dragging this behemoth all the way into the mountains, cutting the road ahead of him as he struggled to reach Magdala before the British arrived. Reading the accounts from 1868, it had almost seemed as if some supernatural force had been attempting to prevent both sides from reaching the plateau, but having been here now him-self and experienced the terrain, Jack knew that this was no more than the overwhelming challenge posed by nature, a catalog of physical obstacles that would make retracing either expedition a monumental enterprise even today.

"Jack. The Patriarch is ready to see you now." A lean, wiry man wear-ing a shirt with the IMU logo over the breast pocket came up to him carry-ing the large picture-frame-sized package that Jack had brought with him from England. Zaheed was IMU's representative in the Horn of Africa, an archaeologist trained in Britain who had worked in Egypt with Maurice and Aysha, excavated extensively at the ancient site of Axum in Ethiopia, and recently relocated to Mogadishu to help get the Somali na-tional museum back on its feet after years of civil war. Jack had only met him briefly before, but had warmed to him greatly on their two-hour he-licopter flight from Addis Ababa into the mountains that morning. He was earnest and enthusiastic, with a deep-rooted love of his country and many contacts that had facilitated not only this encounter at Magdala but also the next stage in the trip, one that should see them meet up with Costas at Mogadishu airport that evening and then travel on to the Somali naval headquarters the next day. It was a tight schedule, with *Deep Explorer* now approaching Somali territorial waters, but the chance presence of the Patriarch of the Orthodox Church of Ethiopia at Magdala on a routine visit had meant that this was an opportunity not to be missed, particularly given the extraordinary item in the package that Jack had been able to bring with him.

He took a final photo of the mortar, focusing on the founder's mark near the breech. The verdigris on the bronze made him think of the in-credible image Maurice had sent him of Lanowski with the Ba'al sculp-ture at the bottom of the trench at Carthage, something that Jack had been unable to get out of his mind since they had spoken on the phone outside the nursing home; the gorilla skin was even more astonishing. Then he put his camera away in the old khaki bag that he had slung over his shoul-der and followed Zaheed along the path toward the church.

He was thrilled that there had been time to trace Captain Wood's move-ments in the final hours of the assault on that day in 1868. While Zaheed had hurried ahead to announce their arrival to the Patriarch, Jack had fol-lowed his path more slowly, making his way from the ledge where the helicopter had landed across the battlefield and up the boulder-strewn track, beside the precipice where the executed Abyssinian hostages had been found. At the ruined entranceway, the Koket-Bir, he had passed the place where Private Bergin and Gunner Magner had won their Victoria Crosses, the walls still pocked with bullet holes, and on the plateau itself he had found the stone that marked the spot where Theodore had shot himself and the British had cremated his body after pillaging all they could from his citadel and its churches.

Wood's diary had remained unopened since it had been brought back to England by Jack's great-great-grandfather in the 1880s, and discovering it in the family archive had been a huge excitement. After reading it, Jack had pieced together what he could of Wood's life in the years after Abyssinia, up to his sudden death from cholera in 1879; he had been particularly fascinated to read Wood's book on the expedition he had undertaken in 1875 with the Russian Prince Constantin down the River Oxus to Lake Aral, making archaeological discoveries on the way that Jack intended to follow up when he had time. The box in the archive contained one other extraordinary item, something that had stunned Jack when he had first unrolled it. He had taken it straight to the IMU conservation department and had received it back from them stabilized and framed just before leaving for his flight. It was that item that had made the presence of the Patriarch here so opportune, and that made Jack's pulse quicken as he followed Zaheed toward the circular thatched building with the cross on it at the western end of the plateau.

"He knows who you are, and is up to speed on IMU," Zaheed said. "He has a doctorate in theology from the Sorbonne and speaks English better than I do. He will quickly get down to business."

Zaheed opened the hanging curtain at the entrance and ushered Jack in. Sitting on a low chair in the center of the church was an elderly Ethiopian wearing a white robe and skullcap, with an elaborate metal cross hanging from his neck. On his right side was a low table, and behind him stood another man in white, evidently his assistant. The Patriarch raised his hand and Jack strode over to shake it.

"Dr. Howard. I apologize for staying seated. I greatly relish doing the rounds of these remote churches once a year, but I am not the spring gazelle I once was."

Jack sat on the stool that had been placed in front of the Patriarch, and

Zaheed pulled up another and sat alongside. "This is a very peaceful church," Jack said. "I like the simplicity."

"It is not exactly Westminster Abbey. Most of what was once here is now gone. The original church was destroyed when the British took Magdala in 1868."

"Before flying out here, Zaheed drove me past the Church of our Lady Mary of Zion, and the Chapel of the Tablet."

"Are you going to ask me whether you can see the Ark of the Covenant? Is that really why you are here? Then you would disappoint me."

Jack shook his head. "I have no justification for seeing the Ark. How could I, when for millions of believers the time of revelation is not yet here? To see it, to touch it with my hands, would be a marvelous thing, but to do so would be a travesty against those for whom the continuing conceal-ment of the Ark, the mystery of it, is what gives them hope."

The Patriarch's eyes twinkled. "Then you are not like other archaeolo-gists who have come asking me this question."

"Because most of them are not archaeologists. Most are treasure-seekers, chancers, looking for a best-selling book and a media sensation. To be an archaeologist you have to see that artifacts such as the Ark have a tran-scendent quality, a meaning greater than their physical presence. And knowing that to reveal an artifact to the world might shatter that mean-ing, as an archaeologist you have to be able to stop, to draw a line in the sand."

"And yet as an archaeologist you are driven by the quest."

"The quest to find the truth, to discover what happened. My line in the sand stops in front of the Chapel of the Tablet."

"Then I think we might have an understanding, Dr. Howard."

"Zaheed has filled you in on the background of why I'm here, the di-ary of the British officer who was present at the siege of Magdala in 1868. I now wish to make a gift, to the Ethiopian Church and to the people of Ethiopia, of something that was taken from this place on that day."

Jack nodded to Zaheed, who passed him the package. Jack withdrew a framed picture about two feet square and held it up for the Patriarch to see. "This was found with the officer's diary. He made a note that he intended on his eventual return to England to pass it on to Richard Rivington Holmes, later Sir Richard, the British Museum curator who accompa-nied the Abyssinia expedition, and this would perhaps have happened had

Wood not died suddenly of cholera in Bangalore in 1879. In the lower right corner is a note in his hand saying it was taken from the church at Magdala—this very church—on the day of the final assault, the thirteenth of April 1868."

The Patriarch stared at the picture, and then gestured for his assistant to come over. The two men talked excitedly in the Amharic language of Ethiopia, gesturing at the frame, and then the Patriarch turned to Jack. "This is an astonishing rediscovery for us. Do you know what it is?"

"It's a woven woolen tapestry. We were able to get a radiocarbon date in the IMU lab for a sample from one corner of the fourth century AD, the time of the Kingdom of Axum. But the image of the man with the braided beard looks much older, Sassanid perhaps, something that would fit more comfortably in Mesopotamian art of the early to mid-first millenium BC. And that doesn't take into account the image of the two large black men ahead of him, and what they're carrying. According to everything I now believe, that means that this image is drawn from an actual historical event of the early sixth century BC."

"A memory of this tapestry has been passed down through the Church, but I hardly dared imagine that it might still exist," the Patriarch said. "According to tradition, the man with the braided beard was Phoenician, and had brought the Ark by ship."

Jack reached over and pointed at a cluster of riders shown behind the man, one of them clearly a woman, with long dark hair and swirling a whip. "Do you know who these people are?"

"They look as if they're chasing him, but they're not. They're actually protecting him from the brigands of the coast, riding to his rescue. According to tradition, the prophets Jeremiah and Ezekiel had mandated a Judaic warlord of the coast to protect the Phoenician and escort him to the mountain cave with his cargo. She was Yusuk As'ar, meaning 'she who takes vengeance.' There were other Jewish female warriors like her throughout history—the mother of Dhu Nuwas of Yemen in the sixth century AD, the Berber Jewish Queen Dihya in North Africa a century later—but Yusuk As'ar may have been the fiercest of them all, a scourge of the Babylonians and the marauders of this coast."

Zaheed nodded in agreement. "A colleague of mine who is an expert on these traditions thinks she might even be the model for the stories of Makeda, the legendary queen who married King Solomon of Judah.

The traditions may contain a conflation of historical reality from those centuries."

Jack passed the tapestry back to Zaheed, and leaned forward intently. "The looting that took place after the death of Theodore is well known. I'm also interested in another period when Ethiopia was desecrated by outsiders. Do you have any knowledge of the Nazi Ahnenerbe coming here on the hunt for artifacts?"

The Patriarch pursed his lips. "The period of fascist rule from 1936 to 1941 was a dark time for us. Some of the looting was brazen, such as the ancient obelisk from Axum that still stands in Rome. My predecessors did their best to conceal the treasures of the Ethiopian Church. You've seen the Chapel of the Tablet, so you see we have some experience in that regard. But many lesser items went missing."

"Not just from the churches and monasteries, but also from the museums," Zaheed added. "We attempted an inventory a few years ago. Much of the material never resurfaced, so we think it must have been cached somewhere and never recovered, perhaps because it hadn't been removed before Mussolini's soldiers were driven out of the country in 1941. By then it would have been difficult to get anything back to Italy or Germany."

"You say Germany. So the Ahnenerbe *were* here?"

The Patriarch was quiet for a moment, and then nodded gravely. "I have never told anyone else this. But they were here, in this village on this plateau. The priest here now was a boy at the time and remembers it, but is still so stricken by what happened that I fear he would not talk to you. Three Germans came, two of them claiming to be archaeologists and the other some kind of thug from the SS, the sort Ethiopians had become used to under the fascist regime. They spent many days here, measuring, digging, going from hut to hut, interrogating. The priest, the boy, had been trained in his vocation by a German in Addis Ababa, so understood some of what they were saying. They appeared to be looking for anything that might have been left over when the British left in 1868. They had high hopes of treasure. They too were after the Ark of the Covenant."

"Did they find anything?"

The Patriarch pointed to the floor of the church. "There used to be a cavern under here, now filled in. For centuries it had been used to store the valuables of the church. When the British soldiers broke in, they ransacked it, taking that tapestry among many other items, but they failed to notice a sealed chamber at the back. Unfortunately, the Germans were very thorough and tested all of the walls, eventually discovering a hollow space. In it was the only great treasure we lost to the Nazis, a treasure that we had kept secret for centuries and a loss that we have not spoken of until now."

He turned and spoke to his assistant, who reached into an old wooden chest embedded in the floor behind the Patriarch's seat and pulled out a worn leather folio volume. He put it on the Patriarch's lap and opened it up, the parchment crackling as he turned the leaves. After about a dozen pages the Patriarch put out his hand, and the man stopped turning and stood back. The Patriarch swiveled the folio on his lap so that it was facing Jack, and looked at him. "This is an old illustration of it, made in the sixteenth century. That is what they stole."

Jack stood up for a better view and stared at the image, a faded painting of an inscription picked out in gold with the letters in black. For a moment he thought he was hallucinating, and he sat back down again, stunned, needing a few moments to marshal his thoughts.

"As you can see, the artifact was a bronze plaque with ancient lettering," the Patriarch said. "It was brought to us in the early sixteenth century by the Lemba people of southern Africa, who had safeguarded it for many centuries before that. They took it from their own safe place because of the arrival of the Portuguese, and the fear that this and other treasures might be discovered and taken away. They brought it all the way to us because in their tradition it had been they who carried the Ark up the mountains to this place, to the cavern in the rock; they could think of no better place of safety for their plaque than here. Their tradition was that the plaque had been set up at the southern cape by the mariner who had brought the Ark from the north, who took them on board to help him with his task."

"The Phoenician, the man with the braided beard in the tapestry," Jack said, coursing with excitement. "His name was Hanno. Without looking again at that illustration, I can tell you that there's a crude pictogram at the end showing two men carrying a chest on poles between them, surely a representation of the Ark. I know this because a little over a week ago, I was staring at that actual plaque, closer to it than I am to you now."

"Where could you possibly have seen it?"

"About a hundred and twenty meters deep, inside a Second World War shipwreck off the west coast of Africa. Seeing that plaque was what set me on this trail to begin with. We found it embedded among a consignment of gold bars from South Africa, and had reason to believe that it had been Ahnenerbe loot. But now we know where they found it, everything is suddenly falling into place."

"Can we see it?"

"You'll see the images soon enough, splashed around the world, along with some incredible finds that our colleague Maurice Hiebermeyer has just told me about from his excavations at Carthage. One of them, amazingly, is a gorilla skin, just as Hanno described in his *Periplus* as having taken back to Carthage. What's most astonishing is that it was flecked on the inside with gold in the shape of a box. I think it can only have been a cover for the Ark, removed on this mountaintop after the Ark had been taken away and concealed, perhaps inside the cavern in this very church."

"Perhaps," the Patriarch said, closing the folio. "Perhaps that story one day too will be told, of how a treasure that had been here for all those centuries, for a full two millennia before the plaque was placed inside with it, was taken out in secret and brought to its present place of waiting."

Jack nodded. "Perhaps it will. But for now we've nearly come full circle on our journey, just as we now know Hanno must have done, circumnavigating Africa, coming here, taking the skins back to Carthage, fulfilling a bargain he had made with those who had entrusted him with their sacred cargo."

The Patriarch put the folio on the table beside him. "Before you go, I have something I want to give you." He gestured behind him, and his assistant gave him a package. He unwrapped it, taking out an object about six inches square inside a blue covering, and passed it over, putting his hands around Jack's and the object as he spoke. "You will know not to open this. It's made of acacia, what the Israelites called *shittim* wood. Many Ethiopians have one of these. We call it a *tabot*, a tablet of the Commandments. This is our Ark, and now it's yours."

He withdrew his hands, and Jack got up, carefully placing the *tabot* in his bag. "I'm very grateful to you. Thank you for seeing us today. You've filled gaps in an incredible story, one of the most amazing I've ever been involved with."

"The tapestry will be a prize exhibit in the National Museum in Addis Ababa," Zaheed said. "It will join other artifacts from the 1868 looting that are being returned. We'll take it back with us in the helicopter."

"Where are you going now?" the Patriarch said. "Zaheed tells me there might be trouble brewing off the Horn of Africa. You need to be very careful if you're going to Somalia."

Jack gave him a steely look. "Being on the trail of the Ark has set us on another trail, one involving a particularly insalubrious treasure hunter and the possibility of a cache of loot from seventy years ago that might include some lethal weapons material."

"Is that Jack Howard the archaeologist speaking, or Jack Howard the former naval commando? Zaheed filled me in a little on your background."

Jack held out his hand. "Both. I've enjoyed talking with you."

"Perhaps, if you're on the trail of those Nazis, you'll come across some of those other lost artifacts from our museums and churches and be able to return them to us?"

"That would be my very great pleasure."

Part 5

19

Somalia, the Horn of Africa, present day

Almost exactly twenty-four hours later, Zaheed pulled up at a fenced compound on the outskirts of Mogadishu, the flat scrubland of the coastal plain on one side and the azure expanse of the northern Indian Ocean on the other. Jack was sitting in the jeep beside him and Costas was in the rear, having been picked up at the airport after his flight from England two hours previously. The compound was surrounded by rolls of razor wire and patrolled by pairs of Somali marines with Kalashnikovs, two of them having already approached the vehicle with their rifles at the ready.

"This is the new Somali navy operational command center," Zaheed said, switching off the engine and unclipping his seat belt. "It's used as a base for training marines, but you can see a couple of patrol boats in the harbor. Security's tight because they've recently had to fend off an attack by the Al-Shabaab extremists, a drive-by shooting, and then a drive-in suicide bombing. Stay here while I do the formalities."

He opened the car door, raised his hands to show the marines they were empty, and then got out, allowing them to surround the vehicle and frisk him. They gestured for Jack and Costas to do the same. An officer took Zaheed's papers and Jack and Costas's passports, scrutinizing them on the bonnet of the jeep. He spoke into a radio and asked Zaheed to follow him, and the two of them disappeared into the guardhouse at the entrance to the compound. A few minutes later they reappeared, Zaheed looking more relaxed, and the officer gestured for Jack and Costas to enter the compound. Zaheed spoke quickly to them on his way back to the jeep. "I'm leaving you two here while I go off to attend to some business. You'll be seeing the base commander, Captain Ibrahim, the second in command of the Somali navy. He's a good guy, one of the best. Where we go next really depends on what transpires here. Call me when you're finished."

Jack nodded, and they stood back from the dust as the jeep roared off. Two of the marines escorted them past the guardhouse and toward a complex of buildings that abutted the wharf. "Amazing," Costas said, gesturing at the patrol boat they could now clearly see in front of them. "That's an old Soviet-era Osa II missile-armed fast attack craft. Last time I saw one of those, it was hurtling toward my ship off Kuwait during the Gulf War."

"I remember them well," Jack said, following the marine to the entrance of one of the buildings. "While you were in the engine room of your destroyer, I was up the Shatt al-Arab laying charges under three of those boats with my team."

"To think we were so close, but we didn't even know each other then."

"It was a different world. There may have been a war on, but at least back then you could sail past the Horn of Africa without being attacked by pirates."

They entered a conference room with British Admiralty charts pinned around the walls and a table in the center. "Sit here," the marine said curtly, pointing at the chairs on the opposite side of the table.

"That's sit here, *sir,*" said a Somali officer who had followed them in. "This is *Captain* Howard, Royal Naval Reserve, and *Commander* Kazantzakis, United States Navy Reserve."

"I am very sorry," the marine said, flustered, looking at Jack. "It is my poor English. I meant no disrespect, sir."

"No problem," Jack said, smiling at the marine and then leaning across and shaking hands with the officer. "Captain Ibrahim? Thanks for meeting with us at such short notice."

"It's my pleasure." He shook hands with Costas and they sat down. Two other officers had followed him in and took chairs on either side.

Ibrahim was a slender, fit-looking man with a neatly trimmed gray-flecked beard and two rows of medal ribbons on his shirt. Jack looked at them, intrigued. "UK Operational Service Medal and Distinguished Service Cross?"

Ibrahim nodded. "After school in England and Dartmouth Naval College, I spent twelve years in the Royal Navy before transferring here. My father was a Somali diplomat in London and my mother's English. I was in Afghanistan with the SBS."

"Huh," Costas said. "Jack's unit. We were just talking about old times."

"My experience was nothing like Afghanistan," Jack said, waving his hand dismissively. "I was only on the active list for a year."

"You say that, but we knew all about you," Ibrahim said. "One of the chief petty officer instructors with the SBS had been with you during the Gulf War. They still use your operation up the Shatt al-Arab as a model for how to insert an underwater demolition team at night from an inflatable."

"That was a long time ago." Jack gestured at the window, where three patrol boats were visible. "What's the state of the Somali navy today?"

Ibrahim gave him a rueful look. "You've just seen it. Altogether we've got five of those patrol craft and two search-and-rescue boats. You'll recognize the Osa-class missile boat, obviously. It's the same craft you were up against in the Gulf War, with a few modifications. The P-15 Termit anti-ship missile is a bit of a Cold War relic, but it's still reliable. There's always a large amount of unexpended fuel in the nose tank of those missiles even after a long-distance flight, and that acts as an incendiary to complement the hollow-charge warhead, meaning you get something like an old-fashioned sixteen-inch battleship shell combined with napalm. Put that into a pirate trawler and it's curtains for them."

"Infrared as well as active radar homing?" Costas asked.

"Correct. We've just finished the upgrade. It increases the missile range to more than ten nautical miles."

"Any interdictions yet?"

Ibrahim shook his head. "We're only on the cusp of becoming properly operational again. The navy didn't even exist a few years ago, having been disbanded more than twenty years back when the country went into meltdown. That's how the problem with piracy really took hold. Even now we're barely effective as a coast guard, with three thousand kilometers to patrol."

"What's the range of your vessels?" Costas asked.

"Eighteen hundred nautical miles at fourteen knots," he replied. "The two boats that aren't here are based further up the Horn of Africa, so we can reach anywhere in the Economic Exclusion Zone within twelve hours. It's not enough boats to give us the response time to a call of distress from a merchant ship that we'd like, but it's better than nothing. From the northern base we've operated joint patrols with the Yemeni navy into the Red Sea and around the island of Socotra."

"What's their armament other than missiles?" Costas said.

"Two AK-230 twin thirty-millimeter guns, two thousand rounds apiece. It's yet more ex-Soviet equipment, but we look after it well and it works."

"What is the situation with piracy at present?" Jack asked. "The current commander of Combined Task Force 150 in Bahrain is an old friend of mine, but I've left contacting him until liaising with you first."

Ibrahim leaned back. "CTF 150 have kept things at bay over recent years and the number of incidents has dramatically decreased. But with the new US administration reconfiguring its role in the war on terrorism, the increased focus on tension with Iran, and the need for a greater Mediterranean naval presence to counter terrorism there, the naval assets off the Horn of Africa are no longer what they once were. We've learned the hard way that once a problem appears to be resolved and others take the limelight, the political will of supporting nations to continue their commitment dries up."

"There's just too much else going on," Jack said.

Ibrahim nodded. "The continuing refugee crisis in the Mediterranean, the war in the Middle East sucking in more and more players, the conflict with the terrorists in Libya, our own battle against Al-Shabaab in the south of the country. Meanwhile, the fishing economies of the Somali coastal villages have collapsed again, as the foreign factory ships have returned to transgress in our territorial waters, something we're virtually powerless against with a few patrol boats. As a result, our fishermen have become desperate and are open once again to offers of money to go out and prey on foreign merchant ships, and the problem with piracy has reignited. Over the last six months alone there have been eight attacks, with millions paid in ransoms. Of course, hardly any of it goes to the men who actually do the dirty work."

"There's always a paymaster," Jack said grimly. "Who's behind it all?"

Ibrahim pursed his lips. "For the terrorist organizations, the Somali coast is more important as a recruiting ground for foot soldiers. We're not talking about suicide bombers, fanatics, but about cannon fodder, low-cost mercenaries who are expendable and easily replaced. It's these guys we're killing when we take on the terrorists just as much as the naïve Western recruits and the hard-core jihadists."

"So the extremists aren't interested in the actual piracy operations."

Ibrahim shook his head. "A few million dollars raised annually from ransoms would be nothing for them compared to the huge amounts they're making from controlling the oil supply in the Middle East and Libya. They know that if we detected that kind of involvement in piracy, the Western response might count badly against them. We're not talking drone strikes, military action, but about cyber warfare, shutting down bank accounts and stopping transactions. Unless a ransom is paid in hard cash, those demanding it have to reveal banking details somewhere along the line in order to get paid, and that's their Achilles heel. Most of the terrorist organizations have astute financial management and are very careful to avoid anything like that. Even their recruiting activity among the villages is difficult to pin down, because they use the same agents as the ones used by those who bankroll the pirates. A few hundred dollars changes hands, a few more young men disappear either out to sea or to the terrorist training camps in the north, and some of them never return. Gradually the fishing communities have the lifeblood sucked out of them. It's become the way of life here."

"So who pulls the purse strings for the pirates?" Costas asked.

Ibrahim gave them a grim look. "Western investment consortia, hedge fund operators, working through so many layers of financial complexity that they're impossible to identify. We're not talking about some evil mastermind here, just about those same brokers who will quite happily put money into arms companies that sell to despotic regimes, or drug companies that hike up their prices when they have a monopoly. When you try to understand how a child soldier can gun down his neighbors in central Africa, or a mother die untreated in a village because she can't afford the drugs, it's the same as seeing a bullet-ridden pirate floating in the sea off Somalia or a terrified hostage in a ransom video. The real culprit is the ordinary investor living in Western affluence where these realities can barely be imagined, who hands his money to a broker with instructions to reach a certain profit margin. For those down the line who channel the money to the frontlines, it makes no odds whether it's oil exploration or mining or pharmaceuticals or armaments or piracy, and morality rarely comes into it.

"You can add to that list the problem we have with overfishing. With the upwelling of the current along this coast, these should be the richest waters off Africa, and yet our fishermen are among the poorest. Why? Because foreign fishing companies underwritten by Western investors took advantage of the anarchy in Somalia to dispatch large trawlers and factory ships into our waters, knowing that we had no way of policing them. The result is that our fish stocks were decimated and have only just begun to recover. More Western investors reap profits, more of our people fall below the breadline as a result. That's the reality of capitalism and the Third World for you."

"We see something of the same with treasure hunting," Jack said. "The investors who fund it through similar kinds of consortia are often decent people who are likely to be appalled when they see images of the destruction of ancient sites by terrorists, and who love to visit museums with their children. Few of them have any idea that their money is contributing to the wanton destruction of archaeological sites in the search for loot."

Ibrahim nodded thoughtfully, and then straightened up, looking at his watch. "So. What can I do for you? Zaheed is an old friend, and of course I wanted to meet the famous Jack Howard. But you didn't come here to fight pirates."

Jack took out his phone, opened a photo, and pushed it across the table. "What do you know about this vessel?"

Ibrahim glanced at the image. "*Deep Explorer.* Zaheed told me you were on her trail. We've been tracking her for the past three days, since she came up on our screens. She's owned by a salvage company of the same name, specializing in shipwrecks. You, of course, will know all about them."

"Costas and I were the UN monitoring team two weeks ago that checked out a Second World War wreck off Sierra Leone they were intending to rip apart. Let's just say the outcome didn't exactly go in their favor. I know their boss personally, a guy named Landor, what makes him tick. Our own IMU satellite monitoring told us that they'd sailed from Sierra Leone around the Cape and into these waters. Have you seen anything to indicate why they're here?"

"They've stayed just beyond territorial waters, so they're outside our jurisdiction. When they first appeared, we ran the usual background check and everything seems legitimate: registration, officer qualifications, all the paperwork in order. There was no obvious cause for concern—that is, until yesterday morning."

Jack stared at him. "Go on."

Ibrahim gestured to one of the officers beside him, a young bearded man, immaculately turned out. "I'd better let Lieutenant Ahmed take over. This has been his operation."

The officer stood up abruptly, speaking perfect English. "Firstly, Dr. Howard, let me say what a huge pleasure it is to meet you. I'm a keen diver and an avid follower of all your adventures, those of Dr. Kazantzakis too," he said, nodding toward Costas. "If there's anything I can do to help, especially underwater, please let me know."

"Much appreciated, and we will," Jack said, smiling. "Now, tell us what you've got."

Ahmed pointed at the chart on the table. "At about 1100 hours yesterday, four crewmen from *Deep Explorer* came ashore in a Zodiac at this village on the northeastern Somali coast. We have informants in all of the main coastal villages, so we were kept abreast by phone of everything that went on. They recruited one of the most notorious of the pirate gangs. The pirates call themselves *badaandita badah,* 'saviors of the seas,' which the leader of this gang has abbreviated to Badass Boys. Unlike the local Somali men who have been forced into piracy by unemployment, the Boys are thugs from Mogadishu and further inland, former street gunmen who have only known war. Their leader, who spent his teenage years in America and goes by the name of the Boss, has only just got out of jail. Each time he's imprisoned he gets out on a technicality, we think because the Western investment operatives who fund him pay backhanders to the judiciary. He and the Boys have orchestrated half a dozen ship seizures over the past year and several million in ransom payments. He's also a brutal sadist, responsible for numerous murders, including his own gunmen when they displease him."

"I can't believe the *Deep Explorer* people have gotten involved with piracy," Costas said, shaking his head. "They may be unscrupulous, but that would be sheer madness."

"They've recruited the pirates as players, but we believe their objective has nothing to do with piracy." Ahmed sat down, pulling his chair up and leaning forward, looking at Jack intently. "My club has dived the Somali coast extensively since things became more settled here, and we know the location of many shipwrecks. Several of us have a special interest in wrecks of the Second World War, and we've researched them comprehensively, including original documentation from Italian, German and Allied observers who were based in this region. There aren't that many along this coast because it was away from the main theaters of war, but one of the most intriguing is the account of a Type XB U-boat, *U-409.*"

Jack stared at him. "What do you know about it?"

"She was last seen on the twenty-sixth of May 1945, almost three weeks after the war with the Nazis had ended. Her last known position was off the southern Somali coast, when she was spotted by a USAF Liberator out of Aden carrying out a routine patrol. It was assumed that she'd surfaced preparatory to surrendering, but she dived after the aircraft came into view and was never seen again."

"What was her course?"

Ahmed laid a ruler on the chart. "According to the Liberator's log, the U-boat was heading at approximately 230 degrees. From her recorded position, that puts her on a course directly for the Socotra archipelago."

Jack looked keenly at Ahmed. "Is anything else known about her?"

Ahmed shook his head. "Very little. It's as if she'd been erased from history."

"At that point there were U-boats taking fleeing Nazis and their possessions to safety, weren't there?" Ibrahim said. "Isn't that how some of them reached South America?"

"The northwest Indian Ocean seems a pretty unlikely place to try and establish a new Reich," Ahmed said.

Costas looked at him. "Weren't the Type XB cargo subs used in the secret trade between Germany and Japan?"

"Exactly what I was thinking," Jack replied, remembering what Louise had told them a few days earlier. "The exchange of gold for raw materials and technology. *U-234* is a documented example, captured at the end of the war in the North Atlantic with arms, medical supplies, optical glass, even a broken-down Me 262 jet fighter, all destined for Japan in exchange for gold."

"If gold is in the offing and the *Deep Explorer* researchers have got wind of it, then that's surely enough to explain their presence here," Ibrahim said.

Jack thought hard for a moment. He remembered his encounter at the

National Archives with Collingwood, the indications that he had been on to something new for *Deep Explorer* and Landor to find in these waters. Everything was beginning to fall into place.

"*U-234* was carrying something else, wasn't she, Jack?" Costas said quietly.

Jack felt himself go cold, and swallowed hard. "Yes, she was," he said. "It was classified for years after the war, kept secret by the US intelligence officers who emptied her after her capture. She was carrying fifty lead cubes about ten inches across labeled U-235, as well as gold-lined lead cylinders with the same label. U-235, just to be clear, is not a U-boat designation."

"Uranium-235," Ahmed said. "Uranium oxide."

"About twelve hundred pounds of it, enough to yield almost eight pounds of U-235 after processing," Jack said. "It's thought that the Americans who captured it sent it on in secret for use in the Manhattan Project, and that it may even have ended up in the Hiroshima and Nagasaki bombs, a terrible irony if so, given that it had been destined originally for use by Japan. It would have made up about ten percent of the fissile material needed for one of those bombs. In its unrefined state, anyone with basic bomb-making knowledge could use it to make dozens of dirty bombs, enough to irradiate cities across the world."

"Good God," Ibrahim said quietly. "That raises the stakes horrifyingly."

"Landor wouldn't stoop to that, would he?" Costas said. "The only possible takers would be terrorists."

Jack gave him a grim look. "I don't think he has much in the way of morality left."

Costas tapped the map. "What I still don't understand is where the U-boat was going. Were there any supply bases in this area?"

Ahmed leaned forward, looking at Costas intently. "With this coast being under Italian control in the early part of the war, it seemed conceivable that they might have built a secret pen for their long-distance submarines. The breakthrough came when my club was diving off the village of Bereeda in the northeastern extremity of Somalia, only fifty nautical miles from the nearest islands in the Socotra archipelago. An old fisherman who knew of our interest in Second World War wrecks told us that he had seen an Italian cargo ship anchor close to one of the islands during the summer before the war started, and unload heavy machinery. The ship remained

there and men carried on working at the island for several months afterward, and then they disappeared. There was little to be seen for all their
efforts except a small naval coast guard station, and he and the other
fishermen were warned off when they got too close. He never returned to
the island after the war, as the fishing was no longer any good."

Costas looked at Jack. "What drives a U-boat captain to take his sub to
a secret pen way off the route between the Atlantic and Japan after Germany's war is finished?"

"Turn the question on its head," Jack replied. "What would drive a
U-boat captain to continue delivering his cargo to Japan? Not all U-boat
captains were fervent Nazis, and by that stage many of them probably just
wanted the war to be over. And even for the Nazis among them, there was
little love lost for the Japanese and little interest in furthering their cause
after Germany had been defeated."

"So you're saying he found a bolthole to ride it out, a secret pen far
from the war zone?"

"Possibly more than that," Jack said. "If he was also carrying a consignment of gold, he and his crew might have been able to get something out
of the war after all."

"Providing they hadn't irradiated themselves as well," Costas said.
"Maybe that's why the fish all died out."

Jack turned to Ahmed. "Can we speak to the fisherman?"

Ahmed glanced at Ibrahim. "He disappeared two days ago. His boat is
still in the harbor, and his wife said that men came in the night for him.
I'm afraid that happens quite a lot around here, but there's been a particular development that might explain this case. Over the last few days, since
Deep Explorer arrived offshore, there have been questions asked all along
the coast about the location of wrecks. The men asking the questions are
the same agents who normally recruit for the pirates or for the terrorists,
and we think they've been paid by someone who came ashore from the
ship. One of them was questioning fishermen in Bereeda the day before
the old man disappeared."

Jack exhaled forcefully. "Do you know where the island is?"

Ahmed put a finger on the chart. "Near the islands of Samhah and
Darsah, within the archipelago that lies between Socotra and the Somali
mainland. The island is uninhabited, though nominally under Yemeni
control. We haven't had a chance to get out there yet."

Jack turned to Ibrahim. "Let's assume that our friends on *Deep Explorer* have got hold of this account of *U-409*. How do you think they are going to play it?"

Ibrahim thought for a moment, and then pointed at the chart. "*Deep Explorer* is here, about two days' sailing from Socotra. We know they've employed the Badass Boys from their base about two thirds of the way up the coast, only about a hundred nautical miles from the island. During piracy raids, the Boys operate from a trawler that acts as a mother ship to the fast skiffs they use to board the merchant vessels. Here maybe *Deep Explorer* is the mother ship, and the trawler is the vessel that's going in. The trawler would be far less conspicuous, a factor of particular concern with the Iranians beginning to fly aggressive sorties along that sector."

Jack's mind was racing. If there were a secret U-boat base on the island, could it also have been a place used by the Ahnenerbe to store the artifacts they had stolen during their expeditions in northeast Africa, from places such as Magdala? It would have made sense to transport the artifacts back to Germany by U-boat, a plan that might have been stalled indefinitely while the sea lanes were controlled by the Allies. He stared at the chart, looking at the island of Socotra and the smaller cluster to the west, midway between the Horn of Africa and the Arabian shore. Then he glanced up at Ibrahim. "You say you have good cooperation with the Yemeni navy?"

The other man nodded. "The trouble is that they're about as well equipped as we are, and preoccupied with their own civil war as well as the Iranian situation."

"I'll speak to my friend in command of Combined Task Force 150," Jack said. "But my guess is that they'll only be able to react if there is an imminent threat or an incident, and what we're able to tell them now with certainty won't be enough to justify sending a warship when they're under such pressure elsewhere. Our own research ship, *Seaquest*, is getting here as fast as she can from her current project off Sri Lanka, but that will be several days, and I'd only be willing to commit her to those waters with a CTF 150 escort, especially given the increasing threat of air attack from the Iranians."

Ibrahim sat upright. "Then we have no choice. This is a situation that calls for direct action. I'm going to authorize the deployment of our own assets."

"How soon can you get us out to that island?"

Ibrahim glanced at the officer on his other side. "Commander Fazahid and I will work up the operational details. My plan would be to send one of the two missile boats based in the northeast of the country, the closest we have to the island. We'll fly you up with a section of marines by helicopter to join the boat and be ready to embark within twelve hours. I will take command of the vessel myself. Even if we overtake the trawler, we have to work on the assumption that the pirates might already be on the island, and that there could be a showdown. The Badass Boys sound like a joke, but I assure you they are not. They're hardened fighters from Mogadishu who were involved in numerous atrocities before they were recruited into the gang. They show no mercy, and we will show them none either. With these people, you shoot to kill."

Jack got up, took out his phone and glanced at his texts. "Zaheed's outside waiting for us now. I need to update him and get in touch with IMU, and then visit the British Embassy."

Ahmed got up as well, picking up his cap. "If we're looking at a submarine pen dug into the rock, it's going to be at least partly submerged. I'm guessing that we might be needing some diving equipment."

"Always a good idea," Jack said. "You can liaise with Costas about that. And he had a point about the possibility of radioactivity. We'll want NBC suits just in case, enough for all of the marines and crew as well."

Ahmed nodded, and Ibrahim got up too. "We plan to meet back here at 1800 hours ready to go. We'll gear you up and feed you in the mess. And one thing before you go. Are you armed?"

"Zaheed is, but we're not."

"You need to watch your back in Mogadishu. This place is crawling with kidnappers, and with informants. By now someone will have noticed you and passed on the word, and your friends on *Deep Explorer* will probably know. If that old fisherman could be snatched in broad daylight, then so could you. The last thing we want is Jack Howard being held for ransom, or, more likely, found floating face-down off the coast with a bullet in the back of his head. On your way out, the corporal here will escort you to the armory and have you issued with side arms and body armor. Only do what's absolutely necessary in Mogadishu and get back here as soon as possible. Two of my marines will accompany you in Zaheed's vehicle."

"Understood," Jack said. "Thank you."

Ibrahim gave Jack a steely look and offered his hand. "It will be a pleasure working with you."

Jack gripped it. "Likewise."

Costas finished penciling a list of equipment requirements, and slid the note over to Ahmed. "No expense spared. We'll cover it all and then give you and your club the dive trip of your lives when *Seaquest* arrives and this is all over."

Ahmed beamed at him. "That would be excellent. I can't wait to tell them."

Costas scratched his stubble and peered up at Jack. "Looks like we're in it again. Game on?"

Jack pocketed his phone and took a deep breath. "Game on."

20

Two hours after leaving the Somali naval headquarters, Jack stood inside the heavily fortified compound of the British Embassy in Mogadishu, itself within the security perimeter of the international airport. He was wearing the body armor that they had been issued at the naval armory along with side arms, but he had removed his helmet and handed in the Beretta to the Royal Marines sentry when he had entered the compound an hour before. He looked up at the Union flag flapping over the entrance, feeling the heat of the sun on his face. Like the Somali navy, the embassy had been shut down when the city had descended into anarchy in 1991, and had only been re-established at its new site a few years ago.

Gone were the days when Mogadishu was the most dangerous place on earth, a lawless battleground for rival clans, but the war against the Al-Shabaab extremists was a constant backdrop, and gang violence bubbled just beneath the surface, kept at bay only by the African Union military presence, which meant that large parts of the city were in virtual lockdown. Three times on the way in they had heard eruptions of gunfire, the distinctive clacking sound of Kalashnikovs, and Zaheed had driven at breakneck speed between the checkpoints. Like so many who were now trying to save Somalia, he had fled Mogadishu in 1991 as a teenager to live in the West, but he had been back long enough to know the dangers of travel through a city that was always at risk of another meltdown.

Jack returned to the entrance and retrieved his helmet and Beretta from the sentry, checking the magazine before replacing the gun in the holster on his waist. He had needed to visit the embassy to explain their presence in Somalia to the ambassador, and to outline a possible aid program for the fishing communities with a visiting UK international development official. Meanwhile, Zaheed and Costas had gone to the National Museum to deliver a restored Arabic manuscript that Costas had brought with him from the IMU conservation department; they had dropped Jack at the embassy and sped off in the Toyota, Zaheed still at the wheel and the two Somali marines in the rear seat. That had been over an hour ago, and they were due back soon.

Jack checked his phone, seeing only the text that Costas had sent him ten minutes before, saying that they had left the museum. He wanted to get back to the naval base so that Costas could liaise with Ahmed and check through the diving equipment they had requested. He was feeling jittery, anxious to get on the move, his thoughts already dominated by the long trip on the patrol boat toward the island they had planned for that night, excited and apprehensive about what might lie ahead.

There was another burst of gunfire, this time much closer than previously, somewhere near the airport perimeter. Two long bursts of Kalashnikov fire were followed by a succession of single shots from a handgun, and then there was silence. The marine sergeant in charge at the sentry post spoke into his shoulder mike. "Shooting incident on the outer perimeter. Red alert. I repeat, red alert."

Four of the marines immediately assumed prone positions behind sandbags on either side of the entrance, their rifles aimed, and another hurried from the sentry post with a scoped sniper rifle, taking position behind a berm some ten meters along the wire. The marine sergeant glanced at Jack. "There's usually some kind of shootout on the airport perimeter a couple of times a month. A suicide car bomber is our main concern, the possibility of a vehicle getting through the perimeter security and heading our way."

Another four shots rang out, handgun again rather than rifle, followed by another burst from a Kalashnikov. Jack had been counting the pistol shots. That was fifteen, a full Beretta magazine. He suddenly felt a cold jab of apprehension, and then his phone rang. It was Costas, barely audible. "Jack, I'm all right. Zaheed's been hit. We got as many as we could.

I think they're going to take me. I'm . . ." There was a loud crackling sound, and the phone went dead.

Jack turned to the marine sergeant. "You need to get me there. Those are my people."

The sergeant nodded, pointing to two others in the sentry box. "Anderson, Bailey. On me." He ran to the jeep that was parked behind the box, followed by Jack and the other two. They all got in, the two marines in the back and Jack in the front passenger seat, and the sergeant gunned the vehicle through the entrance and down the airport approach road, screeching round a corner as they approached the perimeter. He had radioed ahead as he drove to the commander of the African Union detachment providing airport security, and the gate was already open. He pulled to a halt, leaned out of the window, and spoke briefly to the Kenyan officer in charge, then gunned the jeep forward. "It wasn't a terrorist attempt on the perimeter after all," he said. "It looks like it was specifically targeted at your people. A contract killing or a kidnapping. Sounds pretty bad."

They rounded another corner, racing out of the perimeter into the city streets, and then came to a screeching halt. A scene of carnage met their eyes. Zaheed's four-by-four was resting at a crazy angle half on the pavement, smoke pouring out of its engine, its tires all shot out. Sprawled around it in pools of blood were six bodies, two of them the Somali marines who had accompanied Zaheed, the rest evidently attackers. Cartridge casings were strewn everywhere, but all the weapons had been removed and there were tire tracks through the blood and over one of the bodies.

Jack saw Zaheed on the far side of the jeep, leaning over one bullet-ridden door. "Wait here," he said to the sergeant. "There's one still alive." He took out his Beretta, opened the door, and got out, running over to the vehicle.

Zaheed dropped heavily to the pavement, sitting upright for a moment and then falling on his elbows, twisting to one side. Jack knelt beside him, and he gestured weakly with one arm. "They've taken Costas. Not Al-Shabaab. The Badass Boys. I recognized them from the fishing village. One of them was the Boss. They headed off in a Toyota, going north."

Jack could see where a bullet had penetrated Zaheed's chest under his left arm, one place that was not protected by the body armor. He coughed, bringing up blood, and then lay back, a slew of blood spreading beneath him from the wound and more coming from his mouth and nose. Jack knelt down and held his head, trying to make him more comfortable. His face was ashen, and he coughed more blood, this time weakly. "Jack," he whispered, his breath rasping. "In my wallet."

Jack quickly felt in the zip pocket of the combat trousers Zaheed was wearing and pulled out his wallet, opening it up. Zaheed raised one arm weakly and fumbled in it, half pulling out a photo and then letting his arm drop. Jack pulled it out completely, showing it to him. "I can't see it," he whispered, barely audible, his eyes staring sightlessly past Jack. "My wife and daughter. We talked about them. I wanted you to see them." His face crumpled, and then he was gone, his eyes half open and his jaw slackening.

Jack pulled off the blood-soaked scarf that Zaheed had been wearing and placed it over his face, then got up and looked around. Already a crowd was gathering, the children with the glazed eyes of those who were used to this kind of scene, their minds already elsewhere. A police car swerved up onto the pavement, and he could see two African Union armored cars hurtling toward them from the perimeter post. The police would assume that this had been an Al-Shabaab attack, and soon the whole area would be in lockdown, roadblocks in every direction. If he did not get out now, he could be trapped here for hours.

Jack knew he had no time for sentiment, only for cold, clinical reaction. Costas would be kept alive only as long as he was useful to the kidnappers' paymaster, and that might be no longer than the instant of their arrival at the island and their discovery of the U-boat pen. He stepped away from Zaheed's body, keeping the wallet and the photograph, and ran back to the jeep, where the marines had stayed put with their weapons at the ready. He jumped back into the passenger seat and turned to the sergeant. "I need you to take me to the Somali navy command center. You know where it is?"

"Yes, sir. We help train their marines."

"I've got to get there now."

"I should get clearance."

Jack gestured at the naval ID card for the embassy that was still hanging from his neck. "You know who I am?"

"Yes, sir."

"Then you've got all the clearance you need."

"Yes, sir."

The sergeant shoved the gearstick forward and roared off, swerving around a corner and then hurtling along the main road parallel to the shore in the direction of the naval headquarters. "We can't use lights and sirens, as it makes us a target for Al-Shabaab," he said, dropping a gear to pass a donkey cart. "Fortunately there are no speed limits."

Jack was coursing with adrenalin, his hands shaking. He took out his phone and punched the number he had preset for Captain Ibrahim. The phone was answered almost immediately, and Jack quickly filled him in. "This is what I'd like you to do. We go ahead with the mission as planned. You dispatch the patrol boat toward the island, with a marine contingent on board. We can't know for certain that's where they've taken Costas, but if the kidnappers were who Zaheed said they were, then there's a good chance they'll drive him up the coast and put him on the trawler. But I'd like to take a small diversion first, if you can help me. The Somali defense force has a couple of Hueys, right? I'd like to be dropped on *Deep Explorer*. There's someone on board I need to have a word with. And you might want to follow that up by sending a team to intercept them with your second patrol boat. I have a feeling *Deep Explorer* will be changing course and heading into Somali territorial waters, without permission and with suspicious intent. You won't even need to invoke international law to seize them."

He gave Ibrahim the license plate number of the jeep they were in so that the naval guards at the compound would be forewarned, and then he pocketed the phone and stared ahead, bracing himself against the potholes and bumps in the road. They would be there in ten minutes, probably less. He felt preternaturally alert, as if he were seeing the people they were passing in slow motion, slow enough for him to scrutinize them as threats. He knew that it was the result of adrenalin, a natural defense mechanism. He thought of Zaheed. He was still clutching the picture, the blood already drying on it. Zaheed had planned to stop by his home on the way back that afternoon so that Jack could meet his wife and daughter. They had talked about the trials and joys of fatherhood, and Jack had told him about Rebecca. When this was all over, he would go and see Zaheed's family. Right now, there was only one thought running through his head, only one thing he had to do. *Payback*.

Four hours later, Jack gazed out over the Indian Ocean from the door of the UH-1N Twin Huey as the distinctive red hull of *Deep Explorer* came into view, her wake showing that she was continuing to steam north toward Socotra, exactly as the satellite surveillance images had revealed. He leaned forward beside the door gunner, his helmet muffling the worst of the rotor noise and his visor giving the sea an unearthly green hue. He remembered the last time he had seen *Deep Explorer*, two weeks earlier, as he and Costas were taken off by the British Army Lynx following their dive on *Clan Macpherson*.

He remembered how he had felt then. His relief had been tempered by the uneasy feeling he always had after his encounters with Landor. With his close knowledge of Jack, and his press conferences that so adeptly white-washed his operations as legitimate archaeology, Landor had always seemed one step ahead, like a criminal taunting a detective who never quite had the evidence to make an arrest. Jack had dealt with some intractable enemies in his career, with warlords who ruthlessly controlled the antiquities trade, with sadists who were driven by twisted ideology. With Landor, it was different, more complex. Archaeologists and treasure hunters were inevitably at loggerheads, their motivations so radically different, the moral case for archaeology unambiguous. Yet the personal element, the old friendship and the shared passion for diving in those formative years, had always stopped Jack from confronting him head-on, and Landor knew it. Sometimes it seemed as if Landor were his doppelgänger, a parallel version of himself in a universe with little morality, with no higher purpose, and yet with that shared passion that had set Landor apart from so many of the others he had come up against in the past.

This time, though, was different. This time Landor had gone one step too far, had let his greed and his bitterness, his desperation after his failure to raise the gold from *Clan Macpherson*, lead him into waters that were over his head. Jack was certain that he had ordered the gang to kidnap Costas as a bargaining chip to keep Jack out of the way until they had found the U-boat at the island. He had known that Landor would one day make a mistake that would destroy him, something more than his minor run-ins with governments in the past, but he had never guessed that it might be something this personal. He had spent most of the flight trying not to think of where Costas was now and what might be happening to him. He still had Zaheed's blood under his fingernails, and that photo of his wife and little girl in his pocket. One thing was for certain: the Jack that Landor thought he knew was very different from the one who was going to be confronting him now.

The gunner drew back the bolt on the 50-caliber Browning machine gun and trained it on *Deep Explorer*, traversing it so that those watching from below could see. The pilot expertly maneuvered the helicopter over the stern of the ship, dropping to fifty feet and mimicking the ship's course and speed. The loadmaster hooked Jack's harness to the winch and gave a thumbs-up as the door light went green. Jack dropped out, feeling the rush of air from the rotor, and seconds later was down on the aft deck of the ship. There had been no formalities, no courtesy call to explain their intentions. *Deep Explorer* was just outside the exclusion zone, so the Somalis had no jurisdiction here. But legal niceties mattered little on the high seas when a ship was confronted by a machine gun capable of ripping apart the bridge and any crew in its sights, not to speak of the destructive potential of the twin rocket pods under the airframe. Landor had hired pirates whose livelihood was attacking unarmed ships in international waters; now the tables were turned, and he was about to reap his own whirlwind.

Jack took off his helmet, unclipped the carabiners, and cast off the line, pushing it out of the way as the loadmaster winched it up. The Huey drew forward and clattered deafeningly over the bow, the helmeted gunner with his machine gun clearly visible through the side door. Jack knew exactly where he was going, and went quickly up the steps to the bridge, pushing past several crewmen who had been ducking against the downdraft from the rotor. He pulled open the sliding door and stepped inside. The captain was at the helm, staring up at the helicopter with a mike in his hand. Jack shut the door noisily, and the captain turned round and saw him.

"Where's Landor?" Jack snarled. The captain paused, as if judging the best response, then quickly picked up a phone. "Make a call now and they *will* shut you down," Jack said, pointing out at the helicopter. "Your ship will be impounded and you will relocate to a stinking Mogadishu jail while I do all I can to block any attempt to release you."

The captain held the phone and the mike for a moment longer, then lowered them both and jerked his head toward the door of the chart room at the back of the bridge. "Mr. Landor isn't here, but Macinnes is. You can take whatever problem you have to him."

Jack gestured at the helm. "Change course to bearing 320 degrees."

"But that will take us into Somali territorial waters."

Jack pointed up at the Huey again. "Do it, or he'll empty one of those rocket pods into your rudder and screw, and you'll drift with the current toward shore anyway."

The captain pursed his lips, but stood behind the helm and did as he had been told. Jack checked the bearing, and then took out several plastic ties from his pocket. "Hands behind your back." He put a tie around the man's wrists and used another to attach it to a rail. "Apologies for the plastic," he said. "The Somali navy officer who'll be boarding in about half an hour when you enter territorial waters and impounding your ship has some real handcuffs."

Jack pulled open the door to the chart room. Macinnes, the operations director he had last encountered off Sierra Leone, was sitting in the easy chair behind the chart table, tapping a mobile phone and putting it up to his ear, then trying again. "It's called electronic countermeasures," Jack said coldly. "No comms to or from this ship while the helicopter's outside. That's the Somali navy."

Macinnes put the phone down, leaned back in the chair, and put his hands behind his head. "So, Dr. Howard. We meet again. The Somali navy? That's a joke. We're in international waters, and they can't touch us. Mr. Landor has gone ashore in our helicopter to broker an agreement with the Somali government so they get a cut of anything we find, our usual percentage. We find that generally works in Third World holes like this. Whichever naval officer is in charge of this puny operation is about to lose his job. Now, get off this ship and go home."

"We're talking murder," Jack said. "The murder of three Somali citizens, two of them marines, the third one a government employee in the museums service. That gives the Somali navy the right to make an arrest."

"You're in way out of your depth, Howard. You should stick to your dinky toy excavations and your bits of broken pot. This is the big time."

"Yes, it is," Jack said. "If you had any nautical sense you'd have noticed by now that the ship has changed course. In fifteen minutes you'll have crossed into Somali territorial waters. That means you and everyone else on this ship will be arrested as accessories to murder. Next stop Mogadishu central jail, a really nice place for Westerners accused of messing around with this country, I hear."

Macinnes got up, angrily pushing the chair aside. "This is outrageous. Get out of my way. I need to see the captain." He advanced on Jack, who unholstered his Beretta and leveled it at him.

"One step closer, and I shoot."

Macinnes sneered at him and tried to shove him aside. "Get out of my way. You haven't got the guts." Jack pushed him back, leveled the Beretta again and fired a round close to Macinnes's ear, a deafening crack that made him reel back in pain. Then he kicked him into the chair, keeping the gun leveled.

"I know Landor's not at some meeting in Mogadishu, as the naval commander has explained his implication in the murders to the Justice Minister and he'd be arrested on sight. In fact, he's nowhere near Mogadishu. He's gone for a trip to an island with your new friends, hasn't he? Right now, I don't care about that. I can deal with him later. All I want to know now is *where is Dr. Kazantzakis?*"

Macinnes held his left ear, blood trickling down his hand. He looked at Jack, and guffawed. "That loser? I'm amazed you bother with him. That dive off Sierra Leone was one of the most incompetent things I've ever seen, all that fancy IMU equipment that doesn't work. But when a little birdie told us you'd arrived in Somalia and were probably on our trail again, we knew your clown sidekick would be along as well. Lo and behold, he shows up. Take my advice, you're well rid of him."

That was enough. If Landor knew they were in Somalia, there was no question about who was behind the kidnapping. Jack remembered the last time he had seen Macinnes, having to toe the line and endure his snide comments after he and Costas had boarded *Deep Explorer* for the UN inspection. This time, Jack was in charge. He lunged forward, kicked the chair back, and reached for the scruff of the man's neck, pulling him up bodily and slamming him against the bookcase behind. He punched him as hard as he could in the face, let him collapse, and then picked him up again, the blood pouring out of his nose and down his chin. He pressed the Beretta behind Macinnes's ear, pushing it as hard as he could, his other hand around his throat. "I don't think I heard your answer. *Where is Dr. Kazantzakis?*"

21

The trawler slammed into the waves again, sending a tremor through the hull that seemed to jar every bone in Costas's body. Over the past few hours he had learned to accommodate himself to the boat's movements, tensing as it dropped into a trough and then relaxing as it rode the swell, the engine grinding against its mounting one way and reverberating and shuddering the other. Twice he had nodded off and lost the rhythm, and had paid the price in an excruciating jolt. Sleep, he knew, would be an impossibility as long as the sea was this rough, but they were probably past the halfway point and the rest of the trip was a matter of endurance. He guessed they were heading toward the island near Socotra, the one that Ahmed had identified as the site of the U-boat pen; from their embarkation point at a fishing village several hours north of Mogadishu they should reach the island not much after first light. It was a question of lasting out the remainder of the night, of keeping alert and learning anything he could from the noise and the smell, of seizing any opportunity that presented itself to overcome his captors and escape.

He shifted slightly, bracing his feet against the engine mounting and his left shoulder against one of the timber frames of the hull, trying to find a better angle for his wrists. They had been handcuffed behind his back with a cable tie, and for several hours now he had been trying to cut the cable, pressing it hard with each jolt of the hull against an upturned metal

edge beneath him. He had been blindfolded since being hustled out of the
Toyota in the village and could only guess at his surroundings, but he knew
that it was a large fishing vessel, undoubtedly the trawler that Captain Ibrahim had described, the mother ship for the pirate gang. He knew it was a
fishing vessel from the appalling stench that had hit him when he was first
pushed down the hatch into the hold, and the fish guts that slopped around
his feet as the boat pitched and yawed. That and the stale sweat of the
crew had made him gag and retch, but as soon as the engine had coughed
to life he had been engulfed by diesel fumes and the reek of overheated
oil. All he had been able to sense for some time now was a cloying in the
back of his throat, whether from diesel fumes or blood from the beatings
he could not tell. He felt as if he were a mountaineer in the death zone,
knowing that no matter how much he breathed there was never going to
be sufficient oxygen in this place to keep him alive. He desperately needed
fresh air, and soon.

The engine coughed and spluttered, running on idle for a few moments,
and then hacked back to life again. The hatch above him clanged open and
someone dropped into the scuppers. He could tell from the stink that it
was his captor, his tormentor. He clenched his jaw tight, knowing what
would come next. The blow when it came was still a shock, snapping his
head sideways, and he felt his mouth fill up again with blood. A hand
roughly grasped his jaw, and he smelled the man's breath again, the reek
of tobacco and khat and marijuana. "Hey, English," his captor said, his voice
heavily accented. "I bring you water."

"I'm not English," Costas said hoarsely. "For the last time, I'm American."

"No Americans here," the man said, taunting. Costas felt the muzzle
of a gun thrust under his chin. "No American Embassy, no George Bush,
no Obama, no Clinton. No help for you, English."

Costas strained his head up. "Your engine," he said. "It's bad, kaput.
I can fix it. I'm an engineer."

He heard the rasp of a lighter and a deep inhalation, and then he smelled
the smoke. The last thing they needed down here was a spark to blow them
all to kingdom come—himself, his stoned captor, the others on the deck
above. "The engine," he tried again, speaking more loudly. "It's kaput,
finished. I can fix it."

The mouth of a bottle was pressed hard into his teeth, ripping at his gums. He drank as much as he could, trying to ignore the coppery tang of his own blood. The bottle was upturned as he drank, and most of the water spilled down his front. He heard the man inhale again, and his voice close against his ear, blowing smoke as he spoke. "No George Bush, no Obama, no Clinton," he repeated. "No one to help you, no ransom. Soon it is you who will be kaput, English."

The engine spluttered again. A voice shouted down from above, and the man answered, speaking quickly in Somali. The other replied angrily, and there was a heated exchange. The man seemed to concede, and spoke to Costas again. "Okay, English. The Boss wants you to look at the engine. You look, you tell me what to do. Anything funny, *you* kaput, you understand?"

Costas flexed his wrists, trying to keep the circulation going. He had no way of knowing how close he had come to cutting the tie, but he knew that he had at least made a notch in it. He felt the blindfold being pulled off, and then a searing pain in his left eye as the pressure was removed from it. He remembered the blow to his head after Zaheed and the marines had been gunned down, and then a confusion of memory as he recovered consciousness in their attackers' vehicle some time later. He blinked, able to see nothing through the swollen eye, and then caught sight of his captor for the first time, leering at him in the gloom.

The man was scrawny, with sunken cheeks and eyes and yellow teeth, and of indeterminate age, probably much younger than he looked. He wore a grubby vest, and on one shoulder Costas saw the distinctive Badass Boys tattoo that Ibrahim had shown them, a stylized bird with a crescent above, and beneath that a dozen or so raised welts signifying how many people he had killed. He was holding a Kalashnikov with the wire butt folded in, the muzzle aimed at Costas's gut. He leaned close, his eyes hazy and his chin covered with wispy hair, and took a final drag from his joint, flicking what was left into the scuppers and causing a small eruption of blue flame where leaked diesel ignited. Then he grabbed Costas by the hair and pulled him forward on his knees in front of the engine, holding the rifle to his head. "Now, English, you fix, okay?"

Costas pretended to scrutinize the engine, and then got up on one knee, nodding toward the stern. "I need to see over there, the propeller shaft," he said. The man backed off slightly and Costas started to rise, lurching sideways with the roll of the boat, his head bowed under the low ceiling of the deck. The boat jarred into another wave, and in that instant he saw his chance. He pulled his wrists apart and broke the tie, in the same movement swinging his arms around and slamming his hands into his captor's head, pushing him off balance. The man fell hard against one of the frames, clutching his left leg in agony, his weapon falling into the bilge. Costas lunged for it, but was brought up short by a savage blow to the head. He fell forward on his knees, a searing pain in his neck, and looked up blearily to see the Boss standing over him, his own Kalashnikov raised.

"Not so fast," the man said, an unlit cigarette hanging from his lips. "Has my boy been giving you trouble?" He swung his rifle toward the downed man, firing a ten-round burst that ripped up his chest and into his head, exploding it like a watermelon. Costas stared in horror, his ears ringing from the noise, and then slumped back, wiping the spatter of blood off his face. The Boss grinned, showing a mouth full of gold. "See? No more trouble." He took out the cigarette and spat a jet of khat juice on to the corpse. "Plenty more where he came from." He sniffed exaggeratedly. "*Man,* it stinks down here. We need to get you some fresh air."

Costas rolled back, looking at the man. He had spent hours listening to him in the Toyota and through the hatch in the boat when it had been left open, but this was the first time he had seen him. He was young, too, but better fed and sharper-looking than the other one had been, his eyes less hazed by drugs. He spoke in a curious patois that seemed to owe something to hard-edged Hollywood gang movies of recent years, but that could have been a result of time spent in the US or Canada. Now he sat down beside the body, placed the Kalashnikov across his knees and offered Costas the cigarette. When he refused, the Boss leaned forward, looking him over with an exaggerated expression of surprise and contempt. "I'm examining my merchandise, and I don't like what I see," he said, digging a lighter out of the fallen man's pocket and flicking it under Costas's chin, examining his bruises and shaking his head. "I don't see anyone paying a ransom for you any time soon, my man."

"If you kill me, your paymaster from *Deep Explorer* isn't going to be too pleased, is he? Nor are my friends in the Somali navy."

The Boss stared at him, his jaw dropping theatrically, then sniffed and spat at his feet before suddenly letting out a high-pitched peal of laughter and slapping his knee. He jabbed the hand with the cigarette at Costas. "You trying to frighten me, man?"

"Just putting you in the picture."

"I'll tell you about the picture." The Boss leaned forward, his face contorted. "That man Landor? He's here now, upstairs. He's different, he understands us, knows what makes us tick. The rest of you are all the same, Americans, English, you come here thinking you can take us on, and you run away as soon as you get a bloody nose. The Somali navy? Give me a break, man. And you know what? I'll take his money, yes. But he and I have an agreement. Part of what's on that island is mine. What we're going to find now."

"You might want to take care. It may be a little hot for you to handle."

The Boss got up, staring, the whites of his knuckles showing where he was clutching the rifle. "Are you doing it again? *Are you doing it again?*"

"Just a friendly word of warning."

Costas knew what was coming. He had provoked it, but he had known it was going to happen again at some point and he just wanted it over with. The blow when it came threw him back against the side of the hull, a blinding pain exploding behind his eyes. Then he felt nothing.

Jack gunned the Zodiac forward, twisting the throttle as it rose out of a deep trough and then easing it back again as he dropped down the other side, trying to keep a steady speed. Rather than taking the patrol boat's larger rigid-hulled Zodiac he had opted for the four-meter inflatable with its forty-horsepower outboard, keeping their profile as low as possible and reducing the chances of anyone on the trawler spotting them. If he had tried to plane over the waves, the shriek of the propeller rising out of the water between the peaks might have given them away. Stealth was of the essence, and their progress so far had been good enough, meaning that they should be closing in on their target before dawn.

He lowered himself to the floorboards, sitting with his back against one pontoon and his feet against the fuel tank, holding the tiller of the outboard with one hand and the painter line with the other. Wedged in the bow was Lieutenant Ahmed, keeping as far forward as possible so that his weight would stop the boat from flying upward as they rose above each trough. As soon as Jack had extracted confirmation from Macinnes on *Deep Explorer* that Costas was on the trawler, Ahmed had immediately volunteered for the mission, and Jack had seen the necessity of having two men in the boat, doubling the firepower. This operation was about rescuing Costas, but confronting the pirates was also a Somali naval responsibility, and Ahmed was the spearhead of their new rapid-reaction force, trained at the US Navy SEALS base at Quantico. With the plan they had devised with Captain Ibrahim for dealing with the trawler, Ahmed's diving skills would also come in very useful.

They were about two nautical miles ahead of the patrol boat and less than half a mile now from the trawler, all of them heading in a line toward the little island to the west of Socotra. Jack glanced back, throttling down even further to reduce the phosphorescence in their wake, thankful for the rough seas that should help to keep them concealed. He pulled the tiller sideways to aim at a rogue wave, climbing it and then pushing the tiller to get back on course, trying to keep his profile as inconspicuous as possible in the event that anyone in the trawler ahead was actually keeping a look-out. Everything was as close to black as they could make it—their wetsuits, their faces—and it was a moonless night, still more than an hour away from dawn. He ran again through a mental checklist of their equipment. Both men wore three-liter air tanks that would give them about twenty minutes or so underwater, with octopus rigs so that they had two regulator mouth-pieces each. In backpacks beside the cylinders they carried small fins and low-volume face masks, with Jack carrying a second set. Around their waists they wore equipment belts with holstered 9mm Beretta pistols, spare magazines, fragmentation and stun grenades, and in Jack's case a flare gun as well. Ahmed also had an MP5 submachine gun and a bandolier on his chest with additional magazines, his role being to provide suppressing fire to allow Jack to find and extract Costas.

All they could do now was to keep going, to hope that the timing was right, to pray that nobody in the trawler saw them. An hour earlier, a drone launched from the patrol boat had seen the trawler's skiff leave and go on ahead, taking one white man who could only be Landor and at least a dozen others of the gang toward the island. It meant that there would be a reception for Jack and Ahmed if they did get to the island themselves, but that was too far ahead in the plan to think about now. The immediate conse-quence was fewer men to deal with on the trawler itself, a slightly higher chance of success if they did get on board. It was an audacious plan, but there had been no other way of interdicting the trawler without making their presence known in advance, potentially jeopardizing Costas's chances even further.

Jack had tried not to think about that, having blocked the worst-case scenario from his mind. Costas was only valuable to Landor as long as he thought his capture was deterring Jack from following him to the island. Landor himself might have bitten off more than he could chew. The gang boss was by all accounts a shrewd operator, wily enough to guess that the value of whatever lay on that island was a lot greater than he had been promised as payment. Landor might have offered him a cut, but that in itself might be seen as a sign of weakness, as if Landor were desperate. What seemed certain was that Costas would have little interest to them as a hostage for ransom, that his life would be forfeit the instant they knew that Jack was on their trail, the moment any of them saw the Zodiac approaching. Even if he were not killed immediately, Jack knew there would be little chance of reasoning with the gang, most of them probably off their heads on drugs, their boss a ruthless psychopath. All he cared about now was Costas, and the certainty that without their plan his friend would die.

He kept his eyes glued ahead, seeing the dark shape of the trawler each time the inflatable crested a wave, and ahead of that the first hint of the island, a low shape on the horizon. He glanced at his watch, and nodded at Ahmed. They knew that Ibrahim on the patrol boat would have his binoculars trained on them, and that the larger Zodiac with a section of Somali marines would be prepped and ready for the follow-up action. He watched Ahmed crouched at the ready in the bow, holding his MP5 close to him against the spray. Less than an hour from now they would know one way or the other.

Jack huddled beside the outboard, checking his equipment with his spare hand, making sure the regulator hoses were wound around his neck to keep them from catching on anything, feeling for his holster. He remembered what had happened to Zaheed, the look on his face in those final moments, and what Ibrahim had told him about their adversaries ahead: that these were not fishermen forced into piracy but sadistic thugs from inland, murderers and torturers and rapists. He felt his adrenalin flow, his body tense. He would show them no mercy.

22

Twenty minutes later, Jack angled the Zodiac into the wake of the trawler, now no more than five hundred meters ahead. He could see a dim light from the deckhouse, but still no sign of movement. With the skiff having departed for the island full of men, it was impossible to know how many were left on the trawler, but he and Ahmed had guessed at least half a dozen, perhaps twice that. Ahmed extended the retractable stock on his MP5, pulled the cocking handle to check that a round was chambered, and held it slung over his shoulder, the silencer poking out above the pontoon. His job was to take out anyone who might happen to appear at the stern railing; the silencer would reduce the chances that the noise might alert any others. They had entered the critical phase of the operation, within gunshot range of the trawler. A single round from the pirates into the inflatable and it would be game over, with any hope of rescuing Costas instantly lost.

They were closing in now, with less than two hundred meters to go. Jack concentrated on keeping within the slipstream of the wake, riding the wave that was angling out from the starboard quarter. A momentary lapse of attention and the Zodiac might be swept off the wake into the sea alongside, where it would be more visible; getting back into position would mean gunning the throttle, also attracting attention. As they followed the churning phosphorescence behind the trawler's screw, Jack ran over what he would do once Ahmed had leaped aboard. He would need to make sure that the Zodiac was not pushed away, that he kept it against the hull so that he could attempt to get on board himself. With nobody to man the throttle to keep it in position, it was going to have to be a split-second leap, a matter of finding any handhold before the inflatable was taken by the waves and spun away out of control.

In the pre-dawn glimmer, he could now see the condition of the trawler more clearly: the rusting hull, the derricks for dragnets at the stern, which had probably been unused for months, the deckhouse above the accommodation block. He had never encountered pirates before, but he had been thoroughly briefed by Ibrahim and Ahmed and he had some idea of what to expect. Hostages released after ransom had said that the Badass Boys were continuously high, making their behavior erratic, more dangerous. Jack was sure that he could smell the marijuana above the diesel fumes that were now enveloping them. It meant that the danger for Costas was multiplied, the risk that one of the pirates might decide on a whim to murder him, but it could also mean that his guards were less alert, easier to overwhelm. Jack's role was to go below and search for him while Ahmed held off any opposition above. He checked the holster with the Beretta on his right side, making sure it was shut. He would know the nature of the opposition soon enough.

They were less than fifty meters away now. One of the pirates suddenly appeared at the back rail, lurching, a Kalashnikov swinging from one hand, a joint in the other. Without hesitation, Ahmed snapped up the MP5 and fired a five-round burst. The man toppled over the rail and fell into the wake, his body bobbing past them. The gunshots had barely been audible, little more than a staccato coughing, but the man had dropped his own gun with a clatter and one of Ahmed's bullets had pinged off something metallic behind him, ricocheting into the distance. Another man appeared, evidently alerted by the noise, and Ahmed repeated the exercise, this time dropping the man onto the deck.

Jack gunned the boat forward. It was now or never. Ahmed slung the MP5 over his back and picked up a grapple line from a bucket in the bow. The Zodiac rammed into the stern of the trawler, bounced against it and then held fast, the engine screaming. Ahmed threw the grapple, watching as it caught on the stern rail, and leaped out, impacting the hull hard as he pulled himself up above the wake. Jack throttled back, swerved sideways out of the wake, and came back again at the trawler along her starboard side. Above him he heard a ripping sound as Ahmed emptied his MP5 forward, and the noise of ricochets and shattering glass. He squatted up on the floorboards, holding the tiller with one hand and his own grapple with the other. He swung the tiller hard, threw his grapple and then leaped out himself, slamming into the side of the trawler just as a deafening burst from a Kalashnikov ripped into the inflatable, shredding one pontoon and causing it to flip over and spin off in the wake.

He hung on to the line, the spray lashing his face, his body half in and half out of the water. He summoned all his strength and pulled himself up until he reached deck level, swinging his left leg until his foot caught behind one of the railing posts aft. He heaved himself up against the railing and looked across the deck. A few feet away lay the crumpled body of the man who had fired the Kalashnikov, rivulets of blood spreading along the divides of the deck boards around him. Ahmed had already advanced forward of the main hatch, and was squatting behind the derrick machinery, his MP5 aimed at the deckhouse. Jack stared at the hatch, the place where fish would normally be spilled through into refrigerator compartments below. If Costas was anywhere, that would be it. He looked forward again to Ahmed. There was no need for stealth now, just speed. "I'm right behind you," he bellowed. "I'm going for the hatch. I need suppressing fire."

"Roger that." Ahmed dropped the half-empty magazine from his weapon and loaded a new one. "On your call."

Jack flexed his arm muscles and peered at the top of the railing, judging his timing. He took a deep breath and yelled, "Ahmed. *Now.*" Ahmed fired a long burst that shattered the remaining deckhouse windows, spraying rounds from left to right. Jack heaved himself up the railing, dropped over the other side, unholstered his Beretta, and scrambled over to the hatch, pulling at the handle. From somewhere ahead a Kalashnikov opened up and rounds went everywhere, ricocheting off machinery and gouging sprays of splinters from the deck boards.

Jack ducked down, his hands over his head, and looked across at Ahmed, who had taken out a stun grenade and pulled the pin. "Fire in the hole," Ahmed yelled. They had agreed not to risk fragmentation grenades until they knew for certain where Costas was being held, but a stun grenade might at least buy them time. Jack pressed his hands against his ears, and watched Ahmed toss the grenade at the deckhouse. Seconds later there was a deafening crash, followed by a few seconds of silence and then sounds of commotion, high-pitched voices yelling orders in Somali. "I can just about make out what they're saying," Ahmed called. "I think there are three of them, and one down below. He must be guarding Costas. You need to get down there now."

He fired another long burst at the deckhouse, and Jack got up on his knees. Over the port railing he could see the island clearly now, no more than half a mile away. He held the Beretta ready with one hand, and pulled hard at the handle with the other. It suddenly gave way, and he pushed the hatch up, staying behind it for cover. A burst of fire came up from below, two rounds tearing through the wood only inches from his torso. He let the hatch drop open, in that instant seeing his assailant and firing half a dozen rounds into him, the impact throwing the man back down the ladder. Jack followed, Beretta at the ready, swinging it round as he peered into the gloom. "Costas," he yelled. "*Costas*. Are you there?"

He listened hard, hearing only the throbbing of the engine and the slapping of the sea on the hull outside. He reached the bottom of the ladder and turned forward, slopping through fish entrails in the scuppers, trying to keep himself upright as the ship pitched and rolled. He called again, but there was still no response. Then he saw a body splayed backward between the hull frames, the head an unrecognizable pulp. Whoever it was had been killed some time earlier; the blood had dried and was swarming with flies. It looked like an execution. He suddenly felt sick. *They could not be too late.* He peered more closely, seeing the unfamiliar clothes, the brown skin. He heard a moaning from further forward and squatted down beside the body, pistol at the ready. As he crept slowly ahead, he saw the Hawaiian shirt, matted and bloody, and the battered face. "Costas. Can you hear me? It's Jack. We're here to rescue you."

One eye opened; the other was black and sealed shut. "It's about time," he mumbled. "Got whacked on the head. Dude over there with the tattoo."

"Okay. He's gone. Anyone else down here?"

"Nobody alive."

"We need to get out of here. Can you manage it?"

Costas blinked hard. Jack picked up a half-empty water bottle that had been beside him and put it to Costas's lips, holding his head up. He drank noisily, shook his head, grimaced, and then pushed himself up on his elbows. "Okay, Jack. Get me out of this hellhole."

Jack squatted beside him, heaved Costas's arm up over his shoulder, and helped him to his feet. Costas lurched sideways, and Jack caught him again, holding him upright. "We're going up the ladder through the hatch. Ahmed is there and most of the crew are gone. It looks as if the Boss has already gone ashore with some of his boys."

"He's the one I want," Costas said, reeling. "Point me in his direction."

"Time for that soon enough. Right now we're going for a swim. Some friends of ours are about to light this boat up, and we need to be out of here."

"You're wearing a three-liter cylinder with an octopus rig," Costas slurred, staggering sideways. "So I kind of guessed that. The tool belt I like. Anything in it for me?"

"All in good time. We need to get you out of here first." Jack shouted up through the hatch. "Ahmed, I've got him. We're coming out now."

"Roger that," Ahmed shouted back. "Suppressing fire now."

Jack heard the familiar rip of the MP5 as he pushed Costas ahead of him up the ladder and then jumped round to finish pulling him out. He helped him to his feet and they staggered to the back railing. "A swim will do me good," Costas murmured. "Clear the head. I need that if I'm going to take on that guy. Which I am."

Ahmed backed off from his position until he was alongside them. The shoreline was now alarmingly close, only a couple of hundred meters away, and the engine was still going full blast. Ahmed took the second grenade from his pouch and pulled the pin. "Fragmentation this time. Fire in the hole." As he tossed it, Jack pushed Costas behind the port-side derrick, holding his hands against his ears. A deafening blast blew a hole in the left side of the deckhouse, sending burning chunks of wood clattering onto the deck around them. "There might still be a couple of them left," Ahmed said. "We need to get out of here now."

Jack turned to Costas. "There's a Somali navy patrol boat commanded by Captain Ibrahim closing in on us. As soon as they see this flare, a P-15 Termit missile will be launched at this trawler. Do you understand?"

Costas looked back at him, less groggy now, nodding. "Sounds like a plan."

A burst of gunfire erupted from the remaining part of the deckhouse, one of the bullets grazing Costas in the left forearm and another knocking the flare pistol out of Jack's hand. He lunged for it, catching it just in time as it spun across the deck toward the stern. Ahmed leveled his MP5 at the deckhouse, firing off the remainder of his magazine, then quickly loaded another, emptying that too in one long burst. He dropped the gun, grabbed Costas and yelled, "Now!" just as another burst erupted from the deckhouse. Jack fired the flare gun high in the air, and then hurled himself at the other two, all three of them going over the stern railing and hitting the sea together as rounds jetted into the water on all sides.

He pulled them underwater, swimming down as hard as he could. After a few meters he stopped and quickly unwound one regulator, passing the mouthpiece to Costas, who began breathing off it as he helped Jack with his; Ahmed did the same a few meters away. They equalized their ears as they sank deeper, and Jack struggled out of his backpack, opened it and passed Costas a mask and fins. He grabbed his own and let the pack drop, then put the mask on, blowing air into it to clear it and seeing that Costas had already done the same. Pulling on their fins, they powered away from the shadow of the hull, Ahmed close behind, knowing that every second counted.

A minute after they had hit the water, a shock wave threw them forward, and a flash of red lit up the surface. Looking back, Jack could just make out the shattered form of the trawler sinking to the seabed, the bodies of the gunmen pirouetting away from it, smudges of blood shrouding the ones who had just been killed in the missile strike.

Costas tapped Jack on the shoulder and pointed at the blood curling up into the water from the bullet wound on his arm, then made a biting motion with his hand. Jack peered at the injury, a nasty graze rather than a penetrating wound, and scanned the reef around them. Costas was right: blood in the water would act as a magnet for sharks, and they would go for the living before they went for the dead. They were only a hundred meters or so from the rocky shoreline of the island, but even that would consume most of the air in their tanks. He pointed emphatically up the slope, and Costas and Ahmed both gave okay signals. Without buoyancy compensators or weight belts, they were struggling to counter the natural tendencies of their bodies to sink or float—Jack the former, Costas with his greater bulk decidedly the latter, with only Ahmed having something close to neutral buoyancy.

About five minutes into the swim, Costas transferred from Jack's to Ahmed's octopus regulator, knowing that Jack's tank would be close to depletion. They had been swimming at about eight meters' depth, below the oscillation of the swell, but as the bottom shelved up, they were forced into shallower water where they began to be pushed around by the ocean's movement. There were fewer coral heads in the shallows than in the deeper water but plenty of jagged limestone outcrops to scrape against, not to mention numerous spiny sea urchins that seemed to loom up toward Jack every time the swell dropped him close to the seabed.

They had not included pressure gauges with their tanks to economise on space, but Jack knew that he must be down to his final few minutes of air, and he looked along the surf line for a possible egress point. Ahmed and Costas were off to the right, and Costas gestured forcefully for him to follow, his arm trailing tendrils of blood. A white-tipped reef shark appeared below them, swimming in wide circles, and then another joined it. Jack tensed; where there were small sharks, bigger ones were sure to follow. The last thing they needed was for it all to end in a feeding frenzy, just when they were so close to their goal. He swam determinedly toward Costas, keeping at least two meters below the surface. Ahead he saw a cavernous opening between rocky outcrops and the shoreline that he knew must be Costas and Ahmed's objective, somewhere that promised calmer waters beyond, a place where they might surface unseen. He sucked hard on his regulator, knowing that he only had a couple of breaths left, but kept going. To surface now, still more than ten meters from shore, would be to risk being driven against the rocks before reaching that entranceway, and also being seen by those of the gang who were ashore and might be searching for survivors from the trawler.

He dropped down to the shingle-strewn entrance to the cavern, took a final breath from the tank and then powered forward behind the other two, swimming beyond the protective rock wall of the entrance and ascending inside, exhaling to avoid an embolism as he came up. As he reached the surface, he spat out his regulator, took a few deep breaths and then looked around, treading water hard to keep afloat. The sun had risen above the eastern horizon and bathed the rocks in light, sparkling off the water. They were in a small pool that formed a narrow inlet, protected on both sides by a rocky shoreline that rose several meters above the level of the water, the shingle sloping to form a rough beach. The other two were already making their way out, and Jack followed them, pulling himself up and sitting in the shallows. He stripped off his mask and fins and unstrapped his cylinder, dropping it beside him, and then crawled over to Costas, who was lying inert on the shingle, the sun on his face. He leaned over him, dripping water, and opened Costas's good eye, inspecting the pupil.

"Hey, what are you doing?" Costas said, sounding half asleep. "This is my beach time."

"Just checking for concussion. You look fine. Anything broken?"

"A few teeth. Maybe my jaw. Nothing too serious."

Jack unzipped the main pouch on his belt, took out a bottle of coagulant powder and spilled it on the wound, then wrapped it in a shell dressing and pinned it. Ahmed scrambled down from the side of the inlet where he had gone to check out their surroundings. "Okay," he said, squatting down, speaking quietly. "There are two guys with Kalashnikovs about three hundred meters west, inspecting the bits of wreckage that have come ashore. Another guy's marching up and down talking on a phone, gesticulating. I'm guessing he's the gang leader, the Boss. The skiff's nowhere to be seen, but I imagine the entrance to the submarine pen must be somewhere nearby, and that's where it's gone. I can see where we need to go."

Jack peered at Costas. "If you're not up to it, you can hold down the fort here while we go in. If all goes according to plan, there should be a section of Somali marines coming ashore from the patrol boat within the hour."

"Are you in contact with them?" Costas asked.

Ahmed shook his head. "Radio contact is too risky. There's a chance of being overheard. But I've set a locator beacon on that rock above us, something they can follow. This inlet will be a good beaching point for their Zodiac."

Jack reached into the pouch on his back and pulled out a waterproof package, passing it to Costas, who unwrapped it, revealing a second Beretta in a holster. "Thoughtful of you, Jack."

"What was it you said a few days ago? The buddy system. We look after each other."

"Right on." Costas staggered to his feet, shook himself and pulled back the slider on the pistol, chambering a round. "Full mag?"

"Full mag. Two more with the holster."

Costas slotted the holster over his shorts, held the gun down and paused.

"I wanted to ask about Zaheed. Last I saw of him he'd taken a round in the chest."

Jack gave him a grim look and shook his head. Costas nodded slowly. "I thought so. No way am I waiting this one out. There's someone here I want to meet again."

"Me too," said Jack. He stared down at the shingle. For the first time in as long as he could remember, the thought of Landor did not make him feel apprehensive, uneasy, the old sense of guilt. Seeing what they had done to Costas had removed all that. Now all he wanted was to get into that pen and end the job, to see Landor finished for good.

Costas looked at Ahmed. "You good to go?"

Ahmed pulled the slider on his own pistol. "Good to go."

"Okay," Jack said. "Let's move."

23

Ahmed led them forward over the rocky edge of the inlet, Costas following and Jack bringing up the rear. Before leaving, Jack had made Costas eat the energy bar that had been in a pouch on his belt, and they had checked him again for signs of concussion. The Somali naval base doctor and two medics had come along in the patrol boat in anticipation of casualties, with a standby arrangement for medevac by helicopter to a French fleet auxiliary ship with a full operating theater, part of the Combined Task Force flotilla currently off the coast of Yemen.

Jack's friend who headed the anti-piracy force had offered to divert a Royal Australian Air Force P-3 Orion surveillance aircraft over the island, part of the routine anti-piracy patrol carried out between Oman and the Horn of Africa that had recently been retasked to deal with the threat of naval incursion from Iran. Captain Ibrahim had advised against it until they were certain that Costas was safe. Like the terrorists, the pirate gangs were not easily intimidated by Western military force, having seen it come and go with political change and knowing that the task force might be prevented from interdiction by restrictive rules of engagement. Seeing an aircraft might only stoke up the pirates' defiance, and result in even more erratic violence. Ibrahim could request task force assistance once his marines were engaged and under fire, but until the landing team arrived in their Zodiac the three of them were on their own. Their priority now was to discover the U-boat pen and secure its contents before any damage could be done, particularly if those contents included potentially lethal radioactive materials.

Ahmed signaled for them to stop, and they squatted down among the rocky outcrops, looking around. A light breeze had sprung up from the east, bringing with it the smell of burning from the wreckage of the trawler. For the first time Jack could see the island in its entirety, a desolate rocky outcrop less than a kilometer across, almost flat and with hardly any vegetation. The rock had been eroded by sea and wind into a variegated surface of fissures and gullies, something that might slow their progress but would provide cover as they approached their target. Ahead of them, where Ahmed had earlier seen the two men inspecting the wreckage, lay the beginning of another inlet like the one they had just left, only much wider and cutting deeper into the island. There was nowhere else obvious for the skiff from the trawler to have gone, and this was their best bet for the U-boat pen.

Ahmed signaled them forward, and Jack acknowledged. They crept on, weapons at the ready, and a few minutes later reached the edge of the inlet, taking cover behind a crest of rock that overlooked the water about twenty meters away. "We need to get in there fast," Ahmed said. "If they discover we're here, they'll make a fortress of it, and this could go on for days. But from inside we can clean them out like ferrets in a rat hole."

Two men appeared seemingly from nowhere on the rough ground about thirty meters in from the back of the inlet. Ahmed took out a small pair of binoculars from his belt, stared for a moment, and then put them away again. "I think that's an entrance into the pen," he said. "But it's going to be tricky for three of us to take it by storm. The same problem applies: that once they know we're outside, they can make it virtually impregnable."

Jack looked at the inlet. "How much air did you have left in your tank?"

"Not yet sucking, but can't be more than a few minutes' worth."

"I have an idea. We think the U-boat got into that pen, right? There must be a channel underwater large enough to take it. If I can swim through there, I might be able to achieve an element of surprise."

Ahmed thought for a moment. "Okay. Let's do it." He scrambled back and returned a minute later with his diving rig and Jack's mask and fins. "I've got two fragmentation grenades left. You can have one, we'll have the other. As soon as we hear yours go off, we'll toss ours down that entranceway."

Jack quickly put on the gear, checked his Beretta and made his way down the rocky slope toward the inlet. A man with a Kalashnikov suddenly appeared a few yards in front of him; he had barely had time to register his surprise when three jets of blood spurted out of his back and he fell. Jack glanced over his shoulder and saw Ahmed's Glock with its silencer poking out from behind a rock, a wisp of smoke curling up from the muzzle.

When he reached the water's edge, he slipped in, then pulled on his mask and fins and dropped down, putting his regulator in his mouth and swimming quickly in the direction of the inlet. As he had suspected, the inlet was deep, eighteen meters according to his dive watch, and wide enough for a U-boat to make its way in. He swam toward the dark patch that he knew must mark the entrance into the pen, swiftly finning under the rocky overhang and hoping that none of the men had spotted his bubbles. Ahead lay blackness, and no certainty that he would be able to get through; he doubted he had enough air to make it in and out again if the way was blocked. But he had no choice now, and he kept going, running his hand against one rock-cut wall for guidance in the dark.

His breathing began to tighten as the tank emptied, but he tried to keep cool, to keep his swimming measured. A few seconds more and he saw a smudge of green light, and then it became clearer, the shapes around him more defined. He realized that the huge bulk that had appeared to his right was the stern end of a submarine, its rudder and screw now clearly visible. He had no time to be astonished at the sight; his air was almost gone. He saw an iridescent patch above him and rose into it, taking out his mouthpiece as he broke surface and trying to keep as quiet as possible.

He was on the edge of a rock-cut platform forming one side of a dock that had been designed to take two submarines. There was artificial light from bulbs strung up on the far side of the chamber, and he could hear the hum of a portable generator. Glancing at the submarine, he could now clearly see that it was a U-boat, rusted but intact, with its forward gun still in place. On the conning tower he could see its designation painted in black letters: U-409. Ahmed had been right. The U-boat had been sitting there for over seventy years, since the end of the war, with a cargo inside that could be as lethal to the world today as it might have been back then, had it reached its intended destination.

He crawled up onto the dock, slipped off his fins and mask, and began to unstrap his rig. Suddenly there was a shout from the platform ahead, and he froze. The crack of a rifle reverberated in the chamber, and a bullet slammed into the rock just behind him. He quickly pulled out his Beretta, found his target, and fired five rounds, dropping the man. Then he got to his feet and ran forward behind a concrete revetment. He could see where four more men had been coming down the rock-cut stairway that must mark the entrance, about fifteen meters away; they were now all crouched down. He pulled out the grenade, pulled the pin and threw it in their direction, falling prone with his hands pressed hard against his ears.

He felt the detonation more than he heard it, a shock wave that coursed through his body. He remained where he was, hoping and praying for the second grenade from Ahmed, and seconds later it detonated, sending a shower of rock fragments in his direction from the entranceway. He got up again just as Ahmed and Costas appeared at the top of the stairs, advancing down in a flurry of gunfire as they finished off any of the pirates who were still alive.

While Ahmed replaced the magazine in his Glock and began to skirt round the dock, Costas walked cautiously along a gantry toward the deck of the U-boat. Jack ran toward him, passing a slew of carnage where the grenades had exploded, and joined him beside the conning tower. Costas beckoned him forward. "The Boss wasn't among them," he whispered. "Nor was Landor. The Boss had a lot of interest in what he thought might be inside the U-boat, so I think he'll be in there."

Jack nodded, then followed Costas up the ladder and into the conning tower, holstering his pistol as he made his way down the rungs. At the bottom, Costas brought his finger to his lips and put on a headlamp that Ahmed had given him, and together they crept round the control room, heading toward the forward torpedo tubes. Costas took out something else that Ahmed had brought, a small Geiger counter, and activated it, sweeping it over the deck. As they approached the tubes, the pinging became more frequent. One of the tubes was open, and they could see that it was stacked full of lead cubes labeled U-235. Jack felt his stomach go cold. "How safe is it?" he whispered.

"A bit heightened, but nothing for us to worry about as long as we don't linger. Someone has recently opened that tube up, as you can see. My guess is we've got company forward."

They turned and headed back toward the conning tower. Further forward, Jack saw a smudge of light and heard noises. They crept past the periscope and the wardroom, watching intently. Suddenly a shot rang out, then another. Jack ducked into the captain's cabin. To his horror, he saw a skeleton slumped over the table, the mildewed remains of a Kriegsmarine uniform shrouding it and a Luger pistol in one hand. What had happened here was anyone's guess, but the captain had not died peacefully; a large section of his skull was missing. Another shot rang out, and Jack followed Costas further down the corridor. Costas caught Jack's attention and pointed at his Beretta. "It's jammed," he whispered. "And it's the Boss ahead, I can smell him. He seems to be out of his head and talking to himself, but he's still got his Kalashnikov. I need a weapon."

Jack remembered the Luger he had seen in the captain's cabin. It had looked in reasonable condition, and there was a chance it might still be functional. He peered along the passageway, and then slowly got up and made his way back, stepping through the cabin doorway. He went over to the skeleton and prised the finger bones from the pistol, peeling the mummified skin off the grip. He had no thought of repugnance for what he was doing, only of survival. He quickly inspected the Luger. It had been well oiled and had a layer of discoloration on the metal parts, but there was no obvious rust. He pressed the catch on the grip and pulled out the magazine, seeing that it still held rounds. He had no time to eject them and check the number, but the two he could see at the top, along with the one in the chamber, would at least give him a fighting chance. He pulled the toggle; at first there was resistance, but then it opened entirely and he ejected the round that had been in the chamber. He worked the toggle several times to loosen the action, pressed the round into the magazine, pushed the magazine back in and cocked the pistol with the toggle, letting it snap forward.

Out in the corridor again, he kept hold of the Luger and passed his Beretta to Costas. "Twelve rounds," he whispered. "Be careful."

Costas pointed ahead. "He's mine."

They advanced along the corridor, weapons at the ready. Sitting against the hatch through the next bulkhead was the Boss, his Kalashnikov over his knees, a dusty half-finished bottle of brandy with a Nazi label in one hand and a joint hanging from his lips. "Eh, Landor, my man, about time," he said, waving the bottle without looking, taking a drag on the joint. "Where you been?"

"Not Landor," Costas said coldly, the Beretta aimed at the man's head. "English, remember?"

The Boss looked at him hazily, then waved the bottle again. "Ah, American, yes. Sit down, have a drink."

Jack saw to his alarm that the Boss had several of the lead cubes in a pile on one side of him, and under a cloth he saw something else, the dull yellow of a gold bar. "Where's Landor?" he demanded.

"Eh?" The man's eyes rolled. "Who are you? Gone to get me some more gold bars. More of my cut. Then we're going to get out of here, find a helicopter to pick us up and take us away. What was all the shooting outside? Some pretty big bangs."

"Come on, Costas, let's go," Jack said. "He's out of it, and this place stinks."

"Hey, not so soon, English." The Boss whipped out a Glock and aimed it at Costas. Jack pulled the trigger on the Luger, and at the same time Costas fired three rounds from his Beretta. The Boss slumped back, his eyes half open, blood running from his chest.

"That's for Zaheed," Costas said quietly. "And for my black eye."

From above they heard a clattering, and then Ahmed's voice shouting down. "Jack. Costas. I think I've found what we're after." They quickly retraced their steps back to the conning tower and climbed out, following Ahmed down onto the deck and across to the dock on the other side of the U-boat. "Up there," he said, pointing at a rusted metal ladder leading to a balcony about ten feet high, robustly built and with a rock-cut entranceway at the top.

They heard a noise from the entrance passageway on the other side, and all three turned and trained their weapons. A Somali marine came cautiously down, his rifle at the ready, followed by two more. Ahmed whistled and showed himself, and then pointed to Jack and Costas. More marines entered and began to spread around the pen, checking and searching, kicking the bodies of pirates on the way. Jack turned to Ahmed. "Only one bad guy still missing. Where the hell is Landor?"

Ahmed pointed up to the balcony. "Let's go and check it out."

Jack climbed the metal ladder onto the balcony and peered round the corner into the passageway, Luger at the ready. Ahead of him, recessed into the rock, was a metal door, the bolt open, with a symbol the size of his palm stamped into the front. He stared at it, his mind racing. It showed a sword facing downward within a loop, and surrounding it an exergue with the words *Deutsches Ahnenerbe*. He turned back to Costas, who had followed him up, Ahmed close behind. "This looks like a strongroom."

Costas edged closer, panning his headlamp beam over the door. He put his shoulder to it, but there was no movement; it presumably opened outward. "I don't suppose you packed any C-5 into that belt of yours?"

"I didn't, but Ahmed did."

"Just a word of warning. This door would normally be padlocked and bolted from the outside. It presumably has some kind of latch on the inside as well. What I'm saying is that there could be someone in there."

Ahmed passed Costas a plastic-covered package that looked like plasticine, and a pair of pencil-shaped detonators. Costas immediately set to work pressing a wedge of the explosive into the edge of the door, and slotted one of the detonators into it. "Okay. I'm setting a thirty-second timer. We need to get out of the way. Ready?"

They quickly backed out, taking shelter behind the rock face on either side of the entrance. Costas looked at his watch. "Fire in the hole." They covered their ears and pressed themselves against the rock. Seconds later the charge went off with a violent crack, sending a spray of debris out over the balcony and clattering onto the U-boat below. They waited while the dust cleared, and then Costas ducked back around, followed by the other two. The metal was dented, but the door was still intact. Jack and Costas each held one of the padlock retainers and pulled hard, inching the door outward. Once it had moved far enough, Costas went behind it and heaved, coughing in the dust, until the door was completely open and they were staring into the chamber beyond.

At first Jack could see very little, the dust still filling the space and his headlamp beam only penetrating a few meters. Then, as the dust settled, he saw a breathtaking sight. What had seemed a narrow passageway was in fact a wide chamber stacked from floor to ceiling with gold bars, hundreds of them, a cache that must have represented more than one U-boat cargo. Beyond the gold lay the open door of a further chamber, stacked trays and racks with objects on them just visible on either side.

In that instant Landor emerged from the dust, lunging toward Jack, barreling into his midriff and pushing him out onto the balcony. Costas and Ahmed watched in shock, their weapons out but unable to shoot for fear of hitting Jack. Landor swung him round against the railing above the water, putting a knife to his throat. "This is our final showdown, Jack. You lost me that gold on *Clan Macpherson*, but you're not going to lose me this."

Jack looked up, feeling the vice-like grip, remembering that it was Landor who had always won the wrestling matches at school. There was no point in struggling, and with the edge of steel against his neck, even the slightest movement might prove fatal. He could see Ahmed trying to aim his Glock to get a head shot, but it was too close to try. "Tell your friends to drop their weapons," Landor snarled.

Ahmed and Costas did so without being prompted, laying them on the balcony and backing off. Jack could feel the knife against his throat as he spoke. "Do you remember our dive in the quarry, Anatoly? Amazing we made it back up with the gear we had. Me jamming my valve against that beam, us buddy-breathing all the way up, you dropping our only flashlight. And then the next day we went back and did it all over again. Those were the days."

"Don't try to sweet-talk me, Jack. Diving doesn't mean anything to me any more. What I remember is that you turned away from me to go and grub around in the dirt with Hiebermeyer."

"Wrong. I turned away from you because of what you were becoming. What you've become now."

"You're not getting out of this one. Not this time."

"Do it, then. Just do it."

Jack tensed. In that instant of hesitation he knew that he had been right, that Landor could not do it. In one swift movement he brought his left elbow hard into the other man's abdomen, making him drop the knife and double back against the railing, taking Jack with him. Ahmed and Costas quickly retrieved their weapons, trying to train them on Landor. Jack twisted round, holding Landor back by the chin, struggling to keep his balance. "It looks as if we're going diving again together after all," he said, jerking his head down to the water beside the U-boat. "It's about ten meters deep, and I've got a minute or so of air left in this little tank on my back."

Landor went wide-eyed, tottering on the edge, his arms wrapping around Jack's regulator hoses as he tried to get at his throat. "You know my medical condition. You know even that would give me a bend."

"That's your call. You can stay up here and be shot, or go down there and take your chances."

They had both leaned out too far, and suddenly they were falling, tumbling down beside the U-boat into the water. They hit the surface in a tangle and went down a few meters, and then Landor released himself and swam down quickly into the gloom toward the base of the chamber, his weak leg trailing behind him as he pulled with his arms. Jack grabbed one of his regulator hoses and put the mouthpiece in, taking a breath and dropping after him. Without a mask, the water was a blur, but he could see Landor on the bottom, looking up, his arms held wide, blowing the remaining air out of his lungs.

Landor had deliberately gone too deep to surface by himself without drowning. But Jack knew him well enough to know that this was not suicide. Landor was playing him, again, and Jack had no choice but to go along with it. Landor knew that Jack would not let him die, not like this, not underwater, when there was a chance of rescue. It would go against all their training, everything they had learned together all those years ago. It was not suicide, but the depth was enough that if Jack gave him air from his tank, it would almost certainly bring on another bend, enough to require immediate medical attention. Landor would have guessed that they would have brought medics with them, and that a naval vessel from CTF 150 would be on the way, probably with the only recompression chamber in miles and one to which the medics would be obliged to send him. He knew that the game was up, that he was not getting away now with any of the gold, and he was seeking a way out. To be captured unharmed by the Somalis would mean festering in a Mogadishu jail; to be medevacked out to a ship in international waters might mean a chance of escape, a chance for Deep Explorer's lawyers to get involved and for Landor to live to play this game another day.

All of that flashed through Jack's mind as he sank to the bottom. He pulled in the octopus rig and tested the purge valve, holding the mouthpiece at the ready. He could see Landor watching him, eyes wide, suddenly terrified, wondering if he had miscalculated. Then Landor grabbed the regulator and breathed from it, hard and fast, the bubbles billowing above

him. Jack knew they only had seconds before the tank would run empty,
and he pulled at Landor's arm, trying to kick up toward the surface. Landor
resisted, hyperventilating, knowing that the more air he breathed under
pressure the more likely he would be to have a bend. Jack felt his own
breathing tighten, and then he pulled the octopus regulator away, pushing
Landor back. This time Landor kicked hard and began to ascend, breathing out as he did so, Jack following close behind. They both broke surface
to the glare of headlamps from the Somali marines who were standing on
the dock with their weapons trained, Costas and Ahmed squatting alongside, ready to help.

Jack gave an okay signal, and looked over to where Landor was bent
double in the water, struggling to keep his head up. "Get him on pure oxygen," he said, seeing the medic among the marines. "And then get him
out of here."

Half an hour later, Jack stood with Costas again at the entrance to the Ahnenerbe chamber. He had stripped off his tank and his tool belt and drunk
several water packs brought along by the marine medic, quickly revitaliz-
ing himself after his encounter with Landor. All of his attention now was
on what lay in front of him. The scene beyond the bullion room was astonishing, one of the most extraordinary sights of his archaeological career.
The chamber revealed by their head torches was small, the size of a modest
bedroom, but was crammed from ceiling to floor with ancient artifacts, as if
they had opened the treasury of a latter-day King Tut. Jack could immediately make out objects of Abyssinian origin on one set of shelves to his left,
elaborate gold crosses of a distinctive Ethiopian shape, chalices and cups, a
golden crown set with emeralds and rubies. On the other side were trays of
artifacts that he recognized from the report that Zaheed had shown him of
material that had disappeared from the museums in Somalia and Ethiopia
at the time of the fascist occupation, and from the churches.

"Congratulations, Jack," Costas said. "It looks like we've hit pay dirt."

"It's fantastic," Jack replied. "When I was reading Captain Wood's account of his Abyssinia experience in 1868, I researched all of the treasures
known to have been looted from Magdala, and their present whereabouts.
Hardly anything was recorded of the drumhead auction that General
Napier held afterward, and a lot of artifacts disappeared without a trace

into private hands. But this collection shows that some of the missing items thought to have been looted then were in fact taken from Abyssinia years later by the Nazis."

"You told me that the Patriarch mentioned that secret chamber beneath the church at Magdala, and the Ahnenerbe men spending days scouring the place. Maybe they found other secret caches that the Abyssinians had managed to conceal from the British."

Jack held up the crown, and looked pensively at the ground. "I only wish Zaheed had been able to see this. It would have made his day. It's going to put Ethiopia and Somalia back on the map archaeologically."

"Finding this stuff and getting it back to the museums is the greatest credit you can give Zaheed. We wouldn't have got here without him."

Jack made his way through exotic furniture and other artifacts cluttering the floor to a heavy wooden chest in the far corner of the chamber. He lifted the lid, and gasped. "I've never seen anything like this outside a Hollywood movie."

Costas came over and knelt down beside him, his jaw dropping too. The chest was full of gold and silver coins, thousands of them, of all shapes and sizes. Jack plunged his hands in, grasping what he could and pulling them out, letting the overflow cascade back down and inspecting what was left. "Incredible," he said. "I'm seeing lots of medieval issues of the sultanate of Mogadishu, and Axumite gold coins of the fourth and fifth century, many of them mint issues. Look at that one: the inscription reads 'Basileus Axomitus,' King of the Axumites. I'd say the Ahnenerbe must have got hold of a couple of hoards. But there are also lots of others, Egyptian, Arabian, Indian, gold dinars, lots of Byzantine Roman issues of Theodora and Justinian. Some of those have holes in them showing they were reused as jewelry, very common in India. It looks as if the Ahnenerbe scoured the whole of the Indian Ocean region for this, not just the Horn of Africa. It's a fantastic porthole into the Indian Ocean trade in antiquity, and it's going to occupy numismatists for years to come. Not to speak of being a spectacular centerpiece for a museum display."

Ahmed appeared at the entrance, leaning in. "That's the place secured. Landor's in custody pending evacuation to a secure military hospital in Mogadishu. We're not letting him out of the country. Captain Ibrahim has radioed to say that a second patrol boat is on the way, as well as a frigate from CTF 150, with a team prepped to deal with removing the uranium. And it's game over for the Badass Boys. None of them are left alive. We're scouring the place in case there are any Nazi munitions that need to be made safe."

Costas looked up, dropping the gold coin he had been holding. "Ordnance disposal? Count me in."

"Not a chance," Jack said. "You're helping me here."

Ahmed suddenly saw what Jack was doing. "Merciful Allah," he exclaimed. "That's incredible. It looks as if you've got your hands full here too."

Costas rocked back on his haunches, looking thoughtfully at Jack. "Yo-ho-ho and a bottle of rum," he sang quietly.

Jack turned to him, his arms half buried in gold. "Don't go there. I mean, just don't. We are *not* pirates."

"Have you seen yourself? I wish I had a camera. Jack Howard gone over to the dark side."

Jack hastily withdrew his hands, self-consciously brushing off a few coins. "Remarkable find," he murmured. "We need to get these cleaned and into plastic sleeves."

"Not all pirates were bad, were they?" Costas continued. "I mean, Robin Hood was a kind of pirate, and he took from the rich and gave to the poor. And you can't tell me that all your Howard nautical ancestors were goody-goody. There must have been the odd Blackbeard among them, right? You must have just a *little* bit of pirate in you."

"I like the sound of giving to the poor. That's where all those gold bars outside are going. As for this stuff, getting it into museums in the countries where it belongs is going to enrich far more lives than just my own."

"You're telling me that kneeling there up to your elbows in gold, you didn't just slightly reach out to your inner pirate?"

Jack looked around at the room, at the treasures he had been holding, suddenly awash with excitement at what they had discovered, at the wonders he would soon be able to reveal to the world. He turned to Costas, his eyes glinting. "My inner pirate? What do *you* think?"

Costas slapped him on the back. "I think you're a hopeless case."

Jack put his arm around his friend, tired but elated. "You know me. I'm just an archaeologist."

Epilogue

Three days later, Jack sat on the shore of the island, watching the waves lap the rocks and the evening sunlight cast a rosy hue on the surface of the sea. The last of the naval team who had been working in the U-boat pen had departed half an hour before, leaving one remaining Zodiac for him to drive out with the others when they were ready. *Seaquest* was holding position half a mile offshore, flanked by warships from the anti-piracy force, one a frigate of the Royal Canadian Navy, the other a US Navy destroyer. They were a reassuring presence, security against any unwanted incursion while the pen was being cleared. Once the uranium had been removed and the Ahnenerbe chamber emptied, the plan was for a naval demolition team to blow the entrance and collapse the cavern. The residual radiation levels in the U-boat were unlikely to pose a long-term hazard, but the site was a war grave, the last resting place of those who had died here in 1945. There was every prospect of the islands becoming the front line in a new war, not against pirates but against Iran and its terrorist affiliates, and the Yemeni and Somali governments had agreed that the archipelago should be a no-go zone until the situation improved.

Jack watched three figures make their way over the rocky ground from the helipad that had been cleared above the cavern entrance. Rebecca and Jeremy had arrived on *Seaquest* two days before to help with clearing the Ahnenerbe chamber, due to start tomorrow. The Lynx from *Seaquest* had dropped them on the island a few minutes ago, and had then clattered off back to the ship. Trailing behind them was a third figure in familiar Hawaiian beach gear, his left arm trussed up in a sling and carrying something on his back. Jack smiled when he saw them, and raised his hand in greeting. They came over and sat down around him, Costas dropping his sack on a flat rock beside the sea. "I had the catering people on *Seaquest* make me up one of those portable barbecues, with real charcoal. This place isn't exactly a beach, but it'll do."

"What are we eating?" Jack said.

Costas reached into the sack, pulled out the foil barbecue tray, and then a wet bag. "Fish," he said, spilling the contents onto the rock. "Red mullet, wrasse, sea bass. Jeremy speared them this afternoon."

Rebecca stared at Jeremy in mock disbelief. "I didn't know about that. No way. Jeremy couldn't hit a tin can in front of his nose."

"Yep," Costas said, pulling out a box of matches and a stack of paper plates. "This afternoon while you and your dad were busy, I drove him around to the reef at the back of the island and showed him the fish identification chart, and an hour later we were on our way back with the cooler full."

"What was it you said a few days ago?" Jeremy said, eyeing Rebecca. "There's a lot you don't know about me."

"I still don't believe it. I challenge you tomorrow. We'll catch lunch for the entire team."

"You're on."

Jack smiled and turned to Costas, inspecting his swollen eye and the cuts and bruises on his face. "You sure you're okay being out of sick bay?"

Costas dropped a lit match into the tray, and stirred the charcoal with a stick. "I checked myself out. No way was I staying cooped up in there. How about you?"

"My back hurts from bouncing around in that Zodiac, and my right knee is playing up. Nothing that won't be fixed as soon as I'm back in the water again."

"Let's face it, you two *are* getting a bit old for this kind of thing," Rebecca said, taking another stick and poking at the fire. "No offense, but you know what I mean. Maybe it's time you passed the baton to the younger generation."

Jack turned and looked at Costas, and they both stared at Rebecca.

"Maybe it's time the younger generation went back and finished school," Jack said.

"I didn't mean the diving, I meant all the commando stuff," Rebecca continued, looking at them deadpan. "You could delegate that to your up-and-coming protégés—Jeremy, for example."

"Whoa," Jeremy said. "Spearfishing is one thing, wielding a Kalashnikov is another. I'm an epigrapher, not Indiana Jones."

"Long may it stay that way," Jack said. "Without your expertise with the Phoenician inscriptions, we'd be telling a different story."

Costas put the grill on the tray and sat beside it. "So, Jack. We found our gold after all. We made up for what we lost on *Clan Macpherson*."

"What *you* lost, you mean. I didn't try to defuse that torpedo."

"You weren't ever going to let it fall into the hands of Landor, were you?"

"It's true. You made it easier for me."

"So what's the plan with this new haul?"

"There are some formalities to get through with the Yemeni and Somali authorities, but nobody's going to claim ownership or stand in the way of the plan I'd envisaged for the *Clan Macpherson* gold. The South African government has agreed to take the bars and rebrand them under UN ownership, and our UN rep has already secured approval for a new agency specifically to disburse the funds. We're looking at half going to West Africa, to alleviate child poverty and for disease prevention, and half going to the Horn of Africa, to the coastal communities of Somalia, for development aid. How does that sound?"

"Pretty amazing, Dad," Rebecca said. "I'd like to be part of that."

"That kind of aid in Somalia might help to wean young men away from piracy," Costas said.

"Not just piracy, but the lure of the extremists," Jack replied. "This coast is a prime recruiting ground, with so many young men unemployed and directionless. I had a long discussion about it with the naval force commander yesterday. It'll be a challenge to get the balance right, but we envisage a combination of poverty alleviation, funding schools and educational programs, and seeding economic initiatives, especially those focused on rebooting traditional subsistence activities. None of it will work without effective policing of the offshore territorial zone to exclude the foreign trawlers that have nearly destroyed the local fish stocks, the main factor that has driven the men to piracy. We want to see the patrol boats policing against outsiders, not against the Somalis themselves. That gold will help to extinguish piracy along the coast."

"Amen to that," Costas said, wincing as he held his arm. "And a big finger to the Nazis and their schemes. Whoever once might have owned that gold, this is the best place for it."

"So what about the Ark of the Covenant?" Rebecca said.

Jack said nothing. He was staring out to sea, looking south toward the huge stretch of coast that the ancients called the Runs of Azania, toward the island of Madagascar and the very extremity of Africa, to the cape where a Phoenician adventurer had put up a bronze plaque with an extraordinary message to posterity more than two and a half thousand years ago. In his mind's eye he imagined the scene, saw Hanno tapping in that final symbol as the wind howled and the sea churned against the rocky headland below; for a moment, gazing out to sea, he saw not *Seaquest* and the two warships but a lone Phoenician vessel battling its way up the coast, carrying a cargo to a secret destination in a covenant with a people who knew they might not see their most sacred treasure for many generations to come. He was convinced that what he was imagining was real, not just a flight of fancy; he had seen the plaque with his own eyes, as real as the flecks of gold on the animal hide that Maurice had excavated in Carthage. And he remembered standing with Zaheed in front of the Chapel of the Tablet at Axum, sensing with sudden clarity why it was that the ancient prophets of Israel had wanted their treasure concealed, and why the time was not yet right to reveal it, even though their descendants ruled once again in the Holy Land and might need the strength of their covenant more than ever.

Costas laid the first of the fillets on the grill, and they watched as the steam rose above them into the darkening sky. "Another one of those biblical passages I can remember," Costas said, staring into the embers. "Jeremiah, chapter three, verses sixteen and seventeen. 'And it shall come to pass, when ye be multiplied and increased in the land, in those days, saith the Lord, they shall say no more the ark of the covenant of the Lord; neither shall it come to mind: neither shall they remember it; neither shall they visit it; neither shall that be done any more. At that time they shall call Jerusalem the throne of the Lord; and all the nations shall be gathered unto it.'"

"What does it mean?" Rebecca asked.

"There's another passage in Second Maccabees, chapter two," Costas continued. "You won't find it in the King James version, but it's considered canonical by the Greek Orthodox Church. After the Ark is sealed up in its cave, the prophet Jeremiah reprimands his followers for leaving waymarkers to it. He tells them that the place shall remain unknown until God finally gathers his people together and shows mercy to them. 'The Lord will bring these things to light again, and the glory of the Lord will appear with the cloud.'"

"I'm just a dirt archaeologist," Jack said, "but I do believe in the power of artifacts for their symbolism, for maintaining hope and strength in times of adversity. And sometimes that's best maintained when an artifact is just beyond our reach, a hidden treasure that forever fires up our imagination. It's the yearning for it, the quest, that keeps us going, not the thought of actually holding it in our hands."

"And the world of peace the prophets hoped for, the time for the revelation, has not yet come about," Rebecca said.

Jack nodded grimly. "The Middle East is a cauldron, worse than it ever has been before, worse even than at the time of Nebuchadnezzar and the destruction of the Temple, when the Ark was spirited away. All the peoples of the Holy Land, whatever their beliefs, need symbols of hope to sustain them. The Ark is where it should be."

"So what's going to happen to Landor?"

Jack paused again, pursing his lips. "Captain Ibrahim assures me that he'll be put on trial for conspiracy to murder, attempted murder, and aiding and abetting piracy. They hold him responsible for the deaths of Zaheed and the two marines killed during the kidnapping shoot-out, as well as the casualties here."

"Do you think it will stick?"

"I doubt it. With the Badass Boys history now, the Somalis may be unable to find anyone who can testify that Landor ordered the kidnapping. He's a wily customer, very experienced at covering his back, no paperwork or emails, everything done by word of mouth and payments in cash. Deep Explorer Incorporated may go under, but not Landor. He'll probably never walk again, but he can do what he does just as well from a wheelchair. He'll spend some unpleasant months under guard in a Mogadishu hospital, then his lawyers will get him bail on a technicality and he'll be out of the country before you can say treasure wreck. He did the same thing in Colombia early in his career, and will doubtless do it again before he gets on the wrong

side of someone really big-time—the Russian or Chinese mafia perhaps—
and someone puts a bullet in the back of his head."

"And *Deep Explorer*?"

"That's a happier outcome. I don't think there's any chance the investment consortium are going to try to reclaim their ship. They've cut their
losses before and moved on under a different name, and they'll do the same
now. This morning Ibrahim and I had a teleconference with the British
ambassador in Mogadishu to discuss the possibility of UK aid funding to
convert her to a fisheries patrol and research vessel, run by the Somali navy
but with a scientific role as well. She'd be modeled on *Seaquest* and *Sea
Venture*, and we could do the conversion in our own yard. I think we'll get
the go-ahead."

"The situation with fishing remains the critical factor out here," Costas said.

Jack nodded. "I talked about that with the ambassador just before the
gun attack that killed Zaheed. We agreed to work up a strong case for an
aid package that would see surplus UK equipment go to the Somali navy,
as well as more personnel secondments and training initiatives. The UK
has put a big commitment into Somalia with the new embassy, and the
ambassador thinks there's a good chance of our package being approved.
She thinks the US will come on board as well, once they re-establish their
presence in Mogadishu."

"Have you been in touch with Zaheed's wife yet?" Rebecca asked.

Jack stared into the embers. "I'll be visiting her in Mogadishu as soon
as we're out of here. The embassy people have been with her and her daughter round the clock. They know that IMU will look after them financially
for as long as is necessary, including her daughter's education and their re-
location to the West, if that's what they want. We'll provide for them as
Zaheed would have done had he lived."

"Zaheed talked to Lieutenant Ahmed, you know," Costas said. "Outside the naval headquarters before we took our fateful drive. They were
planning to present you with a proposal for a beefed-up IMU presence in
Somalia, with Ahmed's club providing the divers."

"Ahmed's spoken to me about it, and it's already green-lit," Jack said.
"That's part of the plan for *Deep Explorer* as well, to serve as an operational
base for wreck investigation. It allows us to make use of quite a lot of the
existing equipment in the ship, redirecting its purpose from salvage to

archaeology. I've invited Ahmed to spend his next leave with us in Corn-wall. If only Zaheed had been able to come with him. But it's great to see something good emerging from all this."

"Ahmed's still on the island and is coming up here shortly," Costas said. "Apparently he's got something to show you. He's pretty excited."

"Where are you going next?" Rebecca said to Jack, resting her head on her knees and hugging her legs.

Jack looked again at *Seaquest*, and then around to the north, following a dark streak of cloud that seemed to envelop the horizon. Somewhere up there, somewhere beyond the Arabian shore, a black hole of destruction was threatening to swallow the cradle of civilization itself, sucking into it the very essence of history. Ever since returning from the clutches of ex-tremism in Egypt, Jack had known that his destiny was to return, not to Egypt but to the very maw of the hole itself, to the place where history was being wiped clean. Nothing else he could do now, no other quest, was as important as trying to protect the treasures of the oldest civilizations from desecration, a task he could no longer stand by and watch others fail to achieve while knowing that he might have the ability and resources to make a difference.

"You're going back there, aren't you?" Rebecca said quietly. "Into the cauldron."

Jack stared into the fire, watching Costas turn the fish. "I don't know. But I can't just ignore it. None of us can." He exhaled forcefully, then looked at her. "What about you?"

"Me?" Rebecca took off the headscarf she had been wearing, and gave him a brazen look. Instead of the long, dark hair he was so used to, he saw that she had shorn it almost completely, to above the ears. He stared, flabbergasted, and then slowly smiled. Suddenly she was no longer a girl but a young woman, tough and ready for anything.

"I had no idea," he said. "That looks great."

"I didn't do it for the look of it. I did it because it's more practical in this heat, for what Jeremy and I have planned."

"Which is?"

"We talked it through with Captain Macleod on *Seaquest*. He has to stay on station for another five days at least, while they finish clearing the pen. The warships will be here as well for our protection, and the Yemeni official in charge of Socotra has given us the go-ahead."

"You planning to invade the island? Costas said.

"Intensive archaeological survey off the south coast. We can put four Zodiacs in the water from *Seaquest*. The diving units on both warships are excited about it too, an excellent training opportunity for them. With the possibility of war looming, when are we ever going to get another opportunity like this? These islands were bang in the middle of one of the most incredible trade routes of the ancient world, between the Mediterranean and the Red Sea on the one hand and the Indian Ocean and the world beyond on the other. We could get anything: medieval Arab traders, Chinese junks, Greek and Roman merchant ships, you name it. My hope is for an ancient Egyptian ship coming back from India laden with treasures of the East. Maurice thought that would be really cool."

"You've discussed this with him?" Jack said.

"It was his idea, actually. Apparently he's always wanted to explore Socotra. Something about Egyptian Middle Kingdom artifacts dug up here years ago by a British adventurer, in the mid-nineteenth century, I think."

"Ah, yes," Jack said. "That would be Captain Peter Hall of the Bengal Sappers, one of the men on the 1868 Abyssinia expedition. I found out about his Socotra excursion in one of my great-great-grandfather's letters, and made the mistake of telling Maurice about it."

"Actually, he's itching to get out here," Rebecca said.

"Maurice is coming?"

Rebecca looked at her watch. "Should be in the air in a couple of hours. Almost all finished at Carthage. He just needs to clean up in his trench and get it backfilled."

"Good of you to keep me in the loop."

"You and Costas are welcome to join us. That is," she said, eyeing Jack mischievously, "if you're not too old for that kind of thing."

"That reminds me," Jack said, suddenly remembering something. "Louise, the Bletchley girl back in England. I owe her an update."

"Don't worry about it," Jeremy said. "I've kept her posted since the get-go. She seems to have taken a particular shine to me."

"Still, I'll Skype her tomorrow," Jack said. "She opened up to us about the war, about her work at Bletchley, and I owe it to her. Finding the gold helps to bring the story of *Clan Macpherson* and that whole secret operation to a kind of resolution, something she's been wanting for more than seventy years."

"She'll love to hear what you're planning to do with it," Jeremy said. "One up on the Nazis. A lot of people like her who put their all into it back then are still fighting the war, you know."

Twenty minutes later, Lieutenant Ahmed came along the rocks from the direction of the inlet, wearing Somali navy fatigues and carrying a plastic bag. "A few more for the barbecue," he said, handing the bag to Costas. "My men did some spearfishing after their final inspection of the inlet."

"How goes it?" Jack said.

Ahmed sat down on a rock and accepted a bottle of water from Costas. "All the radioactive material is now in the frigate, destined for disposal. We've got everything set up for the team from the museum who are arriving tomorrow to begin clearing that treasure chamber. Are your people still good with that?"

Jack nodded. "The IMU conservators are due this evening at Mogadishu and will be brought out by the Lynx from *Seaquest* in the morning. With any luck we'll have all the artifacts flown out and in a secure laboratory by the end of the week."

"This is going to cause a huge stir," Ahmed said. "It looks as if those Ahnenerbe men were quietly stealing everything they could find of value in the places they explored in Africa. One of my friends who works for the museum has had a look at the records, and there were items that disappeared mysteriously while this place was under Mussolini's control in the late 1930s, most of it gold from the ancient Axum civilization. Restoring those artifacts to their rightful place will give a big boost to the sense of identity and pride among the people here, something much needed after the past couple of decades."

"IMU will do everything it can to help," Jack said.

"There is one other thing." Ahmed took a swaddled package from his pocket and leaned forward, eyeing Jack intently. "Do you remember I told you my plan to enlist local fishermen in our search for wrecks, a way of getting a program of maritime archaeological research on a proper footing in Somalia?"

"Putting out an APB," Costas said, taking Ahmed's fish and laying them beside the grill. "It's always the best way. Use local knowledge first."

Ahmed nodded. "Well, we've already come up with something very interesting. One of the fishermen, a grandson of the man who led us to this island, regularly goes along the northern Somali coast into the Red Sea as far as Eritrea, to Annesley Bay. One of his favorite spots is not far from the town of Zula, near ancient Adulis, the port of Axum."

"Where the British landed during the 1868 Abyssinia expedition," Jack said.

"Right. It's a big area of salt flats, and there's still some evidence of the British engineering works: piles for jetties and the remains of wooden causeways. At one of those places our man came ashore and saw the remains of an old hull poking out of the mud, with strange-looking markings on the bow. He took a picture of it on his phone and forwarded it to me."

Ahmed tapped his phone and passed it over to Jack, who enlarged the picture and stared at it, swiping from side to side to get a full view. "That's old all right," he murmured. "*Very* old. Ancient mortice-and-tenon construction."

"Could be Egyptian," Rebecca said, peering over his shoulder. "The ancient Egyptians sailed down the Red Sea to the Land of Punt, and they were the originators of that construction technique. At least that's what Maurice says."

"Not with this on the bow." Jack passed her the phone, and Jeremy and Costas leaned over to see. "Good Lord," Jeremy said. "It's a painted eye. An apotropaic eye."

"You don't see those on Egyptian boats," Jack said. "But you do see them on ancient ships of the Mediterranean, where the eye is still used today to ward off bad luck."

"Specifically, you might see it on a Phoenician ship," Jeremy said, taking the phone and swiping the screen to get maximum magnification. "*Definitely* on a Phoenician ship."

"What else can you see?" Jack asked.

Jeremy handed the phone back, pointing. "That."

Jack stared at the image. It was a section of planking just below the bow, half buried in mud, with a symbol faintly visible on one of the planks. "It's a carpenter's mark," he said. "The letters *alpha* and *gamma.*"

"The letter A is toppled over on one side," Jeremy said. "That's the Phoenician letter A. Can you see it?"

"What could a Phoenician ship possibly be doing in the southern Red Sea?" Costas said, looking at Jack with a half-smile on his face.

"Pharaoh Necho's expedition?" Rebecca said. "Didn't he employ Phoenicians to sail south down the Red Sea on their expedition to circumnavigate Africa?"

"Phoenicians came in the other direction too, didn't they?" Ahmed said. "Circumnavigating Africa from the west. You told me your theory about Hanno."

Jack nodded slowly, his mind racing, staring at the photo. "He may not have sailed the entire route back into the Mediterranean, but he made it back to Carthage, and I'm convinced it was from this side of Africa."

"Then you'll be very intrigued with the other thing the fisherman found." Ahmed unwrapped the package, carefully taking out an encrusted potsherd. "This was in the shallows just beyond the hull. It looks like an amphora sherd to me. I've been following the blog on your Phoenician wreck off Cornwall over the past few weeks, so I'm pretty sure I can recognize Phoenician letters when I see them. I think I can read that first word."

He passed the sherd to Jack, who held it so the others could see it. One side, the interior, was covered with worm castings and accretion, with some of the pitch lining of the amphora still visible. The other side had the faint lines of letters scratched on it, clearly done in antiquity. Jack stared, astonished. *Two words; two brothers.* One was the man he had followed on his venture around the coast of Africa, an extraordinary expedition with an extraordinary cargo; the other was a man who had gone to the far side of the known world, whose final moments they had charted in the waters of the cove in England where Jack had been diving less than a week before, where Costas had found the sherd inscribed in the last moments of duress, when that man too could only think of his brother.

"Hanno and Himilco," Rebecca said quietly. "Hanno thinking of his brother when he leaves his ship, wondering if he'll see him again."

Jeremy took out a pocket magnifier and scrutinized the sherd, angling it against the firelight. He snapped the magnifier shut and handed the sherd back to Jack. "I thought so," he said.

"What is it?" Jack said.

"Between the names. You can barely see it, but it's there. That pictogram."

Jack stared. Suddenly he could see it, the image on the plaque from *Clan Macpherson* that had been on the sherd from the Cornwall wreck. "Well

I'll be damned," he said, passing it to Rebecca, pointing at the symbol of the two men carrying the box. "That's incredible. It's exactly the same."

Costas reached over and shook his hand. "Well, you didn't find the Ark of the Covenant, but then neither did those Nazi bastards. But when it comes down to it, there's nothing like a potsherd to keep an archaeologist happy."

"Oh, but I did find it," Jack said, taking the sherd again and holding it up. "And you're right. This sherd is my gold, all the gold I need." He grinned at Ahmed. "I think I owe you a place on our next big wreck excavation, your duties permitting, of course."

"I'd love that."

"Right, grub's up," Costas said. "There's beer and water in the bag for everyone. Plates, please."

Jack took a bottle of water and uncapped it. He picked up a plate, waiting his turn, and took a deep drink, looking at the stars that were just becoming visible above the horizon. He thought of all those he seemed to have been shadowing: Hanno and the Phoenicians, the soldiers who had scaled Magdala in 1868, the men of *Clan Macpherson,* and those in Bletchley Park who had decided their fate. For a moment he imagined himself looking down from far above, seeing only the red speck of the fire, the bare rock and the great expanse of the sea around them, imagining those lives that had gone before, all of them navigating routes that seemed to have converged at this place.

He took another swig and watched Rebecca sit down on the same rock as Jeremy with her plateful. He looked back at the sea again, thinking about diving. Macleod had told him about Rebecca's project as soon as she had introduced it, but he had let her take it forward. They would need to sit down tomorrow with the Admiralty charts to talk about currents and reefs. He had already scoped out the island for the most likely places for wreckage, the places nearest to the sailing routes where ships might have been blown ashore. They would have to take account of the variegation of the seabed he had seen on their hurried dive from the doomed trawler. A few hundred meters of easy-looking coastal water on the surface could be a jumble of rocks and gullies underwater, hard to navigate and impossible to survey systematically. It would be Rebecca's project, but he would make sure they did not come away empty-handed. And she might well be right. There could be a great treasure lurking under these waves in front of them, something to add to IMU's rich bank of projects for the future.

Rebecca passed her phone over to Jack. "Maurice just sent me this. He wanted you to see it."

Jack stared at the image, a selfie of Maurice holding a small Egyptian statue of a god and beaming at the camera. "Huh," he said. "A *shabti,* a funerary figurine. That looks like the one he found when we excavated the Roman villa as schoolboys, the find that really turned him on to Egyptology. Good to see him looking happy again."

"No," Rebecca said. "That's one he's just found in Carthage. *That's* why he's so happy."

Jack smiled broadly. "Well I'll be damned. Good on you, Maurice."

"It was at the bottom of the harbor entrance channel, below the bronze of Ba'al and the gorilla skin. He says he knows it doesn't prove anything, that it could have been dropped overboard by a passing ship, but he does say that it's the right date—ninth century BC—for an Egyptian presence in the early trading post at Carthage. He says finding it makes him feel as if he's come full circle. He says from now on he's not going to hold back on telling you what he's found. From now on he's going to tell you *everything.*"

"That sounds like the old Maurice. I knew he'd be back."

Costas slapped a fish on Jack's plate and sat down beside him, grunting with satisfaction as he contemplated the pile on his own plate. He nudged Jack along on his rock to make more space, and peered at him. "You've got that look again."

"You always say that. I've just been thinking, that's all."

Costas picked up a fish by the tail and pulled the flesh off the bone, then cracked open a beer. "Is there something you want to ask me?"

"About what?"

He took a swig. "You know. The usual. About my plans."

"About your arm."

"My arm? What about it?"

"Salt water would do it good. Clean up the wound."

Costas stuffed some fish into his mouth and waved dismissively. "It's only a scratch. I can take this thing off tonight."

"It's just that I was wondering . . ."

"Yes?"

"You ready to dive tomorrow?"

Costas took another huge swig of beer, swallowed noisily, and slapped Jack on the back, grinning broadly. "What do you think? Those are the best words I've heard all day. I can't wait."

Author's Note

When the power of Carthage flourished, Hanno sailed round from Cadiz to the extremity of Arabia, and published a memoir of his voyage, as did Himilco when he was dispatched at the same date to explore the outer coasts of Europe.

Pliny, *Natural History*, 2:169

The kernel of this novel came early in my career as an archaeologist when I was standing beside the ancient harbor of Carthage in Tunisia, having just come up from a dive to examine the submerged remains located a few meters offshore. A year earlier, exploring underground passageways near Temple Mount in Jerusalem, I had wondered whether any of the treasures concealed at the time of the Babylonian conquest in the early sixth century BC might still be there, and afterward I had gone down to the Mediterranean coast of Israel to dive at the old Phoenician port of Caesarea Maritima. At Carthage, nothing remains above ground of the early Phoenician settlement, but excavations since the 1970s have revealed much of later Punic date—Punic being the term the Romans used for the Carthaginians—that allowed me to envisage the city at the time of the Babylonian conquest of the Holy Land by Nebuchadnezzar.

Nowhere in Carthage is the Punic past more visible than in the harbors, their landlocked form strikingly reminiscent of the harbor of Carthage's mother city of Tire in modern Lebanon. Not far from where I was standing was the Tophet, the supposed site of Carthaginian child sacrifice, another tangible link to the old world of Phoenicia and Canaan, to the biblical story of Abraham and Isaac. I began to wonder about the strength of the connection in the sixth century BC of Carthage with old Phoenicia, and by extension with the kingdom of Judah. After Tire and the other ports of Phoenicia had been subjugated by the Babylonians, and with Carthage in the ascendancy—and home of the greatest navigators of the day, men such as Hanno and Himilco—could it have been to Carthage that the Israelites turned to safeguard their treasures? Could the greatest treasure of them all, Aron Habberit, the Ark of the Covenant, have been spirited away by Carthaginian mariners on an incredible journey to a far-distant place, to await the time of revelation prophesied in the Old Testament?

The appearance of the Ark of the Covenant is well known from the account in the Book of Exodus (25:10–22) quoted at the beginning of this novel. Another biblical source is the Second Book of Maccabees, accepted as part of the canon by the Roman Catholic and Greek Orthodox churches (though not in the Jewish or Protestant traditions); in it we read of Jeremiah on a mountain putting the Ark inside a "cave-dwelling," and then sealing up the entrance (2 Maccabees 2:5). There is no mention of the Ark in surviving ancient secular literature, for example by the Roman encyclopedist Pliny the Elder, and all modern discussion must therefore rest solely on the biblical accounts.

   The plausibility of the Ark as an actual ancient artifact was given sharp focus by the 1922 discovery in Tutankhamun's tomb of the Anubis Shrine, a gilded portable chest bearing close similarities to the description of the Ark and dating from the same period—especially if, as I suggest in my novel *Pyramid*, the biblical Exodus did indeed take place at the time of Akhenaten, Tutankhamun's immediate predecessor. One oft-cited difference, between the seated dog Anubis on the chest and the two golden *kerubim* of the Ark, who "spread out their wings on high . . . with their faces one to the other" (Exodus 25:18–21), may arise from a mistranslation. The word "cherub" in Western art, referring to an angelic child, appears to derive from a rabbinic tradition that defined the ancient Hebrew word *kerubim* as "like a child." However, the word at the time of the Old Testament most probably referred to the lion or bull with wings and a human face commonly represented in ancient Middle Eastern art, and appearing in Egypt as the sphinx. The seated Anubis dog and the *kerubim* may there-

fore have been similar in appearance, and served a similar protective function over the contents of the box—sacred funerary equipment in the case
of the former, the testament of the Ten Commandments in the latter.

If such an artifact, modeled on Egyptian processional chests familiar
to the Israelites, did indeed survive the ravages of Nebuchadnezzar, then
its whereabouts since the sixth century BC remains a mystery. One theory,
associating the Ark with the Lemba people of South Africa, who claim to
have carried the *ngoma lungundu*, "the voice of God," to a mountain hide-
away, may be given weight by a similarity in genetic signature between the
Lemba and peoples of known Semitic origins, and by the similarity of some
practices and beliefs among the Lemba with those of Judaism. A more deep-
rooted tradition places the Ark in Ethiopia, where the Ethiopian Orthodox Church claims that it is kept in the Chapel of the Tablet at the Church
of Our Lady Mary of Zion in Axum. For the guardian priests of Temple
Mount in the early sixth century BC, hemmed in on all sides and with the
Babylonians at the gate, the lands south of Egypt might have seemed
the best bet for concealing their treasures, away from Babylonian raiders
yet within reach of future recovery when the time was right—the "promised land" that was to become the early Christian Kingdom of Axum,
flanked to the south by nearly impenetrable mountains that might have
provided just the kind of cave refuge for the Ark described in the Second
Book of Maccabees.

If such a scenario is correct, then a decision by the priests of Jerusalem not
to send their greatest treasure on the perilous overland trip south, fraught
with the possibility of brigandage and capture, but instead to use the much
longer sea route across the Mediterranean and around Africa, may have
been spurred by the greater security offered by their Punic kinsmen in
Carthage—masters of sea trade at that time, and expert handlers of cargo—
and by the recent success of Phoenician navigators in completing a circumnavigation of Africa. According to Herodotus, writing in the fifth
century BC, the Egyptian pharaoh Necho ordered a Phoenician crew to
"sail round and return to Egypt and the Mediterranean by way of the
Pillars of Hercules," the Strait of Gibraltar (*Histories*, 4:42). Necho ruled
*c.*610–595 BC, so that voyage may have taken place only a few years before
Nebuchadnezzar captured Jerusalem. The success of those Phoenicians

may have led Hanno of Carthage to attempt his own circumnavigation in the other direction, counterclockwise, at the same time that Himilco set off toward the British Isles. Dating these famous voyages of discovery to the early sixth century BC is consistent with Carthage suddenly being thrust into the limelight as the new center of the Phoenician world, both for those already settled in the western Mediterranean and for their kinsmen fleeing the Babylonians, and with the need for Carthaginian traders to assert their dominance over sea routes leading beyond the Strait of Hercules, to the north as well as to the south.

The oldest surviving version of Hanno's *Periplus* is a tenth-century copy of a Greek text in the *Codex Palatinus Graecus* in Heidelberg University Library. The original Punic account is said in the introduction to have been inscribed on tablets hung up in the temple of "Chronos," a Greek rendition of a Punic god and probably referring to the temple of Ba'al Hammon at Carthage. The idea that Hanno did indeed complete the circumnavigation—the Heidelberg *Periplus*, which may be incomplete, has him abruptly turning back somewhere near modern Senegal—derives from Pliny's assertion that he sailed from Cadiz to the "extreme part of Arabia" (*Natural History*, 2:169). Pliny, writing in the first century AD, probably had access to an early Greek or Latin translation of the *Periplus*, perhaps one made after the Roman capture of Carthage in 146 BC. He himself reveals that the tablets were still there to be seen at that date in his other famous reference to Hanno's voyage—his assertion that the skins of the females he calls "Gorgons," the *gorillae* of the Greek version (a word perhaps taken verbatim from the original Punic inscription, and of southern African origin), were hung up in a temple "to prove his story and as a curious exhibit," and were still there when Romans captured Carthage (*Natural History*, 6:200).

On the other hand, the *Periplus of Himilco*, if it ever existed, does not survive even in part; the only indication that there might have been such a work is a remark by Pliny that Hanno "published an account of his voyage, as did Himilco." A circumnavigation of the British Isles would have been at least as worthy of celebration in Carthage as Hanno's voyage, and if a *Periplus* did exist in Pliny's time, it seems surprising that he should not have made more of it. For that reason I have imagined that Himilco did not, in fact, survive his voyage, that his brother Hanno waited in vain for him in Carthage until all hope was lost, and that the only news that eventually did come of Himilco—none of which mentioned a successful circumnavigation of the British Isles—originated with those who had left the expedition earlier, and who could report nothing that Pliny centuries later could regard as interesting or reliable enough to put in his *Natural History*.

The chapter set in Carthage was inspired by my own experiences codirecting investigations at the ancient harbor site as part of the UNESCO "Save Carthage" project when I was a post-doctoral research fellow at Cambridge University. Just as Hiebermeyer does in the novel, we watched while a digger excavated deep into the sediment at the harbor entrance, eventually revealing the gray-black sludge of the channel; on the way it exposed a skeleton, perhaps of a sixteenth-century Spanish soldier, that our students dubbed "Miguel." At the time, I wondered whether the unexcavated seafront flanking the channel might have been the site of a monumental harbor entrance, just the kind of place where the achievement of the great navigators might have been celebrated—perhaps even the site of a temple precinct of Ba'al Hammon that contained the tablets of the Periplus and the *gorillae* skins from Hanno's voyage.

A harbor-front platform might also have been a place where propitiatory child sacrifice was performed before great voyages, rather than at the Tophet sanctuary some distance inland. As of yet, nothing has been found of the horrifying furnace described by the Roman author Diodorus Siculus (20:14.6), a "bronze image of Ba'al Hammon extending its hands, palms up and sloping toward the ground, so that each of the children when placed thereon rolled down and fell into a sort of gaping pit filled with fire." However, recent analysis of child cremation burials from the Tophet, suggesting that most were healthy infants, not premature or stillbirths, strongly supports the picture of Carthaginian child sacrifice presented by Diodorus and other Roman historians, something that would fall in line with similar practice evidenced among the ancient Semitic peoples of the Near East.

One of my most exciting recent discoveries has been in Gunwalloe Church Cove, Cornwall, the site of the fictional Phoenician wreck in this novel, after winter storms had stripped away meters of sand and revealed the well-preserved hull of the steamship SS *Grip*. You can see a film I took of that dive on my website, as well as images of cannon found on other wrecks in the vicinity. Beyond the *Grip* was an expanse of shingle just as I describe Jack seeing in this novel, and as I swam over it I imagined the wreck I had always dreamed of finding in these waters—a Phoenician tin trader, blown inshore by the prevailing westerlies like so many other ships through the centuries that had foundered in the cove. No such wreck has yet been found off Britain, but several Phoenician wrecks recently investigated in the Mediterranean give an idea of the artifacts that might be uncovered. One off Cartagena in southeast Spain from the seventh or sixth century BC has produced amber from the Baltic, tin and other metal ingots, artifacts inscribed with Phoenician letters, and, most amazingly of all, sections of elephant tusk from northwest Africa. Seeing those tusks reminded me of elephant and rhino ivory of East African origin that I had handled from a late Bronze Age wreck off Turkey, part of a cargo that showed the interrelationship of Canaanite, Egyptian and other traders and suggested a similar model for trade in Phoenician times, with goods being sought by men such as Hanno and Himilco from the very farthest reaches of the known world and beyond.

The idea of setting part of this novel in the wartime Government Code and Cypher School at Bletchley Park came to me while I was sitting in Alan Turing's reconstructed office in Hut 8 during a visit to Bletchley with my daughter. The recent Hollywood films, the large number of books and TV documentaries, and the revitalization of the site as a tourist attraction have lifted some of the veil of secrecy from wartime operations at Bletchley, but much remains poorly known—in particular, some of the uses to which Ultra intelligence was put, including difficult decisions not to act on all intercepts of U-boat movements for fear of alerting the Germans that the code had been broken. Nazi organizations monitored at Bletchley undoubtedly included the Ahnenerbe, Himmler's "Department of Cultural Heritage," whose schemes included the search for lost Jewish treasures; another would have been the organization responsible for the exchange of high-grade raw materials and gold between Japan and Germany, carried out by

Japanese and German submarines. The characters and the special operations hut in my novel are fictional—as is the letter in Chapter 14 from Fan to Louise—but my account is based as closely as possible on the types of people who worked at Bletchley, on the procedure for conveying intelligence to the Admiralty, and on the circumstances of the Battle of the Atlantic during those pivotal months of April–May 1943.

My account of the British merchant ship *Clan Macpherson* is based on the actual circumstances of her wrecking on May 1 1943, when she was one of seven ships in convoy TS-37 torpedoed by *U-515* some seventy-five nautical miles off Freetown in West Africa. No attempt has ever been made to locate the wreck, which could lie close to the edge of the continental shelf as I suggest here. The names of the four engineer officers who went down with her can be seen on the Tower Hill Memorial to the Merchant Navy in London, along with the names of thousands of other merchant seamen who died as a result of enemy action during the war. The correspondence in Chapter 7 between the Admiralty and *Clan Macpherson*'s master, Captain Edward Gough, OBE, Lloyd's War Medal—a veteran of two previous sinkings—is quoted from letters in private hands reproduced in part in Gordon Holman's *In Danger's Hour* (1948), the Clan Line Second World War history. A file containing further correspondence relating to the sinking and the adequacy of the escort is in the National Archives (ADM 1/14944), and extracts from it can be seen on my website.

My grandfather, Captain Lawrance Gibbins, was an officer with the Clan Line during the war, and only a few months earlier had sailed the exact route taken by *Clan Macpherson* on her final voyage, including the Takoradi and Sierra Leone convoys. I was very fortunate to be able to talk to him about his wartime experiences, and to use that as a basis for researching the ships, convoys and actions of his service, the results of which can be seen on my website. I myself have dived on two Clan Line wrecks, the *Clan MacMaster*, which ran aground off the Isle of Man in 1923, and the *Clan Malcolm*, which foundered off the Lizard peninsula in 1935, not far from Gunwalloe Church Cove and the wreck of the *Grip*. Both of those Clan ships were built in 1917 and were similar to *Clan Macpherson*, with triple-expansion steam engines and comparable dimensions. My image of the wreck in Chapters 2 and 3 derives from numerous wartime merchantmen I have dived on over the years, from the Red Sea to the English

Channel, including one deep wreck in the Mediterranean with an unexploded torpedo lodged inside its hull just as described here.

In this novel, the ancient hull found in 1868 at Annesley Bay on the Red Sea, the tapestry depicting Hanno discovered at Magdala in Ethiopia, and the underground chamber in the church there are all fictional, though based closely on actual historical circumstances. In the preparations for the 1868 British campaign against King Theodore of Abyssinia (Ethiopia), the Royal Engineers officer responsible for building the head of the pier in Annesley Bay—site of the fictional hull discovery—was Captain Herbert William Wood of the Madras Sappers and Miners, the basis for my fictional officer. A veteran of the 1857–9 Indian Mutiny, Wood later went on to join Grand Duke Constantine of Russia in an expedition to the Oxus and wrote a fascinating account of it in *The Shores of Lake Aral* (1876).

At the time of Wood's early death in Madras in 1879, my great-great-grandfather, Lieutenant Walter Andrew Gale—the basis for Jack's fictional ancestor—had been in the Madras Sappers for almost two years, and I have therefore imagined Wood handing on his account and the tapestry to the younger officer. The tapestry is based on an actual painting on woven wool that you can see on my website, showing fighting involving Axumites in Ethiopia; the painting is Egyptian in origin but thought to be based on a Sassanid silk that may be copied from a much older depiction. In the center is a bearded man, the basis for my fictional image of Hanno on the tapestry. Much of the loot taken by the British at Magdala, ranging from gold crosses and church vestments to weapons, manuscripts, and *tabots*—representations of the Tablet of Commandments—was auctioned in the field under orders of the force commander, General Napier, the proceeds being distributed among the soldiers of the expedition. Hundreds of manuscripts were acquired by the expedition archaeologist, Richard Rivington Holmes (later Sir Richard), and are in the collections of the British Museum, the British Library and Windsor Castle, among other places. You can see images of some of those treasures and read an account of the ongoing attempt to restore them to Ethiopia on my website.

The church at Magdala was guarded after the assault by soldiers of the 33rd Foot, who had been the first to enter the fortress along with an advance party of sappers, including Lieutenant Le Mesurier of the Bombay

Sappers, but the guard appear to have done little to limit the plunder. Two men of the 33rd, Private Bergin and Drummer Magner, won Victoria Crosses for their exploits in climbing the fortress wall, the only decorations awarded in a campaign that was decidedly one-sided—the British did not suffer a single soldier killed in action against at least 700 Abyssinians killed and 1,200 wounded (to that figure should be added the many hundreds of his own people murdered by Theodore—Abyssinian hostages or others who displeased him—many of whom were hideously mutilated by having their hands and feet chopped off). Among the casualties of the final assault was Theodore himself, killed by his own hand with a pistol that had been sent to him as a present by Queen Victoria. The numerous eyewitness accounts of the assault of Magdala and the plundering include *Coomassie and Magdala* (1874) by Henry Morton Stanley, the Welshman-turned-American who was to find fame a few years later by discovering Dr. Livingstone near Lake Tanganyika.

The Abyssinian campaign was an engineers' war, entirely dependent on the officers of the Royal Engineers and their Indian sappers for the construction of piers, railways, and roads, for supply, survey, and communication, and for many other necessities, including the operation of condensers by the sea to make fresh water. Another role was photography, and it is the extensive photo archive—much of it now online—that makes the Abyssinian campaign stand above many others of the period, not least because of the extraordinary landscape it depicts. One of those images, of the plateau overlooking the route to Magdala, I have imagined being taken by Captain Wood and Sapper Jones from their ledge the day before the assault. Many men present were struck and even unnerved by the spectacular environment in which they found themselves, so far removed from their previous experiences. One of them, the expedition geographer Clements Robert Markham (later Sir Clements, Fellow of the Royal Society), wrote in *A History of the Abyssinia Expedition* (1869) of seeing a celestial phenomenon in a manner that sounds like an ancient author writing of portents before a battle: "Early in the forenoon a dark-brown circle appeared round the sun, like a blister, about 15° in radius; light clouds passed and repassed over it, but it did not disappear until the usual rain-storm came up from the eastward late in the afternoon. Walda Gabir, the king's valet, informed me that Theodore saw it when he came out of his tent that morning, and that he remarked that it was an omen of bloodshed."

Photographs are not the only images to survive from the campaign. Another historical character in my story, Major Robert Baigrie of the Bombay Staff Corps, painted watercolors that were published as etchings in the *Illustrated London News*; before beginning to research this novel I had been familiar with his work because a decade earlier he had painted another of my ancestors when they had been young officers together during the Indian Mutiny. It was one of his paintings in Abyssinia, *Half-way to Senafe*, showing a towering mountain ridge over a valley on the route to Magdala, that inspired me to think that the mountain called the "Chariot of the Gods" in Hanno's *Periplus* could refer to a mountain in present-day Ethiopia—to Magdala itself, perhaps—with the light of the sun at dawn or at dusk rippling along the ridge like fire.

You can see Baigrie's painting and much else of interest on my website (www.davidgibbins.com; www.facebook.com/DavidGibbinsAuthor), including photographs and videos of me diving, discussion of artifacts, shipwrecks and ancient texts, and links to online source material mentioned in this note.